THE RED WIDOW

THE RED WIDOW

A Story of Journalism, Treachery, Betrayal and Murder

T. CASTLE FURLONG

Yards220 Publishing

DISCLAIMER

The main characters in this novel are entirely fictional. None represents any individual, dead or alive. Any similarities of name or identity are entirely coincidental.

Dedicated to Thomas Raphael Furlong, my late father and senior Chicago Tribune editor whose exemplary life has always been my North Star.

CONTENTS

Peter Bainbridge: Deputy foreign editor of the *New York Herald*

Harry Terwilliger Berger: Night copy desk chief at the *Herald*

Shamus Callahan: FBI agent in charge of the Manhattan office

Lt. Gino Carella: NYPD cop in charge of city's anti-terrorism unit

Ike Citron: PR man to the superrich in New York

Vic Cox: Sydney-based private eye and retired homicide cop

Rembrandt T. Dabovitch III: Investigative reporter and two-time Pulitzer winner

Dion DeStefano: Brooklyn mobster

Angela R. Flanagan: *Herald* reporter/photographer in Sydney

Rafer M. Flanagan: *Herald* bureau chief in Sydney. Angela Flanagan's estranged husband

Sgt. Candy Garcia: NYPD chief deputy to Lt. Carella

Zbigniew Zeke 'Ziggy the K' Koslowski: Hit man in northwest Australia

Sheila Koslowski: Ziggy's wife and partner in crime

Julius J. 'The Jackal' Levitsky: NY hedge-fund tycoon

Peter Lynch: *Herald* bureau chief in Hong Kong

Margarite T. Maye: *Herald* Editor and novelist

Rocco Mazilli: Toyota salesman in Darwin

Conor McCann: Mysterious *Herald* news source in Sydney

Kathleen Q McGiffin: FBI agent in Manhattan

Clementine B. Murphy: Agent in charge of the Darwin office of the Australian Federal Police

Vito Papadakis: Runs iconic Roebuck Hotel in Broome, Australia

Jack Quinn: Aussie tourist official and Mrs. Flanagan's lover

John J. 'Black Jack' Reilly: Mrs. Flanagan's father

Jim "The Rim' Robison: Brooklyn gangster and fitness guru

Wilbur Ross: *Herald* 'numbers guy'

Michael 'The Ice Man' Scanlon: Retired cop in Wyndham, hottest town in Australia and salt-water crocodile hot spot

Stacey McKenzie Simpson: Sydney police reporter and Mrs. Flanagan's ex-lover

Ari Steinberg III: *Herald* Publisher

Ari Steinberg Jr.: Father of *Herald* Publisher

Roberta Steinberg: Wife of *Herald* Publisher

Christian Turnbull: *Herald* night managing editor

Kellen Williams: *Herald* foreign editor

Dan Wirthin: New Jersey state trooper

Betsy Wright: *Herald* PR chief

Zoe Z. Zelinsky: TV talk-show host

Prologue

A NIGHT TO FORGET

Monday, April 27, 1983
Metro Section, Chicago Tribune, Page 3

Coed Attacked
In Drug Deal
Gone Bad

By Joe Morang
©Tribune Police Reporter

Chicago police combed a low-income apartment complex on the near north side Sunday, searching for suspects in connection with the assault on a college student late Saturday night.

The victim was found in a vacant first-floor apartment after a neighbor called police, saying she had heard a woman's cry for help.

Police sources told *The Tribune* the attack is believed to be connected to a late-night drug trade where college students go to buy marijuana and cocaine.

After police found the victim, she was taken to Cook County Hospital for treatment. A hospital spokeswoman said the woman was in stable condition after undergoing surgery for a broken nose.

The victim, whose name was not released, is a student at Northwestern University's Medill School of Journalism in north suburban Evanston, according to sources at the university's school newspaper.

PART ONE

CHAPTER 1

The Full Monty

Home of John J. (Black Jack) Reilly,
Baldwin Farms Road
Greenwich, Connecticut
Friday, September 7, 2001
4:19 p.m.

Raffy Flanagan drained two ounces of colorless liquid—straight up, no ice—in the recycled jelly jar and put the glass down in the grass next to his blue-padded deck chair. The 72-degree pool waters beckoned a few feet away under the late-afternoon, late-summer sun.

"Angela," he intoned, "we have to talk."

His hard-bodied, red-haired estranged wife, face still flush from her daily workout, sat impassively a few feet away. Wearing a skimpy crème-colored robe, she glared at Raffy, green eyes radiating irritation and ennui.

"I'm done talking, darling,' she replied, her Texas accent still twanging after 15 years of living overseas. "Now that you're coming back to New York, only thing that matters is the terms of the split. Just business from here on out. Nothing personal."

Raffy eyed his tart-tongued wife impassively, most of his anger spent after three years of living apart in Sydney, Australia. And, of course, they still had appearances to maintain. After all, the *U.S. Journalism Review* once labeled them "The Model Tandem Couple" among all American foreign correspondents working abroad. Put their photo on the cover of the magazine back in 1988, two years before he won his Pulitzer Prize for economics writing.

"Daddy's been through four of these splits," she added, smiling coyly, "so I'm just getting started."

Raffy laughed despite himself. There was something about Mrs. Angela Reilly Flanagan that still charmed his Brooklyn Irish soul. One minute she sounded like a sweet southern belle at a Dallas debutante party, the next a foul-mouthed waitress in an East Texas truck stop.

"Angela, I'm meeting with Kellen next Tuesday," Raffy said, referring to *New York Herald* foreign editor Kellen Williams. "I'm going to fight this recall as hard as I know how. Coming back to New York to work on Metro is not—repeat not—an option for me."

"Honey, I have my own fucking career to worry about," she shot back, shifting position in her deck chair and brushing back her long curly wet hair with both hands. "I'm staying in Sydney. I want the bureau chief job. I deserve it. You've pretty much been a bust down there."

Raffy absorbed the left hook and countered with a right cross of his own.

"Angela, you don't have the experience to be a bureau chief," he said matter-of-factly. "You're a feature writer and a photographer. Besides, I think the paper wants to close the bureau if I leave. No hard news in the South Pacific. Wasting money down there. Probably put another reporter in Hong Kong or Shanghai. That's where the real action is. With my economics background, I'd be perfect for Hong Kong."

Angela sat up straight and stared hard this time, eyes flashing hurt and anger.

"Rafer McCann Flanagan," she said quietly, slowly, "may I remind you that when I followed you overseas, I did all the inside stories— the cultural and business crap—and you got all the front-page glory. I followed you from one hellhole to another—Nairobi, Cairo, Delhi—and never complained. But you never noticed."

She paused, lighting a joint and taking a long drag. "Then," she continued, following a deep exhale, "I persuaded Mr. Steinberg—who by the way adores Australia—to send us to Sydney to reopen the South Pacific bureau and you go into this deep funk. Start drinking again big-time, lose interest in the job, lose complete interest in me."

"Angela, stop," Raffy cut in. "May I remind you I didn't want to go to Sydney. Ari Steinberg's not the editor. Maggie Maye is. She runs the newsroom. I love Sydney, it's a great city, but her editors don't care about Australia. No hard news. I went there because of you, but it's tanked my career. I haven't been on the front page in years."

"Well, I love it there," Angela shot back. "The people there don't shit in the streets like they do in India. God, that place was so gross. I don't care if we had 10 servants in Delhi. I hated it. Not that you noticed--or cared."

She took another hit on the joint and plunged on. "Only thing you cared about was that Pulitzer you won. It spoiled you, Raffy. You got lazy. You only wanted a repeat. When that didn't happen right away, you fell off the wagon--again. Fucking prize was the worst thing that ever happened to you—and us."

She's got a point, Raffy thought, though certainly can't concede that in the heat of this battle.

"Problem isn't Australia, baby," she said, voice more sorry than angry, "it's you. If you keep drinking like this, you're going to die young just like your father and the rest of his fucked-up Irish relatives. You've got to get help."

"You should talk, Angela," Raffy fired back. "Look at you. You can't get through the afternoon without a couple of joints, and you do so much coke your nose leaks like a bad faucet."

"It's just allergies," Angela replied, back on defense. "I've always had 'em. Anyway, I can't deal with that now. Daddy doesn't have much longer. He is my only close living relative. I'll deal with all that other stuff later."

She paused again, brushing back her wavey red hair with the left hand this time, an unconscious reflex Raffy still found endearing and sexy.

"You should know," she said after a time, "I'm going to talk to Ari while we're here in New York. I want to stay in Sydney no matter what Maggie Maye and Kellen want. She's a hard-hearted shrew and he's a corporate limp-dick who does whatever she wants. By the way, I hear they used to do the wild thing back in the day when they were both reporters in Europe."

Raffy said nothing this time, failing to see the relevance of some long-forgotten office fling—even if it was good gossip, the coin of the realm for all great reporters.

"Anyway," Angela said, "Mr. Steinberg reopened the bureau for a reason, and I want to prove him right. They need a colorful writer to showcase the entire South Pacific and, frankly, Raffy, your stories are boring. Lifeless and obsessed with policy."

"Last word to you, as usual, Angela," Raffy shot back, standing up abruptly. "I'm headed down to Brooklyn tonight to see if I can find Dion in his old lair. His old phone number doesn't work anymore."

"Dion DeStefano?" Angela asked, surprised. "Your old high school basketball pal? Good God, Raffy, glad you haven't forgotten the old neighborhood. That Dion's a piece of work. Wonderful family."

The unhappy couple laughed for the first time, clearing some of the foul air around them. Sensing a break in the hostilities, Angela made her move in typically theatric style.

"Listen, Raffy, I want to ask you a serious question," she said, standing up and shedding her pool robe, giving her startled husband the full Monty.

"Angela, what on earth are you doing?" he gasped, averting his gaze momentarily. "What if Jack comes out here?"

"Honey, Daddy's napping," she said nonchalantly. "I do my pool laps like this. He knows I'm a naturist in private."

"Exhibitionist is more like it," Raffy fired back. "And where did you get that tattoo on your back? What is that? The Queen of Hearts? You've got to be kidding."

Angela just smiled, saying nothing and doing a slow graceful pirouette on her toes, as though warming for ballet class. Audrey Hepburn's style, Raffy thought, Demi Moore's body.

"Do I do anything for you anymore, Raffy?" she asked as she twirled around. "You used to love it when I danced around nude when we were first married. That magic twanger of yours would go from zero to sixty in about three seconds. Now the rumor is you're spending all your time in those homo bars in King's Cross. I hope you're using a condom, darling. Is that why you used to do me from behind all the time?"

"Angela, pleeeease," Raffy said, suppressing a laugh. "Homo bars? It's 2001. I haven't heard that term in 20 years. Even the Aussies say 'gay' now."

"Well, that's what Mama used to call them down in Texarkana," Angela replied, sitting back down and relighting her joint, not bothering to cover up. "There was one on the Arkansas side that everyone knew about. Cops raided the place and beat the stuffing out of everyone in there."

"Angela, please put your robe back on," Raffy said, tone softer now. "Why are you so concerned with my private life? We haven't been together in years. And I hear you're sleeping with Stacey, the office manager. Are you two homos?"

The pair laughed again, longer this time. Standing, they hugged hard for the first time in years. Shudders of regret coursed through both as they teared up and shared a warm kiss.

After a time, Angela stepped back and gave Raffy a full-body scan. "My, darling," she said gently, "you've gotten so thin. Feels like you're going to blow away in a gentle breeze. Let me get a better look."

She expertly peeled off his sleeve-less t-shirt and cutoff jeans in a fluid one-two motion, followed by the blue-cotton briefs that she tossed into the pool. Save for his green flip-flops, he was now as *au naturel* as she was.

"Angela," he protested weakly, "we shouldn't be doing this."

"Let's just see what happens," she said soothingly, moving her kisses slowly down from his neck. "I'm so sorry it had to turn out this way,

Raffy. I really am, darling. Anyway, it's good to see Pinto again. Let's see how fast I can get him to stand up. Oh, my. Almost like the old days."

CHAPTER 2

The Texas Tornado

Office of the Foreign Editor, New York Herald
Herald Tower, Midtown Manhattan
Friday, September 7, 2001
6:06 p.m.

Kellen Throckmorton Williams IV, dandy foreign editor of the august *New York Herald*, ran his soft hands through his silvery mane, rubbed his temples and groaned quietly.

Yet another Flanagan flop, he thought sourly, reading a few graphs into the computer printout on his desk before sailing it in the direction of a nearby trash can. True to recent form, Rafer M. Flanagan—Raffy to his friends and colleagues—had authored another feature dispatch from the South Pacific that had no pop, snap or style. Guy is a total burnout case, Williams mused. Has been for years, ever since he got to Australia. Perfect candidate for a second career in PR at Con Ed—once he dries out.

"Kellen," said his assistant, Kathy Stankowski, suddenly filling his doorway, "Maggie wants to see you right away. Says it's urgent. Doesn't sound happy."

Williams shot an angry glance at Stankowski, who was chewing gum as usual, hands on her ample hips, obviously loving the drama that ensues when the fearsome Margarite T. Maye—the first female editor in the *Herald's* 113-year history—issues one of her curt summonses.

"Tell me something I don't know, Kathy," Williams snapped. "She's always unhappy and it's always urgent."

"Now, now Kellen," Stankowski fired back, "I'm just the messenger, remember? Isn't that what you journalists always say? I'm outta here. See you *manana*."

"God, I hate this job," Williams said out loud to himself, carefully putting on his Savile-Row, blue-pinstriped jacket and rubbing down the sleeves. Even my own assistant disses me, he thought sourly.

Managing a slowly dying business is a drag, Kellen mused, making his way through the dumpy, frills-free newsroom to Maye's office just off the city room floor. All these writers and editors—focused like lasers on the stories *du jour*—are a doomed lot, dead men working if you will, particularly the younger ones.

In the 100-yard slow walk to Maye's office, Williams reminded himself to lose the sour mood. The editor demanded that her senior staff— the all-important department and deputy department heads—be positive, upbeat team players in these uncertain business times. While she didn't know a football from a *futbol*, she loved sports clichés.

"We must work together every night as a team to get the ball into the end zone," she liked to say at the daily afternoon story meetings. Competitive she was, Williams thought, original she wasn't.

"Hi, Maggie," Kellen said, popping his head part-way through the door. "You need something? I'm on deadline."

"Come in," Maggie ordered. "Sit down. Shut the door."

Fuck, he thought, look out below.

"Two words, Kellen," Maye said grimly, staring hard at her foreign editor. "Angela Flanagan."

Williams winced but said nothing. Not her again, he thought, the infamous East Texas tornado, wife of the Sydney bureau chief, herself a *Herald* feature writer, the distaff side of the tandem couple from hell covering the South Pacific. Charming, cunning, impossibly self-centered, the woman has been a managerial nightmare for years.

"You know Wilbur Ross, right?" Maggie asked sharply, not really a question because everyone in the newsroom knew of the paper's chief numbers guy.

Kellen nodded, still not daring to say a word. Maggie was leaning forward now at her teak-wood desk, arms down, hands folded, eyes locked—the sure sign she was about to launch like a Roman candle.

"Wilbur was in my office not ten minutes ago and he told me—this is completely off the record—that Angela hired a girl Friday in Sydney off the books to manage the office and do Raffy's job. With no authorization from anyone. She's been there almost a year. Gets paid in cash. From the bureau operations fund. Thirty thousand dollars a year!"

Maggie was really smoking now, Kellen thought. Head looks like it's about to explode. Best not to volunteer anything at this point and look *really* stupid.

"Christ, nobody in the newsroom knew about this? She's writing stories under Raffy's byline? No wonder they're so bad, Kellen. We can't spend money like this just because the bureau chief 's a lush."

"You know, Maggie," Williams cut in, seeing his opening, "$30,000 really isn't that much money in a foreign-correspondent budget of $20 million a year. Hell, I once rented a plane in the African bush that cost $5,000 for one story."

"How do I get through to you, Kellen?" Maggie fired back, glare intensifying. "Wilbur usually rubber-stamps our expenses in the bureaus. If he dives too deep, we're in a world of hurt. Drunks at Mardi Gras spend their money more carefully than your reporters."

Look out, Williams thought. Here it comes.

"You ought to know, Kellen. You're still a legend for those expense accounts from London. Loved those $1,000 bottles of French wine with the, quote/unquote, unnamed sources at Buckingham Palace. When the fuck did you ever write any stories about the Queen? I never saw one."

Ouch, he thought. She's right but she doesn't have to be so nasty. Maggie was once a foreign correspondent herself—and not a very good one, he remembered—and she didn't exactly stay in youth hostels on the road. She once spent $400 at one London hotel—it may have been the Savoy—for a "beauty treatment" that included a full-body massage, manicure, pedicure and pubic-hair wax.

"Don't say it," Maggie said, reading his mind perfectly. "What you and I used to do on the road doesn't cut it anymore. We're managers now. New business in a new era in a new century. Hell, a new millennium. Adapt or go home."

Maggie paused for a moment, drew a deep breath, sat back in her faux-leather chair and rubbed her eyes. She then snapped back to an upright position and refolded her hands, looking directly at Williams.

"Now," she said, "let's get back to Angela and Raffy, our tandem couple gone bad. We must do something here. Their marriage is over. They hardly even speak, I'm told. Raffy, our Pulitzer boy, needs help big-time. He's got to go into rehab, rejoin AA and stay in this time. If not, his career is toast.

"Angela is a different problem—and a lot scarier one, in my opinion. First, she's not that good. She's a first-rate photographer and a fourth-rate writer. Her stories have no sense of place, and the quotes all feel canned. Her travel pieces are the only stories she does well."

"No argument there," Kellen chimed in eagerly. "You know, the foreign desk doesn't edit her stuff. We just hand them off to business or features or whoever."

"Then," Maggie plowed on, ignoring the self-serving comment, "there's all that other stuff that has been rumored for years—the cocaine, the lifestyle, the hold she has on our publisher. All in all, a ticking time bomb for all of us."

Maggie paused and took another deep breath before plunging ahead.

"So, what we have is a deeply dysfunctional professional couple in a country that no one—save our publisher—cares about, where there is virtually no hard news, and where all we do is manage their messes.

"They're back in New York next week, right? I want Raffy recalled, put into rehab, and then assigned to the investigative team on Metro. He could really help us there."

"What about Angela?" Kellen asked.

Maggie paused and stared out for a long while at the high-volume human traffic in the newsroom just outside her office window.

"Well," she said finally, "she'll want Raffy's job and title as South Pacific bureau chief, but she's not qualified. Not today, not tomorrow, not ever."

Neither editor spoke for a time, both enervated by the messy personal issues that involve Ari Steinberg III, the publisher and CEO. One misstep and they knew their carefully nurtured careers could crash and burn.

"Have you ever asked Ari about Angela?" Kellen asked, smiling slightly. "We know he goes through women like a sickle through wheat. Is she part of his wheat field?"

"Kellen, Kellen," Maggie replied, smiling for the first time, tone mocking, "you must understand you never ask the royal family about personal stuff like that. We're the hired help to the Steinbergs. Nothing more."

"It would be fun to match up Angela's expense reports with Ari's over the past five years," Kellen said. "Bet there would be a lot of overlap in hot steamy Bangkok."

"Let's not go there," Maggie said humorlessly, waiving her left hand indicating the meeting was over. "Let's talk more after you meet with him next week. Raffy was a great reporter when he was sober. He won that Pulitzer for a reason. Let's reel him back in gently.

"Maybe he can be our answer to Rem Dabovitch over at the Daily News. His series on the mob control of the construction unions—the one that won the Pulitzer last year--was fabulous. I want someone on our Metro who can do that too."

CHAPTER 3

Bye-bye Mrs. Flanagan?

Behan's Ale House
Atlantic Avenue, Brooklyn Heights
September 7, 2001
9:19 p.m.

Raffy spotted Dion DeStefano in the distance, standing alone at the far end of the bar—all six-foot-six, three hundred pounds of him. My God, Raffy thought, Dion looks just like Big Sal, only bigger and scarier.

Making his way down the bar at Behan's, Raffy was bathed in a soothing familiarity that took him back 15 years. It was as though the Friday night clock had frozen in place. The awning outside was still black, the front door still red and battered, the ambient bar noise still loud and raucous. The photos of the Irish writers and poets still adorned the walls—Joyce, Shaw, O'Casey, the huge head shot of Brendan Behan himself. No wonder I feel so at home here, he mused. What did Brendan once say? Writing is the curse of the drinking class? Something like that.

Dion's eyes were locked on three hot young women—yuppie types who had discovered Behan's in recent years—playing darts nearby. Judging from their high fives and squeals of delight, you would have thought every dart was a bullseye, Raffy noted as he passed them by.

"Dion," Raffy said loudly over the barroom din, catching his old pal off guard, "what's up, Dude?"

Dion's coal-black eyes narrowed through the semi-darkness, radiating suspicion, showing little hint of recognition. The DeStefanos never did like being caught off guard, Raffy thought.

"I know you, motherfucker?" Dion growled. "I can't quite place you. Step back and state your business."

"Whoa, D.D., it's Raffy, you blockhead. Rafer Flanagan."

"*Jesus, Jose and Maria,*" Dion said slowly, enunciating each name slowly and carefully, before letting out a roar and enveloping his oldest childhood friend in a wraparound bear hug.

"Raffy," he bellowed, "what the fuck are you doing here? You're supposed to be in Australia. I didn't even recognize you. What happened to the beard? The long hair? Christ, you must have lost 50 pounds."

"Yeah," Raffy said sheepishly, backing up several steps, still feeling the impact of Dion's iron grip. "A lot's changed since I last saw you. Angela and I are back on home leave for a while. Staying up in Greenwich at her dad's house. Thought I'd pop down here to see I could find you."

What the fuck happened to my old pal, Dion wondered. Nothing like the hoops magic-man I played high school basketball with—the guy they used to say could be the next Jerry West. Pale and gaunt now, sparkle gone from those piercing aqua-blue eyes. Resembles the POWs in those yellowed World War II photos, he thought.

"Jesus, Raf," Dion said bluntly, "you look like you've been on some sort of Jap death march. What up with that?"

"Yeah, I know," Raffy replied. "Had a rough go of it lately. Let's sit at your old table over there. I can't believe how little this place has changed. I love it."

As the pair settled into a corner booth in an alcove away from the crowd, Dion bellowed out drink orders. "George," he yelled at the Jamaican bartender a few yards away, 'bring us two black-and-tans right away and keep them coming whenever my friend, Mr. Flanagan, and I get low."

"Yes, sir, Mr. DeStefano," George replied evenly. "Coming right up."

"So, what the fuck happened to you," Dion asked, skipping the verbal foreplay as always. "Last time I saw you everything was great. When was that? Ten, eleven years ago? You'd just gotten that Pulitzer. Everybody was talking about you being the next editor of the paper."

"What can I say?" Raffy replied sheepishly. "Marriage is over. Career in ruins. Australia is a wonderful place to live, but there's no big news there. Pulitzer just a faded memory. A dot in the rearview mirror."

Jesus, Dion mused, been 36 years since Raffy swished probably the most memorable shot in New York City high school basketball history. Tiny St. Brendan's Memorial in Bensonhurst upset Bronx powerhouse DeWitt Clinton 69-68 in three overtimes in the city finals. Raffy hit the winning shot at the buzzer and the crowd mobbed him for five minutes.

"Sorry to hear that, Raf," Dion replied. "You are my only friend from St. Brendan's who ever really amounted to anything. Famous foreign correspondent for the *New York Herald*. Really made us all proud back in the hood—even if no one really reads the paper. Way too far uptown.

"You know," he added, "most of the guys from the old team are either dead, in jail or—in my case—up to their usual no good."

Dion flashed his signature crooked smile for the first time, making Raffy laugh out loud.

"Lots of memories in this place," Raffy said wistfully, already draining the last of his first pint. "Met Angela in here. She was a photog for the *Bergen Record* over in Jersey. She thought I was Mr. Big because I worked for one of the metro dailies. Lust at first sight."

"So what happened with all that?" Dion asked. "I still remember the huge wedding party at St. Ignatius Loyola up in Darien after you got married in Africa. Never seen so many legally rich people in all my life."

"Yeah, well," Raffy answered glumly, already several ounces into his second pint, "as the old Stones refrain goes: 'It's all over now.' Haven't been together in almost three years. She's living at the *Herald* mansion near the beach in the Sydney suburbs and I live in a dumpy flat near the airport. She's strung out on drugs, into kinky personal stuff. Even wants my job if I have to come back to New York."

Raffy paused, allowing the litany of blues to marinate for a bit, the alcohol already starting to muffle the voices in his head and insecurities in his soul.

"How about you, D.D.?" Raffy asked. "What are you up to? Still got the PI business?"

"Yeah, you know, my brother Guido, pretty much runs it day to day. Divorces, insurance fraud, civil stuff, all that crap. People in the hood come to the DeStefanos because they know we always get it done. Then, I handle the things that need to be—how should I say it?—'adjudicated beyond the arm of the law.'"

Dion winked and smiled wider this time, adding no elaboration, making Raffy laugh again. Jesus, he thought, D.D. not only looks like his dad, he *sounds* like him. Sal DeStefano was the terror of Bensonhurst —until prosecutors put him away for good on criminal RICO charges.

Dion said nothing for a time, leaning back in the booth, arms behind his head, composing his thoughts about this brainy Paddy Boy whom he always had to protect when they were growing up. He finally sat up straight and leaned across the table, speaking in a voice usually reserved for serious family issues.

"Listen, Raf, let me tell you a story about Big Sal. When he was dying of colon cancer a few years ago at Attica, I visited him in the prison hospital. We made small talk for a while. He asked about Salvatore the deuce, what kind of grades he had, the usual family stuff. He also asked about you. Loved you like a third son."

Raffy said nothing, but thoughts of his own parents flashed through his head. His Mom, a kindergarten teacher, so Italian, dead at 42 from a ruptured aorta. His Dad, a *Daily News* truck driver, Irish to the core, dead a few years later from alcoholism and a broken heart.

"As I was leaving the hospital room," Dion continued, "I finally asked him the question everyone used to ask me: 'Sal, how many people did you personally take out in your life?

"He didn't hesitate. 'Maybe 19, 20, depending on how you do the numbers.' And then he says: 'Let me tell you something, Dion.' (He never called me D.D. Said it was a girl's name.) 'It was never personal. Never got rid of *anyone* without a good reason. Never forget that.'"

"Hmmm," Raffy said finally, "kind of like the DeStefano family honor code."

"Fucking A," Dion shot back. "That was just about the last thing Sal ever said to me. He died two weeks later."

Raffy stayed quiet this time, draining the last of his second pint and starting the third that George the bartender had just left on the table. Raffy knew Dion was just getting to some point or another.

"In my business," Dion said quietly, "when someone's relative or associate gets out of line—drugs, skimming, flagrant affairs—they often disappear. Word goes out they probably moved to Vegas."

Dion paused for effect. Raffy stayed mum.

"I could get Angela a one-way ticket to Vegas if that would help. No charge. Like Rod Steiger in 'No Way to Treat a Lady.' Bye-bye, Mrs. Flanagan, bye-bye."

"Whoa, Dion," Raffy responded, sitting up holding out his palms like stop signs. "Hold on, Dude. Let me figure out my job situation first. I have a meeting with my editors next week on what's next for me. I'll worry about Angela after that."

"Where is she now?"

"At her dads in Greenwich. He doesn't have much longer himself. Stage four lung cancer. Angela and I have declared a truce while we are here."

"Well, my offer stands," Dion said, leaning back, body language returning to normal. "Listen, Raf, I still consider you my best friend. You know that, right? I'd do anything for you. Beating those niggers in the Garden that night is still the highlight of my life."

Jesus, Raffy thought, wincing at the slur, looking over at George. He was only about five yards away.

"Speaking of that, guess who works for me now?" Dion asked.

"Haven't a clue."

"Jimmy Robison."

"The Jimmy Robison?" Raffy asked. "As in 'Jim the Rim.' The center for DeWitt Clinton. The guy you got in a fight with in the third overtime?"

"Yep," Dion said, "the one and only. Does black ops for me now, so to speak. After he got tossed out of Boston College on that point-shaving scandal, he did 25 in Attica for killing a guy in a bar with one punch. Got to know Sal there. Called me when he got out and I put him on the payroll. Been friends ever since. Give him my toughest assignments."

"I can only imagine," Raffy deadpanned.

"Get this, Raf. Every so often when we have a beer here in Behan's, the Rim mentions your name. Still calls you B-29. Says: 'I still can't believe we allowed you honky motherfuckers win that game. The brothers have never let me forget that.'"

The old friends laughed hard this time, clinking glasses and doing a fist bump.

"You know," Dion said, standing and staring down the bar, "Robison is supposed to meet me in here about now. We got some business to conduct. I think I see him coming through the front door now."

Turning around in his seat, Raffy saw a tall figure making his way slowly towards Dion's alcove, the yuppie patrons parting like the Red Sea.

Even from a distance Raffy marveled at the fearsome figure Robison cut—the beret, the turtleneck, the leather jacket, all in black. As he got closer, Flanagan could see a huge diamond earring in Robison's left lobe and giant silver crucifix around his neck. A modern gangster right off a Hollywood movie set, Raffy thought--except he's real.

"You sure he's not going to punch me?" Raffy whispered, only half joking. He stood and felt his palms starting to sweat. "He doesn't hold any grudges, does he?"

Dion laughed, waving at Robison to come over to the booth. "Jimmy, come here," he yelled. "Got someone I want you to meet."

Robison approached, eyes focusing on the pale skinny white guy his partner was standing with. Tallish, nerdy looking, buzz cut, clean shaven, looked harmless enough. Must be one of Dion's accountants.

"Jimmy," Dion said, smiling widely now, "you recognize this guy?"

Robison gave Raffy another once over and shook his head. "Sorry dude," he said smoothly, a West Indies lilt in his voice. He extended his huge hand toward Raffy. "To whom do I have the pleasure of speaking?" he asked with mock formality.

"Two hints," Dion said. "First one: March 21, 1965."

"That's easy," Robison shot back. "DeWitt Clinton vs. St. Brendan's. Madison Square Garden. Worst day of my life, best day of yours. What's no. 2?"

"Very good," Dion said. "You know this guy as B-29--the mad bomber."

Robison straightened up like he had been shocked and looked harder a third time at Raffy. He broke into a huge smile, showcasing the gold crown on his left front tooth.

"Mother fucking dawg," Robison said slowly. "Raffy Flanagan in the flesh. The man who haunts me to this day. Thought you lived in Africa or something."

"Australia, actually," Raffy replied, relieved by the friendly reception, palms still moist. "Great to see you again, Rim. Amazing how you and Dion hooked up again after all these years."

Robison looked remarkably the same, Raffy thought, save for the dreadlocks instead of the Afro. The unlined light chocolate skin, the XXXL fingers, the dazzling dark-blue eyes. Where did he get those eyes, Raffy wondered.

"Yeah," Robison replied, "I still have that article by Tim Weigel, the *Herald* sportswriter, about the night you guys beat us. It's framed on my wall. Constant reminder to never, ever underestimate your opponent. Serves me well in my line of business."

The three aging ex-hoopsters laughed easily and sat down at the wooden table in Dion's alcove. As always, Dion took the seat looking down the bar. The demise of Bill Hickok was about the only lesson he took away from his American high school history class.

"Rim, you still a personal trainer at that gym down in Rockaway?" Raffy asked. "My wife showed me an article several years ago in the *Daily News* about you and your clients on the Jets and Giants. She knew we played basketball against each other in high school."

"Yeah, that article was great for business," Robison said. "Still getting referrals from that. Best thing is it's the first item that comes up on Google now, not the Attica shit."

"You think you could help me?" Raffy asked plaintively.

"Help you what?"

"Get back in shape. Gain some weight. Add some muscle. Looks like I may have to come back to New York in a few months and I need to get the old mojo back. Get my life back on track."

"Sheeeit," Rim said, "give me six months and I'll have you looking like the Mojowski Brothers—Big Mo and Little Mo. Little Mo is 260, Big Mo is 240. Both all muscle. They work out there in the off season. I'll introduce them to you. Great guys."

"That would be great, Rim," Raffy replied. "Really need a lift. Been bouncing along the bottom for a few years now."

"Buck up, bro," Rim said. "you don't know bottom until you've lived in Attica. All relative."

The three clinked glasses.

"Listen, Raf," Dion said, standing up suddenly and looking at his watch, "me and Rim gotta go. It's Friday night. Got people to visit, business to conduct."

Dion paused and stared down at his pale friend, still seated, and grabbed him by the shoulders.

"You ever need anything—money, job, roof over your head—you know where to find me, Raf," Dion said. "You're still my skinny half-breed brother—half mick, half wop. I got to protect you, dawg. Just like the old days."

With that, the two mobsters shook hands with Raffy and began a slow stroll out the bar, the patrons eyeing them carefully as they exited stage right. Make way for Mad Dog and Jim the Rim. They some bad mo-fos.

CHAPTER 4

The Captain's Quarters

Office of the Publisher, New York Herald
Herald Tower, Midtown Manhattan
Monday, Sept. 10, 2001
5:15 p.m.

Maggie and Kellen were always taken by the majesty of Ari Steinberg III's corporate suite compared to the dung-heap of a newsroom one floor below.

Up on 15, the carpets were fit to sleep on, the furniture made for a prince, and the paintings all Monets. Down on 14, the floor was linoleum, the aluminum desks gun-metal gray, and the walls a bulletin-board mishmash of notes, announcements and photos.

From the engine room to the captain's quarters, Kellen mused, always a jarring climb.

"Maggie, Kellen, please come in," Ari said, bouncing out of his high-backed leather chair to greet his top-tier editors. "I heard you wanted to see me *toute de suite*. What can I do for you?"

What struck most people when they met Ari III for the first time is that he appears to be a Yiddish version of that J. Peterman character on "Seinfeld." The stilted speech, the lecturing tone, the born-on-third-base pomposity, the French *bon mots*. It was Ari to a tee.

But he was revered in the newsroom because he continued to invest big bucks in the dead-tree edition even though the internet tidal wave was now clearly visible on the horizon. The fact that he was a stuffy twit—and not the brightest bulb--bothered no one so long as he kept writing the checks.

"Afternoon, Ari," Kellen began, tone deferential as always in these gilded surroundings. "Thank you so much for seeing us on such short notice. We know how busy you are."

"You're most welcome," Ari replied, smiling, hands behind his head, Gucci loafers on the edge of his antique desk, a picture of relaxed royalty. "What can I do for my two favorite editors?"

"Ari," Maggie cut in, taking charge, "let me go right to the chase: Kellen and I have decided to close the South Pacific bureau and redeploy our scarce reporting resources over there to China. Our tandem couple in Australia has not worked out as we had hoped. We're going to recall Rafer to work in New York as an investigative reporter on Metro. We're going to tell him tomorrow."

Ari winced but said nothing. He stood up and walked to the picture window overlooking the heart of the city's honky-tonk tourist district. After a long look down, he slowly turned his gaze back to his underlings, gently stroking his chin with his left hand.

"What about Angela?" he said finally.

"What about her, Ari?" Maggie replied sharply. "She and Rafer are getting a divorce and she's not that valuable to foreign. It was a fluke of marriage that foreign got her in the first place. Maybe we could send her back to India. I haven't given it that much thought. She's a terrific photographer but a lousy reporter. We can't tolerate that on foreign."

Again, Ari did not react immediately, letting Maggie's harsh words hang in the air and marinate as he slowly—as always—collected his thoughts. He sat back down.

"Maggie, Kellen," he said, moving into lecture mode, "I need to take a few moments to explain an issue with which you are probably both unfamiliar."

OMG, Maggie thought, not another one of his virtual soliloquies about Australia. I don't think I can take hearing this story again.

"I wanted the Sidney bureau reopened in the mid-1990s when you were in London, Kellen, and Maggie, you had just gotten to Washington as bureau chief, I believe. The reasons I did so remain valid today, though my senior editors have always been non-believers. So, allow me to explain in more detail."

Lie back and think of Paris, Maggie thought.

"When I was a young reporter back in the day—when Ari Jr. wanted me to learn the business from the bottom up—I read all the stories from Australia by a correspondent named David Lamb from the Los Angeles Times. We had our own reporter there but, frankly, his dispatches tilted toward the dull side."

Just like you, Maggie thought.

"The Los Angeles Times, on the other hand, was in the early stages of a Grand Awakening under the great Otis Chandler and Lamb was a member of a new generation of foreign correspondents who were daring, imaginative, unpredictable. He wrote about the Aussie love affair with pubs, gay rights in the land of the macho man, the legendary Aussie racehorse Goondiwindi. Those kinds of dispatches. Marvelous reading, just marvelous. Made me fall in love with the place all over again. As you may not be aware, I sowed some wild oats down there as a young college student."

Ari smiled slyly and paused. As always, he was immensely enjoying the opportunity to lecture his senior editors on what really constituted great foreign reporting.

"Anyway, when I became publisher 10 years ago after Ari Jr. retired, I began applying pressure to reopen in Sydney—we closed it in the 70s—because I felt we could bring fresh eyes and first-rate journalism to the first world's most underreported region."

Fabulously fit from years of cross-training, Ari sprang to his feet like someone in their 20s (he was 51) and returned to the picture window. Looking at the crowds below, he droned on, oblivious to his audience's ennui.

"The top editors at the paper at the time all opposed the idea—no news down there, they said—but I insisted. Though the idea was outstanding—if I do say so myself—the execution failed. They sent Rafer Flanagan, a great digger and dogged reporter who wouldn't know a good feature story if it bit him on the bottom."

Ari stopped again, chortling at his choice of words, his audience smiling and feigning interest. Ari sat down again and looked hard at Maggie this time.

"Thank God for Angela," he said. "She has authored nifty business stories and her travel dispatches from all over the South Pacific are a huge magnet for advertisers. I get to Asia at least once a year and I always get rave reviews about her from the business community south of the equator. And you're right about one element, Maggie. Her photographs are simply marvelous. Beautiful tableaus that bring her stories alive. Saves us a prodigious amount of money. Our other correspondents should be so gifted."

"Ari," Maggie blurted, trying to jump in.

"Stop, Maggie," Ari shot back, holding out his left hand. "Let me finish. The bottom line here is the Aussie visitors board is a huge advertiser in our Sunday travel section with all those FYI South Pacific ads and they adore her. She's our great goodwill ambassador down there—unlike her inebriate of a spouse whom no one has seen in years."

Ari cracked a slight smile, pleased with his argument and choice of words. This man is dangerous, Maggie thought. His sisters are right: he is a fool.

"Maggie, Kellen, I don't want to close Sydney yet," Ari declared. "Fine to recall Rafer but I want to meet with Angela to mull the possibilities."

Hmmm, won't be a lot of mulling in that meeting, Maggie thought. Speaking of pictures, I'd like to get a shot of that little get-together.

"One last point," Ari said, putting his $400 tasseled loafers on his desk again. "I expect both of you to act in the overall best interest of this great newspaper, whose long-term financial future is, unfortunately, problematic at best. It does not matter what the journalists themselves think. Most of them don't know how to run anything except their mouths. They have never made a payroll and they haven't the foggiest notion what it takes to run a profitable news enterprise. We move them around like chess pieces for the greater good of our readers and, yes, our advertisers. Maggie, every foreign correspondent doesn't need to be David Halberstam. We need good feature writers as well."

"Yes sir, I hear you," Maggie said quietly.

"Let's talk tomorrow after Kellen has met with Raffy," Ari concluded enthusiastically, bounding to his feet and rubbing his hands. "I've got a good feeling about all this. Making lemonade out of lemons. It's going to be a win-win-win.

Something's Rotten Down Under

Office of the Editor, New York Herald
Herald Tower, Midtown Manhattan
Monday, Sept. 10, 2001
5:53 p.m.

"Win-win-win, my fat ass," Maggie said sarcastically. "Do something, Kellen. You're the foreign editor."

Both editors laughed, shaking their heads at the opaque world of Ari Steinberg III and the rest of his dysfunctional family organization. It's like watching your favorite soap opera but the tv is fuzzy and the voices are scrambled. You sort of get what's going on but you're not certain.

"Something is rotten in our little South Pacific outpost," Maggie said. "I can't see it but I can smell it. Not sure I really want to know."

As the pair chatted, lower-level reporters and editors buzzed outside Maggie's office, preparing for the evening news meeting that would determine the content and look of tomorrow's front page. It was a special time of day in a beloved ritual and routine that was slowly coming to an end.

"Maggie, let me ask you a serious question," Kellen said. "If Ari wants Angela to be Sydney bureau chief, why fight him? Who gives a flying frog about that place? Most Americans probably think Sydney is the capital of Sweden. Or Austria. Besides, Ari says he wants half our 25 bureau chiefs to be female by the end of 2003. He has told the board of directors that. This is just part of that effort."

"I don't buy it," Maggie snapped. "She doesn't have the intellect, experience or temperament to be a good bureau chief. We certainly couldn't count on her if the *merde* ever hits the fan down there. I have to be able to sleep at night."

Maggie paused and looked out into the newsroom. "This is the worst kind of affirmative action," she added. "There are plenty of women in this newsroom right now who could do that job better than Angela. But all you need to do is look into Ari's eyes when he talks about her. She has a serious hold on him—and she knows it."

Need to lighten up here a little, Kellen thought.

"Maggie," he said, smiling, "remember how a certain comely young female correspondent used to schtup the Paris bureau chief back in the day? Just wondering how this is any different."

"Hah, hah, Kellen," Maggie said with a snicker. "All that comes to mind is a brief tryst at the end of a long liquid lunch on the Champs Elysses. Or was it the Left Bank? I can't remember. Whatever happened to that guy?"

"He went on to become the London bureau chief of the *New York Herald*," Kellen shot back. "Rumor has it he played a major role in mentoring that correspondent, who became the first female editor in the paper's century-old history."

Maggie laughed. "Tell that guy he wasn't that good, believe me. Now get out of here Kellen. I have a news meeting to run. Bring Raffy around after lunch tomorrow and I'll get him jazzed about Metro. And thanks for the trip down memory lane."

Maggie laughed again and dismissed her foreign editor with a flip of the left hand.

Hmmm, Kellen thought, his pale face reddening as he made his way back to his office. What exactly did she mean, he wasn't that good?

CHAPTER 6

The Unhappy Reporter

Office of Lieutenant Gino Carella
NYPD Headquarters, Lower Manhattan
Monday, Sept. 10, 2001
6:36 p.m.

Sargent Candy Garcia, chief deputy to Lieutenant Gino Carella, strolled casually into her boss' windowless office at police headquarters, a transcript in her hands, a look of mild amusement on her face.

"Lieutenant." she said, "can I show you something interesting?"

"Make it fast, Sergeant," Carella said. "Terror squads got a huge softball game tonight with Engine Co. 66. Game's down in Brooklyn Heights at 8:30. We're going to smoke their Irish asses."

"Sorry I can't be there," Garcia deadpanned. "I love watching 50-year-old men running around in tight tee shirts and spandex pants. The way their bodies jiggle—it's so hot."

Carella looked up from his desk and glared at his wise-ass deputy—and good friend—looking drop-dead fit in her perfectly tailored NYPD uniform. He instinctively sucked in his ample stomach.

"Sargent Garcia," Carella said evenly, "I'm going to bust that cute butt of yours down to meter maid if you keep implying how fat I've gotten—even if it's true. Now, whatya got there?"

"You know that wiretap we got on that booth down at Behan's Ale House in Brooklyn Heights where those Saudi guys have lunch?" she asked. "Well, we just got an interesting hit."

"Fantastic," Carella said, grabbing the transcript out of her hand and scanning it quickly. "Give me the headline."

"Well," Garcia replied carefully," it's not what you might think. It's not about the Muslims, it's about those dago dudes you used to chase."

"Dago dudes," Carella said, laughing. "I like that. For a Rican, you're pretty clever. What do we have here?"

"I just read it quickly," she replied, "but it sounds like Sal DeStefano's son, Dion, is offering to ice the wife of some reporter at the *New York Herald*. Some guy named Ralph or something like that. Guess she's a coke addict and ruining his life."

"Listen, Garcia," Carella said impatiently, standing and starting to pace, "that tap in Behan's is to investigate a possible terror cell, not snoop on some *Herald* reporter. Hell, half the men in New York want to kill their wives. Tell me something I don't know. Besides, I could care less about the *Herald*. It's a rag. They hate cops."

"I like their style section," she offered.

"More to the point," Carella continued, "I'll never get promoted again—and you won't either—if we don't get something on those A-rabs. There's been a lot of buzz lately about a possible terror attack on New York. Where are we on that?"

"Don't know yet," she replied. "They always speak in the mother tongue and it takes a while to get those translated. You speak Italian, I speak Spanish, we both speak English and none of it does us any good."

Both cops yukked it up over that one.

"Look, Garcia, I gotta go," Carella said. "Game's for the championship and I gotta get loose. I'm the star centerfielder if you'd like to attend."

"Hmmm," Garcia said, "if you are the star, who's the batboy?"

"Hah," Carella shot back. "You should really come watch us play. You might just finally find yourself a boyfriend. Didn't you just turn 30? Your poor mother must be beside herself."

"Believe me," Garcia said, laughing, "I've got higher standards than that. I'd rather go it alone."

"Suit yourself," Carella said, tossing the transcript into the bottom drawer of a metal filing cabinet on his way out the door. "Let me know if we get anything more specific on the unhappy Carl Bernstein. And we should at least make sure Brooklyn organized crime knows what Dion DeStefano is doing these days. He's turning out to be worse than Sal.

CHAPTER 7

The Lord's Work

Home of John J. (Black Jack) Reilly
Baldwin Farms Road, Greenwich, Conn.
Monday, Sept. 10, 2001
10:33 p.m.

Black Jack Reilly struggled mightily to emerge from his soft leather chair and go over to the bar in his beloved library. Though the gait was unsteady, the spirit was willing for one last call.

"How about just one more, Raf, and we'll turn out the lights?" Jack said, words starting to slur slightly. "I know you have a big day tomorrow."

Jack and his books, Raffy mused, a love affair pure and simple. The bookcases jammed to capacity and lining all four walls from top to bottom, this is the spot where he wants to spend his final months on earth. Looks more like a third-hand bookstore.

"Make it a light one, Jack, please," Raffy said. "This Wild Turkey can sneak up on you."

"Cheers, Raf," Jack said, handing his son-in-law a whiskey glass filled with four ounces of 101-proof bourbon, three ice cubes and no water. The pair clinked glasses.

"Listen, Raf," Jack began, "if they make you return to New York, why don't you stay with me until you get your sea legs? You can take the train to mid-town. I know Angy wants to stay in Australia. She loves it there. It's her home now."

Raffy tried to break in but Jack waived him off.

"I don't have much time left and it's just me now, all these rooms and ghosts of memories past. I've still got a few rounds of golf left in me and I'd love it if you would join me."

"Jack," Raffy replied, "I really appreciate the offer, but I've got to work through this mess. Maybe hit reset and get sent to China. Really hot there now. Great economics story. And that's the area, after all, where I won my Pulitzer.

"Fact is, Jack, this is all I know. I just can't tell you how humiliating this recall to headquarters would be. I think it might just kill me."

Startled, Jack looked at his favorite son-in-law for several seconds and nodded. "You know, Raf, I have five other sons-in-law and they're all jackasses—country-club types, all born on the opposing 10-yard line and act like they've run the ball back 90 yards. Just like that knucklehead in the White House.

"On the other hand, you're like me: Irish, blue collar to the bone, work hard, work smart. You know, I love the *Herald*. It's my bible. And you're the best. I have so enjoyed seeing your stories on the front page—Africa, Middle East, Asia. You've had a great run. Give yourself some credit."

Jack took a long sip of his bourbon and plowed ahead.

"You reporters do the Lord's work, but your bosses have done a terrible job telling the public why what you do is so important. It's not enough just to say your work speaks for itself. Doesn't work that way anymore. You need to tell your story. Rush Limbaugh has been killing you guys for years."

"Yeah," Raffy replied absently, "that's beyond my pay grade. Listen, Jack, your friendship means everything to me. Sorry what's happened with Angela and me. We're trying to make this parting as painless as possible."

"She's a handful, I know," Jack replied. "Had a hard upbringing down there in east Texas. Mother was an addict, stepfather abused her.

"Funny," he added, "she appears so normal—charming, smart, beautiful. Damage is all in the head."

"Yeah, I know the feeling," Raffy said. "You know what they say in AA, don't you? 'Normal is a setting on a washing machine.' How about another, Jack? I'm feeling pretty good right now. I think I'll be able to pull this off tomorrow."

CHAPTER 8

Tangled Web

New Jersey Turnpike, Exit 14E
Tuesday, Sept. 11, 2001
8:33 a.m.

Head pounding, bloodshot eyes shielded by tinted glasses, Rafer Flanagan reached for his driver's license as New Jersey state trooper Dan Wirthin approached the car on the passenger side of the turnpike.

"Sir, do you know you were going 77 in a 55?" the trooper asked, bending over and looking through the window that Raffy had opened. "That borders on reckless driving. What's the rush?"

"Sorry, Officer," Raffy answered meekly, handing him his driver's license and the Hertz registration card on the 2002 Cadillac SUV. "Got a little lost and ended up in Jersey. Trying to get to an 8:45 meeting at the World Trade Center."

"Well, you can forget that," Wirthin said. "Are you okay, Mr. Flanagan? You don't look so good."

"I'm fine, thanks," Raffy lied. "Just a little jet-lagged. Flew into JFK last night from Sydney."

No harm in a little bullshit, he thought.

"Okay," Wirthin said. "Wait here."

What a mess, Raffy thought. Did he and Jack really finish that whole bottle last night? All lost in a bourbon-shrouded fog. Worse, he left his cell phone in Greenwich. No way to call his breakfast interview, Burton Smith, to tell him he would be late.

What a great friend and source Bertie is, Raffy mused. So glad I can hook up with him while I'm here. High-level exec at Citicorp, lives in both Sydney and New York, great contacts in Aussie law enforcement and has intelligence agency contacts all over the world, including the CIA and MI6. Meet several times a year to swap gossip, story ideas and sources.

"You're not Australian, are you, sir?" Wirthin asked, reappearing at the passenger window. "You don't sound like it." The cop handed him back his license, along with the car registration and speeding ticket.

"No, I'm American but I've lived in Sydney several years and I had to get an Aussie driver's license when I got there. They drive on the left side, you know. Back on holiday now. I'm South Pacific bureau chief of the *New York Herald*."

"The *Herald*, eh?' Wirthin said, unimpressed. "Never read it. They hate cops."

"Sorry you feel that way, officer," Raffy said lamely. "They really don't."

"One other thing, Mr. Flanagan. You said you flew into JFK from Australia last night, right?"

"Yes, sir."

"Then why did you rent this car a week ago in Greenwich, Conn.?"

Christ, Raffy thought, what an idiot I am. Just keep your mouth shut. He stared across the Hudson River at lower Manhattan, gleaming in the morning sun. Several seconds passed.

"Oh, what a tangled web we weave, Mr. Flanagan," Wirthin said finally. "You can pay your ticket by mail. Have a nice day."

Lord, what else could go wrong, Raffy thought. He looked at his watch. It was eight forty-five.

CHAPTER 9

So Long Cruel World

New Jersey Turnpike, Exit 14E
Tuesday, September 11, 2001
10:44 a.m.

Scared sober, Raffy had a front-row seat to the horror flick playing out in real time at the south end of Manhattan.

Why am I paralyzed, he thought? Even after two hours. I should be rushing toward the smoke. That's what good reporters are supposed to do.

A gorgeous day west of the Hudson River, to the east it was Satan's show. His brain could barely absorb that the twin towers had collapsed —yes, just fucking crumbled—before his very eyes. How could that happen, he asked over and over? Steel just doesn't melt, does it?

"I was in Vietnam during Tet and it wasn't nothing like this," Raffy heard one New York cop tell a radio reporter for the all-news channel.

Poor Bertie, Raffy thought for about the fourth time. No way he could have gotten out of that north tower when the first plane hit. If I hadn't overslept, I would have been with him at the very end, he mused for the first time.

Though late in arriving, the realization jolted him like an electric current from a defibrillator for a patient in cardiac arrest. A feeling of warmth began to flow through him. Everyone—Angela, Jack, Kellen, Maggie--all knew he had an 8:45 meeting at Windows on the World.

Maybe it's time to begin anew, he thought, looking hard at the black-and-white dust cloud still shrouding the chaos across the river. The cloud in his head, however, was starting to lift. Chance for a fresh start in a new century, hell, a new millennium. Put all his wreckage in the rear-view mirror where it belonged. No more Angela, partner from Hell. No more buzz on the foreign staff about the tragic dimming of one of its erstwhile bright lights. No perp walk through the newsroom to get the official edict from Maggie the Ball Buster.

What's that Army Airborne motto? Death before dishonor? So brave, so strong, so pure. My honor will be salvaged, my reputation restored. No more depression, no more booze, no more insane voices jabbering incessantly in my head. Goodbye to my beloved profession that is headed straight into a Cat 5 hurricane.

Taking a deep breath, he started the car for the first time since being stopped and steered it back onto the turnpike, heading who knows where.

Rafer McCann Flanagan—Brooklyn high school basketball star, elite foreign correspondent, Pulitzer Prize winner—disappeared along with thousands of others in the World Trade Center collapse. Cut down in the prime of his life, going full stride, head held high.

RIP, Raffy Flanagan. You will be missed.

CHAPTER 10

Goodbye to an Irishman

Section Two, Obituary Page
New York Herald
Sunday, September 16, 2001

Herald Scribe Feared
Dead in WTC Collapse

By Foxx Buttermilk
©Herald Staff Writer

Pulitzer Prize-winning foreign correspondent Rafer M. Flanagan is missing and feared dead in the terrorist attacks on the World Trade Center last Tuesday, it was announced Saturday.

Flanagan, 52, was the South Pacific bureau chief of the *New York Herald*. Based in Sydney, Australia, he was in New York at the time in an interview at the Windows on the World restaurant when the first of the hijacked commercial airliners slammed into the north tower.

Police said nobody above the point of impact on the 78th floor survived, including senior Citicorp executive Burton "Bertie" Smith, the man Flanagan was believed to be interviewing at the time. Senior bank officials confirm that Smith has not been seen since the attacks.

In a phone interview, *Herald* foreign editor Kellen T. Williams explained that Flanagan and his wife, Angela, also a *Herald* reporter in Australia, were on home leave at the time of the attacks.

Williams said Mr. Flanagan was being groomed for a senior editing position with the paper at Herald Tower in midtown Manhattan. "As impressive as his reporting career had been, his best days as a newspaperman were still ahead of him," Williams said.

In a press release, *Herald* Editor Margarite T. Maye called Flanagan a "key part of the paper's foreign correspondent network who will be sorely missed. The newspaper business was in his DNA." Flanagan's late father was a delivery truck driver for the *New York Daily News* in the south Brooklyn neighborhood of Bensonhurst.

Flanagan won the prestigious Pulitzer Prize for foreign reporting in 1988 for a collection of stories on the gales of economic change blowing through East and South Asia, primarily China and India. He was based in New Delhi at the time.

"Rarely has a foreign correspondent written so perceptively and authoritatively about matters of such great economic importance," the Pulitzer board said in its citation of Flanagan's work.

Ms. Flanagan, in a phone interview from Greenwich, Conn., where she is staying temporarily, spoke of the "heartbreak of losing my soul brother and best friend," adding she intends to "carry on as a reporter in my late husband's best tradition. I'm sure he would want me to return to Sydney and continue where he left off."

"He loved Van Morrison, his fellow Irishman," she added, voice cracking. "If you want to remember Raffy, please play 'Reminds Me Of You.' It was his Irish national anthem."

Mr. and Ms. Flanagan were among several elite couples in the newspaper business who handle their overseas assignments as a team. They were featured in a cover story in the *U.S. Journalism Review* in 1990 about how they carried out their shared duties on an equal basis.

"Just as their marriage is sown seamlessly by a deep love," the article stated, "so their joint reporting efforts are bound by a deep sense of unity, pride and purpose."

CHAPTER 11

A Bad Porn Movie

Plaza Hotel, Room 1313
New York Herald Suite
Central Park South
Sunday, September 16, 2001
4:44 p.m.

Angela Flanagan gazed over the south end of Central Park, expertly inhaled two lines of white powder on the black marble writing table, and nimbly gulped from a three-ounce tumbler of freezer-cold Stolichnaya, her favorite chaser.

God, what a week, she thought. Five awful days for New York City and America, five great ones for me. So long drunken husband, goodbye money worries, adios back-bench reporter. Unless I fuck this up, she thought, the bureau chief job is mine. About bloody time.

As the cocaine coursed through her divine 41-year-old body, focusing her on the task at hand, she fixed her long red hair in a ponytail and glanced over her shoulder at her most important "client." Save for the blue-silk underpants around his left ankle, he was as naked as one of those old Playgirl poster boys. Wrists tied to the headboard, he was lying on the bed face down on a thick blue comforter, head resting on a soft pink pillow.

What a scene, she thought. The world's most influential newspaper publisher is her own personal butt boy. Sporting a mid-thigh fish-net t-shirt, silk underwear, and four-inch spiked heels, the lady in all black stared down coolly at Ari Steinberg III. Have to give it to him, she mused. Has a great body for a guy in his early 50s. Firm butt, nice abs, strong legs, well hung. No wonder women throw themselves at him.

"Honey," she drawled, thin leather whip in hand, "I love these little sessions of ours. Scene out of a bad porn movie, don't ya think? The ruthless female subordinate punishing the powerful publishing tycoon for his misbehavior. You love it too. It's the one time you don't have to be in charge."

Angela giggled before prattling on: "If they ever make a movie about us, I want Glenn Close to play me. One tough chick. Always gets what she wants. Loved 'Fatal Attraction.'

"Are you kidding?" Ari replied, lifting his head off the pillow and looking back. "Do you remember what happened to her at the end?"

"So," Angela said, shifting gears, "when is the big announcement? Maggie is fighting this, I know. She hates me."

"Angela," Ari said, exasperated, "give it a little time. We just ran Rafer's obituary this morning. You just lost your soul mate, remember?"

Angela just smiled. He can be amusing, she thought, even at a time like this.

"Job is yours," Ari purred. "Don't worry, baby. Announcement by month's end, I promise."

Angela smiled contently. Just love the way his heart and mind follow when I have him by the *cajones*, she thought. No way Maggie can fight me on this.

CHAPTER 12

Raining on this Parade

Office of the Publisher, New York Herald
Herald Tower, Midtown Manhattan
Monday, September 24, 2001
11:55 a.m.

Tanned and well-rested from the usual long weekend in East Hampton, the publisher of the *New York Herald* was in a rare expansive mood —animated, excited, defiant, really *enjoying* the job for a change.

Leaning back in his leather chair, hands behind his head, feet on his grandfather's desk, Ari Steinberg III was basking in the accolades raining down on the paper.

"Maggie, Kellen," he raved, almost yelling, "the 9/11 coverage has been fantastic, off the charts, *incroyable*. Circulation is up eight percent. We're selling 100,000 more papers a day all over the country. New readers flooding the web site in staggering numbers. Everybody's emailing me. Bravo, they're saying, bravo, bravo."

Ari paused, virtually leaped out of his chair and walked to the picture window, looking down on the late morning throng, the tourists and office workers flooding the midtown zone. His editors—spent from two weeks of 16-hour days—smiled as brightly as they could but remained mum. Both braced for the point.

"I know you guys are exhausted," Ari continued, "but this is where the rubber meets the road. I feel multiple Pulitzers here. Democracy's highest calling. When the going gets tough, we get going."

He didn't really say that, did he, Kellen thought. His clichés are more banal than Maggie's.

"Thanks, Ari," Maggie said finally. "We appreciate your support. It means the world to us."

Ari nodded, returned to his desk and sat on the edge, directly in front of his two editors. Here it comes, Maggie thought.

"Now," Ari began, "let's get to the point of this little get-together, shall we?"

Ari smiled awkwardly and looked directly at Maye. "Maggie, I'm going to overrule you. Angela Flanagan will replace her late husband as South Pacific bureau chief. She will get his salary and all his duties. She has earned this chance. This decision is final. *Fini*, as the frogs like to say."

Maggie didn't react, though her complexion started to turn from cream to crimson. She looked away, masking her disgust.

"Look, Maggie,' Ari began, argument well-rehearsed, "you know what a priority it has been for me to promote women in the newsroom. Making Mrs. Flanagan a bureau chief is simply in line with that strategy."

Again, silence from his audience.

"Come on, Maggie," Ari said, almost pleading. "Say something. Work with me on this. Tell me what you really think."

Maggie finally laughed. "I can't, Ari. You'd fire me on the spot. Look, it's your paper. Do what you want. I'll simply repeat that she's not qualified to be a bureau chief. She's a terrific photographer who didn't even begin her reporting career until she went to Nairobi with Raffy. That doesn't clear the bar. She can't do real news and analysis. You will regret this one day."

"Kellen?" Ari asked, turning to his foreign editor.

"We'll make it work," Williams replied crisply. "I'll have her report directly to Peter Bainbridge. He's coming back from Joburg to be my chief deputy. He'll keep her on a short leash."

Ari will get that imagery, Maggie thought, smiling slightly.

"Perfect," Ari said, jumping up again and clapping his hands like a football yell leader. "I adore solutions. Give her a year max. If she flops, I'll fire her myself."

Ari clapped his hands again and started to pace. "Now, I want Betsy Wright to orchestrate the press release on this. Maggie, put the story inside this Sunday's business section. Use good color photos. Get Foxx to write the story. He did a great job on Rafer's obituary. I loved the ending."

"That was total bullshit," Maggie snapped.

"Of course it was," Ari said soothingly, smiling, "but we don't display our dirty clothes in public. We only do that for everyone else."

The three laughed and rose to their feet, the dreaded meeting finally almost over.

"On to the next edition," Ari said, almost giddy now. "I can't wait to inform the board of directors about Mrs. Flanagan, of whom they think the world. Our directors are great supporters of my distaff promotion program."

"How big is the board these days," Maggie asked matter-of-factly, heading toward the exit.

"Hmmm, about 15, I believe," Ari replied.

"And how many are women?"

"Two, I believe," Ari replied, oblivious to Maggie's trap.

"Sounds like the board could use a distaff promotion push of its own," she sneered. "Might try to set an example for the rest of the employees."

"Now, now, Maggie Maye," Ari said, smile curdling noticeably, "no raining on this parade. Just think Pasadena on one of those beautiful mornings on New Year's Day."

Snippy bitch, Ari thought, after showing his editors the door. I've always been a trailblazer for female advancement and this is the thanks I get?

CHAPTER 13

New Ouagadougou Bureau

Office of the Editor, New York Herald
Herald Tower, Midtown Manhattan
Monday, September 24, 2001
12:17 p.m.

Now it was Maggie's turn to take her head in her hands and rub her pounding temples.

"Thanks for backing me up in there, Kellen," she said sourly. "Something besides: 'we'll make it work.'"

"Stop, Maggie," Kellen fired back, holding out his palms. "Just stop. We have a war to cover. I have five reporters in Afghanistan and four in Pakistan. That's what I need to focus on—not some silly melodrama in Sydney. That's community theater in Omaha for a paper like ours."

Maggie threw her pen down on her legal pad in disgust, knowing full well her foreign editor was right. Kellen was a good journalist, she thought, even if he was a dud in the hay and useless in management range wars.

"You're right," Maggie said wearily, rubbing her eyes and brushing back the sides of her longish, graying black hair, now in a ponytail. "I have to let this go. Too many important things to worry about."

"Maybe Angy the Cat will surprise us," Kellen said without much conviction, glancing at his watch. "At any rate, I'll make clear to Bainbridge that his ass is on the line here. If she fucks up, he'll be opening our new bureau in Burkino Faso."

Maggie laughed, lightening the mood momentarily.

"I just can't help it," she said. "The woman makes my skin crawl. The obsequious southern accent that always seems to sweeten around the big swinging dicks. Did you see her a couple of years ago at that Asian correspondents' meeting in Tokyo? She was all over Ari like a bad aftershave."

Kellen said nothing, hoping the silence would end the meeting. He shifted uncomfortably on the couch and looked again at his watch, conspicuously this time. This is getting old, he thought. The newsroom calls.

"And she's so obsessed with her appearance," Maggie rattled on. "The long red hair. That must be a dye job. The designer clothes. That body—God, it's just perfect. She just doesn't *look* like a foreign correspondent for the *New York Herald*."

"Ease up, Maggie," Kellen replied. "Cut her some slack. I've never seen Ari so happy as he was just now. Give the gentleman what he wants. Angela is his kind of correspondent. She's good for business. She's sexy, glamorous, smart in her own way, talented in her own way. Just the kind of reporter who might attract the less literary younger readers."

Kellen paused, looked out into the newsroom and stood to go.

"Ari doesn't want any more reporters from Smith College who want to write about poverty in the Horn of Africa. Australia excites him. There's money there, adventure, beautiful women. Let him have it. We don't have time to care."

"It's going to be your ass if she fucks up, Kellen," Maggie warned as he moved out the door. "You will be opening that new bureau in Ouagadougou. I hear they have a great film festivals there."

Kellen roared with laughter as he exited into the newsroom, just now awakening to the sounds and scents of the next edition. I'm glad he thinks I'm kidding, Maggie thought.

CHAPTER 14

The Elephant Wears Pink

Office of the Publisher, New York Herald
Herald Tower, Midtown Manhattan
Tuesday, September 25, 2001
11:22 a.m.

Ari Steinberg looked uneasily across his desk at the unwelcome visitor—Wilbur Ross, the paper's chief auditor, the ogre who always tells the publisher what he doesn't want to hear.

My God, look at him, Ari thought. Dresses like he gets his style tips from the "The Man in the Gray Flannel Suit." Way beyond old school. The man radiates mustiness.

Problem is, Ari reminded himself, Wilbur knows where all the money goes—when to wink yes or shake his head no—and he's still married to Jenna, my looney older sister. Last time the clan gathered at Dad's in Palm Beach, when I wasn't there, Jenna bad-mouthed me mercilessly. Said I was totally inept. Thankless bitch. Entire family, except for Dad and Wilbur, are a bunch of loathsome freeloaders who live *la dolce vita* on *Herald* dividend checks.

"So, Wilbur," Ari said impatiently, drumming his manicured fingers on his desk, "give me the headline on this overseas trip of yours. What are you recommending for foreign? I don't want to wait for the written report."

"Cost structure in Asia is a nightmare," Wilbur replied bluntly. "Riddled with fat. Looks like a bad steak. Expense accounts and living costs are obscene."

"So what's the answer?" Ari asked irritably.

"Close Sydney for starters," the numbers man said. "We closed it once 27 years ago. Time for a redo."

"Wilbur, listen to me," Ari shot back, "since you took your trip to Asia in August—which cost $16,000 by the way—we've had 9/11 and our Sydney bureau chief was killed by terrorists. I can't cut back in this environment. We're at war. Everybody is working sixteen hours a day. The paper is at the top of its game. Look at circulation, look at web traffic. Closing Sydney now would send a terrible message. No, the decision will have to wait until next year. Write up your report and I'll read it when I have time."

Neither man spoke for a while, Ari starting to drum his fingers again.

"Anything else, Wilbur? Got a lot on my plate today."

"Well, there is an elephant in the room and she's wearing pink," Wilbur said mildly. "Name is Angela."

"What about her?" Ari snarled. "She's getting her husband's job. Announcement TK. She's perfect for the job. Business leaders down there love her."

"Ari, I'm a numbers guy," Wilbur said patiently. "I look at the cost side of things. She hired that office manager last year with no ok from anyone. All off the books. You don't do that with a public company. Even our outside auditors didn't know. The SEC wouldn't like that."

"Look, Wilbur, don't be so literal here," Ari shot back. "The SEC doesn't care about petty stuff like this. Take my word on this. I'm the lawyer.

"Look, Flanagan is dead. No more $175,000 salary, no more health insurance. We're replacing him with someone already on the payroll. Do the numbers. Costs cut. Problem solved. Besides, our ad revenues down there have been terrific--better than any other overseas region except Canada, Mexico and Britain."

Wilbur sighed and jumped back in.

"Look, the cousins confide in me," he said carefully. "They're worried you're not paying enough attention to the web site, that you're spending way too much time and money on the newspaper, a doomed product in their view. And they worry about your relationship with, quote/unquote, that Flanagan woman, as they call her. Everyone except Roberta seems to know about her. Even your dad asked me about her."

"God damnit," Ari barked, slamming his palm down on his desk, "fuck the relatives and fuck my dad. Fuck them all. They have no idea the pressure I'm under. I never wanted this fucking job. If my brothers hadn't been killed in that plane crash, I'd be in Silicon Valley working on cool things with Steve Jobs. Instead I'm stuck in an industry that has more in common with the 19th Century than the one we're in now. And the fact is, I have to support the newspaper. I have no choice. It makes all the money and I don't see that ending any time soon. The cousins wouldn't know anything about that. They've never paid a fucking bill in their life."

Wilbur didn't react to the outburst, waiting to make sure his brother-in-law was finished with the latest version of a familiar rant. Wilbur noted he had never heard the Steve Jobs reference before. Must be because the two met for the first time a few months ago at a tech conference in Palo Alto.

"Look, I know the stories," Ari said, tone softening slightly. "I've never had sexual relations with Mrs. Flanagan. Those rumors have been around for years and nobody has any proof they're true.

"The truth is I promoted Mrs. Flanagan because she hears a more melodious drum," he added, switching to J. Peterman mode. "Her feature stories are beautifully written, rainbow-like in their color. Like a bright blue hole in a slate gray sky. Most of our dispatches from overseas are so ponderous, they make me want to cry. Hers always have so much energy and life in them."

"Whatever Ari," Wilbur said, standing to go. "Just be careful. She's not like the other bureau chiefs. Did I mention I discovered that she spent $10,000 of company money last spring to celebrate her 40th birthday?"

"And that seven-bedroom palace we rent near Bondi Beach, where the party was held, is costing us about $100,000 a year. The woman is living like an English crown princess."

"Chump change, Wilbur," Ari said, more relaxed now, patting his bro-in-law on the shoulder. "The revenues from down there on the travel promotions alone make Sydney worth it. And that birthday party was fabulous PR for the paper. Everybody who is anybody was there. Society pages raved about it. Packwood Kerry, who lives down the street, gave me a first-hand account."

"Just don't let the tail wag the dog," Wilbur warned. "That's all I'm saying."

"Tell the cousins everything's under control," Ari said, showing Wilbur out with a smile. "Please inform them not to worry their empty little heads about anything. I got the waterfront covered."

CHAPTER 15

Red Star Rising

Business Section, Page 5
New York Herald
Sunday, Oct. 7, 2001

Herald Picks Widow
To Fill Aussie Post

By Foxx Buttermilk
©New York Herald Staff Writer

Angela R. Flanagan, veteran overseas reporter for the *Herald*, has been named the paper's new bureau chief in the South Pacific, the newspaper announced Saturday.

Ms. Flanagan is the widow of Rafer M. Flanagan, the previous bureau chief who died in the collapse of the World Trade Center on Sept. 11. Mr. Flanagan was on home leave at the time and was conducting an interview near the top of the north tower when the skyjackers struck.

"While we continue to mourn Mr. Flanagan's death, we are delighted his widow is available and ready to fill her late husband's very large shoes," *New York Herald* Publisher Ari Steinberg III said in a press release.

Ms. Flanagan, 40, began her journalism career as a photographer for the *Bergen Record* in northern New Jersey. Known then as Angela

Reilly, she met her future husband while he was a city hall reporter for the *New York Daily News*.

They met at Behan's Ale House in Brooklyn Heights in the 1980s. "It was Friday night after a long week for both of us," Ms. Flanagan recalled in a phone interview from her father's home in Greenwich, Conn. "It may not have been love at first sight but it was definitely electric."

In the past two decades, Ms. Flanagan has photographed and written travel, business and culture stories from Mumbai to Melbourne and Tasmania to Timbuktu. In her latest posting to Australia, she has done articles on the Sydney Opera House, the mining boom on the west coast and an intrepid American named Roff Smith who circled the entire country on a bicycle.

Since going aboard 16 years ago, the Flanagans have been based as a tandem couple in Nairobi, Cairo, New Delhi and, since 1996, Sydney. They were married at the summit of Mt. Kilimanjaro in a ceremony overseen by a Tanzanian faith healer.

"They worked together fluidly," *Herald* foreign editor Kellen T. Williams IV said in an email sent from his home in Rye, N.Y. "They each brought unique talents to inform and entertain our readers. We are delighted Ms. Flanagan will carry on in the finest tradition of this paper's superb correspondents in the United States and overseas."

Margarite T. Maye, the paper's first woman editor, said Ms. Flanagan's promotion is also part of the paper's goal to have half its 25 bureau chiefs be female as soon as possible. The number now stands at about 30%, she said.

"Our goal is to bring news to our readers from as diverse a group of journalists as possible," Maye said in the paper's press release. "Born in upscale Connecticut, raised in hard-scrabble East Texas, college educated in the suburbs of Chicago, Ms. Flanagan has a broad understanding of how Americans live and what they want to read. That will serve her well in her new assignment."

In a phone interview, her voice breaking, Ms. Flanagan read a prepared statement: "I am so honored by this promotion but I'm sorry it had to happen this way. I will miss my husband the rest of my life and will do everything possible to live up to his high standards." She declined further comment.

Ms. Flanagan was raised in Texarkana on the Texas side and attended the prestigious Medill School of Journalism at Northwestern University. She is the youngest child of Connecticut homebuilder John J. Reilly.

Mr. Reilly, battling lung cancer at age 78, said by phone that only a proud father could understand how he feels now. "I'm glad I lived to see this moment," he said.

Winifred Reilly Morgan, Ms. Flanagan's mother, is deceased, as is her stepfather, Army Lt. Col. Peter Morgan.

CHAPTER 16

A Natural Redhead

Office of Lt. Gino Carella, Department of Public Security
NYPD Headquarters, Lower Manhattan
Sunday, October 7, 2001
9:19 p.m.

Lieutenant Gino Carella eyed the half-eaten piece of pizza in his left hand—thick crust with pepperoni, onions, mushrooms, heavy on the Wisconsin cheese—and threw it into the metal trash can next to his desk.

My God, he thought wearily, rubbing his bloodshot eyes, was this his 24th straight day on the job or the 25th? Protecting this city will never be the same, he mused. Maybe it's time for a dinosaur like me to check out.

"Lieutenant Carella, you look like hell, honey," Candy Garcia, his chief deputy, said as she appeared in the doorway of his new office. "You should go home and get some rest."

"Don't sugarcoat it, Garcia," Carella said wearily, glancing at himself in the wall mirror and wincing. "And don't call me 'honey.' I'll have you brought up on sexual harassment charges."

The two friends laughed.

"That would look great on the front page of the *New York Post*," Garcia quipped. "You know: 'NYPD Boss Harassed by Hot Young Latina.' Your buddies at Engine Co. 66 would have loved that one."

"Makes me sad to even think about those guys," Carella said, quietly shaking his head. "They beat us 14-4 in the championship game and the next day most of them die just doing their job in the trade center. I still can't believe it happened. They're God's angels now."

Carella paused, adding: "You may still be hot but you sure as hell ain't young anymore."

"Hah, hah," Garcia shot back, not laughing. "By the way, did you read the business section of this morning's *Herald?*"

She pulled the section out of her huge leather purse and handed it to him. "Take a look at page five," she said.

"You know I don't read that rag."

"Just take a look. It won't bite."

"Whoa, who's this?" Carella asked, looking at the full-page color feature spread on Angela Flanagan. "Yabadabado."

"You're such a retard, Lieutenant." Garcia said, laughing. "Woman's name is Angela Flanagan. Same female mentioned in that tap at Behan's I told you about a few weeks ago. Husband ended up dying on 9/ 11. Thought you might want to see the woman that mobster offered to kill."

Carella laid the section out on his desk and dove deep into the promotion story that was accompanied by three color photos. The largest picture, taking up about a third of the page, featured Angela in a stylish hiking outfit at the famous Ayers Rock deep in the Australian Outback.

"Jesus," Carella said finally, "I never saw a newspaper reporter who looked like this. She really works for the *New York Herald?* Might have to start subscribing."

Carella stared at the photos for a long time, turning the broadsheet sideways and upside down for better angles, as if analyzing pictures of a crime scene.

"Man," he said finally, "she's hot, gonna get millions from all these insurance settlements and has a fab new job. A real hat trick. Wonder if she'd like to meet the new head of the NYPD Intelligence Division, fresh off divorce number three?"

"The woman lives in Australia, Lieutenant," Garcia pointed out.

"Yeah," he said absently, "my schlong's long but it ain't that long."

"Don't be a pig."

"I am a pig, So are you."

They laughed.

"You know," he said seriously, "I've wanted to go to Australia for a long time. Maybe next year. Maybe I'll be retired by then. Stop by her office and say hello. Who knows what will happen? She probably won't be in mourning anymore."

"She's not in mourning now, you blockhead," Garcia pointed out. "Read that transcript I gave you. They loathed each other. This article is total bullshit. 'Remember him the rest of my life,' my Puerto Rican pussy. She's probably already forgotten who he was."

"Don't call me a blockhead, Sargent," Carella said mildly, taking out a magnifying glass from his desk drawer to examine the photos even more closely. "God, her hair is fantastic. Must be a natural redhead. Look at those arms. This woman does some serious body work. Her nose looks a little crooked. Wonder what up with that?"

Carella sucked in his stomach and stood to go. "God, I feel awful, look awful," he said. "All this takeout food, no exercise, no fun. You know, I think I've gained 10 pounds in the last month. Maybe I'll get on my Harley and head over to Behan's for a beer. Not too far from where I live. Always wanted to check that place out."

CHAPTER 17

The Last Call

Home of John J. (Black Jack) Reilly
Baldwin Farms Road
Greenwich, Conn.
Monday, October 8, 2001
10:33 p.m.

Hearing the knock on his study door, Jack Reilly put his book aside and struggled to his feet.

Angela opened the door a crack, sticking her head in part-way. "Daddy, can I come in?' she asked. "Want to let you know my travel plans."

"Certainly, please, by all means," Jack replied. "How about a Stoli?"

Jack opened the small fridge under the wet bar, took out the quart bottle of the Russian vodka and poured triple shots into two highball glasses.

"Cheers, darling," Jack said, as father and daughter clinked glasses. "You make me very proud."

"Cheers, Daddy," she replied. "Love you more than you know."

Jack looked carefully at his youngest child, the product of his fourth —and final—marriage that lasted less than three years. Even without makeup, red hair tied in a bun and wearing a ratty pink bathrobe once worn by her late mother, she looked beautiful, Jack thought--despite the slightly crooked nose. Just like her fashion-model mother, Winifred, Jack remembered. He used to call her 'Freddy' in their happy early days.

The pair nursed their drinks in silence for a while, enjoying the late-night solitude on an early-fall evening, knowing this was almost surely the last time they would spend quality time together and talk honestly.

"Daddy," Angela said finally, "these last four weeks have been just a blur for me. I feel like the ground is still shaking. It just won't stop. I need to go home."

Angela took a sip and continued. "The scary thing is my future never looked better. I've got Raffy's old job and I'm getting all this insurance money. Made me an instant multi-millionaire. Just like I won the lottery. In a way, I guess I did."

"You know how much you'll get?" Jack asked.

"It's several million," Angela replied. "There's the double indemnity policy from the *Herald*—Raffy was working at the time—and then there's this special victim's compensation fund. I don't know how all that will sort out but it will be a lot of money.

"Funny thing is I didn't think of Raffy as my husband anymore. He fell off the wagon as soon as we got to Sydney and he never climbed back on. He was a complete mess. You saw him. He looked awful. So thin and frail."

"Yea, it was bad," Jack said. "Don't get it. I thought he was on track to be the editor of the paper. Won that Pulitzer, local Catholic high school basketball legend, beautiful and talented wife, son of a news-paper delivery truck driver. Had printers' ink in his bloodstream."

"He hated Sydney, Daddy," Angela said. "Called it the graveyard for his career. Never forgave me for pushing to go there. Sad. He was drunk all the time. Moved into a flat in a crappy part of town. Became a fag."

"Don't say fag," Jack said sharply. "Makes you sound ignorant, like you never left East Texas."

"Sorry, Daddy," Angela said sheepishly. "Sometimes you can't take East Texas out of the girl. I don't mean anything nasty. I don't care who he sleeps with."

"Listen, honey," Jack said, looking directly at his daughter, "don't look back. Not worth it. No regrets, no fear. This is your big chance. You're on the verge of something exciting. That's what matters now."

"Fact is, Daddy, I am afraid," Angela said, undoing her bun and allowing her long curly hair to cascade over her right shoulder. "I'm not sure I can do this job. The editors in New York hate me."

"What about all those nice things they said about you in the paper yesterday?" Jack asked. "Liked that they said you were part of the best the paper had to offer. Something like that."

"Oh, Daddy, that's just PR. Never believe that management crap, even from a newspaper. It's a public company. Bullshit the readers and stockholders at all costs."

Jack drained his highball glass and put it down. "Another drink, honey?" he asked. "Think I can handle one more."

"I don't think so, Daddy. One's enough tonight."

"As you can see, I've never been able to swear off the booze," Jack said. "Tried many times. Even was a grateful member of AA for a few years. Hey, why stop now? Dr. Stetson told me last week I probably have less than a year left."

"Daddy, please," Angela said, eyes suddenly welling up with tears. "You're going to be around much longer than that. Maybe you could come live with me in Australia. Talk about a country that knows how to drink."

They laughed.

"Well, Angela," Jack said, rising slowly to his feet, the clock in the study sounding the first of eleven chimes, "probably best if I stop too. I have a tee-time in the morning with the widow McGinley. Want to join us?"

"No, thanks, Daddy," Angela said, standing as well. "I have to start packing. So many clothes in the house I want to sort through and give away."

"Anyway," she added with a smile, "three's a crowd, at least in your generation."

"What's that supposed to mean?"

"Never mind, Daddy," Angela said, laughing and kissing him on the cheek. "I love you. Thanks for the chat. See you in the morning."

CHAPTER 18

Farewell My Lovely

City Room, New York Herald
Herald Tower, Midtown Manhattan
Tuesday, October 9, 2001
7:17 p.m.

Decked out exquisitely in cream-colored Australian pearls and black low-cut sleeveless dress, Angela made her way through the newsroom like a modern Grace Kelly sweeping by the adoring throngs at Oscar time. Every head in the office swiveled as she glided by, the intra-office e-mails spiking off the charts. Angy the Cat was in the house, on the red carpet.

Smiling, waving, shaking hands, blowing kisses, she certainly didn't look as if her mourning period lasted very long, Kellen Williams mused sourly as he awaited her in his office just off the newsroom floor.

"Angela, do come in," Kellen said, air-kissing her on both cheeks. "Thanks for stopping by. We'll make this quick."

Kellen shut the office door and closed the blinds so the nosey newsroom couldn't read their body language and spray gossipy e-mails hither and yon. Both took their seats, Kellen at his desk, Angela across from him on a well-worn red couch.

"I know you're in a hurry," Kellen began.

"Let's cut the bullshit, shall we, Kellen?" Angela interjected. "I know how you and Maggie feel about me. Good thing I have Ari on my side. I have to be in his office in ten minutes. He's taking me to a farewell soiree tonight at Elaine's. Tom Wolfe and Gay Talese will be there. They have been *such* a comfort to me since Raffy passed."

OMG, Kellen thought, not a lot to say to that.

"When are you going back," he asked blandly.

"Tomorrow night. Eight p.m. from JFK on Qantas. Lose a day on the way. Will be at my desk Saturday morning Sydney time."

"You met with Peter Bainbridge this afternoon, right?" Kellen asked.

"We talked on the phone," Angela replied curtly. "I didn't have time for a meeting."

"Peter is the best," Kellen said. "A real pro. You'll report right to him."

"Why the special treatment?" Angela shot back. "None of the other foreign reporters has to answer directly to him. Why do I?"

"Look, Angela," Kellen replied, voice hard now, stare direct and unblinking. "let's get something straight here. This is your chance to show you can play at the next level. No more travel stories about sunset camel rides on the beaches of western Australia—good as they were. We want smart analytical pieces about the entire South Pacific—how it's being changed by Asian immigration, how its economic ties to China and India are growing exponentially, how national defense strategies are evolving. We also want to break hard news. We want scoops that echo around the world and redound to our benefit. Always, always tell me something I didn't know or expect. Understood?"

Angela didn't respond at first, staring down at her red-polished fingernails and shifting her position on the couch. She uncrossed her legs and leaned forward.

"You know, Kellen," she said, "Ari also has lots of story ideas for me. He just loves Australia, as I'm sure you're aware. I'm told he lost his virginity down there. Even got a green kangaroo tattooed on his left hip to celebrate the occasion."

She paused before adding: "Or at least so I've been told." She smiled smugly and leaned back.

Not going there, Kellen thought. Just wasting my precious time. This woman is an empty dress—and radioactive to boot. Pardon the mixed metaphors, he mused.

"Good luck and Godspeed, Angela," he said, abruptly standing and showing her out. "Have a safe trip. Think big thoughts. Do great stories. Make us proud."

Kellen watched from his doorway as she made her way to the staircase in the newsroom that would take her to Ari III's suite one floor up. Have no idea where her ship is heading, he mused, but I do know those seas have never been mapped.

CHAPTER 19

Fire Down Below

South Pacific Bureau, New York Herald
Diplomat Road, Bellevue Hill, Australia
Friday, October 12, 2001
4:14 p.m.

The sun funneling through the skylight, the couple lounged lazily on the twin bed, nothing on except a Bob Seger CD, consumed with each other and catching up after the unexpectedly long separation.

"Angela, I still can't believe what happened to Raffy," Stacey McKenzie said, head resting on Angela's breasts. "What a bloody nightmare."

"I know, darling, I know," Angela said, lying on her back, arms around her young lover. "No more tears. Let's just hold each other. It's all good now."

Angela's piercing green eyes scanned the small study, her secret trysting spot in the seven-bedroom mansion, a world removed from the bureau's newsroom one floor below. Only her most important "sources" were allowed in there—Ari III; Jack Quinn over at the Aussie visitors bureau; Packwood Kerry, the media mogul and neighbor; and, of course, Stacey, a regular visitor. There were others, mostly advertising types, but they were the junior varsity.

Aside from the ceiling's well-hidden cameras, there was nothing unusual about the hideaway—just a simple wooden writing desk and chair, a single bed along the far wall and a brown leather couch along the other wall. The wall on the left as one entered was blanketed with photos—all Angela's handiwork—documenting the Flanagans' helter-skelter life along the zig-zag correspondent highway. The hippie-style wedding on Kilimanjaro; Indian sunsets in Goa; China's great wall; the Pyramids, of course; and so on. Oddly, Raffy had not been allowed in this room, which Angela kept under separate lock and key. Her V-cave, she called it.

"Angela," Stacey said, suddenly sitting up, "let me look at you, luv. Flip over. Gained a little weight, have we? Your bottom looks flabby."

"Thanks so much," Angela replied, rolling over on her stomach. "In fact, I do feel fat. All that insanity up there. Most people stop eating when they're stressed. Look at Raffy. I do the opposite. I ate myself sick the last night in New York."

Angela moaned with pleasure as Stacey did her magic massage, the long fingers so adept with a basketball kneading Angela's derriere and lower back. It was a ritual Angela never tired of.

"Did you see Mr. Steinberg when you were there?" Stacey asked.

"Of course, silly," Angela replied. "How do you think I got the bureau-chief promotion so quickly? That man is sooooo predictable."

Both women laughed easily and stayed quiet for a time, Seger going on in the background about "Night Moves" and "The Fire Down Below."

Angela flipped over on her back again and gently guided her young lover's head toward the fire of her own down below.

"Everything's going to be different now, baby, I promise," Angela purred, eyes wide open, starring through the skylight at a cloudless afternoon sky. "We're going to be partners from here on out. Show Maggie and all those snooty correspondents we have the right stuff. We'll be the stars of the foreign staff."

CHAPTER 20

New York's Not Happy

South Pacific Bureau, New York Herald
Diplomat Road, Bellevue Hill, Australia
Friday, July 12, 2002
6:16 p.m.

Fuck, Angela thought, slamming down the landline. Fuck, fuck, fuck. This stupid story on the Australian Stock Exchange is a dud—no spark, no bark, no bite. Who cares if Sydney is now the southern hemisphere's premier financial center? People in New York could care less. Story won't even make the cover of the Sunday business section, she thought sourly. Can't get anywhere at this paper on page D8. Even my dear departed father—God bless his literate soul--wouldn't look for a story that deep in the paper, she told herself.

"Stacey," she yelled out from her first-floor office, "get in here. We need to talk."

Silence. Christ, Angela thought, has she already gone home to hump that stockbroker boyfriend of hers? This stupid story was his idea. Why on earth did I listen to him?

As was her nightly ritual around this time, Angela carefully lined up two thin rows of white powder and expertly inhaled them in one quick motion. The Stoli chaser followed.

"Stacey, where the fuck are you?" she bellowed, louder this time. "Get that cute ass of yours in here."

That phone call from Peter Bainbridge this morning was a total buzz-kill, she thought. The man doesn't know Australia from Madagascar, other than they're both islands south of the equator, and he lectures me on what kind of stories I need to write to get on Page 1. All he gives a damn about is being the next editor of the paper, she thought sourly. Nobody kisses Steinberg butt better than Peter.

Angela blew her nose and tossed the tissue into the wicker basket next to her desk. She gazed out at the waning early-evening light over downtown Sydney, a beautiful tableau that did nothing to muffle her nasty mind-set. God, she mused for the umpteenth time, this bureau chief job is harder than it looks.

"What can I do for you, Angela?" Stacey said warily, appearing in her office doorway. Handbag in hand, she had already changed into her Friday-night pub-crawl outfit—designer jeans, pink blouse, three-inch black heels. "I'm running late. I was supposed to meet Scott 15 minutes ago at Biddy Mulligan's."

"Sit down, Stacey," Angela ordered. "And for God's sake button your blouse. You're a reporter for the *New York Herald*, not a hostess at Hooters. Act like you've been here a while. You might even try wearing a bra."

"Angela," Stacey replied wearily, balancing on the edge of her boss' desk, "what's wrong now? Luv, you've got to go easy on the cocaine. It's frying your bloody brain."

"That's my business," Angela fired back. "We have big problems. New York's not happy. At this rate they're going to shut down the bureau by the end of the year. We've got to do something—anything— to get some real news. I haven't had a front-page story since I got back here."

"Angela," Stacey said, standing to go, upset now, "that's your issue. You're the bureau chief. Frankly, I'm sick of this job. You told me nine months ago when you got back from New York last year we were going to be partners. Some partners. You yell, you swear, you order me around like an indentured servant. And I feel like I'm your own personal sex toy whenever you need to let off steam. Talk about sexual harassment. I don't *care* if your handcuffs are the real deal from the NYPD."

The two laughed despite their anger.

"You know, I have an open offer from the *Morning-Telegraph*," Stacey said seriously. "Maybe I should take it."

"Christ, the *Morning-Telegraph*," Angela shot back. "It's not even the best paper in Australia. Even if it were, that wouldn't be saying much."

"That's it. Goodnight, Angela," Stacey said, moving out the door. "Help is out there. You might try the Narcotics Anonymous meeting on the beach tomorrow morning. All kinds of head cases there. You'd fit right in. Have a nice weekend."

With both head and heart pounding now, Angela walked over to the picture window, looking at the horizon, the last signs of light nearly gone. "She's right, God, I do need help," she said out loud. "I'm in way over my head."

CHAPTER 21

Help is on the Way

South Pacific Bureau, New York Herald
Diplomat Road, Bellevue Hill, Australia
Thursday, July 25, 2002
5:44 p.m.

Stacey McKenzie stared at the black landline, now in its second ring, and glanced behind her at the yellow wall clock, shaped like a dazzling Queensland sunflower. Who can that be at this hour, she wondered? Phone hasn't rung all day and now it chirps to life just as I'm about to head down to the beach to play some pickup basketball.

Finally, on the fifth ring, curiosity winning out, she picked up. "McKenzie, *New York Herald*," she barked into the phone in her best reporter voice—flat, hard, all business. "Talk to me."

"Talk to me. I love it," replied the voice on the other end, accent somewhere in the British Isles, probably Ireland. "That's the way they talk in Hollywood."

"How nice. Never been there. May I help you, sir?"

"No," the caller shot back, "but I can help you. I've got a bunch of great story ideas for you guys. Judging from the look of things, you're the ones who could use the help."

"Beg your pardon, sir. I didn't get your name."

"Didn't give it. Just call me C.M. I knew Raffy Flanagan back in the day. Old Africa hand. I'd like to help his widow. His death was devastating."

"Ok," Stacey said carefully, still noncommittal. "Ms. Flanagan's in Canberra until next week. Can I have her call you when she gets back?"

"You know O'Rourke's tavern in King's Cross?" C.M. asked.

"Sure."

"Good. Meet me there now. You can't miss me. Old guy, beard, white hair, black tee-shirt, yellow pants. Playing darts."

The line went dead before Stacey could reply. Why not, she thought. Basketball can wait. We do need help.

CHAPTER 22

Bare Naked Lady

South Pacific Bureau, New York Herald
Diplomat Road, Bellevue Hill, Australia
Tuesday, July 30, 2002
10:10 p.m.

This bare, naked lady is one exhausted dudette, Angela mused as she unwound in the 104-degree waters of her rooftop spa and listened to the sounds of Steve Page singing what he'd do "If I had a Million Dollars."

Well, I've got the million dollars, she thought, and a lot more, but otherwise it's just not working. That story conference with Kellen and Bainbridge a few hours ago was a disaster. Just returned from a few days in Canberra and Bainbridge wants a story about what a dull, insipid place the Aussie federal capital is. How the sidewalks roll up at 9 p.m., how the food sucks, how there really is no there there. Alluded to some writer named Gertrude Steinberg—or something like that. Also mentioned Bill Bryson. Do that kind of edgy feature, Bainbridge says, and I'll get the story on the front page.

Problem is, Angela thought, I really liked the place. The people were nice, the atmosphere congenial and the Chamber-of-Commerce hosts who showed me around were thrilled the *New York Herald* was going to profile their underrated jewel of a town. I don't want to mock them, she thought. Bainbridge is such a dickhead, she thought with a smile. Such a perfect description of him. Switch-hits with the best.

A loud knock on the rooftop door interrupted her story-meeting rehash. "Angela, are you up here?" Stacey asked, sticking her head partly through the door. "Are you alone? I've got some great news."

"Come on in," Angela replied. "The water's wet. Just grooving to Barenaked Ladies."

"Oh, I just love them," Stacey said, peeling off her sweat-stained workout clothes and slowly easing into the bubbling spa waters. "Canadian, aren't they?"

"Haven't a clue," Angela said, leaning back and closing her eyes. "What's up? I need some good news."

"Angela," Stacey said, voice dripping drama, "I just got this unbelievable tip: there is a lawsuit that going to be filed in Sydney Friday against a tour operator on the Great Barrier Reef. Seems like the charter operators left a couple on the reef after a long day of snorkeling and didn't discover them missing until a day later. They're trying to cover the whole thing up."

"What?" Angela blurted, sitting up straight, practically shouting. "You can't be fucking serious."

"I know, I know, it's unreal," Stacey said excitedly, feeding off Angela's vibe. "Get this: when they finally figured out what happened, they went back to where the couple was snorkeling and found nothing. Zip, nada, zero. No wet suit, no snorkeling gear, no body parts. Just the great whites."

"*Mon* fucking *Dieu*," Angela said, breathing out slowly. "When did this happen?"

"Monday," Stacey said. "I'm told that your buddy, Jack Quinn, is lobbying to sit on the story until they can figure out how to spin it. Aussie tourist types are totally freaked. The reef is the most popular draw in the whole country."

"What do we know about the couple?" Angela asked, in full reporter mode now, reflexively stroking her long wet hair into a ponytail over her right shoulder. "They're American, I hope."

"They are American," Stacey replied, "and guess what? They were *Peace Corps* volunteers returning to the States from New Guinea after their tour ended. They were making a stop here and New Zealand before heading home. They're from Omoho, or something like that."

"Fan-fucking-tastic, "Angela said, taking another deep breath. "It's Omaha, in the American outback."

"Whatever," Stacey shot back. "This story is just too good to be true. Just what you're looking for."

"Listen," Angela instructed, "have we confirmed this? Where did this tip come from?"

"A source of mine," Stacey said matter-of-factly. "First called me last week. Said he knew Raffy in Africa. Wants to help us get good stories. Met him at O'Rourke's. Kind of mysterious. Struck me as a spook type. Says his name's C.M. Anyway, he just left me a phone message a couple of hours ago and I called him back."

Angela was quiet for a time, story-planning wheels turning in her head.

"Ok," she said finally, "you call C.B. in the morning and find out when exactly the suit is going to be filed, where exactly it's going to be filed and who's the lawyer filing it. We need a copy of it right away."

"It's C.M."

"What?"

"His name is C.M.," Stacey said, "not C.B."

"Whatever," Angela said. "C.M., C.B. Who cares?"

The women laughed, breaking the tension a bit.

"Listen," Angela continued on, "I'll call Quinn first thing in the morning. He'll have to come clean with me. I own him."

"What do you mean?"

"Never mind. I'll tell you later. Suffice it to say, we have a very special relationship."

Angela went quiet again, starting to relax and laid her head back against the edge of the spa. She smiled ever so slightly at her junior partner and reached for her hand.

"Stacey," she said, "good work, darling. This is the front-page news I've been looking for since I got back. Finally. Not a moment too soon."

She put her arm around Stacey and kissed her on the lips. "Tell me about C.M. I never heard Raffy mention anyone like that. What's he like? Good looking? Married?"

CHAPTER 23

It's Osama's Fault

Aussi Visitors Bureau
AHP Building, Sydney, Australia
Wednesday, July 31, 2002
11:11 a.m.

Jack Quinn's sumptuous 20th-floor office was little comfort to him this morning, despite its magnificent views of Sydney Harbor and the iconic Opera House. In fact, his long and comfortable career as senior flack with the national tourist bureau had suddenly veered off course into hostile territory.

"You don't understand, Sid," Quinn yelled into the phone at Sidney Greene, the bureau's main man in Cairns, near the Great Barrier Reef. "I've already had two calls this morning from the *New York Herald*. They've already talked to the lawyer who's going to sue on behalf of the victims' families. We've got to get ahead of this story. Find out what really happened. See if we can blame the couple somehow. The cops say they can't keep it secret much longer. They disappeared two bloody days ago, for God's sake."

Quinn, standing beside his mahogany desk, ran his pudgy, well-manicured fingers through his thinning blond hair and listened impatiently to Greene's non-update update.

"God-damn it, Sid," he broke in angrily, shouting now, "I don't give a frog about the company's internal investigation and I don't give a fig about what their lawyer is telling them. You get the fuck over there this afternoon and inform them if they don't have a coherent narrative by 11 a.m. tomorrow, the bureau will make sure their operating permit is yanked by sundown. The publicity will be so bad they'll be bankrupt by the weekend."

Quinn slammed down the landline so hard—it sounded like a high-caliber rifle shot—that his support assistant, Vera O'Connor, came rushing into his office.

"Are you all right, Mr. Quinn?" she asked. "Sounded like one of your paintings came crashing down. What a racket."

"It's fine, Vera, just fine," Quinn assured her, shooing her back to her station just outside his glass-office door. "Just a little frustrated with Sid. He makes me crazy sometimes. World's laziest white man."

Quinn closed the door and stared out at the magnificent harbor and the famous bridge connecting downtown to North Sydney. Normally, the scene reassured him how well he had done for the seventh and youngest son of a Melbourne railroad engineer.

Not lately, though. The bad news had been nonstop since 9/11. Tourism from North America—a growth area in recent years—has plunged and this Great Barrier Reef fiasco would only make horrid headlines around the world. A flack's worst nightmare. Peace Corps volunteers from America, he mused with a wince. Why couldn't they have been from France? Nobody cares about the frogs. AP story at worst.

"Mr. Quinn, Angela Flanagan on the phone for you again," Vera said over the intercom. "Third call this morning and it's not even lunch. Cheeky Yank, she is. Bloody awful woman. A red-headed witch if you ask me."

"That's quite enough, Vera," Quinn said sharply. "Mrs. Flanagan is a consummate and courageous professional. I'll take the call on number two, please. No interruptions."

Quinn drew a deep breath, sat down and hit the button with the blinking light. "Angela," he said, with all the faux enthusiasm he could muster, "still awaiting those reports from Cairns. Should have something for you soon. This is a tough one to untangle."

"Jack, Jack," Angela shot back, twangy voice dripping sarcasm, "cut the crap, darling. All I want from you is a confirmation that these two Americans have been eaten and what happens now to the Aussie tourist industry. Can't wait to hear what that sorry-ass charter company says. This is going to be good."

"Angela, please," Quinn replied weakly, trying to maintain his dignity, "don't say 'eaten'. We don't know that. They could still be alive somewhere. We can't have a rush to judgment here. We have to establish the facts first."

"Jack," Angela shot back, "I hear you guys are the main ones pushing to keep the story hushed up until the weekend. Put it out late Friday night when all the reporters have gone home. Speaking of that, this is a *Herald* exclusive. Don't even think about leaking this to the locals. Fuck me on this, honey, and those cute little gonads of yours will be in my meat grinder. You'll be a falsetto the rest of your life. Count on it."

Fucking cunt, Quinn thought. She's serious.

"No need for those kinds of threats, Angela," Quinn replied, sweat stains starting to show on his blue button-down shirt from Brooks Brothers. "I would never do that to you."

"One other point," Angela barked, "Ari Steinberg mentioned to me that the visitors bureau may be cutting back on its FYI South Pacific ads because of 9/11. Not smart, Jack, if you get my drift. Wouldn't want to have to give *Sydney After Dark* my photos of you up in the spa doing those lines of coke."

"Angela, stop, please," Quinn replied, in full plead mode now. "We can't continue spending all that money with you guys right now. Blame Osama bin Laden, not me."

"Fuck Osama," Angela fired back. "It won't be good if you slash those ad buys. Cut a little, ok, but no more than 10%. Get it? Ari would really appreciate it."

"I'll do my best," Quinn replied, manhood obliterated. "Maybe there's something we could do. Geez, Angela, you were a lot nicer when you were just a travel writer."

"Get me a statement on the reef, Jack," Angela ordered. "I want it by the end of the day."

The line went dead before Quinn could reply. The woman is out of control, he thought. She's got to be stopped. Where did she get those pictures? Good God, what a mess.

CHAPTER 24

The Aussie Jaws

Page One Conference Room, New York Herald
Herald Tower, Midtown Manhattan
Thursday, Aug. 1, 2002
5:05 p.m.

Stifling a yawn, Margarite T. Maye scanned the faces at the weekend news meeting—the department heads or their deputies at the conference room table, along with the back benchers and production types seated behind them along the four walls. My God, she mused, there must be 40 or 50 people in this room. What on earth do they all do?

Much as she loathed the numerous story conferences she had to attend each day, there was something about the Sunday meeting on Thursday afternoon she rather enjoyed. Picking the six best stories to run on the most important day of the week on the front page of the most influential general circulation paper in the world was still a rush. (The paper was so fat with ads and news that almost three days of focused planning were needed to ensure it landed without fail on reader doorsteps early Sunday morning.)

What the stories would be, what graphics would run with what story, how the front page would be laid out—all Maggie's call at this meeting. Enjoy it while it lasts, she mused. The paper version of what we do is fast headed to the Obsolescence Hall of Lame.

"Ok, Kellen," she said, bringing the meeting to order and looking at her natty foreign editor, "what'd ya got? Please, no more tedious thumb-suckers about post-9/11 life in Uzbekistan--or any of the other Stans for that matter. No offense, but we could use a little pop from our foreign staff."

Kellen jumped on the challenge like a slow curve ball just inside the outside corner—right in the old wheelhouse.

"No offense taken, Maggie, I assure you," he began grandly. "Just so happens our newish bureau chief in the South Pacific has a monster scoop. Seems a young American couple was left behind on the Great Barrier Reef while they were snorkeling a couple hundred yards from the charter boat. When the charter boat operators realized the mistake and went back the next day, they didn't find a thing. Nada. No trace. Eaten by sharks, most likely."

An audible gasp erupted from the room, a rare show of emotion in a meeting where holding your cards close is normally *de rigueur*.

"Ok, Kellen, not bad," Maggie deadpanned. "Tell me more. When did this happen? Have we confirmed it? Is it exclusive?"

"Monday Sydney time, yes and yes," Kellen replied quickly. "Local media totally asleep at the guard post of this one. Relatives of the dead couple are suing the charter company late Friday afternoon Aussie time. That's in a few hours. That will top our story. We got an advance copy of the litigation.

"We also have a reporter, Dave Freed from Denver, and a photog from Chicago, Kari Rene Hall, in Nebraska with the family. Very nice people, real salt-of-the-earth farmer types. Not surprisingly, they're in a state of shock. Get this: the victims were Peace Corps volunteers returning home at the end of their Asian tour. They were stopping in Australia and New Zealand on the way back."

"Jesus," Maggie commented, "the detour to Hell. Sounds like a bad movie."

"Yeah, Hollywood will eat this one up, "Kellen replied. "Pun intended."

"Peter, are you handling the editing on this?" Maggie asked, looking over at Peter Bainbridge sitting with the back benchers.

"Indeed," Bainbridge replied crisply. "Talked to Flanagan an hour ago. It's Friday morning there. I've seen her first draft. About 2,500 words. Needs work but it's all there. I'll send a copy to our lawyers just to be safe."

For the first time, Maggie leaned back in her chair and exhaled audibly.

"Barring other late-breaking news, this story leads the Sunday paper," she ordered. "Get it in the early edition. That means it must be ready to go by tomorrow night at 7. I want lots of photos of the family on an open page inside, maybe a double truck if we have enough good stuff. Tell Freed to write the Nebraska sidebar as long as he wants. I want color, I want heartbreak, I want pathos. He's good at that."

"Yes, mam," Kellen replied with a smile. "Never let it be said foreign doesn't break news."

"Let's not get carried away, Kellen," Maggie deadpanned. "Tell Angela good job and tell her to be prepared. This is going to cause a *merde* storm."

CHAPTER 25

Haunting Way to Die

New York Herald
Page A1, Column 6
Sunday, Aug. 4, 2002

YANK COUPLE FEARED LOST
ON AUSSIE REEF

Snorklers Left Behind in Shark-Infested Waters

By A. Reilly Flanagan
And S.I. McKenzie
©New York Herald Staff Writers

Cairns, Australia—A vacationing American couple returning home from the Peace Corps has disappeared at sea after a charter boat abandoned the pair on the Great Barrier Reef and didn't realize what had happened until 24 hours later, the *Herald* has learned exclusively.

The victims' relatives, who live near Omaha, filed suit in Sydney late Friday, accusing the charter company of "unspeakable gross negligence" and are seeking at least $50 million in damages. A massive search of the shark-infested waters found no signs of life where the couple was last seen wearing wet suits and snorkeling gear.

"Fraid they're part of the food chain now," said Clem Davis, grizzled owner of a rival charter company here in Cairns, jumping off spot for the one million-plus tourists who visit the famous reef every year. "Hate to imagine it."

Diver's Delight, the charter company that lost track of the couple, identified as Randy and Sandy Dana, declined comment. A brief statement from the local police department said only that an investigation "was underway but no conclusions have been reached. The search for the missing couple is continuing."

A shirtless, sunburned man slammed the door in a *Herald* reporter's face when she inquired about the incident at the company's trailer-park headquarters on the outskirts of town. The man, believed to be charter skipper Michael Tyler, answered the door at 10 in the morning with a 24-ounce beer can in his right hand. Tyler was named as a defendant in the suit.

Jack Quinn, chief spokesman for national visitors bureau, said the incident should have little effect overall on foreign tourism. "A few foreign tourists get killed every year down here," he noted. "Hey, stuff happens."

The incident took place last Monday afternoon Australia time but wasn't disclosed until the Herald broke the story Saturday morning New York time on its web site. The time in Sydney is 16 hours ahead of New York.

Meanwhile, 50 miles northeast of Omaha, grief-stricken relatives and friends gathered at the Dana family farm *(continued on Page A8)*

CHAPTER 26

Kick Butt, Print Names

South Pacific Bureau, New York Herald
Diplomat Road, Bellevue Hill, Australia
Thursday, August 8, 2002
11:11 p.m.

Finally off deadline, the two reporters sipped their first beers of the night and relaxed as the unrelenting intensity of the past ninety-six hours was finally starting to lighten. Sitting in the rooftop spa, bone tired and buck naked under a cloudless night sky and three-quarters moon, they basked in the cool winter air and the attention cascading down from around the world.

"I still can't believe the shit storm we set off," Angela said, finishing off her beer and belching loudly. "Ooops, excuse me. Not very lady-like and you know what a lady I am."

The pair laughed and clinked cans. "This is the best story, the most satisfying I've ever done in 15 years in this business," Angela added. "What a rush, what a ride."

"You know, Angela" Stacey said earnestly, "you did a great job on that CNN interview with Aaron Brown. You looked great, sounded great, a real natural. And thanks for mentioning me. Made my day. My dear ole mum in Perth saw it. Called me right away. Never heard her so excited about what I do."

"Gotta keep on top of this," Angela said. "Great running story. Need to keep milking it. Remind our editors in New York that we can break real news. Need to follow that Parliament probe into slip-shod tour operators. That's a good one. Be careful with the local reporters. They're furious they got scooped by a couple of babes at a foreign newspaper. Maybe talk to the Time magazine stringer down here. See if he'd like to do something on us for their media section. And we've got the business establishment calling for Jack Quinn's head because of that stupid comment about dead foreign tourists. He's mad as hell as me. Claims he was speaking off the record."

Angela paused for a moment and opened another Fosters. "God, I love this so," she said. "Nothing more fun than lobbing grenades at a hornet's nest."

The two women clinked cans again and stayed quiet for a time.

"I must have had 100 emails since the story ran telling us what a great job we did," Angela said finally. "Maggie. Kellen. Peter Bainbridge, first time he's ever given me a compliment. Tom Wolfe, for God's sake. Guess who didn't email me?"

"Let me guess: Jack Quinn?"

Angela laughed. "Definitely not Jack. Like I said, he claims I made him look like a fool. Hard to argue with that. He is a fool—but he is our fool. Aussie press, though, is eating him alive."

"You think he'll be fired?"

"Hope not," Angela replied. "He's our golden goose and Ari wants me to keep him happy. And I always have, at least until this story. Which leads me back to my original question. I never heard anything from Ari. He's usually so supportive. Always sends me those stupid: 'You go, girl,' notes. Didn't send one this time."

"Well, his buddy Jack did look terrible in the original news story," Stacey said. "Even I know as a rookie reporter that corporate and government flaks get into a lot of trouble when they try to be honest-- or funny."

"Ari's got to understand I'm not a cute little travel writer anymore," Angela said. "I'm a bureau chief now and I don't pull punches. We kick butt and print names here."

"So, what now with the not-so-mighty Quinn?"

"Tell you what," Angela replied. "Jack and I do have a special relationship. He does what I tell him and he is important to the paper on the business side. I want you to write a follow-up story for the weekend saying what a great job he is doing coping with this mess. Tourism damage control and all that. Put it in the business section. That should help him keep his job a while. Ari will like that."

Angela smiled smugly and stood, grabbing a towel off the wall next to the spa. "Problem solved, darling," she said. "You just have to be creative in these jobs and not worry about breaking a few stupid journalism rules. Just watch how I roll. You'll learn soon enough. Now let's go downstairs. Have some fun. I want to be nice and relaxed for my interview with the BBC tomorrow morning. You can handcuff *me* this time."

CHAPTER 27

Ship of Freeloaders

Office of the Foreign Editor, New York Herald
Herald Tower, Midtown Manhattan
Tuesday, August 13, 2002
4:44 p.m.

"Got a minute, Kellen?" Maggie said, barging into her foreign editor's small office and sitting down before he had a chance to answer. "Jesus, your desk is a mess."

"Empty desk, empty mind," Kellen shot back. "What if I said no?"

"No? No, what?"

"No, I don't have a minute."

"Hah," Maggie laughed. "Just rhetorical. You always have time for me. You better."

"In that case, Ms. Maye," he replied with mock formality, "to what do I owe the honor of this visit? You don't visit the hired help very often."

"Yeah, I know," she said absently. "Just trying to rally the troops. Look, I just ran into Ari upstairs and he seemed out of sorts. Sullen, angry almost. Didn't even mention Angela's blockbuster. His favorite Lois Lane breaks a huge story, it's followed by every major news organization on the planet, she's all over CNN, Fox, the BBC, looking great, sounding incredibly literate and articulate, and bringing us all this great attention—and Ari says nothing. Not a peep. I don't get it."

"You don't get Ari, period, Maggie," Kellen explained. "The man is miserable. He hates his job. If he had his druthers, he'd be racing cars, skiing the great mountains of Europe and schtupping even more beautiful women than he does now. Instead, he's stuck as the CEO of this mortally wounded business dying this incredibly drawn-out death. No fun in that."

"Kellen," Maggie shot back, "the man makes $5 million a year, is worth at least $100 million and is treated like a rock star wherever he goes. I should be so miserable."

"Fact is," Kellen said, "the secretaries up on 15 tell me confidentially that the last few months have been particularly brutal. Ari Jr. has really been on his case about the stock price. It's gone nowhere for years now. And his sisters have been even nastier than ever. Jenna told a family gathering in Palm Beach recently that the III at the end of his name was a constant reminder that he's three points shy of a triple digit IQ."

"Ouch," Maggie said.

"Really," Kellen said. "How would you like to be the captain of that ship of fools? Ship of nags and freeloaders is more like it."

"Look, Kellen," Maggie said, "we know third and fourth generation newspaper families are invariably like that. Fact is, Ari does need to figure out this internet stuff. How to tame it, make money off it, make it work for everyone. How do we gradually phase out the newspaper and phase in quality on-line news in a way that makes good money. Everyone is counting on him to ferry them safely to the other side—employees, readers, advertisers, shareholders, stakeholders. Doesn't matter if he got this job by accident. The *Herald* brand must endure."

"Nice speech, Maggie," Kellen said, "but save it for the troops. I wouldn't bet the ranch on Ari figuring this out. What were you doing up in corporate?"

"Chatting with Wilbur Ross. Love that guy. Only sane person on the business side. Got a nose like a bloodhound. He's smelling something rotten."

"Go on."

"Well, we were talking about Angy the Cat," Maggie said. "Guess she really dazzled old Wilbur on his trip down there a year ago. I mean, the woman is drop-dead hot and charming. Don't imagine Wilbur meets women like that very often. But he also says something's amiss in that office. Same creepy feeling I've had. He's looking into these FYI South Pacific ads that run in Sunday business. Thinks there's something un-kosher about them."

"Like what?"

"Let's have a drink at the Back Page some night after work real soon," Maggie said, bouncing to her feet and heading to the door. "What I really wanted to tell you is I think Angela's reef story will keep the sharks at bay for a while—bad pun intended. A couple more stories like that and we may have to keep that godforsaken outpost open. Never looks good to close foreign bureaus. Glad I pushed so hard for her to get that job."

Maggie laughed and disappeared into the newsroom, which was starting to come to life for yet another edition. There really is nothing else like it in American business, Kellen mused: the magic feel of the newsroom on deadline; the mad dash to edit stories and send them to the composing room; the thunderous roar of the presses at the print-ing plant shortly before midnight; and, finally, the papers landing with a thud in several hundred thousand driveways all over the New York metropolitan area shortly before dawn. God help me, he told himself, but I'm starting to like this editing gig. It's the bottom of the 8th, he mused. Might as well stay for the rest of the game.

CHAPTER 28

Basking in the Glory

South Pacific Bureau, New York Herald
Diplomat Road, Bellevue Park, Australia
Monday, August 19, 2002
9:39 a.m.

Feet on her desk, still dressed in her workout sweats, reading the *Morning-Telegraph*, Angela was in pause mode, taking a breather from the couple-eaten-by-sharks frenzy. The unopened mail on her desk was at least a foot high. Who cares, she thought. Most of it is just garbage—stupid press releases that aren't worth the paper they're written on. PR people are so pathetic, she thought. Just hope I never have to become one.

CNN was saying something about America preparing to invade Iraq in the wake of 9/11. What up with that, she thought. Even I know how stupid that sounds. She muted the sound on the wall-mounted flat screen and absent-mindedly pulled an oversized brown envelope from the middle of the pile that had an NYPD return address. She opened and skim-read it just as Stacey came breezing in.

"Good morning, Angela," she said happily, looking every inch the modern Sydney working woman in black slacks and cream-colored blouse, not a long blond hair out of place. "How are we today? See you are taking your time getting started this morning."

"My, don't you clean up nicely," Angela replied sarcastically. "You must have gotten laid last night."

"No comment," Stacey replied laughing. "Scott and I had a wonderful dinner at home last night. That's all you need to know. He asked me again when the three of us are going to get it on. He thinks you're superhot for an old babe."

"Can't remember the last time I had sex with a real man," Angela groused. "Ari doesn't count. He usually lasts about ten seconds. And tell Scott not to hold his breath. Boys shouldn't try to do a man's job."

Both women laughed.

"By the way," Angela said, "your infamous dirty-dozen group photo is bouncing around the internet again. Got a voice mail last night from my buddy at *Sydney After Dark*. Said he just wanted to confirm that *New York Herald* reporter S.I. McKenzie is the same Stacey McKenzie who played center on the Aussie national women's basketball team a few years ago. You know, he said, the one with you naked as a blue-jay in the middle holding the basketball."

"That bloody photo," Stacey said crossly, sitting down on the chair next to Angela's desk. "Damn thing is going to follow me to my grave. It was just a fundraiser for the team and breast cancer awareness. All side shots. A little T and not much A. For God's sake, the *Sports Illustrated* swimsuit models reveal more than we did."

"Life's not fair, baby," Angela said unsympathetically. "Talk to any man about breast cancer awareness and it's only the breast he'll focus on. I just don't want the editors in New York making the connection. Just give them another reason not to take this bureau seriously."

"You know," Stacey said, still upset, "I just read a blurb in Time magazine about a movie coming out soon that has a bunch of old babes taking their clothes off for charity. Think it stars Helen Mirren. That's all we did."

"What's the latest update on Jaws 2.0?" Angela asked, done with Stacey's jeremiad. "I took yesterday off. Hung out at Bondi. Didn't take one call or read one e-mail."

"Still going strong," Stacey replied. "We need another follow soon. Diver's Delight is now officially out of business and the tour-boat captain has disappeared. Police issued an APB for him, saying he is wanted for questioning.

"Then, it was a zoo in Parliament. Saw it on the public channel. During the PM's question period, the loyal opposition had another field day pointing out how the great liberal watchdog press got scooped by a New York newspaper on the blockbuster story of the year. At one point, MP Jeremy Nesbitt pointed up to the press gallery and said: 'Shame, shame, shame on every one of you.' He loathes reporters. Calls us pimps and sluts."

"God, I love it," Angela said gleefully. "I can't tell you the number of times that horny old goat has propositioned me. What about the Hollywood stuff?"

"E-mails just keep coming. Got eighteen more yesterday. All wanting to discuss the quote/unquote 'reporter rights to the story.' And not just Hollywood. We got Bollywood, England, France, Sweden, even Russia.

"Love it, love it," Angela said. "Make sure you put copies of the e-mails in my personal basket. I'll read through them today."

"What else?" Stacey said. "I'm heading out to have coffee with Jack Quinn. He sounds a little better. No so shell-shocked. Think the follow-up story helped."

"Yeah, good work on that," Angela said, handing her the NYPD envelope. "Tell Jack to be a man and tough it out. No, don't tell him that. I'll tell him when he comes over this weekend.

"Take a look at this letter. From a guy who says he's the head of the NYPD anti-terror squad. Gino something or another. Coming down here on vacation. Wants to have dinner. Can you check him out? If he's the real deal, set something up on Bondi. Join us if you wish."

CHAPTER 29

To Our Finest Edition

Back Page Pub, 42d St.
Midtown Manhattan
Friday, August 23, 2002
8:18 p.m.

Kellen Williams finished his first martini of the night—splash of vermouth, two olives—and mulled the wisdom of a couple more. Why not, he thought. Can always take the train home to Rye, or, better yet, get a cab and put it on the paper's tab. Maggie's right: no one pads an expense account better than I do. Whenever and wherever real newspapermen gather to tell their tall tales about expense accounts, my exploits are legend, he mused proudly.

"Another one, Mr. Williams?" asked Yost Nickelsberg, lone bartender at the Back Page, the dive bar near Herald Tower where ink-stained wretches used to drink in droves on Friday night. "Another Manhattan, Ms. Maye?"

"Sure," the editors said in unison, laughing.

"Journalists don't drink enough anymore," Kellen groused, glancing at his watch. "It's not even 8:30 on a Friday night and everyone's already gone home to their apartments and condos in Brooklyn Heights and the Upper West Side. Bunch of anal yuppies. Colorless, joyless, useless. I hate what's happened to this business."

"My, aren't we in a good mood tonight," Maggie said. "You sound like everyone's crabby Uncle Henry."

"I can't help it, Maggie," Williams said. "Turned sixty last week. Hit me hard. Not easy getting old in this business. Most of the people I started with thirty-seven years ago in Chicago are either shameless flacks, clerking in a used-book store, working on a copy desk, or sleeping for eternity in a pine box. It's depressing. I feel like I'm just hanging on by my fingernails."

Maggie laughed and took the first sip of her second drink. "Stop complaining," she said. "You're doing fine. You've had a great career and it's not over. Be thankful for that. And, Kellen, I do remember those Saturday afternoons in Paris. You were a veritable top gun, as it were."

"Yeah, yeah," he replied, "truth is I don't remember the details all that well myself. Shrouded in the mists of time. I think I remember which one you were."

The editors chuckled and clinked glasses. "Is there something else bothering you?" she asked.

"I'm starting to like this editing job a little more but I'm still having trouble being inside all the time," he said. "It feels so claustrophobic, suffocating. In London, I had so much freedom. People there treated me like I was a big deal. They knew my name. Here I still feel like a colonel at the Pentagon."

"That's natural, Kellen," Maggie said soothingly. "Most correspondents feel that way when they return to the mother ship. It can take several years before they get their sea legs."

"Yeah, I guess."

"Anything else?" she asked.

"Show me the money, Maggie," he said glumly. "Where's it going to come from?"

"Say what?"

"Our survival as a business. The management talking points are we're 'platform agnostic.' Doesn't matter if our stories run in the paper, online, on the wire service. More eyeballs than ever reading our stuff. Sounds great but the numbers don't add. It's a mirage. We're desperate and thirsty, and we're seeing things in the distance that aren't real."

Williams drained his glass and set it down hard on the scarred old wooden bar. "Journalists don't understand simple economics," he complained. "The golden goose is withering away and there's nothing viable to replace it. You think a website can finance the kind of reporting we do? That's a bloody joke. Face it, great journalism is really, really expensive but great journalism is a bad business unless there's a healthy newspaper to underwrite the costs."

"Thank you, Dr. Doom," Maggie said. "That is the conventional wisdom but I'm not sure I buy it. If you get enough digital subscribers, web sites could make a lot of money. But, yes, newspapers themselves are doomed."

"Mark my words," Williams said, "the *New York Herald* as a newspaper will not exist in another 15 years max."

"Focus on now," Maggie said. "Look what we did on 9/11. Five Pulitzers, all in the news category. The newspaper mattered that day. Sent circulation off the charts for weeks."

"Yeah, that was unbelievable," Williams said, brightening some. "I kept several copies of that September 12th edition. What we did in those 16 hours was a bloody miracle."

"To September 12, 2001," Maggie said, raising her glass. "As Mr. Churchill might have put it: 'They will surely look back and say this was their finest edition.'"

"Amen Maggie, amen Winston."

"Another drink?" Nickelsberg said, approaching the last two at the bar. "Last call."

"Sure," the two upscale newspaper bar flies said in unison, clinking glasses.

"*Pourquoi pas?*" Maggie said in the French she perfected at the Sorbonne. "*Apres nous, le deluge.*"

CHAPTER 30

Strangers Bearing Gifts

South Pacific Bureau, New York Herald
Diplomat Road, Bellevue Hill, Australia
Saturday, August 24, 2002
6:16 p.m.

Dry vodka martini in one hand, Cuban cigar in the other, Gino Carella pinched himself to confirm he wasn't in some bucolic parallel universe.

Twenty-four hours earlier he had not even met the comely South Pacific bureau chief of the *New York Herald*. Now, 24 hours after that great dinner last night, he was sitting in her rooftop hot tub in one of suburban Sydney's toniest neighborhoods. The only women who look like this on my old beats, he mused, are $2,000-a-night sex workers.

"Angela," he said, putting down his drink and gripping her left bicep. "Where did you get these arms? And the abs? What's the deal?"

Angela beamed, never tiring of hearing hosannas for her middle-aged body. Just part of the Angela Reilly Flanagan mystique, something she loved to rub in the face of her moldy feminist colleagues at the newspaper. My body *is* fantastic, she thought smugly, and I love to show it off.

"No magic formulas," she replied nonchalantly, "just fifteen hours a week at the gym and the South Beach diet."

"Well, it works," Carella replied. "Keep it up. Speaking of that, I wanted to tell you that I'm glad you didn't give up on me after last night. I've been a little out of sorts. Life's been crazy for me since 9/11. All the long workdays, then another bad divorce, kids in trouble. Just fried my nervous system."

"You're most welcome, Lieutenant.," Angela replied smiling easily. "Those little blue pills I keep around do come in handy. Loved that motorcycle ride this morning and the erection this afternoon. Thought we were going to have to call the doctor."

Carella chuckled and felt a return call to action below the water line. He drained his martini, set down his cigar and put his left arm around her. "Listen," he said seriously, "I need to talk to you. The last twenty-four hours compel me to say something you need to know."

" Ok, Lieutenant," Angela said, turning to look at him directly, "but don't get mushy on me. It's only sex. It's the way modern girls network. Think Samantha Jones."

Not having the foggiest who Samantha Jones is, Carella laughed anyway and plowed ahead. "You know Dion DeStefano, right?" he asked. "Old friend of your husband from their basketball days in Brooklyn."

"Sure," Angela replied, surprised at the inquiry. "He was Raffy's best friend. Came to our wedding party in the States after we had gotten married in Africa. Only time I met him. A real character. My Dad loved him."

"What about Dion's father, Sal? You know him?"

"God, no. Scary guy. Died a few years ago at Attica. Where are we going with this, Lieutenant.?"

"I just want to warn you," Carella said, "that I came across some information a while ago that Dion suggested to your husband that he could have you killed if that would solve his marital problems. Raffy told him you were a cocaine addict and ruining his reporting career."

Angela scoffed and sat up straight, green eyes flashing. "I don't do that much coke and, truth be told, Raffy drank himself out of his job," she shot back. "If he hadn't died on 9/11, he would have been dead in six months anyway. Where'd you get this information?"

"Take it easy," Carella replied soothingly. "I can't tell you my source. Point is, you just need to know DeStefano is a bad guy, despite all his charm. His apple fell right underneath dad's tree. And his sidekick, Jim Robison, isn't much better. He's Dion's enforcer. Did time for murder at Attica with Sal."

"Robison is the tall black guy with the blue eyes, right?" Angela asked. "I read a story about him in the Daily News. Said he was born again."

"Yeah," Carella scoffed, "born-again killer. Look, I'm not trying to freak you out. I'm not aware of anything going on—particularly since your husband is dead anyway—but keep checking your rear-view mirror. Beware of strangers bearing gifts. Always, always verify. Never trust unless you do."

"Oh, Gino," Angela purred, putting her right arm around his neck, "you're not going to spoil my pink cloud tonight. Raffy's history—gone, forgotten, good riddance—and those other guys are ten thousand miles away. They could care less about me now."

She reached below the water line with her left hand and began stroking gently. "We have a saying in journalism: 'If your mama says she loves you, check it out.'"

"I always check everything out, Lieutenant. Now how about letting this mama check you out? Maybe sit on your lap? My, sure doesn't feel like you need any more pills."

CHAPTER 31

Thanks for your Service

Qantas International Terminal, Sydney Airport
Sunday, August 25, 2002
2:02 p.m.

What a trip, Carella thought, making his way toward the Qantas security line, hooking up with a free-spirited female who parties like Hugh Hefner. Go slow with this one, he reminded himself.

"Ok, Lieutenant.," Angela said, stopping just short of the end of the security line, "this is as far as I go. Maybe you can get fast-tracked if you tell them you're a New York cop."

"Nah," Carella said, "I don't want anyone to know who I am. I've got plenty of time. Flight doesn't leave for two hours. It's bizarre. My plane lands at JFK an hour ago east coast time. The Yankees are playing the Rangers this evening. Maybe I can go."

The couple laughed and hugged goodbye, as the international herds streamed around them for points everywhere.

"Listen, Angela," Carella said, pulling back. "I'm thinking about putting in my papers—33 and done, lucky to be alive and all that. I'm going to see a guy next week who runs a kind of private FBI network around the world. Hoping he'll give me a job somewhere. He has an office here."

"Ok, Lieutenant," Angela said noncommittally. "Keep me posted. I'm not going anywhere for a while."

She smiled, adding: "We are always here to support our men in uniform, even if they are retired, and thank them in *every* way we can for their service."

"Angela, don't forget what I said. Don't take any wooden nickels."

"Oh, Gino, that's what my Irish grandfather used to tell me. I never did understand what that meant. Stay longer next time, darling."

With that, she kissed Carella hard on the lips, did an about-face with the military precision her stepfather taught her, and walked away without looking back, just a blind wave as she exited the terminal.

CHAPTER 32

Red-Widow Spider

Office of Lieutenant Gino Carella
NYPD Headquarters, Lower Manhattan
Monday, August 26, 2002
9:09 a.m.

Four more months, Gino Carella thought as he gazed out his new corner office at One Police Plaza, and it's over. Three decades on the job, shot three times, adrenalin rush from month three, key cog in the best police force in the world—Amadou Diallo notwithstanding. Am I really ready for Act II, he thought wearily, still badly fatigued from yesterday's flight. Or is it Act III now? How does that work anyway?

"Lieutenant., welcome back," Candy Garcia said, barging into his office. "All relaxed and refreshed, I hope."

"Candy, please come in, as if you ever needed an invitation," Carella joked, giving his good friend a brief hug. "Good to be back, I think. Have a seat."

"Something wrong, Lieutenant?" Garcia asked. "You only call me Candy when you're out of sorts. Usually it's: 'Garcia, where the fuck are you? I can't find'....Fill in the blank."

Carella laughed. He'd miss this woman.

"Listen, Garcia," Carella said. "I'm pulling the cord at the end of the year. I decided yesterday on that god-awful 20-hour flight home. Time to go while I'm still in one piece. Truth be told, I'm worn out. This last year has been a killer. I don't want to die with my shoes on. Thirty-three and done."

"Kind of expected that," she replied. "The last 12 months have been insane. The new normal. I'm exhausted all the time, too."

"I don't fit anymore," Carella said. "This new office is great, promotion is great, love the view. Brass wants me to hang in but smoking out terrorists is different than tracking gangsters. The mob, I understand. Christ, I grew up in Bensonhurst. They usually kill for money or revenge, and they usually kill other bad guys. They have a code of conduct that I understand.

"These Muslim terrorists have no honor, no respect for anything outside their own little dirty worlds. They kill innocents in the name of Allah and they do it in the most hideous ways. And because I've never walked in their shoes, I never have a gut feel of what they might do next and how they're going to strike. That make any sense?"

"Yeah, it does," Garcia replied. "Do what feels right. I wish I could join you. Go make some real money. You've earned it."

"Yeah, I've got an interview this week with Julius Levitsky, the guy who hires all the retired cops and FBI agents. Spooks too. He indicated to me in an e-mail that he may have an opening in Australia, of all places. Who would have thought?"

"Ooooh," Garcia said, laughing and rubbing her hands, "guess it went well with the widow Flanagan, eh? Did you play hump the hostess?"

Carella glared at his deputy, knowing full well that anything he told her would ricochet around 1PP like one of those balls of silly putty in an old Walt Disney cartoon. Like most cops at 1PP, Garcia was an incorrigible gossip.

"We did meet," he said carefully. "It was all very, ah, cordial. Let's just leave it at that."

"Cordial?" Garcia scoffed. "Nice try. That's why you want to move there, right? You can tell ole Candy all about it. Don't leave out any of the details. Is she really a natural redhead?"

Carella gave his deputy another irritated look and shook his head. "Garcia, it's too early in the morning for this and I'm really jet-lagged. Let talk after I've met with Levitsky."

"Be careful with her," Garcia warned. "I was looking at those photos of her again, the color ones in the newspaper from last year. Kept a copy. Something sinister about those green eyes and red hair. Make sure she isn't, you know, some sort of mutant red-widow spider. You know, devours her partner after she mates. Or have you two mated already?"

"Nice try, Garcia," Carella shot back. "Get back to work. I ain't done here yet."

CHAPTER 33

Rock Around the Clock

Office of Julius J. Levitsky, Esq.
Trump Tower, Fifth Avenue
Friday, August 30, 2002
3:44 p.m.

It was the wall of clocks that jarred Gino Carella as he was escorted into the corner office of Julius J. Levitsky—aka "Julie the Jackal" in the colorful lexicon of the New York tabloids.

"Mr. Levitsky will be right with you," said a young assistant named Debi, last name not given. "Have a seat. There is a wet bar in the corner over there. Help yourself."

She disappeared, leaving Carella alone in a wondrous 1,000 square foot office that had hand-woven Kashmiri rugs on the teakwood floor, Picassos on two facing walls and a huge picture window on the 44th floor that had a view of the East River.

The fourth wall had the clocks—24 of them, giving the time in every zone on the planet. So, it was 11:45 a.m. in Anchorage, 3:45 p.m. in New York, 8:45 p.m. in London, and 7:45 a.m. Saturday in Sydney. A sunny photo of Levitsky anchored the middle, around which the clocks revolved like planets in a solar system. Whoa, Carella mused, studying all the time zones, this guy really *is* a master of the universe.

"Lieutenant Carella, you like the clocks, eh?" Levitsky said, exploding into the room, voice booming, all 333 pounds of him moving with Jackie Gleason-like fluidly and elegance, dressed in an elegantly tailored blue-pinstriped suit. "I like them, too. You can always find a time to work and a time to imbibe—my two favorite pastimes."

The two laughed and shook hands like old friends. "Honor to meet you, Mr. Levitsky," Carella said, as they sat on a leather couch facing the picture window. "You're a legend in my world."

"Call me Julie," Levitsky ordered, "and you're the legend, Lieutenant. I remember when you almost bought your final real estate in that gun battle in Brooklyn with those Jamaican drug dealers. My wife and I prayed for you. Guess the Lord was listening."

"Yeah, thanks for that," Carella said, patting his chest. "One inch over and I'd be just another dead cop."

"So, Lieutenant," Levitsky began, rubbing his huge meaty hands, diamond rings on each pinky finger, "your recent e-mail to me was fortuitous, to put it mildly. You mentioned you wanted to see me after you returned from vacation in Sydney. I had just talked to a client of mine, a good friend, about getting a much higher profile in the South Pacific, particularly Australia. They fly mostly below the radar down there now, but there's big money being made there in mining, real estate and tourism. I have only one guy there now—a former CIA agent at Ayers Rock—but I don't use him much. He's on contract."

Carella nodded and stayed mum. The Jackal was just warming up.

"Listen, Lieutenant., you know I'm FBI to the core, right? Spent twenty-five years there before starting this company ten years ago. I don't care if J. Edgar was a faggot and cross-dresser, the rank-and-file is the best and the agency itself is the most professional law enforcement arm in the world. I'll always have that place in my DNA.

"Here's my point: your police background is the real deal: mob squad, Brooklyn narcotics, Muslim smack-down. A real man of the streets, not some office jockey looking for the next promotion. Just want you to know how much I respect and appreciate that. If I were still at the FBI, I'd hire you in a Mumbai minute."

"Thank you, sir. I appreciate that."

"Now," Levitsky said, shifting his huge frame around on the couch to look more directly at Carella, "just between you, me and the lamp-post, it was the publisher of the *New York Herald* who was touting Australia. Says they're making all kinds of money on airline travel ads and some marketing campaign called FYI South Pacific, where they write about how great it is to do business down there and go there on vacation. They're a monster hit."

"Yeah, I'll take a look," Carella said. "Can't say I read the paper much." Hmmm, he mused, better keep my new-found personal connection there to myself--at least for now.

"Anyway," Julie went on, "let me tell you a little bit about this business, Lieutenant. We're just a bunch of high-paid Sam Spades with a very rich, very smart clientele. And you're paid by the hour, just like corporate lawyers and flacks. So billable hours are the mother's milk of what we do. Cops like you usually work til the job is done, maybe get some overtime. You catch the crook, hours be damned. When you do the math our way, however, and total up the fees, you wouldn't believe how much rich people are willing to pay when their testicles are on fire."

Levitsky roared with laughter—an oddly high-pitched sound coming from such a huge head—and plunged on. "So help me God, but I do love it so. The hotter the flames, the more I make and the fatter I get."

He paused for a moment and patted his massive mid-section benignly. "Next point is, we never, *ever* break the law here—I am a lawyer after all—but that doesn't mean we don't stretch and bend it just shy of breaking. We routinely withhold information from the police and public in the best interest of our clients. You've spent your whole career chasing bad guys, but if you work here long enough, you realize some of our richest clients *are* the bad guys. Arrogant assholes who are obscenely rich, and assume their lawyers, PR men and private detectives will keep them out of jail and off the front page."

"Interesting," Carella observed, without much enthusiasm. "There's a whole world out there I know very little about."

"Just remember, Lieutenant. you leave the priesthood when you come work for me. This ain't no morality play. Just cheap, tawdry commerce."

"Can I ask you an impertinent question?" Carella said. "Why is it that Page 2 column in the New York Sun always calls you the Jackal? Seems like they mean it as a compliment."

"Hah, I love that name," Levitsky roared, almost coming off the couch. "I say that's what my middle initial stands for. The jackal is a cunning animal who sizes up his prey with great stealth and, when the deed is done, steals away into the night leaving no evidence behind.

"Fact is, Lieutenant., that's what I do: move quietly, act fast, and leaves no traces behind. Rich people like my publisher friend fuck up and they call the Jackal to make it right. No fuss, no mess, no bullshit, no publicity unless they want it. That's how I roll and I expect everyone who works for me to do the same. No exceptions, none. That make sense?"

"Yes, sir," Carella replied. "I like it."

Levitsky nodded and glanced at one of the clocks on the wall. "I'll be damned if it isn't 6:17 in Halifax. We're way overdue for a drink."

He stood, walked to the white-marble wet bar and pulled out a couple of three-ounce shot glasses along with a bottle of Johnnie Walker Blue Label.

"Let's talk more next week about sending you to Sydney," Levitsky said, filling the glasses to the top. "I like you for that job. Think about it. You know the place now. Remember, I'm the Goldman Sachs of what I do. I only hire the best of the best."

He handed Carella the shot glass of the brown scotch whiskey and toasted: "To the best booze, obscene fees, and--as always--beautiful, brainy women."

Levitsky threw down the shot with a flourish and Carella followed suit, wincing slightly as the 80-proof alcohol went down. "Amen to all that," Carella said. "The women down there are, indeed, something else."

The alpha males did a fist bump and Levitsky poured another round.

CHAPTER 34

HH Didn't Drown

O'Rourke's Ale House
King's Cross, Sydney, Australia
Friday, December 13, 2002
7:17 p.m.

Where did this guy come from anyway, Stacey McKenzie asked herself, eyeing the enigmatic source known only as C.M. as he casually played darts and drank his O'Douls. Cool, poker-faced, almost never smiles. All business, no flirt, no alcohol, no fun.

Looks a little like Richard Branson, she mused, the long white hair swept back on top and flowing to the shoulders, the neatly trimmed white beard, the tight black tee-shirt and gray jeans showcasing great arms and butt. Looks a lot better than my boyfriend, at least with his clothes on, she thought, and he's at least twenty years older than Scott. Might have to dig a little deeper on that one, she told herself, smiling slightly.

Most importantly, he has great sources all over town, indeed all over the country. All three of our best stories recently—three straight on A1—were his ideas, including that one last weekend about fatal attacks by the infamous salt-water crocs along the Northwest coast. What a shocker, she recalled with a shudder, and it caused huge blowback at the visitors bureau. Just when it looked like Jack Quinn was back in the saddle again, he was quoted as saying the deaths "weren't that big a deal because *most* of the victims were locals, not tourists." Poor Jack. Not the brightest bulb. Fired as spokesman for the visitors bureau two hours after the story hit the news wires.

"Stacey, let's sit for a while," C.M. said, gesturing toward a corner table a little removed from the Friday-night din in King Cross' hottest Irish pub. "Got a really big one for you this time."

"What's up?" she asked excitedly as they both took their seats. "I'm loving these Friday-night story meetings. You've single-handedly saved our bureau from being shut down."

"Good to hear," he replied. "Thought you guys would be okay with a little help from friends. Listen, I've just learned that Aussie intelligence is about to release a secret report that claims the drowning of Prime Minister Harold Holt back in the 1960s was a hoax. Turns out he was indeed a Chinese spy, as some suspected at the time. Faked his death to avoid being exposed. Unbelievable stuff."

"I'll say," Stacey said, looking confused, not quite sure who Holt was. "Could you remind me about him? Australian history wasn't my best subject."

"Holt," C.M. replied, "disappeared on the morning of December 17, 1967, about 50 yards off a beach south of Melbourne. Body never found. Always were whispers and rumors about the spy angle. A journalist even wrote a book laying out in detail how it happened, but no one believed it at the time."

"Go on," Stacey said, hooked now.

"In fact," C.M. continued, "my sources now tell me this reporter—he worked for Reuters—nailed it. Aussie intelligence—which you guys call AISO—has in its files a top-secret document that concluded that Holt was likely picked up offshore by a mini-Chinese sub and whisked away to mainland China, where he was reunited with his Chinese lover. The document also suggests that Holt and the lover—a Melbourne import-exporter named Lily Chou Dunn—were eventually executed by a firing squad."

"My goodness," Stacey gasped, putting her left hand to her mouth, "how dreadful. What on earth for?"

"Story is," C.M. replied, "Mao himself ordered the execution in 1975 shortly before he died. He never liked Holt anyway and he wanted to ensure they would never live to tell their story."

"We can write all this?" Stacey asked.

"Yep," C.M. said, "I can get a copy of the report at the end of the month, right around New Year's. But don't breathe a word of this to anyone yet—not even Ms. Flanagan. I want to read it in full before launching, make sure it's all real."

"C.M., this is fantastic," Stacey said, reaching across the table to squeeze his hand. "How can we ever repay you, luv? Angela is dying to meet you. We want to take you to dinner."

"That would be great," C.M. said, standing to go. "Let's set that up after the story runs."

"C.M, sit for a minute," Stacey ordered. "We need to talk. Who are you really, luv? You talk like an Irishman but your vibe is American. What gives? Truth time."

"Told you already," he said, sitting back down. "Just an old friend of Raffy's from back in the day. Just wanted to help his widow. It's what he would have wanted."

Hmmm, Stacey thought, that's about an 8.8 on the bullfeathers meter. Maybe he really didn't know how much their marriage had deteriorated.

"I hardly knew Raffy," she said. "In fact, I never met him in person. Just knew him by his voice. Classic New York accent. Never came into the office. I was hired just to write and report his stories under his by-line. Angela told me he used to talk about the 'sweet relief of death' because everything he loved was dying—career, marriage, newspaper business itself. I'm told his father was a newspaper delivery truck driver and Raffy used to ride with him as a kid on the weekends. Angela said those were the warmest memories of his dad."

"Listen, Stacey," C.M. said, standing again, abruptly this time, "I gotta run. Meet me here next Friday night, same time. Get ready to launch. It's going to light up the night sky all over the world—Sydney, Canberra, Washington, Beijing, London, you name it."

"Not so fast, mister," she said, standing and finishing the last of her pint, her fourth of the night. "The night is young. I love all this intrigue, you know. I loved 'All the President's Men.' Saw it in journalism class in college. All that deep throat stuff. It was so exciting."

Stacey smiled coyly. "You know, Mr. C.M., whoever you are," she said, choosing her words carefully, speaking slowly, sexily, "I could be your deep throat for the night. You know, the other kind. Just as a way of thanking you for all you've done for us."

"Stacey, stop," C.M. replied sternly, stepping back. "You're what? Twenty-four? You're young enough to be my daughter. Secondly, you told me you have a boyfriend. And, thirdly, that's not how female reporters should behave. Not professional."

"Oh, C.M.," she shot back, laughing, grabbing his hand and kissing him lightly on the cheek, "you're so old-fashioned. First of all, Scott and I have an open relationship. He wouldn't care. Second, I love older men, particularly ones in great shape like you. I just adore the way your white hair curls in back. And, thirdly, Angela said I should find out more about who you really are. So, I am just doing my job--wherever that takes me."

He started to object, but Stacey made the whisper sound, putting her right index finger to her lips. "Just come with me and do as you are told," she said softly, leading him to the back-exit door by the hand. "It's no big deal. It's the 21st Century. We can do whatever we want."

CHAPTER 35

Monster Scoop

South Pacific Bureau, New York Herald
Diplomat Road, Bellevue Hill, Australia
Monday, December 16, 2002
9:33 p.m.

Much to Angela's disgust, Stacey's workout clothes were everywhere. The sweatpants and underwear were on the ground, tank top and sweatshirt on the patio furniture next to the spa. The sports bra hung all by itself from the tall shrubbery that surrounded the spa and ensured its privacy from the diplomatic mansions on either side. *Maybe I should invite the new British consul general next door over here some time,* Angela mused. *Brits are always great sources, have their fingerprints on everything.*

Taking a sip of her beer in the soothing waters, she let out a loud belch, her first of the night. "Stacey, everything you touch looks like the wreckage from a typhoon," she groused. "The spa, your office, that filthy car of yours. God only knows what that flat of yours looks like."

Stacey smiled, not taking the bait. "Little cranky, are we, luv?" she replied mildly. "Listen, I've got some more good news. C.M. told me Friday night he's got another blockbuster for us. Says it will "light up the night sky" in New York, Sydney and Beijing. Wouldn't give me the details yet but says it will probably land on New Year's Day. Stay tuned."

Angela slid her body completely below the water line, only her head showing, and smiled widely. "You're doing a great job with him, darling," she said, grump gone from her voice. "His story tips are amazing. He's turning me—I mean us—into the stars of the foreign staff, and I haven't even met him yet. All I know is he may be a retired spook who knew Raffy back in Nairobi. Go figure."

"You'll meet him soon enough," Stacey said. "I'm going to set up a lunch for the three of us after New Year's. You'll like him. He's a real hunk."

It's Go Time

South Pacific Bureau, New York Herald
Diplomat Road, Bellevue Hill, Australia
Wednesday, December 19, 2002
5:05 p.m.

"South Pacific Bureau, *New York Herald*. Stacey McKenzie here. Here's your chance. Talk to me."

C.M. laughed on the other end. Never failed to amuse him: a female reporter with a gruff Aussie accent sounding like a Tinsel Town talent agent.

"Stacey, it's C.M," he said. "Looks like it's a go for New Year's Day. Haven't seen the actual report yet but I was briefed by my sources. Fine with them if the *Herald* gets the exclusive. They think the local media are a bunch of bozos anyway. So, go ahead and write up the A-matter."

"A-matter?"

"Yeah, you know," he said, "the background info. Holt's history, what kind of politician he was, who his friends and backers were, how he supposedly died and where. Stuff down in the story that you don't have to write on deadline. You won't have much time to read and digest the actual report itself. It's going to be a tight deadline."

"Got it," Stacey said, excitement palatable in her voice, "What else? Angela is flying back from Wellington tonight. Can I tell her what the story is about?"

"Go ahead, but tell her to hold back from briefing New York," C.M. instructed. "Just for a while, until I can read the report itself. I'll get an early copy of it. I'm also worried about leaks from Herald Tower. You don't want to be scooped by your own Washington or Beijing bureaus."

"Got it," Stacey said.

"Now here's the order of battle," "C.M. said. "Report is going to be officially released on January 2d, Sydney time. That's a Wednesday. That means if the Herald puts it in their New Year's Day edition, it will scoop the Aussie press by about half a day, given the 16-hour time zone differences. Bottom line: send the New York editors a sked about 4 p.m. New York time on Dec. 31."

"A sked?"

"You know," C.M. said, "about four or five paragraphs that lay out the top of the story. Also give the story's approximate length."

"Ok," Stacey said uncertainly.

"Don't worry. Angela knows the drill. Once you get the report, you'll have about five hours to read it and write the story. You should plan to file no later than 9 p.m. New York time on their New Year's Eve."

"Let me see," Stacey said, trying to translate that into Sydney time.

"That's 1 p.m. Sydney time on New Year's Day.," C.M. cut in. "Angela should tell her editors not to put the story on the website until New Year's morning New York time when the newspapers are landing on doorsteps. We don't want the web site to scoop the paper."

"Wow, this is making my head hurt," Stacey said. "We don't do hard news that much. You've got this mapped out to a fare-thee-well. How do you know all this stuff? Like you've done it before."

"Ah," C.M. replied modestly, "I've just been around a lot of journalists in my day. Picked it up through osmosis."

"Fantastic," Stacey said. "I'll get to work on this right away. I'm going to meet Angela tonight. Oh, C.M., this is so exciting."

"Right, you are, luv. Exciting doesn't begin to describe this."

CHAPTER 37

You Do the Pre-Sell

South Pacific Bureau, New York Herald
Diplomat Road, Bellevue Hill, Australia
Thursday, Dec. 26, 2002
10:10 p.m.

Eyes slammed shut, beer in left hand as usual, Angela sat back in the circular spa, utterly exhausted by a workday that began at 5 a.m. in southern New Zealand and ended an hour ago at Sydney International. The 'Twelfth of Never' was playing quietly on the sound system—the Johnny Mathis love song she sang to Raffy at their wedding party in Darien more than 17 years ago. She thought she meant it at the time.

God help me, she mused: this bureau chief job is never done but I am loving it so—despite those dickhead bosses in New York. The Kiwi story has a great shot at A1, Bainbridge says, but you've got to do it right. The premise is terrific: a yarn about clueless North American tourists driving rental cars on the left side of the road all around the southern island on narrow, windy mountain roads. Bad mix: collisions constantly because the tourists, many elderly, are easily disoriented and make terrible split-second decisions that cause fearsome head-on pile-ups. Great interviews on Christmas day from a hospital in one small town where four Americans and one Canadian were recovering from serious injuries. Locals say it happens so often it's not news anymore--unless someone dies. Make the story "darkly funny," Bainbridge said, and I can sell it to A1. What the fuck is 'darkly funny' about that, she wondered?

Angela sighed hard, finished the last of her beer, and let out a belch that echoed like a human foghorn in the quiet summer night. "Angela, that is so disgusting," Stacey said, seated next to her in bubbling spa waters. "Why do you always do that? Do you want to hear about this Holt story or not? I'm going home otherwise. Scott's waiting for me."

"I'm sorry, baby," Angela replied contritely. "I just need to shut my brain down for a while. You've given me the highlights. Why don't you deal with Peter Bainbridge on the pre-sell and we'll write it together on New Year's Day? Story should lead the paper. Jesus, what a great way to start 2003."

"I get the first byline, right," Stacey said, standing and starting to stretch. "I've done all the reporting and already written some of the background material. Oh, my, I'm so sore. Played beach basketball for two hours tonight."

Angela didn't reply as she watched Stacey put her six-foot-three, 155-pound frame through a series of knee and back stretches in the soothing waters. She does not have an ounce of flab anywhere, Angela noted approvingly. Breasts and butt are perfect, legs all sleek muscle. No surprise she can dunk a basketball from a standing start. Spider Woman: that's what the teenage boys on the playground call her.

"Nice try," Angela replied finally. "I'm the bureau chief. I always get the first one. But you clearly deserve a byline. No more credit lines at the end of the story, like you had with Raffy."

Angela exited the spa, grabbed a white pool towel from a chair and wrapped it around her. She took a cigarette out of her purse and lit it.

"Yuk, that is so gross," Stacey spat, waiving at the smoky air. "I thought you'd quit."

"Give me a break," Angela replied wearily, exhaling the smoke through her mouth and away from Stacey. "These things relax me. I only have about three a day. Haven't had any drugs or booze for a month. I can't quit everything at once."

Both women laughed.

"This is so much fun," Stacey said, continuing her stretches. "I do most of my reporting at O'Rourke's or hanging out in the hot tub. Is that normal?"

The women laughed in sync again. Stacey finished her stretches and also exited the spa. She wrapped a towel around her as Angela, nearly a foot shorter, approached and hugged her hard. Both deftly shed their towels as they slow-danced to the Mathis soundtrack. A comical sight given their height differences.

"Let's go down to the V-cave for a while," Angela said after a time, leading Stacey by the hand. "Tell Scott you had to work late. Gotta keep the boss happy."

CHAPTER 38

New Year's Blahs

News Conference Room, New York Herald
Herald Tower, Midtown Manhattan
Monday, December 30, 2002
5 p.m.

God, I can't wait for the holidays to end, Maggie Maye thought, as she looked at the list of stories being pitched for New Year's Day on Wednesday. There's never enough real news, half the staff is on holiday and the news hole is twice as big as normal because of all the advertising. Same shit every year.

"All right, Kellen," she said, bringing the news meeting to order and glaring at her foreign editor at the opposite end of the conference table. "Whatdaya got for New Year's Day? Let's start 2003 with a pop for a change."

"Maggie, thanks for teeing me up," Kellen shot back. "Just so happens we have some breaking news out of Sydney. Details a little fuzzy but it relates to some super-secret Aussie intelligence report on Chinese spying. Bainbridge just talked to the office down there and they'll be writing something on deadline tomorrow. Apparently, it's exclusive."

"Can you be a little more specific?" Maggie asked impatiently. "Not a lot I can do with this. You don't even have a sked yet."

"Yeah, I know," Kellen replied, irritated at being called out publicly by the editor, the back benchers behind him exchanging smug looks. "Let's talk offline. Situation is a little fluid at the moment."

"So I gather," Maggie replied coldly, turning her attention to national editor Heathcliffe Smythe II, sitting to Kellen's right. "National, what do you got? That won't be hard to beat."

CHAPTER 39

She's on Fire

Office of the Editor, New York Herald
Herald Tower, Midtown Manhattan
Monday, December 30, 2002
8:18 p.m.

Maggie Maye was putting on her winter coat as her foreign editor knocked on the open door and entered without an invite.

"Make it fast, Kellen," Maggie barked. "Bernie and I are going to our place on Candlewood Lake tonight and I haven't even packed. I won't be back until next Sunday night."

"Got it," Kellen replied. "Looks like we'll just have to call an audible tomorrow on the spy story. Bainbridge called the researcher again after the news meeting and they still don't have a good handle on what's going on. She sounded a little disorganized."

"Why is Bainbridge talking to the news assistant?" she asked irritably. "Wasn't she part of that basketball team that took it all off for some stupid calendar promotion? Caused such an uproar down there? Why doesn't that reassure me?"

"It was promotion to raise money for breast cancer," Kellen offered.

"Yea, right," Maggie sneered. "I read where the calendars sold out in four hours, all 10,000 of them at $50—repeat $50--each. All men buyers. I had no idea your gender cared so deeply about breast cancer."

"Ok, ok," Kellen said. "Men are pigs. Listen, don't worry about the spying story. We'll figure it out. Enjoy your New Year's. Leave the Blackberry at home. Christian has the duty, Harry Berger's on the desk. They'll make the call. Done this a thousand times."

"Kellen, take a seat for minute," Maggie said, sitting back down in her chair. "I do want to talk about Sydney, as much as I would like to forget that place."

"Angela's terrific, isn't she," Kellen said, smiling. "Who knew? Ten times better than Raffy for that job. Sorry to speak ill of the departed."

"Listen," she said, "Wilbur told me today that the Aussie visitors bureau has cut its Herald ad buys almost in half for 2003. Slashing those FYI South Pacific ads. Wilbur says Ari's furious. Costing the paper a lot of money. Says it's related to the firing of the bureau's chief flack. He was Ari's man in Sydney. Angela supposedly knows him well also. Something he was quoted saying in her recent story about crocs eating tourists in the boonies."

"That was a terrific story," Kellen said. "My wife read it and was mortified. Said we're never going to Australia on vacation. The guy said the salt-water crocs *usually* only attack locals. All in all, not too much for tourists to worry about."

Both editors laughed.

"Yea, that was him," Maggie said. "The visitors bureau went nuts when the story hit the wires and kicked up a shit storm. Convened a special board meeting and fired the guy on the spot. Three hours later, they told Ari in an e-mail the ads buys were being cut way back."

"Well," Kellen said, "no one disputed the accuracy of the story. Angela did her job. That's what I care about."

Kellen stood to go. "Listen, I'm headed to the Vineyard tomorrow for New Year's and I may stay through the weekend. Don't even think about the Flanagan story. We got it covered. You and Bernie have some fun."

Yeah, right, Maggie thought, as she turned out the lights and watched her foreign editor disappear into the newsroom. Have fun with Bernie? 'Weekend at Bernie's' is more like it. I've got to find out more about this Jack Quinn guy, she thought, closing her door and locking it. Memo to self: call Angela yourself when you get back and find out what she knows. What's with these FYI ads? Who writes them anyway? How does that work?"

CHAPTER 40

To the Manor Born

Office of the Foreign Editor, New York Herald
Herald Tower, Midtown Manhattan
Tuesday, December 31, 2002
9:49 a.m.

A true pure-bred and hard-body handsome, Peter Bainbridge worked the newsroom like a prince amongst the unwashed.

Plucked from the reporter ranks to be chief deputy foreign editor after 9/11, he quickly became a natural in the free-for-all kitchen where the news was prepared and served up to several million readers each day. Only forty-four, he would almost certainly—barring a serious mis-step—be lord of the manor one day. Didn't hurt that Ari III was his biggest booster. They lift weights together three mornings a week in the executive gym.

"Hey, Kellen," Bainbridge said, popping unannounced as usual into his boss's office, "I forgot to tell you. I'm heading to Philly in a little while for the parent's annual New Year's soiree. Back later in the week. You're welcome to join me if you wish."

Hmmm, Kellen wondered, when is Peter going to tell his aging parents—old money aristocrats from the Philly Main Line—his little secret. Certainly, everyone in the newsroom knew he was a facile switch-hitter and famously promiscuous with athletes and models half his age. Unfortunately, his proper parents viewed men having sex with other men as akin to bestiality, so Peter only brought his girlfriends to the annual holiday party.

"Thanks anyway. I've got plans myself," Williams replied. "Give your parents my best. Sit down for a sec, Peter. Got something I need to ask you."

"Fire away, chief."

"Don't call me chief. I'm not Perry White and you're not Clark Kent."

Both editors laughed at that chestnut.

"What's with this Aussie story?" Kellen asked. "It might lead the paper tomorrow and we don't even know what it is yet. Maggie slapped my wrist yesterday at the story meeting. We didn't even have a sked. Heathcliffe loved it. He's such a pompous ass."

"Why would anyone give their child the first name of Heathcliffe?" Bainbridge asked.

"Probably someone with the last name of Smythe, which is just a fancy way of spelling Smith," Kellen shot back. "He's a preppy just like you are. Believe he went to both Lawrenceville and Princeton. Doesn't get any snobbier than that."

"Ah," Bainbridge sniffed, "strictly new money from South Jersey."

"Look, Peter," Williams said, boring in, "is this Flanagan piece worth A1 or not? What the fuck is it?"

"Little vague at the moment," Bainbridge replied, unconcerned. "Won't know until tonight. Christian will call an audible. I briefed him a little while ago."

"Great," the foreign editor said.

"Relax, Kellen," Bainbridge said, standing to go. "It's another Flanagan ten-strike. The woman's on fire. She must have a great editor in New York."

"Yeah, yeah," Kellen said, laughing, "a real fucking Maxwell Perkins."

Bainbridge chuckled and disappeared into the newsroom without further ado. Typical Peter, Kellen thought. Cocky as they come, sets his own rules, hears his own drum. Good thing he's so talented. Just like all the other correspondents—immensely gifted, impossibly self-centered, and can't be bothered with the details necessary to print a world-class newspaper every day.

Good thing we have such a great copy desk, Kellen thought.

CHAPTER 41

This Story's a Joke

City Room, New York Herald
Herald Tower, Midtown Manhattan
Tuesday, December 31, 2002
9:08 p.m.

Harry Terwilliger Berger cut a singular swath through the *Herald's* newsroom, where he'd been chief copy editor on weekends and holidays for nearly twenty years.

Thick glasses low on his nose, the graduate of Harvard College (class of '62) had the cheeks of a serious drinker, girth of a dedicated couch potato and mind of a journalist-scholar whose command of 20th Century factual history was rarely challenged.

Most colleagues referred to him respectfully as The Twigg—or Twiggy, an appellation shorthand he loathed. In fact, Harry loathed many things and said so openly. Sports topped the list even though a distant cousin had been a journeyman infielder for the Washington Senators in the 1950s. Most importantly, the top editors adored him: if The Twigg had the swing shift, they could rest easily that night.

Seated at this desk in a cluttered cubicle and glancing at his Bulova watch, Harry sighed at having to work yet another New Year's Eve. Christ, he mused, another three more hours until that stupid ball drops.

If I have to see too many more of those, he thought, I'm going postal. Good thing the Back Page is open til 5 a.m. Probably time to pull the cord, he told himself for about the 1,000[th] time. Then again, what on earth would I do? Don't have any hobbies. Probably have to carry me out of here.

But first there was this 3,000-word mega-turd that just landed on his desk with a prodigious splat. Supposed to be the news story that leads the paper tomorrow. Christian Turnbull, night news editor, insists it must run. "Monster scoop," he called it.

Fucking Turnbull, Harry thought. What a jackass. He flopped as a foreign correspondent and he's even worse as an editor. Known sarcastically as "cool-hand Christian" for his proclivity to melt down on deadline, Turnbull still thinks he can be top editor of the paper one day. What a joke, Berger thought. He'll probably croak on the nightshift— just like me.

Harry spotted Turnbull, natty as usual in his plaid sweater vest and button-down yellow shirt, moving briskly through the newsroom on another busy New Year's Eve. Harry stood and waved him over to his cubicle, piled high with yellowed newspapers, old magazines and musty reports from deep inside some government bureaucracy or another.

"Christian," Harry said crossly, "we gotta talk about this Flanagan story. I just got all the way through it. We can't run this thing. It's a joke."

Turnbull eyed Berger carefully. No sense in getting Twiggy too riled up, he mused, not at this late hour. Look at him, Turnbull thought disgustedly, what a slob. You could always tell what The Twig had for dinner that night because the remnants were all over the front of his shirt.

"What's the problem, Harry?" Turnbull asked mildly. "Flanagan's really nailed another one. A real ten-strike, as Bainbridge put it. He's her editor."

"Gutter ball's more like it," Berger fired back, struggling to get to his feet and holding the story printout with his index finger and thumb like it was tinged with dog excrement. "Bainbridge is an idiot. He couldn't line-edit a story to save his pampered life. This thing has no comment from any of the Aussie spooks who supposedly wrote the report. Nothing. Nada. Seems like you need *something* in a holy shit story like this. *Ya think?*"

"Harry, Harry," Turnbull said patronizingly, looking at this watch, "it's precisely 1:14 in the afternoon down there on New Year's day. No one's at their desks now. They're all nursing their hangovers. We got in there that no one at AISO could be reached for comment."

Berger scoffed. "My dear Christian, just think about this for a moment. An Aussie prime minister from the Vietnam era stages his own death to avoid being outed as a Chinese spy. Then, he and this Suzy Wong of his are executed by Mao to ensure their silence? By a firing squad at dawn, no less? Are you crazy, Christian? Hollywood wouldn't even believe this."

"Listen to me, Harry, and listen closely," Turnbull shot back, pressure gauge rising fast, "I just got off the phone with Flanagan. We have the report. Stamped top-secret in red letters across the top. This is a huge exclusive for us. Just what Kellen and Maggie want."

"No, you listen," Berger fired back, spittal starting to form on his lips. "Let me try this one more time. I don't give a fuck about an exclusive if the story has not been properly vetted and I don't give a double fuck if Flanagan is the next Oriana Fallaci..."

"Oriana Fallaci?" Turnbull cut in, laughing derisively. "Please Harry, you can do better than that. She is so 20 years ago."

"Turnbull," Berger replied, quietly, slowly, menacingly now, "you call Maggie right now and tell her this story's not ready. It needs another day. I will not approve it for publication."

"Harry, you need to understand something," Turnbull hissed, teeth clenched, face beet red now. "You're not in charge here. I am. I know what I'm doing. I used to be Bangkok bureau chief, remember? I know Australia. Filed from there many times."

"I remember your stories, Christian," Berger fired back contemptuously. "They were long, boring and uniquely uninformative. They always gave me a headache. You were the king of conventional wisdom."

"God damnit, Harry," Turnbull roared, the lid now completely blown off, "you bloody fucking nitwit. Just put the commas in the right place and send the story down to composing, like you fucking copy editors are supposed to do."

"Don't call me a nitwit, Turnbull, you imperious twit," Berger screamed back, the spit flying in all directions now, the entire newsroom listening in, "your ass is on the line on this one. I want that on the fucking record."

"You don't know shit about reporting, Harry," Turnbull snarled, more quietly, backing away from the spit storm. "You've never written a story in your entire sorry career. All you do is sit on your fat ass and flyspeck all the great stuff we do. You're a bloody joke."

"You've got it wrong as usual, Christian," Berger said, spitting out the name contemptuously. He sat back down and turned toward his desktop. "We're here to stop bozos like you from making fools out of all of us. For your sake, you better be right."

"You're disgusting," Turnbull said, backing away and wiping the spit on his face with his shirtsleeve. "You reek of booze, Harry. Help is out there. Go get it."

CHAPTER 42

Who Is Conor McCann?

South Pacific Bureau, New York Herald
Diplomat Road, Bellevue Hill, Australia
Wednesday, January 1, 2003
5:11 p.m

Angela pulled back from the desktop in her office, muttered a triumphant 'yes" under her breath, followed by a Kirk Gibson-style fist pump. She made her way down the marble hallway to Stacey's office two doors down.

"Stacey," she yelled, "we did it. The story has moved to composing from the copy desk. It looks fan-fucking-tastic."

The journalists embraced, gave each other double high fives and took seats on the leather couch in McKenzie's office.

"Happy fucking New Year, darling," Angela said. "Now the fun really starts. We've got to get set for tomorrow's news conference. Where is that report? I need to read it more carefully now we're off deadline."

"Conor came by when you were writing and wanted it back for a while," Stacey replied. "Said he'd get it back to us later on tonight."

"Conor?" Angela asked. "Who's Conor?"

"Oh, sorry, forgot to tell you. Last time I saw him, C.M. told me what his initials stood for: Conor McCann. One n in Conor, two n's in McCann. He showed me his passport. It's British."

Angela stood and stared at her collection of Australian landscape photos adorning the wall directly above the couch, saying nothing for a long time.

"Conor McCann," she said finally. "That's so odd. Raffy once told me he had a cousin in Ireland named Conor McCann. Spelled the same way. IRA type, lived in Belfast. Disappeared just before our wedding party and was never seen again. Raffy said Ulster thugs probably got him."

Angela paused and sat back down. "Oh, well, probably just a coincidence," she said. "So, tell me about the report. I just told an editor in New York we had a copy. Why didn't you make one?"

"Xerox is broken," Stacey said. "Conor said he needed to get his copy back to his source before anyone noticed it was missing. There are only five copies and they are all numbered. Don't worry, I've got it handled. Anyway, same report is going to be officially released tomorrow at the press conference."

"What time?" Angela asked. "It's going to be a real zoo."

"Not sure yet. Conor said he'd let me know."

Angela sprang off the couch like a feral cat and started to pace. "Ok, so let's discuss the next twenty-four hours," she said, all in now. "New York's putting the story on the web at 7 a.m. East Coast time. Right about when people at home are starting to read it on New Year's Day."

Angela paused, doing the math in her head and counting it out on her fingers. "So that means about midnight for us. We'll probably be bombarded with calls late tonight if anyone down here is paying any attention. Otherwise, it will all hit the fan tomorrow morning. This will be Holy Shit 2.0, only ten times more intense. I'll have to do lot of television interviews. God, I've got to wash and braid my hair tonight. I look like hell today."

She paused for a time and stopped pacing. "Give this guy Conor a call now and tell him I want the report back as soon as possible tonight. I don't want to go to bed tonight without it."

"By the way," Stacey said nonchalantly, "I meant to tell you I got a call-back message on my answering machine from some flak about the Holt story. I forget what agency he said he was from. Should I call him back?"

"Nah," Angela replied. "Nothing we can do about it now. Presses are about to roll. Call him back in the morning."

CHAPTER 43

Will Ripley Believe This?

Page A1, Columns 3-6
New York Herald
Wednesday, January 1, 2003

Ex-Aussie Leader Exposed as Chinese Spy;
PM Harold Holt Faked Drowning in 67;
Executed with Lover by Chairman Mao

By A. Reilly Flanagan & S.I. McKenzie
©New York Herald Staff Writers

Sydney—In a stunning development, Australia's top intelligence agency has concluded that one of the country's former prime ministers, Harold Holt, was a Chinese spy and faked his own death in the 1960s to avoid being exposed while still in office, the *Herald* has learned exclusively.

In addition, the Australian Intelligence Security Organization, known as AISO, has concluded in a new report, due to be released soon, that Holt and his lover were executed by firing squad several years later on direct orders from Mao Tse-tung.

The news is certain to send shock waves through diplomatic circles in the South Pacific, East Asia and the West. Spokesmen for AISO and the prime minister's office could not be reached for comment on New Year's Eve in New York.

Sources close to AISO told the *Herald* that the report is based on top-secret files that the current Chinese government has selectively leaked in a continuing effort to discredit Mao and his murderous regime. The notorious Chinese leader died in 1976.

It had been previously believed that Prime Minister Holt, head of the Liberal Party and a leader of no great distinction, supposedly died on the morning of Sunday, December 17, 1967, in a riptide drowning mishap. A good swimmer and a fit 59, Holt was last seen struggling in the surf about 50 yards off shore at Cheviot Beach, 60 miles south of Melbourne.

However, the 88-page intelligence report lays out in considerable detail how a Chinese mini-sub picked Holt up and spirited him to a full-sized submarine several hundred yards further offshore. From there, Holt was taken to the Chinese mainland, where he was united with his secret lover, a Hong Kong-born Melbourne businesswoman named Lily Chou Dunn.

The report explained that Holt agreed to fake his own death because Ms. Dunn kept seeing signs that his long-time role as a Chinese spy was about to be exposed. However, the report said, it now appears those signs were planted by Chinese operatives as a way of getting Holt out of office at the zenith of the Vietnam war.

Holt provided valuable intelligence to the Chinese government about America's escalating involvement in Vietnam. At the same time, however, he increased Australian troop presence in the war—a development that apparently infuriated Mao.

According to the report, stamped TOP SECRET in red letters across the top of the cover page, Holt and Ms. Dunn met an unseemly end in late 1975 *(continued on Page A10)*

CHAPTER 44

My Life's in Danger

South Pacific Bureau, New York Herald
Diplomat Road, Bellevue Hill, Australia
Thursday, January 2, 2003
12:02 a.m.

The buzz of the doorbell was so jarring—long and loud—that each woman, dead asleep one floor above in a teaspoon embrace, bounced off the bed in tandem.

"Jesus fucking Christ," Angela said, fumbling with the lamp on the bedside table, "what time is it? Who can that be at this hour? Christ, I was dead asleep."

"So was I," said Stacey, fumbling around for her bathrobe. "Maybe it's Conor returning the report. Should I go down and see who's there?"

"Yes, but be careful," Angela warned. "Don't turn on any lights downstairs. Take the flashlight from the second drawer. Yell if you need help."

Stacey disappeared down the hall and reappeared less than a minute later, carrying an oversized brown letter envelope. "Here," she said to Angela, "This came through the mail slot. I looked outside, didn't see anyone."

"Please read it to me, darling," Angela said, now in a crème-colored robe and looking for her reading glasses in the bedside table.

"Let's see," Stacey said, "the envelope is addressed to you. Black ink. To 'Mrs. Angelique Reilly Flanagan.' Ooooh, how elegant. Is your first name really Angelique?"

"How would anyone here know that?" Angela snapped. "I haven't used that fucking name since grade school. I hated it. Kids teased me unmercifully. Open the envelope already."

"Let's see," Stacey said, "White piece of paper with the same black handwriting on it. 'Dear Angelique: Congratulations on your 'scoop.' (Scoop is in quotes). If you believe that, perhaps I could interest you in a story about rain forests in the Outback. Let's do have lunch next week. We have other issues to discuss. You owe me. Conor McCann.'"

"What?" Angela shrieked, bouncing off the bed as though it were a trampoline and grabbing the note from Stacey's hand. "Let me see that."

Putting on her reading glasses, she stared at the note, speaking under her breath, repeating key phrases again and again, a look of horror growing.

"Oh my God," she said finally, voice breaking, laying back on the bed, "I think I'm going to be sick."

"Angela, you're freaking me out," Stacey said, sitting down next to her and grabbing her hand. "What the bloody hell is wrong?"

"Just don't say anything," Angela said, pulling a sheet up to her chin, eyes locked on the darkened skylight. "Let me think for a moment. Try to sort this out."

Stacey took the note and reread it. "I don't get it," she said, hopelessly lost. "There are no rain forests in the Outback that I know of. What does he mean by that?"

"Gino Carella warned me to beware of strangers bearing gifts," Angela said quietly, skin clammy now, face ghastly pale. "I'm beginning to see what he meant."

Stacey reached over and felt Angela's forehead. "I've never seen you like this before," Stacey said, eyes welling up with tears. "Is something wrong with our story?"

"Stacey," Angela said, suddenly sitting up, "I need to know more about this guy Conor. What haven't you told me about him?"

"Nothing," Stacey replied defensively. "He's a mystery man, some sort of spook, I guess. I told you. He was an old pal of Raffy's."

"Ok, we need to talk," Angela said, grabbing Stacey's hands. "Look at me. We've got to be calm at all costs. I have to ask you about the night you spent with him."

"Why?"

"Stacey, I think something awful is going on but I'm not sure exactly what. I think we may have been set up. You've got to trust me. Did you see him without his clothes on?

"Of course," Stacey snapped. "Isn't that normally what happens during sex? I just wanted to thank him for helping us."

"What about his penis?"

"Angela, what kind of question is that?"

"Just answer it."

"Well, it worked, if that's what you mean. Twice, in fact. We used condoms both times. I put them on myself."

"What else? Think, Stacey, think."

"Well, since you ask, his donger was discolored--large white patches along with the brown. Like one of those Pinto breeds. I obviously got a good look it."

"Oh, my God," Angela muttered under her breath, fists clenched, going down to one knee. "Raffy? How can this be?"

"Raffy?" Stacey cried. "What does he have to do with this? He's dead."

"Never mind," Angela replied, trying to regain her composure. "Stacey, listen up. Have you noticed anyone suspicious lately, someone following you? A mobster type? Weighs about 300 pounds?"

"What?" Stacey shrieked, face clouding with fear. "No. Why do you ask me that? Am I in danger?"

"Stacey, no, you're not in danger. But please just answer the question, baby. What about a tall black man with dreadlocks and a West Indies accent?"

"Well," Stacey said slowly, trying to stay hinged, "I met a guy at the gym the other night who looked and sounded like that. We talked, had a milkshake at the health bar. Said he was here on business. Something to do with aboriginal development. He did ask me what I did for a living and I told him. We also talked about basketball. I told him I played on the women's national team. He said he played in college. Told me he was born in Bermuda."

"Ok, last question," Angela said, staring hard, hovering over her, grabbing both of her wrists. "Did you notice anything about his eyes?"

"Yes," Stacey blurted. "They were stunning. Dark blue. I told him how beautiful they were."

Angela groaned, saying nothing as she fell to her knees and put her forehead on the hardwood floor, her body starting to shake violently.

"Stacey," she said quietly, starting to cry, "we've been had. The story's a fake. Raffy set me up. My life's in danger. I've got to get out of here."

With that, she rushed into the bathroom where she vomited violently. Trying mightily to regain a measure of control, she struggled to her feet, grabbed her purse and moved toward the door.

"Stacey, honey, listen to me," Angela said, looking as if she'd witnessed a landing of armed aliens. "You handle things tomorrow. I'll be in touch. Call Lieutenant Carella in New York. He'll understand."

With that, Angela disappeared into the hallway and Stacey, back on her feet, abruptly fainted, falling straight back, head hitting the wood floor with a sickening thud.

Downstairs, in the offices of the South Pacific bureau of the *New York Herald*, a paper with a history of distinguished overseas reporting going back to the 19th Century, the landlines were coming to life at 33 minutes past midnight.

It was the start of a day that would live in infamy for the paper. The sneak attack worked to perfection.

We're Toast

Office of the Editor, New York Herald
Herald Tower, Midtown Manhattan
Wednesday, Jan. 1, 2003
11:55 p.m.

Fucking blackberries, Kellen Williams thought, getting off the elevator at 14 and heading directly to Maggie's office. Ten years ago, this kind of tempest would not have ruined a perfectly good long weekend. Happy New Year, my ass.

"Kellen, come in, come in," Maggie barked, hanging up the phone as her foreign editor came into her glass-paneled office. "Take a seat. Have you read this Holt story yet? Good God, what a mess. Have you talked to Bainbridge? Where is that guy when you need him?"

"He doesn't know much," Kellen said, sitting down, sphincter muscle tightening at the look of alarm on Maggie's normally poker face. "He couldn't reach Flanagan. Anyway, he left town Tuesday before he even knew what the story said. So did I. Unfortunately."

"The only good news," Maggie said, "is the prime minister has not flat-out denied the story. He is quoted by the AP as saying: 'We question whether such an intelligence report exists, but we will explore the matter further.'"

"We must have the report," the foreign editor said. "You can't invent something like that."

"Kellen," Maggie said, "this story sounds preposterous. Did anyone read it last night? I just have this awful feeling that Angela was conned. What if the report itself is bogus? Remember *The Hitler Diaries*."

"You should know," Williams replied sheepishly, "that Harry Berger left a message on my home answering machine late last night saying he wanted to hold the story—he thought it was bogus-- but Christian overruled him. I got the message a little while ago."

Both editors went quiet for a time, knowing their newspaper editing careers were effectively over if Berger was right. Doesn't get any worse than allowing a total fabrication on the front page—the most hallowed ground in the newspaper biz.

"Where is Flanagan, for Christ's sake," Maggie snapped. "What is she saying about all this?"

"No one has seen her," Kellen replied lamely. "Disappeared. Gone. Vanished into thin air. Hasn't been seen in more than 24 hours."

"What about the news assistant," Maggie demanded, close to shouting now. "I can't believe we gave her a byline. On the bloody front page, no less. God-damnit, where the fuck are our standards?"

Like the newspaper delivery girl she once was, helping her older brother Max, Maye threw a rolled-up front section across her office, hitting the Plexiglas window with a loud thwack. The few stragglers left in the newsroom at that hour--outside her door trying to eavesdrop on what was going on—scattered like cockroaches.

"Easy, Maggie," Williams said, moving to shut the door. "Everybody's watching. They know something horrible might have happened. We can't lose our cool. Bainbridge did reach the assistant. She's in the hospital with a concussion. She had a really nasty fall. He thinks she and Angela must have had a fight."

"We have *got* to get to the bottom of this right now," Maggie hissed through clenched teeth. "I was just talking to Ari when you walked in. He's beside himself. Getting calls from all over the world. I've never heard him so unglued. Keening almost. He knows his slutty superstar has fucked up big-time."

"Look," Kellen said, "I'll call Peter Lynch in Hong Kong and have him get the next flight to Sydney. He's a real pro. He can give us a damage assessment."

"Ok, that's a start," Maggie replied, a little calmer now. "Ari's in his office. He wants me to come see him. You should come too."

Maggie paused a moment and looked out into the quiet newsroom, the final stories for the last edition almost done.

"Whoever did this knew exactly what they were doing," she said quietly. "New Year's Eve, second-tier editors on duty in New York, third-string reporters in the field, an intelligence report from halfway around the world coming out of nowhere. No time to verify it.

"Someone knew Angela would fall for this. Look at the wires. The Aussies are going wild. They're mocking us terribly. We're the laughing-stock of the planet. I don't think the paper can survive this. I know you and I certainly can't."

CHAPTER 46

Shocked, Shocked

Weekend estate of Ari Steinberg III
Sag Harbor Road, East Hampton, New York
Saturday, January 4, 2003
9:09 a.m.

It was the 'Page Two' gossip column in the New York Sun that first gave the pair their famous nickname: "The Real Odd Couple." It was referring to the tag team of Julie 'The Jackal' Levitsky and Ike 'The Master of Disaster' Citron.

As the paper framed it a few months ago: "They are the guns for hire when the super-rich get into deep do-do with the law and the media. The 6-3, 333-pound Levitsky handles the legal train wreck and the 5-5, 140-pound Citron spins the Fourth Estate. Like an iron hand in a velvet glove, they work seamlessly, total fees approaching $2,000 an hour, chump change for the uber top tier."

Ari III brightened when he spotted the famous duo approaching his veranda overlooking the Atlantic Ocean. Still in his light-blue silk bathrobe, the august publisher of the *New York Herald* was a pathetic sight, unshaven now for the third day in a row, eyes red from no sleep. He looked like he had crawled out from under a freeway overpass.

"Ike, Julie, thank God you're here," he exclaimed, giving each man an awkward man-bro hug. "I'm so worried about Angela. Sit down, please. Coffee? OJ? Danish maybe?"

"We're good, Ari," Levitsky said, as the three men went inside and sat on stools at a kitchen bar overlooking the water on a dreary winter morning. "We have to move fast now. You saw the Wall Street Journal story this morning from Sydney, right? The Aussie CIA flat-out said it never authored such a report. The Holt family is furious, threatening to sue."

"I thought you couldn't libel a dead man," Ari offered lamely. "One of the few things I remember from law school."

"The point is," Citron said, "you need to get a grip, Ari. Take charge. And you can't be issuing statements about how the paper stands by the story when you don't even know what the basic facts are."

"I told Betsy Wright to do that," Ari said. "I didn't know what else to do. That's when I called you guys."

"Ok," Julie said, taking charge, "let's try to understand what happened here—and why. If the story is a hoax, then who's the perp? Where did he come from? And where are the reporters? What are they saying?"

"No one's heard from Angela in days," Ari said. "All I know is she fled the office on New Year's Eve down there, saying 'My life's in danger.' Apparently, she jumped into her brand-new BMW, wearing only a bathrobe and drove off into the night."

"What about the other reporter?" Julie asked.

"She's still in the hospital," Ari said. "Fractured her skull in a bad fall the night Angela disappeared."

"What's her job there, anyway?," Ike asked. "I can't figure it out. I'm told she was an Olympic basketball player but she has very little news experience. Where the hell did she come from?"

"She's the office manager in Sydney," Ari explained. "Real nice gal. Does research for Angela when she needs it. Helps her with reporting as well."

"Great," Ike said. "Less said about her, the better."

"Ok, look," Julie cut in, standing and starting to pace, "we've got to assume the worst: the paper was targeted by a deliberate con artist but we don't know the motive. That's the first thing we need to find out."

"Jesus," Ari said, only half listening, looking at his Blackberry, "our stock fell down another 15% yesterday and Goldman Sachs has just gone from a recommended hold to a sell. There goes the third home in Bermuda."

"Ari, put down the Blackberry," Julie commanded. "Ike, we need a statement yesterday, saying the paper has formed an investigative team to report and write the real story of what happened down there. The *LA Times* did that a few years ago with an ad scandal involving the newsroom and the storm blew over."

"Didn't the publisher get fired after that?" Ari asked.

"Ari," Julie shot back, "stop. You're not going to get fired. Your family owns the company-- the majority voting stock at least."

"That's part of the problem," Ari said. "Dad and I had a screaming match on the phone this morning. He says I'm out as CEO if I don't get my arms around this fast."

Ari paused for a time, trying to compose himself, and sighed deeply.

"There's something you guys need to know," he said slowly, painfully.

"Everything here is privileged," Julie cut in. "I'm your lawyer and I've hired Ike as part of the legal team. Don't worry about confidentiality."

"Good to know," Ari said. "Fact is, how can I put this? You may have already sensed this. Mrs. Flanagan and I have a complicated relationship."

"Gee, you don't say," Ike cut in. "We're shocked, shocked."

"I know, I know," Ari said defensively. "Point is, if a bunch of reporters from the *Herald* are unleashed to do a story, they'll be able to confirm our personal relationship and Angela's reputation will be ruined."

Ari said nothing for a few seconds, looking like he might cry. "I can't help it," he said miserably. "I find her irresistible. She's the only woman who truly understands me."

"Admit that publicly," Ike warned, "and you'll be the lead skit on Saturday Night Live. 'The Scion and the Slut."

"Angela's not a slut," Ari protested. "She's a modern woman and true free spirit. I can't explain it. I've never met another woman like her."

Ari paused again and this time the dam gave way. "I hope she's ok," he sobbed. "I feel so bad for her."

"Ari, listen to me," Julie ordered, standing up and grabbing Ari's wrists with both hands. Looking him directly in the eye, he warned: "This is serious stuff. The paper's future is literally at stake. Fuck the widow Flanagan—and I don't mean literally. You hear me: fuck her. You need to focus on yourself, your family, your newspaper, upon which millions of people depend every day. You've got to deal with this mess. Now."

CHAPTER 47

Actress, Princess, Fish Wife

Dom's Clam House
Mulberry Street, Lower Manhattan
Monday, January 6, 2003
8:18 p.m.

It has been more than thirty years since Joey "The Jackass" Genova was iced in this place, Gino Carella marveled, and the tourists keep coming in droves to see exactly where one of the Mafia's most famous hits played out. Mystique of the mob, he mused bitterly. Look at Tony Soprano on HBO. Show's popularity is off the charts. Why don't they do shows about the cops who put these mobsters in jail? Guess they do sometimes, he thought. Look at 'Law and Order.'

"What are you thinking about, Gino?" Candy Garcia said with a soft smile, finishing her white chocolate mousse and espresso. She reached for his hand: "I can call you Gino now all the time, right? Don't go silent on me. You look so serious. You should be happy. Retired in one piece, new job, new life in an exciting new place."

"Yeah," Carella replied without much fire, "it's all good. I'm just in transition. You know, no more blue light for the top of the car, no more crime alerts on the Blackberry, no more department-issue Baretta underneath the jacket. And this move is just weird. Nobody in New

York even knows where Australia is. They think I'm moving to Europe. One cop told me: "I've heard great things about Vienna."

Garcia laughed, squeezed his hand and let go. "You'll be fine," she said soothingly. "You're a survivor. Speaking of Australia, did you see the news about that *Herald* reporter you had dinner with. She's gone missing. Really got her tits in a wringer."

"Yeah," Carella replied, looking pained. "Not too surprised. The woman is out there. Looks like an actress, lives like a princess, swears like a fish wife."

"Me thinks you were smitten with her," Garcia said with a smile. "You never did tell me what happened with you two down there. Never too late."

"Candy, listen to this," Carella said suddenly, looking down at his Blackberry. "It's from Julius Levitsky: 'Lieutenant Carella: Please come to my home in East Hampton tomorrow at noon. Pack a bag and bring your passport. Need you to fly to Sydney first class on the 5 p.m. out of JFK on top-secret assignment for blue-chip client. Expect a two-three week stay. Regards--JJL

"Wow," Garcia said, "lucky you. It's summertime down there now. Must be the *Herald* mess, eh?"

"Must be," Carella said, standing and signaling to the waiter for the check. "Listen, Garcia, do me a favor, will you? Run Rafer Flanagan's name through the cop computer and see if anything comes up around 9/11. Just throw out the net and see if you catch anything."

"Yes, sir, Lieutenant," Garcia replied, back in loyal subordinate mode. "What difference does it make? The man is dead."

"Just a hunch," Carella said. "See if they ever found any traces of that car he rented. E-mail me if anything comes up. I'll call you when I get back."

With that, Carella slapped a C-note on the table, put on his winter coat, kissed his best friend on the lips for the very first time—to her great surprise and delight—and vanished into the night. He was back in the saddle again. She licked her lips and smiled.

CHAPTER 48

Leading from Behind

Weekend Estate of Julius J. Levitsky
Montauk Road, East Hampton, New York
Tuesday, January 7, 2003
12:12 p.m.

Julie Levitsky was counting the money meter for the Angela-alert mess as Gino Carella's cab arrived in his driveway. Carella's bill alone will be $700 an hour, not including expenses, plus another half million for Ike and me, and we're already north of $1 million without breaking a sweat.

Sweet.

Praise the Lord for the third and fourth generation retards who drive their family businesses into the ground, Julie thought. To be fair, he mused, it was not all Ari III's fault. Steve Jobs himself probably would be hard-pressed to save the newspaper itself from the ocean floor.

Transformative technology and big money *always* crush everything in their path, he thought.

"Lieutenant Carella," Julie said as the big cop exited the back seat of a small cab carrying a suitcase and suit bag. "So good of you to do this on short notice. Really gives you a running start on the new job. Let's go in and see Ari. He's waiting in my private study."

After shaking hands, the pair walked into the eighteen-room ocean-front mansion through the foyer and into the private library where Levitsky spent most of his time working on the weekends. Meanwhile, his athletic trophy wife—half his age and a third his weight—played golf and tennis at the club down the street.

Ari III, standing and staring out the picture window, looked a little better. At least he had shaved and shed his bathrobe, but those doe-like brown eyes were still bloodshot and his short curly brown hair still uncombed. (Or is that the style now, Carella wondered.)

"Lieutenant Carella," Ari said, shaking Gino's hand with exaggerated firmness and trying to smile, "such an honor to meet you. Julie's been telling me all about your record. Sorry we couldn't meet under better circumstances. Hope you know how much my paper values and appreciates the NYPD."

"Thanks, Mr. Steinberg," Gino replied politely. "We take our support wherever we can get it."

"Yeah, yeah, cut the bullshit, Ari," Julie chimed in. "Your editorial page hates the NYPD. It's not personal."

The three men laughed, Ari the hardest. He didn't have tough-guy companionship very often—and it felt good. With these two bad-ass males behind me, he thought, maybe I can survive this fiasco.

"Ok, Ari," Julie said, as the trio settled into leather chairs in a circle, "what's new in the last twelve hours? By the way, Ike couldn't come. He's swamped with calls. Even 60 Minutes wants in on this."

"Well," Ari began, "Angela is still missing and Dad has called a telephone shareholders' meeting for this weekend on what went wrong here. Maggie tells me the newsroom is in a complete uproar, saying all kinds of horrible things about Angela and me, and how she should have never gotten Raffy's job. Nobody seems too worried that she has been missing for nearly a week now."

"We care, Ari," Julie interjected coldly. "Let's get beyond that. Lieutenant Carella is heading to Sydney this afternoon. I've asked him to deliver a confidential report to me within 90 days on what happened here. He's going to interview anyone and everyone who might know something. Spend as much time as he needs.

"Once I read the report, I alone will make a recommendation on who should read it and what we do with its recommendations. I expect all this will have blown over by then and we won't have to do anything except ensure a few editors get fired."

"Fine by me," Ari said dully. "Christ, even my own reporters are calling Betsy Wright and rudely demanding interviews with me. Poor woman is beside herself."

"Focus, Ari, focus," Julie said, staring hard at his bedraggled client. "See the big picture. Betsy will survive. The next few days will be hell. Put on your best business suit, buy lots of Visine, get into the office and show the troops you're in charge. Optics matter here."

"Ok," Ari said unenthusiastically, "Lieutenant, please call me directly as soon as you find Angela. I need to talk to her. You know about Stacey McKenzie, right? She and Angela are very close. She'll know where to track her down."

"I know Stacey," Carella said. "As chance would have it, I had dinner with her and Ms. Flanagan while I was on vacation down there a few weeks ago. Had a very nice time at some great Italian restaurant in Sydney. Every bit as good as New York."

"Oh, shit," Ari said, looking down at his Blackberry, "the AP has just moved a story saying Angela's Beemer has been found at a beach south of Melbourne. Purse found inside, along with a sealed note."

"Let me see that," Julie said, grabbing the phone and passing it to Carella after scanning the story. "Yea, this doesn't look good. Lieutenant, get a copy of that note as soon as you get down there. See if it gets us anywhere."

"Got it," Carella replied crisply.

"I knew it," Ari said, standing up unsteadily, tears forming, voice breaking. "I could feel it. The love of my life is gone. My God, how could this happen?"

Ka-ching, Julie thought.

"Don't worry, Ari," he said reassuringly, standing and putting his meaty hand on the publisher's shoulder. "We won't rest for an hour until we get to the bottom of this."

CHAPTER 49

Strangler Strikes Again

Crime Roundup, Page 14
Sydney After Dark
Thursday, January 9, 2003

An unidentified man was found strangled last week in a rundown motel in King's Cross.

According to the police report, the victim was a middle-aged Caucasian with white hair and beard. He was found face down on the bed, gagged, his hands bound behind him with police-style handcuffs. No identification or clothing was found on him or in the room.

One police official who asked not to be identified said it appeared the victim had been drugged, sodomized, and strangled. The body was taken to the morgue for further testing.

Police said an investigation was underway but provided no other details.

CHAPTER 50

Goodbye Cruel World 2.0

Page A7, New York Herald
Thursday, January 9, 2003

Herald Reporter
Is Missing
in Australia

By Peter Lynch
©Herald Staff Writer

Melbourne—Angela R. Flanagan, South Pacific bureau chief of the *New York Herald*, has been missing for more than a week and likely drowned, law enforcement officials in southern Australia confirmed Wednesday.

Ms. Flanagan's 2003 BMW was discovered Tuesday evening at a national park about 60 miles south of Melbourne. Inside the unlocked car were the reporter's leather purse, with credit cards and nearly $1,000 in cash, and a seal white envelope with the notation '---30---' written in large letters in black ink. Reporters in America sometimes use that notation at the end of their filings to indicate the story is done.

Ms. Flanagan has been missing since New Year's Eve when she abruptly fled her Sydney-area home, telling a colleague and friend: 'My life's in danger.' Her disappearance followed a story she co-authored in the January 1 edition of the *Herald* that turned out to be a fabrication and hoax apparently perpetrated by a mysterious Northern Irishman with close ties to Australian intelligence.

The story said that the Australian Intelligence Service Organization had written a report claiming that an Aussie prime minister in the 1960s, Harold Holt, had faked his own drowning to avoid being exposed as a Chinese spy. A spokesman for AISO denied it had authored such a report and a spokesman for the current prime minister, John Howard, said "this story was dealt with decades ago."

In addition, Anthony Holt, a barrister in Sydney and the late prime minister's eldest son, issued an angry statement, saying: 'The Herald story is unadulterated rubbish and has soiled my father's impeccable reputation. I call on the newspaper to make a front-page apology to my family and the Australian people for being so foolish to believe such a silly story. Otherwise, the newspaper should shut its presses forever because it does not deserve the public's trust.'

Herald Publisher Ari Steinberg III declined to be interviewed but he did put out a statement through a spokesman saying the paper has launched its own internal investigation and "we will not rest until we find out how such a hoax occurred and what can be done to prevent a repeat in the future."

Ms. Flanagan was a well-known journalist in Australian business, cultural and social circles. A distinctive red-head with long curly hair, she authored dozens of stories on all aspects of life in the South Pacific since her arrival in Sydney in 1996. She was named the paper's bureau chief in late 2001, replacing her late husband who died in the attacks on 9/11 in New York.

The *Herald* has been the only newspaper in North America and Europe to maintain a full-service bureau in Sydney. Its status is now unclear, a spokesman for the paper indicated.

Colin O'Malley, chairman of the Australian Chamber of Commerce and Industry in Melbourne, was effusive in his praise of Ms. Flanagan's work. "She wrote about this country in a way that was unmatched by any other foreign news organization," O'Malley said in an email to the *Herald*. "Her travel articles, in particular, opened the eyes of North American readers to the joys of a Down Under vacation and they proved to be a major boost to our country's critically important tourist industry."

Meanwhile, police in southeastern Australia are investigating whether Ms. Flanagan was the victim of foul play, given her final comments to fellow reporter Stacey McKenzie. Police are seeking to interview a mysterious Irishman known as C.M., apparently short for Conor Mc-Cann. He is believed to be from Belfast and carries a British passport. He had close ties to the paper's Sydney bureau but little else about him is known.

Ms. Flanagan's car was found not far from where Holt himself was last seen flailing in the surf 50 yards offshore. The prime minister's body was never found and at the time a police official was quoted as saying it was "likely the PM had been devoured" in the shark-infested waters.

Police sources told the *Herald* that it was possible Ms. Flanagan was trying to prove the veracity of her story by demonstrating she was a strong swimmer, as Holt was, and could easily survive in the warm summer waters. However, it is also possible, they said, that she was simply devastated at being hoodwinked and went swimming in the same treacherous waters, knowing full well she would also disappear without a trace. In any event, her crème-colored bathrobe, her only clothing when she disappeared a week ago, was found on the rocks next to the beach.

Police did not disclose the exact contents of the note but did say it merely amounted to "a farewell note to a close friend."

CHAPTER 51

Vanishing Act

Tape-recorded interview of Stacey McKenzie
South Pacific Bureau, New York Herald
Diplomat Road, Bellevue Hill, Australia
Friday, January 10, 2003
9:33 a.m.

Q: Good morning, Stacey. Are you feeling any better? I know it has been a tough few days.

A: Thanks, Lieutenant. Good to see you again, though I wish the circumstances were different. I am feeling better. And, yes, this past week has been a nightmare.

Q: Call me Gino. When did you get out of the hospital?

A: Three days ago. It was a very serious skull fracture. Doctors have told me to lie low for at least another week.

Q: You know why I'm here?

A: I'm about to be arrested for being criminally stupid. (Laughs). Peter Bainbridge gave me an update. It must be serious if the tape-recorder is going.

Q: Let's just say it's serious but certainly not criminal. Everyone in New York knows you and Angela were doing your jobs and

got horribly misled. Seems like it was very carefully organized and orchestrated.

A: I'll say.

Q: Ok, let's get started. First, the bad news is the paper has decided to close the bureau at the end of 2003. That's when the lease ends. There won't be any public announcement now. The paper will just say, if asked, the future of this office "is under consideration." Now the good news for you is you'll receive a severance payment of $100,000 American right now if you agree not to speak publicly about what happened here for five years. After that, do and say what you want.

A: Consider my mouth taped shut. I want to move back to the West Coast ASAP. I want to teach high school English, coach girls' basketball and marry my old college boyfriend who's a cop in Perth. He doesn't know it yet. (Laughs) Neither does my boyfriend here. (Laughs harder)

Q: Terrific. Wipe the slate clean. Don't look back.

A: Something like that.

Q: Ok, please tell me precisely what your role was here in this office. There's some confusion in New York about what your job was.

A: With good reason. I was hired as office manager, doing support and admin stuff, really being a glorified secretary. You know, answering the phone, emails; ordering office supplies; making sure all the computers and cell phones worked. But as soon as I was hired, Angela asked me to help with reporting and research. You know, conduct interviews and write up notes for her stories. Believe it or not, I never met Raffy in person. He had moved out a couple of years before. Just talked to him by phone. He never came into the office.

Q: Do you have any journalism training?

A: I was a sportswriter on my college newspaper at the University of Western Australia in Perth. Got my English degree there. I learned what an inverted pyramid is.

Q: A what?

A: Never mind. Not important.

Q: I hate to pry but what was your personal relationship with Ms. Flanagan?

A: We were good friends and we did have sex occasionally. Angela was a very lonely woman and she needed someone like me she could trust. She had very few female friends. She once told me the female correspondents at the paper despised her.

Q: How would you describe Ms. Flanagan's style? Her personality?

A: Well, you met her, Lieutenant. You got a taste of her. In public, she was all Texas charm, beauty and style. Men here adored her. She mesmerized them. Always made her interview subjects feel like they were important and interesting.

Q: In private?

A: Ambitious, insecure, crude. Seemed like every other word out of her mouth was some variation of fuck when she was angry.

Q: How would you describe her relationship with Ari Steinberg, the current publisher of the Herald.

A: He was her boy toy. She was in charge and he did whatever she wanted. Fact is, Angela loved being the boss. Slept with anyone she thought could help her—sources, colleagues, complete strangers (like you). She loved spending Saturday night at underground sex clubs in Sydney. Run by women.

Q: (Pause) She apparently was badly sexually assaulted in college. Did she ever talk about that?

A: Yeah, it affected her. Says she had this sexual "dead zone" with men (her words) unless she does cocaine and a three-ounce shot of vodka. Got her in the mood.

Q: What about the assault itself?

A: Yeah, if you notice carefully, her nose is slightly crooked. That's because the guys who raped her beat her up. She was down buying drugs in the city and got into a fight with one of the dealers. She accused him of trying to rip her off and called him an 'asshole.' That was how it all started. Told me once that not a week goes by that she doesn't think about that.

Q: Ok, let's discuss her disappearance. I gather her so-called farewell note was addressed to you. What exactly did it say?

A: Nothing important. "My darling Stacey: I'm so sorry for everything that's happened. It was all my fault. I will always love you very, very much. So long, Angela.' Something like that.

Q: That's it?

A: Yep.

Q: You think she drowned?

A: Not a chance.

Q: Why not?

A: She was afraid of the ocean. Freaked her out. The crocs, sharks, stingrays and the like. No, she didn't drown. She's out there somewhere. That story by Peter Lynch was nonsense. The cops and all the powers-that-be just want this case closed. The publicity has been terrible for their bloody image.

Q: What about all the cash and credit cards they found in her car?

A: Chump change, as you Yanks like to say. She's worth millions. What's $1,000 in cash? Good way to throw the cops off your trail. My guess she already has a new identity, a new passport and new charge cards. That woman sure did love to shop.

Q: Ok, let's talk about the mysterious Conor McCann for a moment. Any more thoughts on who he was and why he did what he did?

A: Not a clue. He was charming, polite, a real gentleman. Didn't drink alcohol or smoke, in good shape. I grew to like him a lot. I still can't believe he scammed us like this.

Q: I heard the general descriptions of what he looked like and the kind of accent he had. Was there anything else about him that was unusual? Scars? Body markings? Piercings?

A: (Long pause) No, not really. I only knew him from our meetings in the bars.

Q: Ok, interview's over. I'd really appreciate it if you would stick around a few days and help me go through Angela's stuff at the

house. Clothes, office equipment, personal stuff. New York wants an inventory of everything in the Bellevue Hill office.

Q: Sure thing. I'll stay as long as you need me. Then just pay me off and you'll never hear from me again. I've had enough of you Americans. No joke: you're all bloody crazy.

CHAPTER 52

Alpha Bitches

Tape-recorded interview of Peter Lynch
Hong Kong bureau chief, New York Herald
Diplomat Road, Bellevue Hill, Australia
Friday, January 10, 2003
3:13 p.m.

Q: Good afternoon, Peter. Thanks for helping me out. You're going back to Hong Kong tomorrow morning, right?

A; Right. Not much more for me to do here, Lieutenant. Kellen Williams is due to arrive tonight. He'll take the baton from here.

Q: Ok, help me out here. Give me your take on how all this could have happened. Where does the real blame lie? Why wasn't it prevented? Keep it simple. I'm a cop, not a journalist.

A: Sure. Of course, the biggest problem here was ARF. Angela. She didn't have the wisdom, grounding or the judgment to do this job, which is a helluva lot harder than it looks. She's the Janet Cooke of this story. Doesn't get any worse than that. The word is she was also a cocaine addict but I can't confirm that.

Q: Janet Cooke, eh? Who's she?

A: Google her. Arguably the most disgraced reporter to ever write for a major American newspaper. Until now. (Laughs)

Q: Please be specific. What exactly did Flanagan do wrong?

A: First, that Holt story was preposterous on its face. Any seasoned foreign correspondent would have known that. Second, Stacey told me Angela never even met her so-called Deep Throat. That's insane. Bob Woodward not only knew his Deep Throat, he knew where he lived.

Q: Stacey said to me this morning that she thinks Angela is also certainly still alive. Says the story you wrote the other day suggesting she drowned was, in her words, "just nonsense."

A: Listen, Lieutenant, this was part of the problem. Stacey's a wonderful person but she is not a seasoned reporter. She's a fine athlete and would make a great model for an ancient Greek statue but that has nothing to do with journalism. She was hired as office manager, not a reporter. Then Angela just throws her into a reporting role to take Raffy's place. That's not how things are supposed to work. I put the blame for that on Angela, by the way, not Stacey.

Q: How about the way this bogus AISO report was handled? What do you make of that?

A: Total amateur hour, a complete joke. Angela was completely clueless early on and she let a rookie assistant handle all the important details. A real partnership of dumb and dumber. Can you imagine a great reporter—say a Dan Rather, for example—going with a story where he wasn't 100% sure of the sourcing? Doesn't even matter if the story is true. You must *prove* it's true.

Q: You think there's a chance the Holt story itself is true?

A: No, not a chance. The narrative is preposterous.

Q: What do you think of tandem couples--the ones where husband and wife share duties overseas equally?

A: I don't like them. Senior editors don't either. Jobs are hard enough as it is without mixing marriage, kids and all the personal stuff. Could get very messy. It seems to work, though, if both reporters are qualified on their own. That wasn't the case here.

Q. Tell me what it's like to be a foreign correspondent and why she wasn't up to the job.

The job is great fun and has great perks. Freedom most reporters would kill for. Get paid a ton of money, at least for a journalist. Get great tax breaks living overseas. Usually live well, with lots of hired help in backwater places. Treated like rock stars by the top brass at the home office. Meet cool and interesting people *all* the time. But we also must be *really* good or we don't make the cut. Need energy, talent, coolness, independence, analytical skills, fertile imagination, determination, superb judgement. It can be a tough job. Have disaster, will travel. Work conditions can be deplorable, dangerous, dirty. It can be isolating, lonely, even boring at times. It ain't for everyone. It was way over her head, that's for sure. Management never should have put her in the job. It's their fault.

Q: Last question, Peter. Help me understand Ari Steinberg. Don't worry. He won't be reading this report or hearing this tape.

A: I love Ari. He adores the foreign staff. Loves visiting the bureaus and hobnobbing with foreign leaders to promote the paper. Highlight of his life was when he flew into the North African desert on a private plane to meet Muammar Gaddafi. Always increases the foreign budget by about 10% a year. But he has some serious issues. His family, for one, is crazy. They're always feuding and it drives him nuts. Then, there's his so-called female problem. The man is a certifiable sex addict. He admitted that to me once at a strip bar in Hong Kong. Says he does not do drugs, hardly drinks at all, doesn't smoke, devoted to his children. What he loves doing, though, are long workouts and beautiful women who have brains, strong wills and drop-dead bodies. Alpha bitches, he calls them.

Q: You mean like Angela?

A: Bingo

CHAPTER 53

Pearl Harbor 2.0

Interview with Foreign Editor Kellen Williams
South Pacific Bureau, New York Herald
Diplomat Road, Bellevue Hill, Australia
Saturday, January 11, 2003
11:11 a.m.

Q: Good morning, Mr. Williams. Thanks for coming.

A: Good morning, Lieutenant Carella. Please call me Kellen. And believe me, I had no choice. (Laughs)

Q: (Laughs also) I know, I know. Sending in the big guns from New York. I thought Peter Lynch was going to see this through.

A: Yeah, Ari III made that call. Wants me to visit that beach in Melbourne where Angela disappeared, get a copy of her goodbye note, go through all her belongings to see what nuggets I can find. I'm told she kept a very detailed diary. He *really* wants me to find that right away and send it to him Federal Express. He's a mess, a total basket case.

Q: Yeah, I saw him at Julie Levitsky's house in the Hamptons a few days ago. He looked a little wobbly. Julie told me right after this happened, Ari just shut down for about four days. Said he started to resemble those homeless veterans begging for money outside Herald Tower. (Laughs)

A: Julie Levitsky: you know you're in trouble when you hire him and Ike Citron. The Two Horsemen of the Apocalypse. (Laughs)

Q: So what is your sense of all this now?

A: Everything bad that could have happened did—and there was no safety net. The one editor in New York who raised a bright red flag was overruled. It was a holiday week, there was hunger for a strong news story to start the year, two greenest reporters on the foreign staff were on the case. Perfect setup for a surprise attack. Like 12/7/41. Great planning and execution. Had to be an inside job, but who?

Q: You think there's any chance there is an intelligence report on the Holt affair?

A: I doubt it but it's funny you ask. AISO's statement said only that it had "authored no such report." Whatever that means. They won't comment any further. If not them, then who? Its headquarters is in Melbourne. I'm going to stop by there to see what I can find out off the record after I visit the infamous beach.

Q: What's the fallout from all this going to be?

A: It's already begun. Peter Bainbridge, Angela's primary editor in New York, was fired late last night, I'm told. No severance, no nothing, after 13 superb years on the job. Just get out—and don't even wave goodbye. This was a guy some people thought would be editor of the paper one day. Then there's Christian Turnbull, the weekend news editor, who green-lighted the story on New Year's Eve. He's been put on paid leave while you do your investigation. He's toast. Only a matter of time. Then there's Harry Berger, the chief copy editor who tried to stop publication of the story. He has already been promoted to assistant managing editor in charge of "newspaper standards."

Q: What does that mean?

A: Who knows? Nothing probably. Just PR. Harry's brilliant but he's also buzzed most of the time. Has two martinis every afternoon before he comes to work and three more when he gets off. That's a lot of gin. (Laughs)

Q: Hmmm, what about you and Maggie Maye? Love her name, by the way. Love that song.

A: Well, they'll be more subtle with the most senior editors. Maggie expects to be gone within a few months—pockets stuffed with cash and mouth taped shut. I'll be granted "my wish to return to reporting" and be sent back to London in some kind of third-tier writing assignment. Fine by me. My wife's a Brit. She hates New York. Besides, I'd rather watch this industry death dance from as far away from Herald Tower as possible. The music hurts my ears. (Laughs)

CHAPTER 54

Shaken, Not Stirred

Weekend estate of Julius J. Levitsky
Montauk Road, East Hampton, New York
Friday, March 7, 2003
8:18 p.m.

Mesmerized by the cackle and dance of the flames, the 'Real Odd Couple' stared into the fire, sunk down in soft leather chairs, taking the first sips of medium dry martinis and mulling how to muffle the serious stupidity of one very blue-chip client.

"So," Julie Levitsky said finally, "I just read the final version of Gino Carella's findings. He dropped it off yesterday. Also gave me the final tally on his expenses and billable hours. His billings alone are almost $600,000. With us added, total bill just shy of a mil."

"Nice," Ike replied, smiling. "What's in the report? What's the headline?"

"You want to read it?"

"Of course not. I'm a public relations man, Julie. I have no interest in knowing the truth."

The partners laughed and clinked glasses.

"Report itself documents what Gino told us when he got back from Sydney," Carella answered. "One thing sure: Ari III is toast if this thing ever gets out."

"Well, that's not gonna happen, right?

"We'll see," Julie said. "Gino did some great work on the report. He discovered that Angela had installed a secret photo system on the roof where she entertained this Jack Quinn, the tourist guy. Has lots of digital photos of him on the roof doing coke and cavorting in the jacuzzi. Apparently used the photos as potential blackmail in case the guy got out of line. He's married."

"Whoa," Ike said. "That's rich. Woman didn't mess around."

"Gino also found out Angela ghost-wrote all the copy for those FYI South Pacific ads. Ari knew all about it. Ads made a ton of money for the paper, and she got big kickbacks. Helped her fuel her drug problem. Quinn was her liaison to the advertisers. He made it all happen."

"Jesus," Ike said. "Ari is a lot stupider than I thought. Did anyone else know about this photo system?"

"Gino and Stacey apparently discovered it when they were doing an inventory of Herald property at the mansion," Julie explained. "Stacey was completely floored by it. Had no idea it existed. Or so she claims."

"So what else do I need to know?" Ike asked, getting impatient now. "This story is starting to make me nervous. Now I really don't want to read that report. I need deniability. Let's bury it once and for all and move on."

"It may not be that easy, Ike," Julie warned. "Gino makes a convincing case that the fickle Flanagans may very well be alive, well and floating around some beautiful body of water on a yacht. Thinks the whole thing could be some an insurance scam those two cooked up on the spur of the moment when the Towers went down. Who knows when or if they will ever surface again."

"Hmmm," Ike said, "you really believe that? I don't."

"Look," Julie said, leaning forward and looking directly in the flames. "Carella uncovered—beyond all reasonable doubt—that Flanagan was not in the north tower at 8:46 a.m. He was due west of there a few miles on the exit 14 spur of the New Jersey Turnpike getting a speeding ticket for going 77 in a 55. God only knows what he was doing in Jersey. Gino found the state trooper who wrote the ticket. He remembers what happened. Just as he was driving away, the first plane hit. He could see it. Flanagan was still parked on the side of the road."

"Do you have the actual ticket?"

"Yes, it's one of the exhibits. A copy of it anyway."

"Okay," Ike proposed, "now that it's certain that Bush will invade Iraq in the next few days, let's just prepare a press release that the *Herald* is closing its South Pacific bureau and redeploying reporting resources to the war in the Middle East. We'll also announce the promotion of this new "standards editor" to assistant managing editor and that all the paper's correspondents will receive special training on how to spot bogus story tips. Some nonsense like that. We'll also say the paper's internal inquiry of the episode is continuing."

"Sounds good," Julie said.

"Then," Ike said, rubbing his hands and getting excited, "once Bush the Retard starts Shock & Awe 2.0, I'll put out the press release, probably three days into the invasion."

"Good, good," Julie said. "I like it. By that time, the Herald's war coverage will be among the best in the world and nobody will give a rat's ass what happened in nowhere Australia."

The pair laughed and clinked glasses again.

"There's only one copy of this report and it's going to stay that way for now," Julie said, pointing toward an office safe in the corner of the study. "Who knows? Maybe it will come in handy one day."

"Once again, the Jackal and the Master of Disaster perform their magic and Ari III lives to fight another day," Ike said grandly, standing, smiling, raising his martini glass. "I propose a toast to Ari III. May he always need our help."

"To Ari III," Julie said, rising and raising his glass. "One of the publishing world's great dunderheads."

The two men roared with laughter, clinked glasses and finished the rest of their martinis.

"Let's have one more," Julie said, smiling like a huge Cheshire cat, rubbing his meaty hands and gathering the glasses for round two. "Medium dry. Shaken, not stirred, with a peel of lemon. Just like you know who."

Julie laughed again, louder this time, his high-pitched cackle echoing around his elegant study. "Lord help me. I do love this so. God bless hourly billing."

CHAPTER 55

Hitting Restart

Sulfide Street Train Station
Broken Hill, Australia
Saturday, March 8, 2003
2:12 p.m.

Lithe and stylishly informal, the 40-ish woman peered down the railroad track and spotted the first outlines of the train in the shimmering desert heat. The temperature on the train station thermometer read 33.3 degrees centigrade, unusually warm for this time of day so late in the summer.

She adjusted her Chicago Cubs baseball cap that hid her shortish curly red hair and glanced at her backside in the train-station window through oversized Prada sunglasses. In Jordache jeans, loose-fitting grey tee shirt and black high-top Converse gym shoes, she was trying—unsuccessfully—to blend in with the ordinary Outback crowd waiting for the passenger train, which goes from Sydney to Perth three days a week.

With both hands, she took the arm of the balding, paunchy man next to her and kissed him on the cheek. "I owe you, baby," she said, accent somewhere in the American South. "You were there when I needed you, when it really got ugly. You got it handled. Hope I made it worth your while."

"You did," he said quietly, looking with dread at the approaching train, now about a half mile away. "Guess we'll always have the Palace Hotel, the honeymoon suite, no less. Who knew? In this backwater town of all places."

"Yeah," she replied unenthusiastically, "I can't wait to get out of this place. And don't get any ideas. I just got rid of one husband. I ain't getting another."

She began testing her carry-on suitcase, making sure the rollers and handle worked.

"When will I see you again?" he asked plaintively. "I'll miss you."

"Don't get sappy on me, Jack, "she said coldly. "Hitting restart is not going to be easy."

She stared hard at the approaching train. "He ruined the job I loved," she mused quietly. "My career is over. Can't go back. I'll probably be running the rest of my life."

She pulled a tattered bible out of her huge leather purse and knelt on one knee. "Will you pray with me one last time?" she asked.

He nodded and knelt. "Yea, though we walk through the valley of the shadow of death, we will fear no evil," they said in unison. "Surely, goodness and mercy shall follow us all the days of our lives and we will dwell in the house of the Lord forever. Amen."

"St. Peter may have a little trouble with that last part," she cracked, rising to her feet and moving toward the stopped train. "So long, baby. It's been real."

As she began boarding, she waved—without looking back—and disappeared into the train.

As the train sprang to life, headed to Adelaide and across the super-bleak Nullarbor Plain and on to Perth, he saw her in her window seat and made the "call me" sign with the right hand next to his ear.

He would regret that one day.

PART TWO

SEVEN YEARS LATER

CHAPTER 56

Making $$$ off the Funeral

East Hampton Tennis & Golf Club
Sag Harbor Road, East Hampton, New York
Saturday, September 11, 2010
5:45 p.m.

Two sets of doubles behind them, tall vodka tonics in hand, the two pals nestled comfortably into blue-padded deck chairs, the late summer sun beginning its nightly dive into the Atlantic Ocean to their right. Locals love this time of year on the East End—when the steady ocean breezes make 80 degrees feel like 70 and the masses on summer holiday have gone home to who-cares where.

Still in *de rigueur* tennis whites, the men had that life-is-fine glow organic to those who own in the Hamptons. After all, this is where the top *one-tenth* of one percent hang—the *real* big swinging dicks— the ones who never fly commercial and whose hourly rates *begin* at four figures.

The pair, along with legendary private eye Frank Jablonsky, stunned the money world three years earlier when they formed Levitsky, Citron & Jablonsky. It was a daring hybrid that put corporate lawyers, crisis flacks and white-collar private eyes under one virtual roof, all working on contract to service the super-rich. As one blogger put it, it was "one-stop shopping for miscreants, scoundrels and flimflam men worth at least $50 million."

Julie Levitsky roared when he read that description. "Couldn't have framed it better myself," he told Ike.

It also worked. Revenues soared and Levitsky, LC&J's undisputed alpha dog, appeared on the cover of the Rolling Stone under the head-line: **Hail Julius**. In the article, he defended the right of his clients to be as obscenely rich as their talent, energy and audacity would allow. Real and wannabe millionaires and billionaires cheered him wildly. Just after the magazine article was published, he appeared on the veranda of the tennis club and received a standing ovation. Go, Julie, go, they roared.

But that was yesterday and yesterday, as the famous song says, is gone. Julie was restless, on the prowl for bigger game. He shifted his huge frame on the lounge chair and, Serengetti sunglasses atop his pro-digious head, eyed the sunset with little interest. He drained the last of his vodka tonic in one gulp and set the skinny white glass down with a crack on the glass table between himself and Ike. He waived for another to the white-jacketed footman hovering nearby.

"Ike," he announced with his trademark feel for drama, "I've got an idea I want to bounce off you."

"Please, Julie," Ike pleaded, "enjoy the sunset. Go smell the rose on that table over there. Shut it down for the night."

"I can't," Julie shot back, standing now and waving to a group of 19th hole golfers a few tables away. He stared down at his diminutive sidekick, saying nothing for a few moments.

"I've been mulling this for a long time," he said finally, formally. "We've all seen how fast your beloved newspaper business is going down the drain. Even faster than anticipated. Newsroom layoffs, papers going into Chapter 11, readers jumping ship by the thousands every year, revenues plunging. If the next ten years are worse than the last ten—as they surely will be—newspapers won't even exist by 2025. A 400-year-old business bites the dust in twenty-five years, all because the technology changed."

"Everyone knows that," Ike cut in, irritated his pink cloud had evaporated. "What's your point?"

"Guess who called me yesterday?" Julie asked, ignoring the irritation. "My old pal, Rembrant T. Dabovitch III. You hear the news?"

"Yeah," Ike replied. "Got the old pink slip. Read it on the Romenesko website. Those newspaper investigative reporters are easy targets. They cost too much, they don't produce enough and they stir up too much trouble for failing publications. Internet roadkill."

"Out of tragedy comes opportunity," Julie said, sitting back down. "A light came on in my head when I was listening to his jeremiad. I thought: 'I can use this guy. His life is such a mess he'll grasp at anything."

"Use him how?"

"Ok, hear me out." Julie replied. "This is a little involved and it's totally off the record. Breathe a word of this to no one. I'm going to buy the *New York Herald* and Dabovitch is the perfect reporter to help me do it."

"What?" Ike yelped. "Are you insane, Julie? LC&J is buying that newspaper? Over my dead body."

"I'm doing this on my own," Julie shot back. "Has nothing to do with you or Frank. Just listen. You remember the Carella Report, right? No one has ever seen that, not even you. Only Gino knows what's in it, and he works for me now in Puerto Rico. And I have the only copy."

"So?"

"So, today's the ninth anniversary of 9/11. A year from now, there will be a media feeding frenzy leading up the tenth anniversary. All sorts of vigils and remembrances at the site, politicians blathering, cable talking heads bloviating, etc. etc."

"And?"

"Rem is a great reporter—he's won two Pulitzers after all—and he happens to be broke, in the midst of a nasty divorce and has three teenage kids drowning in drugs and alcohol. What I want to do is commission him to write a news story and then a full-length book on what really happened to the Flanagans—Rafer and Angela—and time the publication for next summer just as the tenth anniversary hype is starting to build."

"What does that have to do with buying the *New York Herald?*" Ike asked, not illogically.

"Look," Julie explained, "Rafer supposedly died at 9/11 but we now have absolute proof with that speeding ticket that he didn't. That itself is big news. His wife supposedly drowns 16 months later after she says someone is trying to kill her. But her body is never found and her closest friend says it's all nonsense. So the strong suspicion is that this was just a clever insurance scheme that they concocted on the spur of the moment when the towers went down."

"Even if that were true," Ike chimed in, "and I doubt very much that it is, I don't see that as anything more than an episode of Scams, Scoundrels and Suckers. Great scam, the Flanagans make great scoundrels, and, I'm guessing here, Ari III is the sucker. I could sell that to CNBC in a heartbeat."

"As usual, you're playing little ball, Ike," Julie shot back. "I'm going to give Dabovitch access to the Carella Report and have him independently confirm all the shit that went down in the *Herald's* Sydney office. The corruption and how the wall between editorial and advertising completely broke down. Ari's kinky relationship with Angela. The drugs, the photos, the blackmail.

"You know, Julie," Ike warned," if you give Dabovitch that report and Ari finds out, he can sue the shit out of both of us—and win. We told him flat out all that stuff was privileged."

"Relax," Julie replied. "I won't *give* him the report, I'll just let him read it when I'm not looking. That will give me deniability. This is only a roadmap for Rem. He'll have to report everything out on his own."

"You're flying really close to the sun on this one," Ike said.

Levitsky forged on.

"Now, let me tell you the point of all this. I have private equity investors with me who believe we can get the *Herald* at a flea-market price if all this dirty laundry is displayed for the world to see. Idea is to buy the newspaper on the super cheap, shut it down after a certain period and resurrect it as an on-line brand, putting the total focus on quality digital news. The more I can save on the purchase price, the better I can finance the new operation.

"The *Herald* is perfect. It's owned by a completely dysfunctional family, it's run by a misfit sex addict and—this is big—it is still respected as one of the best news outlets in the world. It has a great brand, a rich history. Once the dirt comes out, the Steinbergs will have to sell at a double deep discount. Most of the family wants out of this shitty business anyway and Ari Jr. is in poor health. We figure once the dirt-bombs drop, it will cut the price in half, about $200 million. A true steal."

"What does it matter," Ike asked blandly, "that the Steinbergs stiffed us on most of what it cost to produce the Carella Report?"

"Yeah, it matters," Julie shot back. "You bet it does. It still burns my ass all these years later. Ole Wilbur Ross said he never authorized the money for an investigation like that and gave us only $500,000. Shit, that barely covered our expenses."

"Announcing the closure of the Sydney bureau on a Friday night three days into that idiotic invasion of Iraq was perfect," Ike said. "Not one story appeared, not even down there. Holt scandal dies without a trace. All in a day's work for the Master of Disaster."

Julie glared at his partner but held his tongue. These PR guys are such lightweights, he reminded himself. The things they brag about are so pedestrian, and their jobs dealing with the press have gotten so much easier. Good reporters are so harried by the internet's insatiable and immediate demands and so hampered by shrinking resources that they don't have time to dig deep like they used to. Advantage: spin doctors.

Give Ike credit, though, Julie mused. He does work tirelessly and his clients adore him. Nobody drops names and kisses billionaire butts better than he does. He also knows how to artfully spin the best reporters—the steers who lead the herd. They all regularly check in with Ike on what the latest dirt is—off the record, of course.

"Yeah, Ike," Julie said sarcastically, "you're a fucking genius. PR has always attracted the best and brightest—not. More like the lamest and dumbest."

"Listen, Julie, all your bullshit aside," Ike shot back, "and believe me you sling a ton of bullshit. Fact is killing a great newspaper is not cool. I love newspapers. They've given me—now us—a lot of business over the years. Pols, bureaucrats, CEOs, they all hate it when there's bad news about them on the front page. That's when they hire us. What happens when there's no more front page?"

"I get all that," Julie replied coldly, draining his second drink and signaling for a third, "but the sentimentalists are not going to win this one. Newspapers themselves, for all intents and purposes, are already dead. It's just a matter of who arranges the burial and who profits off the funeral. Somebody is going to lead the way and show the world how to replace them in a way that will make a ton of money on digital subscriptions worldwide. It's very doable. And guess what, Ike? That somebody is going to be me, Julius the Jackal, son of a Russian Jew from Skokie, Ill., proud graduate of the great Evanston Township High School and University of Illinois, Chicago Circle campus. A blue blood I am not, but I'm going to show those Ivy League dickheads how it's done. Dad's up there watching, cheering me on. This is going to be fun."

Julie clapped his meaty hands and roared with laughter, the trademark cackle turning heads across the 19th-hole veranda. The all-male crowd was smiling, wondering what the Jackal was up to now. When Julie's pumped, they knew, it's a great show.

CHAPTER 57

World's Best Profession

Offices of Levitsky, Citron & Jablonsky (LC&J)
Trump Tower, Midtown Manhattan
Monday, September 13, 2010
10:10 a.m.

Rem Dabovitch has seen "Deadline U.S.A." more than a dozen times over the years. Every time he needed reassurance about his life's mission, he threw the 1952, black-and-white movie into an old VCR and watched all 87 minutes of it. When tuxedo-clad newspaper publisher Humphrey Bogart punches the button on the printing press as a gangster is threatening him on the phone, at the end of the movie, Rem would yell: 'Go get him, Bogey. You tell him.' Or something like that.

His wife would only roll her eyes as Rem would repeat Bogey's lines word for word—*before* he said them. "You're crazy, babe," she told him several times. "You really do need help.'" His wife was a psychiatrist at a hospital in the Bronx.

Outsiders just didn't understand, Rem told himself. Being a newspaper reporter for a big-city daily was a heart-pounding, front-row seat on history, take one. Excitement, influence, the impact on the daily dialogue. The adrenaline surge on deadline, the power to comfort the afflicted and afflict the comfortable, the personal bonds among the reporters. It really was—just like they said on Superman—truth, justice and the American way. As Bogie said in the movie: "This being a reporter, it's not the oldest profession on earth, but it is the best."

But as Rem's wife was leaving him for another doctor at the hospital and he blasted through the big 50, another image came to mind when he was fired. It was like riding a beloved racehorse that fractured its ankle entering the far turn at the four-furlong mark. The only option was to put the magnificent animal out of its misery and hope to find another lift to the finish line. In short, Rem needed a new ticket to ride.

"Rem, God damnit, good to see you," Julie Levitsky yelled in the visitors' lobby, wrapping the reporter in his signature bear hug normally reserved for family and close friends. "How long has it been? Come on back. You look like hell. You're almost as fat as I am."

Rem laughed easily, succumbing to the big man's gravitational pull. "Love the new lettering on the door," the reporter said. "LC&J. What a combo."

"Yeah, it's going great," Julie said, handing his guest a tall glass of what looked like tomato juice as they settled into opposite ends of the leather couch that overlooked the East River. "Beyond our wildest imaginations. How's the job search going? Any bites? Cheers, by the way."

"Cheers, Julie," Rem said, clinking glasses but not taking a sip of what he figured was filled with at least three ounces of Russian vodka. "No, it's a tough go out there for me now. Really ugly. Old friends, present company excepted, are avoiding me like I have Ebola. Got my first unemployment check yesterday. Need the money, hate the handout. Very, very sobering, all in all."

"Listen, Rem," Julie said, "I took your call for a reason. You've done great work over the years. You deserved those Pulitzers. Don't lose faith in yourself. I've got a way for you to reinvent yourself. Get a new start. Rebrand. Interested?"

"Of course. All ears."

"There's an empty office down the hall on the right and on the desk you will find aa 99-page document that I think you will find very interesting," Julie said blandly. "Read it through. Take all the notes you want but you can't copy it. If you play this right, there's Pulitzer No. 3 here for you. Real money too. Book and movie rights will surely start in seven figures."

"Whoa," Rem said. "what is this? Hillary Clinton's secret diaries?"

"Not sure that would be very interesting," Julie said, laughing, "but you never know. No, it's a detailed report written more than seven years ago on that *Herald* reporter Angela Flanagan and her not-so-secret affair with Ari Steinberg III. Cover your ears when you read it. Bombshells exploding on every page."

"Is any of this in the public domain?" Rem asked.

"Not only is it not, but I'm going to have no idea where you got this information," Julie replied. "I can't help it that you are snooping around my offices behind my back. Meet me back here at 6 tonight. That should give you enough time. I want a decision fast."

CHAPTER 58

The Perfect Reporter

Offices of LC&J
Trump Tower, Midtown Manhattan
Monday, September 13, 2010
5:55 p.m.

Dabovitch is clearly the perfect man for the job, Levitsky mused, gazing out over the East River. A tireless digger, he has the cred we'll need when the shit hits the fan, as it surely will. If the story has an important fact wrong or misspells a name, the Steinbergs will go for the jugular, saying it's evidence the story is flawed. Dabovitch knows that instinctively, Julie knew. The man digs deep, listens carefully, is painstakingly careful and unfailingly fair.

Career highlights were the two Pulitzers at the *Daily News*—one an expose about the mob's control of the city's trade unions, the other a look at the cocaine and meth epidemic among traders on Wall Street.

Story on the mob took two years to research, Julie remembered. A key interview here, one there, in dive bars, warehouses and high rises across the five boroughs and beyond. All with the careful cooperation of the deputy director of the FBI's New York office--one Julius J. Levitsky.

He couldn't have done that second one without me either, Julie told himself. The heads of every major brokerage in New York City—all clients after I formed my own company—quietly cooperated because they were so appalled at the rampant drug use on the trading floors. The story ran in the tabloid *Daily News* on a Sunday in July, under the banner headline on the front page: 'It's Snowing on Wall Street.' A page turner, it jumped to the natural double truck inside and then to two opens after that. Had great impact, which is why it won the Pulitzer. Several traders were convicted of drug trafficking and a dozen mid-level managers were fired or demoted for being asleep at the switch. The big bosses all skated—naturally. That was the most sensitive—and important-- part of the assignment, Julie remembered.

"Mr. Levitsky, Mr. Dabovitch is done," his assistant, Debi, said over the intercom. "I'm sending him back."

Shaken from his reverie, Julie met Rem at the door, waving him back over to the leather couch. "So, what have you been doing all day?" he asked with a smile. "Tell me what you found that's interesting."

"Jesus, Julie," Rem said, a little dazed. "Insurance fraud. Blackmail. Journalistic malfeasance at its worst. Total tear-down of the wall between news and advertising. She ghost-wrote those FYI South Pacific ads? And got kickbacks to pay for her cocaine? And Ari III was her puppy dog? I don't even know what to say. Not sure anyone will believe it."

"Yeah," Julie replied. "What can you say? The paper would never survive if this gets out, at least under the current ownership. Wave bye-bye to the Steinbergs."

Rem said nothing, pausing to look out the window at the rush-hour traffic along the FDR drive by the East River, the residential high-rises hard by the water bathed in the evening twilight.

"Julie, why did you want me to read this?" he asked finally. "I thought you and Ari III were tight?"

"Not anymore," Levitsky said.

"You know I don't have the high diving board anymore," Rem said. "I'm just an unemployed reporter—one of way too many. What on earth do I have to offer?"

"Glad you asked," Julie replied. "Over the next 12 months, you report and write a news story on your new website—*The Searchlight*, we'll call it—laying out the corruption in the office of the publisher at the *New York Herald*. At the same time, you'll be writing a book entitled: 'The Couple from Hell: How 2 reporters from the *New York Herald* pulled off the most brazen swindle in the history of American journalism."

Julie paused for a moment and plunged ahead.

"Spend as much time as you need traveling the world reporting the shit out of all of this. You've run across this report on your own because you're such a great snoop, but you can use it as a guide only. You're only the third person on earth who knows what's in this, but you must confirm everything on your own. Gino Carella, the author, works for me now in Puerto Rico. He'll talk to you. Start with him. See him in person. You'll know why when you see him.

"The news story and the book will both appear next year, just prior to 10th anniversary of 9/11, and then we'll work on a movie starring, say, Cynthia Nixon as Angela. She'd be perfect—quirky, hot, switch-hitter, red hair, all that. She'd get this role immediately. Matt Damon might make a good Raffy."

"Jesus, Julie, what haven't you thought of?" Rem asked. "I hate to be prosaic but how do I finance this? My wife wants spousal support because she makes less than I do--and I'm broke. In fact, I may have to file bankruptcy."

"Not to worry, bro," Julie replied. "You'll find every month in your checking account a generous living allowance and you will have credit cards that will go to my address here in New York. You are not in my employ. I am not paying you a salary. But I will be your bridge until the money comes in from the book and movie. Believe me, Rem, you will be a rich man when you're done with this. Bet on it. Finalize the divorce soon and your ex won't get a dime."

Rem shook his head in amazement, not as an answer. "You weren't kidding when you said I would have to think differently. This is way, way outside my comfort zone."

"Just think," Julie said, "your third Pulitzer will be the first time in history an on-line investigative reporter wins the prize. That will be in the first paragraph of your obituary, my friend. Well, maybe the second."

"Man," Rem said, still in a fog, "is there anything you haven't thought of?"

"Nope," Julie replied, grinning big. "It's all nailed down, my friend. You just execute."

CHAPTER 59

No Turning Back

Offices of LC&J
Trump Tower, Midtown Manhattan
Monday, September 13, 2010
7:17 p.m.

It was dusk and the traffic along the FDR Drive had returned to early-evening normal—medium volume, thinning nicely.

"'Thank the Lord for the Nighttime'," Julie hummed, looking out his window. Time to pig out. Cell phone in hand, he glanced in the wall mirror and winced at the side view of his Falstaffian waistline. He looked like a taller version of his favorite Chicago Bear—the pro team of his youth—the late, great Abe Gibron whose legendary appetite made his stomach look like he'd swallowed a 16-pound bowling ball.

What a character, Julie thought, smiling to himself. Crude to the bone, Abe used to talk to reporters in pre-season training camp lying on the couch in his office, left hand in his sweatpants, scratching his gonads. Head coach of the Bears at the time, he was asked to confirm a hot story tip by Mike Downey, the legendary Chicago sports columnist. "Give me a break," the 350-pound Gibron scoffed. "Story tips are like assholes. Everyone has one." Good non-denial denial. Tip turned out to be true.

Levitsky's cell-phone ring ('Bad to the Bone') broke his fond remembrance of the incomparable Abe. "Maggie, hi," he said, still staring out the window. "Listen, I'm heading out to have dinner with my *Herald* investors and I want to update you on Rem. It's a go."

He listened for a few seconds and cut in. "No, no, just sit back and wait for him to call you. I told him where you are, gave him your number. You know him from the old days, right? You should be one of his key interviews. You'll know what to do. He's very lonely, if you get my drift."

Julie listened some more, getting increasingly impatient and putting on his suit jacket after switching to speaker. "Listen," he broke in again, "I gotta go. I want you to be his hands-on editor. I've got too much riding on this. I can't afford to have him go rogue on me."

He listened again for a time. "Yeah, yeah, it's got to look real. Best thing would be for him to *ask you* to be his editor. That would be perfect. You figure it out. Gotta run."

High finance ain't beanbag, Julie mused, heading to the elevator. Ethics are fungible and systems are made to be rigged. Five, maybe ten years from now, I'll be the 21st Century version of William Randolph Hearst, my version of San Simeon in the Hamptons, around which the digital news world will swirl, he fantasized.

He entered the elevator and hit G for ground. It's also G for Go Time, he mused. We have finally crossed the Rubicon, he thought, just like the other Julius, the one named Caesar.

CHAPTER 60

Burying the Lede

Office of the Publisher, New York Herald
Herald Tower, Midtown Manhattan
Friday, September 17, 2010
7:07 p.m.

Betsy Wright treaded lightly into the two-room executive suite of Ari Steinberg III, a palpable sense of unease not playing well with her chronic colitis. It was particularly risky on Friday night when 15th floor corporate had largely emptied out, and she hated bearing bad news. Blaming the messenger and all that.

"You want to see me, Mr. Steinberg?" she said deferentially, standing in his doorway, the body language of one of those English servants on PBS appearing before the lord of the manor.

"Betsy, so good of you to drop by," Ari exclaimed, bouncing out of his chair, instantly energized by the sight of his comely PR woman and chief spokesperson.

"Please come in. Have a seat. I just now saw your e-mail this afternoon and thought I'd get some clarity before the weekend."

"No problem, sir," Wright said, walking in and eyeing the infamous leather love couch in the adjacent room that also had a wet-bar, full-sized fridge and even a stove. Legend has it the publisher, facing the prospect of a long, boring weekend with the family, is particularly randy on Friday night. As long as he gets to the weekend home in East Hampton by midnight, his clueless spouse won't have, well, a clue.

"So, Betsy," Ari began, as both took chairs at a writing table that was his grandfather's, an antique the grandson secretly yearned to get rid of, "what's going on? What's the request? Who's the reporter?"

"Well, Mr. Steinberg," Wright began carefully, "the story is a retrospective on the Flanagans, that tandem couple on Foreign from back in the day. Something about how the careers of such a promising and beautiful couple were cut short by terrorism and misfortune. You know, journalism's Camelot. People magazine stuff."

"Yeah, yeah," Ari said dismissively, waving his left hand, "I agree. Not the kind of journalism we do. Besides, they've been dead for ages. We do journalism, not history. Just refer them to our website that honors their memory and say we don't want to intrude on the privacy of their families."

"Since when does that matter to anything the paper does?" Wright asked, permanent smile dimming a bit.

"Yeah, good point, Betsy," Ari replied, surprised and sitting up. Maybe this woman really is more than an empty dress, he thought.

"Just tell them whatever to get rid of them. I barely remember those guys. Who's the reporter, by the way?"

"Well Mr. Steinberg, that's why I sent you that e-mail. It's Rembrandt Dabovitch."

"What?" Ari yelped, jumping completely out of his chair. "Betsy, you buried the lede. Rem Dabovitch doing a sappy feature on the Flanagans? I don't think so. They call that guy the Serbian Assassin. He writes about drugs and the mob."

"Yes, sir, I know," Wright answered blandly, enjoying seeing Prince Ari squirm.

"Find out everything you can on this," he ordered. "What is he up to? Take him out for a meal. All reporters love a free lunch."

"Yes, sir."

"Didn't he just get fired by the Daily News? Who's he writing for now? I hear he's really going through some tough times. Maybe we can use that somehow."

"How?" Wright asked, tone hardening again.

"Never mind," Ari replied quickly. "This is trouble, Betsy. I want you all over this. Update me first thing next week."

"Yes, sir," Wright said, standing to go and moving fast toward the exit. "Have a nice weekend, Mr. Steinberg."

Mouth dry, skin suddenly clammy, Ari moved over to the picture window, peering down on the throngs below--his readers, the little people, the hoi polloi he had to pretend to like. My God, Rem Dabovitch, he thought. He'll eat Betsy alive. Where's Ike and Julie when I really need them? They'd know how to handle this.

CHAPTER 61

Exhuming the Body

Jorge's Trattoria
Dorado, Puerto Rico
Wednesday, Sept. 22, 2010
2:44 p.m.

Rem pulled away from the white plastic table in his white plastic chair in the shaded café courtyard, satiated beyond anything he ever expected in this hole-in-the wall joint.

"I've eaten in every great Italian joint in Brooklyn, and I've never had better meat sauce on my ravioli," the reporter said. "In the suburbs of San Juan, Puerto Rico, of all places."

"Amazing, ain't it," Gino Carella replied. "Candy and I usually come here every Sunday afternoon. Reminds us of home. All kinds of ex-NYPD types hang out here. The owner's an ex-cop who grew up in the Bronx."

Rem reached for his reporter's notebook in the side pocket of his blue blazer on the back of his chair and took out the Paper Mate black-ink pen from the shirt pocket of his blue, button-down Land's End shirt. All standard big-city reporter outer gear and equipment.

"So, Lieutenant Carella," the reporter began formally, "Julie said it was very important that I meet with you in person on this one. Story is so weird and complicated, and you know more about it than any person alive."

"Yeah," Carella replied, "you couldn't make this shit up. Amazing it has stayed secret all these years. Guess that's about to change, eh?"

Carella smiled slightly and continued: "Let me ask you a question before we begin. Julie had me do this investigation almost eight years ago, cost hundreds of thousands to research and write, and then he sweeps the whole thing under the rug like it never happened. Now he wants to exhume the body and do an autopsy. I don't get it. What gives?"

"I don't know either," Rem replied. "He just told me he thinks the true story will make a great read—and a ton of money—on the eve of the tenth anniversary of 9/11. He's on to something, I just don't know what exactly. Above my pay grade."

"Yeah," Carella said absently, "I ain't getting in his way."

"So, how did you get down here, anyway?" Rem began. "Give me the timeline."

"Yeah, so I retired from the NYPD after 33 years at the end of 2002 and moved to Sydney to open Julie's first full-time office in the South Pacific. Liked it a lot first few years but got homesick for New York, came back, hooked up with my former chief deputy, Candy Garcia. Then we moved here—she was born in San Juan—and set up our own private-eye business. Julie is our biggest client."

"Nice," Rem said. "So, I've read the so-called Carella Report but Julie won't give me a copy of it. Can you?"

"Not officially," Carella said. "Julie must be able to say under oath that he never gave the report to anyone, and so do I. And, of course, I was never given an official copy of my own. Unfortunately, I'm going to forget this leather pouch underneath my chair when I leave this afternoon. I won't know whatever happened to it, but you may find the contents relevant to what you're doing."

"Fair enough," Rem replied smoothly. "I can only use what I can independently confirm any way. Speaking of that, I'm going to Australia myself in a few days. Never been there. Where should I start? Who should I see?"

"One, find Stacey McKenzie," Carella said. "She's now a cop reporter in Sydney for the *Morning-Telegraph*. Uses her married name now, Simpson, even though she's already divorced. Left Sydney in 2003 with a big severance, moved back to her hometown on the West Coast, married a cop in Perth, got bored, got divorced and got the cop-shop reporting job back on the east coast for the *SMT*. She was Angela's closest confidante down there. Very colorful, a real piece of work, to put it politely. If you can get her to help you, you're 80% there."

"Got it," Rem said, taking notes furiously.

"Two," Carella said, "find this guy named Jack Quinn. One of Flanagan's boy toys and deeply involved in her FYI South Pacific ad scams. You get him to open up and you're 90% there. He runs a travel agency near Bondi Beach."

"Good stuff," Rem said, still scribbling. "What else?"

"Look for the Flanagans living under new identities somewhere on the Aussie west coast—Perth, Broome, Margaret River, places like that. Or maybe the southern island of New Zealand. Angela loved those places. Wrote a lot of travel stories from there. You should read them. My bet is she and Raffy are hanging out someplace she wrote about."

"So you're absolutely sure Rafer did not die in the Tower collapse?" the reporter asked.

"Positive. Just look at the exact time and location on that speeding ticket. It's one of the exhibits."

"Yeah, I saw it."

"I got hold of the trooper who wrote the ticket. Confirmed everything. He remembered Flanagan. Said he was still in his car when the first plane hit. Said he was acting very strangely."

"How so?" Rem asked. "Didn't see anything like that in the report."

"Trooper told me the guy looked terrible and he seemed to be hiding something," Carella said. "Almost like he knew the attack was coming."

"Whoa," Rem said, "that's a bizarre thing to say."

"This whole thing is bizarre," Carella replied. "Julie's got great intelligence sources all over the world and he told me it's even possible that the discredited Holt story may actually be true."

"Yea, he told me that, too. I'm going to check that out in London. All that James Bond shit. MI6. The invisible hand—everywhere, nowhere, always somewhere."

"Wonder if MI6 and Flanagan knew the attacks were coming," Carella asked with mock seriousness. "Maybe Flanagan worked for MI6."

Carella laughed and added: "Truth is, he apparently did have great spook sources. Did some great stories on India's development of nuclear weapons, Julie tells me. Indian government was furious with him."

Neither man spoke for a time, an indication the interview was pretty much over. "I'm going back to New York tonight," Rem noted. "How about I call you when I get back from Sydney in a few weeks and we compare notes? I just don't have a real good sense where this is all going."

"Australia's a strange place," Carella warned. "I lived there four years, but it never felt like home. They look like us, we speak the same language (sort of), but they're different. Fun-loving and friendly but can also be bigoted and narrow minded. Really quirky when you get outside the major urban areas. Could be the fact that they're so isolated from the rest of the modern world and their founding fathers were convicts. Still waters can run very deep down there. Be careful."

Carella stood to go, grabbing the check off the table. "I'll pay on the way out," he said. "Think you have everything you need."

With that and a handshake, the ex-cop was gone. Rem picked up the battered leather case under his chair and patted it lovingly. Yes, I do, he thought. Off to a good start.

CHAPTER 62

9/11 Truth Time

Behan's Ale House
Atlantic Avenue, Brooklyn Heights, New York
Friday, September 24, 2010
8:18 p.m.

Dug in at this usual spot at the far end of the bar, Dion DeStefano looked up from his cell phone and saw a vaguely familiar figure waving and heading his way.

Guy looks harmless enough, DeStefano mused. Doughy, middle-aged white guy, black-rimmed glasses, probably a writer type. But you can't be too careful these days, he reminded himself, standing and patting the Glock underneath his leather jacket.

"What up, dude?" Dion asked coldly as the man approached. "Having trouble placing your ugly mug."

"Dion," the man said, "Rem Dabovitch. Covered Sal's murder case for the Daily News. I bought you that lunch at Guido's Deli during the trial."

"Holy shit," Dion said, genuinely surprised, drawing Rem in to check for weapons and wires. "Sorry, Rem, didn't recognize you. Ok, you're clean."

Dion waved him over to his booth and the men sat, facing each other, the shouts of the dart players their background noise.

"Somehow I don't think this meeting is accidental," Dion said, never one for small talk. "Am I right?"

"Yeah, I need your help, Dion, big-time," Rem replied. "You have a few minutes?"

"I look busy to you?"

"It's about your old high school basketball buddy, Rafer Flanagan, the *Herald* foreign correspondent. I'm trying to find out what really happened to him."

"So am I," Dion said.

"I'm 99.9% certain he didn't die in the tower collapses," Rem offered.

"I'm 100% certain," Dion said matter-of-factly.

"When did you last see him," Rem asked, suppressing his rising excitement.

"Summer of 2002."

"When did you last hear from him?"

"Winter of 2003."

Neither man spoke for a time, Rem trying to fully absorb the bombshell confirmation that Raffy did not die in the Tower attack.

"Will you help me find him," Rem asked finally.

"Maybe. Depends what you're doing?"

"Writing a news story. I'm a free-lancer now."

"Well, of course, I have no first-hand knowledge of any of this," DeStefano said, smiling slightly, leaning back in the booth. "I got sources, know what I mean? Like you news guys like to say. You know, sources close to Flanagan tell me stuff."

"Go on," Rem said.

"What do I get out of this?" DeStefano asked sharply, sitting up, staring hard.

"Listen, Dion, I'm flying out this weekend to go find him. He was your best friend. Don't you want to know what happened to him? Why you haven't heard from him all these years?"

DeStefano said nothing for a time, at least half a minute, while he scrolled through the e-mails on his iPhone.

"Ok," he said finally, "here's what sources tell me. Not that I can confirm any of this personally. Capiche?"

"Of course."

"He lived in the basement of a friend's house in Brooklyn for nine months after 9/11, changed his appearance completely, swapped out his identity and went back to Australia to get his just due in insurance money and avenge the duplicity of an unfaithful and deceitful spouse. How's that? Detailed enough for you?"

DeStefano smiled widely.

"Might that new identity be an Irishman named Conor McCann who carries a British passport?" Rem asked.

"Might," Dion responded evenly. "You know, I'm told that guy got sober after 9/11. Started lifting weights and putting on the pounds. But the drier—and stronger--he got, the madder—and meaner—he became. Call that a dry drunk. Didn't do AA. Talked constantly about how she had become a rich woman over his so-called dead body and how she'd schemed to get his job. Wanted to even the score--on both counts. You know the Irish. They love grudges. It's all they remember in the nursing home."

Both men laughed.

"So," Rem said, "I take it you think there's no chance that all this was an insurance scheme and the two of them are floating around the Med as we speak on some yacht?"

"Not a chance," Dion shot back. "He was done with her. When I last saw him, he said he only wanted half her money from the insurance and to fuck with her career a little. Bring her down a peg."

DeStefano paused and stood up, indicating the meeting was over. "Talk to me when you get back," he said. "Maybe I can be of further assistance. The more you find out, the more I might be able to fill in the blanks. Know what I mean?"

Time to go, Rem thought. Don't get too close to this flame.

"I know something about people disappearing," DeStefano added, menace in his laugh. "It's often not what you think. Rule nothing out."

CHAPTER 63

Laissez Les Bon Temps Roulez

Capital Hilton Bar
Sixteenth Street NW, Washington, D.C.
Saturday, September 25, 2010
8:08 p.m.

Glancing at the digital clock above an old-school mahogany-paneled bar, Rem mulled the sagacity of a third martini—the one that always takes you across the long suspension bridge to who knows where. He was already engulfed in the numbing glow of the first two—extra dry, straight up, two olives.

"One more Maggie?" he asked. "Need to make this an early night. Taking the 7 a.m. shuttle from LaGuardia, meeting with Julie at 9. Leaving for London Monday night."

"Three is my absolute limit," Maggie replied, draining the last drops of number two. "More than that, you'll have to peel me off the carpet and tuck me in bed."

She gave him a Mona Lisa smirk and signaled to the hovering bartender for another round. She turned sideways on her bar stool, a clear signal her guard gate was going down.

"Is the interview over?" she asked. "You get what you need?"

"Let's talk about your Stella Steele novels," Rem said. "I saw you interviewed by Brian Lamb on C-span not long ago. Ace reporter, battling evil, stupidity and corruption with just a notebook, laptop and website. I love it."

"Yeah, Stella's a monster hit," Maggie said, smiling for the first time. "The millennials love her, especially the guys. Single, kick-ass tough, steam-bath sultry, a lot on the crazy side. The first three books were best sellers. Finishing number four now."

"Amazing," Rem said. "You're back big time."

"Been a long slog," she said. "Ari fires me on my 55th birthday in 2003 and hands me a boatload of cash to keep my big mouth shut. So I do nothing for a year except eat—I gained thirty pounds—and watch cable news ten hours a day. Both bad for your health.

"Then, Bernie comes home and says he wants a divorce. Says he's found someone who 'really understands me.' I almost laughed. He wasn't worth understanding."

"Still, must have been a shock," Rem said. "Going through something like that myself."

"Well, it shocked me enough to get off my fat butt," she said. "Started that cross-fit stuff, doing marathons, writing the novels. All good now. Did the Hawaiian Iron Woman last year and finished third in my group of old broads over 60."

The Maggie Maye of old—the one who was always trying to hire me away from the Daily News—was nowhere around, Rem thought. Gone was that no-frills woman who had a hippie-like disdain for the way she looked on the *Herald* newsroom floor. The long gray hair, granny glasses, no makeup. All yesterday.

The female next to him now was all AARP feminine renewal—muscled and slimmed down; sleeveless low-cut evening dress; shoulder-length light brown hair steaked with yellow; 30-inch pearl necklace accentuating the cleavage. Looks more like Jane Seymour than Betty Friedan, he thought.

"You know, Rem," Maggie said, standing a little uncertainly, her third martini already halfway gone, "with all the training I do now, I look better at 63 than I did at 36. I didn't dress this way by accident."

She giggled like a flirtatious coed and stepped back to better display her wares. She sat back down.

"You're staying here tonight, right?" she asked, slightly slurring her words now. "How about I give you a royal sendoff for your around the world in 50 days? You know: 'Bon voyage, mon cheri.'"

Without waiting for an answer, she waived to the barkeep, hovering nearby in the almost empty bar, enjoying the spectacle of this aging *femme fatale* closing in on her prey.

"Two more, *s'il vous plait*," Maggie ordered. "*Laissez les bon temps roulez.*"

CHAPTER 64

How Pathetic

Room 808, Capital Hilton
Sixteenth Street NW, Washington, D.C.
Sunday, September 27, 2010
9:33 a.m.

Rem rolled over onto his side, pulled the white linen sheet over his head, and moaned at the monstrous injustice of a pulsating headache fired by four—or was it five?—martinis with the unsinkable Maggie Maye.

No sign of her anywhere. Didn't even bother to say goodbye. Modern females for you, he mused miserably. They just use you.

The hotel phone jolted him back to ground. Christ, he thought, looking at his Seiko, the only thing he was wearing, he was supposed to be in Julie's office a half hour ago.

"Rem Dabovitch," he answered as crisply as possible on the third ring. "Talk to me."

"You talk to me, you blockhead," Julie Levitsky roared on the other end of the line. "Where the hell are you? What the pho is going on?"

"Jesus, Julie, so sorry," Rem said, sitting up and putting his feet on the floor. "Must have overslept. Had a great interview last night with

Margarite Maye. Interview lasted longer than I thought. Gave me great stuff, though."

"I can only imagine," Julie shot back. "Be in my office 6 p.m. sharp tonight."

The connectiom went dead on the hotel landline, one those old-fashioned jobs, crème colored with a long curly cord. Rem hung up, put his head in his hands and tried to reconstruct what happened last night. He couldn't remember too much beyond the drinks in the bar. He walked unsteadily to the bathroom, wincing at the flabby sight of himself in the full-length mirror on the inside of the door.

God, I've got to start working out again, he thought, collecting his clothes scattered on the floor near the king-sized bed. Looking around the room, he spotted a blue envelope with his name on the writing table overlooking the hotel entrance, three blocks north of the White House. He went over and took out the note inside.

"My darling," the note read, "thanks for giving this lady what she wanted and needed. You were the cat's meow! Have a fab trip. I wish I were going with you. (Hint! Hint!) Call when you get back. I want to know everything. XXXOOOs, MTM."

MTM. Sweet, Rem thought, his brain still fogged in. Reminds me of Lou Grant, a great newsman if there ever was one—even if he wasn't real. Every time things got crazy in the newsroom—at least in the early days of the Mary Tyler Moore Show—Lou pulled a bottle of bourbon out the bottom desk drawer to help him cope with the chaos.

Hilarious, Rem thought, smiling to himself, but nothing compared to his rookie days as a reporter back in Chicago working for the *City News Bureau*.

Who could forget the late, great Joe Morang, the legendary *Tribune* police reporter who worked the 6-p.m.-to-3-a.m. shift at the police headquarters at 11th and State Streets on the near South Side? Every evening by midnight Joe was asleep on the press room's worn reddish leather couch—only to spring to life the instant the special ring on his phone started buzzing on his desk a few yards away. It was city desk calling, wanting a story about some crime or another in the naked city.

JoMo would get the whole story in about 15 minutes, Rem recalled, usually telling a crime victim or nursing supervisor at a hospital emergency room that he was "Deputy Police Superintendent Walter Vallee" or "Chief Deputy Coroner Peter Spirko." Once he phoned his notes to the rewrite-man back at Tribune Tower a few miles north, Joe would flop back on the couch and fall back asleep.

"Never work any harder than you have to, kid," he would advise Rem every so often. "It ain't worth it."

Hmm, Rem thought, wonder what the former Marine Corps grunt in World War II who survived Iwo Jima and Guadalcanal would think of me now. Probably not much. You let a woman drink you under the table, Joe would have scoffed. That's pathetic. You're pathetic.

CHAPTER 65

Pop, Snap, Crackle

Offices of LC&R
Trump Tower, Midtown Manhattan
Sunday, September 26, 2010
6:06 p.m.

Julie handed Rem a high-ball glass filled with three ounces of brown-colored liquid, two ice cubes and no water. Just what I need, Rem mused miserably.

"So, Rem," Levitsky began, seated at one end of the leather couch, Rem at the other, "get me excited. Tell me something you didn't know the last time we talked. Something you can write, something with pop."

"Well, for starters," Rem began, "Rafer Flanagan not only did not die on 9/11, he went to the home of a friend in Brooklyn where he lived in the basement for another nine months before moving back to Australia in the summer of 2002. He had a phony British passport with the name of a dead cousin, and he looked completely different. Long white hair and beard, 50 pounds heavier, all muscled up, affected an Irish accent. That came naturally. He spent the first 10 years of his life in Ireland. County Wicklow, south of Dublin."

"Nice," Julie said approvingly. "That's a boom, not a pop. To what end?"

"To get even with his putative widow and his share of the insurance money she got after he faked his own death," Rem replied. "Just wanted to even the score."

"Where is he now?"

"Don't know. That's the main thing I want to find out in Sydney. Has not been heard from in eight years."

"Excellent, excellent," Julie said, rubbing his meaty hands. "You're off to a great start. Gino filled me in on Puerto Rico. What else do I need to know? Make it quick. I gotta run soon. Another fucking Wall Street fundraiser at the Plaza. Oprah's the keynoter."

"Well, you should know that Ari's freaking out that I'm doing this story," Rem said. "His flack told me that off the record. Also got a letter from one of his libel attorneys. Said something like: 'We trust you will write nothing to besmirch the reputations of two of the finest correspondents in the history of the *New York Herald*.'"

"Love it, love it," Julie said, laughing. "Send me a copy of that. Ari's not that stupid. He knows his blood is in the water. But, of course, he also knows you can't libel the dead. Hmmm, unless they come back from the grave to contest the facts."

Julie laughed again. "I love this story. It's so weird. I do feel a little sorry for Ari. He's never really been good at anything except lifting weights and scoring with beautiful, smart women. If his older brothers hadn't died, he'd be living in some place like Dallas, selling equities and schtupping SMU society babes. Real responsibility and leadership aren't his strong suits."

"So I gather," Rem said, standing to go, drink untouched. "In any event, I told his flack I would request an interview when I'm almost done with my reporting."

"Yeah, yeah, be careful what you tell her," Julie cautioned. "Keep the cards close. He'll never submit to a real interview, and we don't want anyone to know what we have for the news story until just prior to publication. We're going to kill it on *The Searchlight* launch. Great pub for the book and the movie. That's where the real money is."

"One last thing," Rem said, moving toward the exit, "what are the chances Maggie Maye could help me on this? Just as an informal advisor? She told me last night she could also use some closure on this. Ruined her newspaper career."

Yes, Julie thought. B-I-N-G-O.

"Let me think about that," he said evenly. "I know Maggie well. It would have to be on the q.t., of course. She'll be a player in the book."

"Yeah," Rem said, "a minor one. Fact is I'm going to need a good shadow editor to advise me and back-read this stuff. Nobody better than her."

"I'll let you know," Julie said, showing Rem out. "Keep me posted. Take your time. I just confirmed the London interview at the Savoy is a go. Godspeed. If you don't nail it, don't come back."

CHAPTER 66

Sexagenarian Temptress

Offices of LC&J
Trump Tower, Midtown Manhattan
Monday, September 27, 2010
6:06 p.m.

Julie looked out the picture window and focused on the tiny silhouette of an airliner on its ascent out of JFK heading east. He stood to get a better look.

"That may be Rem's plane," he said casually, keeping his eyes on the horizon. "He was due to leave for Heathrow about now."

Maggie glanced quickly out the window and turned her eyes back to the flat screen, tuned to Anderson Cooper on CNN.

"Did you know Anderson Cooper was gay?" she asked absently. "What a shame. He's a real hunk. Gloria Vanderbilt's son. Still in the closet."

"He's also really good," Julie said, sitting back down. "CNN is the only sanity left on American cable news. Fox and MSNBC just serve up unending political drivel and nasty partisan garbage. Dialogue of the deaf. Not real journalists. Another reason why my new on-line news network is going to work."

"I must admit I'm feeling a little duplicitous and trampy in all this," Maggie said, smiling coyly and sipping her Shiraz. "I'm not used to being a sexagenarian temptress."

"A what?"

"Never mind. Rem's a good guy. I admired him for a long time when he was at the *Daily News.* Tried to hire him three times. He's very serious. Attractive in his own way."

"That's the right attitude, Maggie," Julie said. "Think Samantha Jones. The bedroom is just another space where she does business. It ain't personal."

"So, what now?" Maggie asked sharply, annoyed at the comparison.

"Be waiting for him when he gets to the Sydney Airport," Julie replied. "I have his itinerary. Surprise him at baggage pickup. Be his Maxine Perkins the next couple of months. Low key. Keep him on track. He'll do the rest."

CHAPTER 67

The Invisible Hand

American Bar, Savoy Hotel
The Strand, London, England
Tuesday, September 28, 2010
5:44 p.m.

The spook smoothly took his seat on the bar stool next to Rem as though they'd known each other for years. Fiftyish, wearing a black London fog, good build, with dark red hair and acne-scarred face. Looks like Chuck Norris, Rem thought.

"Mr. Dabovitch, I presume," he said, tone a Bondian cool. "I bring you best wishes from Her Majesty, the Queen."

"Thank you," Rem replied, shaking a surprisingly limp, sweaty hand. "And I bring you best wishes from Julius the Jackal. Says to tell the queen he'll ring her up next time he's in town."

The pair laughed and moved over to a corner table, away from the happy-hour crowd of English locals and Western tourists.

"Ah, the Jackal," the spook-man said. "A true legend. When he asks, we please."

"I sometimes wonder if there is anyone Julie doesn't know," Rem said. "So, I didn't get your name."

"Didn't give it."

"Oh, ok. Mind if I ask where you work?"

"MI6"

"Ok, that's what I thought," Rem said. "Julie said you had something for me. Is that it?" He pointed to a brown envelope the agent had just taken out of his briefcase.

"It is," the spook said, handing him a half-inch thick report, held together at the top by a black metal clamp. "Read through the first few pages. I think you'll soon see what it is."

Rem adjusted his Ray-Bans in the darkish bar and expertly scanned pages one, two and three--second nature to reporters working on deadline. Find the lede—fast.

"Whoa," Rem said finally, "this is that bogus report from Aussie intelligence—the one that got Angela Flanagan and the *Herald* into so much trouble."

"Wrong on two of three counts, Mr. Dabovitch," the agent replied.

"Say again."

"The intelligence report is not bogus and it's not from AISO."

"Go on."

"The report is real. It was written ten years ago by British intelligence —by yours truly, in fact—working on behalf of AISO. Subcontracted out to us, if you will. A sleight of hand to give our very good friends Down Under some cover in case they needed it. Came in handy."

"I'll say," Rem said. "Kind of hung Ms. Flanagan out to dry, didn't you?"

"Ms. Flanagan was a fool," the agent scoffed. "She was a reckless drug addict in way over her head. She hung herself out to dry."

"Why are you willing to show this to me now?" Rem asked.

"Mr. Dabovitch," the agent replied patiently, "democratic intelligence agencies around the world are at war with the Chinese government. They lie, they cheat, they steal on a regular basis. It has gotten much worse in recent years as they modernize. Anything that exposes their historic duplicity and mendacity in this environment serves the interests of all of who believe in democratic ideals. This is for deep background only."

"Has to be," Rem cracked. "Don't even know your name."

The agent smiled slightly and stood to go.

"Rafer Flanagan had this report, didn't he?" Rem asked. "You gave it to him when he was bureau chief down there. He was quietly working on the story at the time of 9/11. And, in fact, this is the report the mysterious Conor McCann showed Stacey Simpson. Even though the narrative was true, Flanagan knew his wife and Simpson would botch and underreport such a bombshell story. He knew the Australian government would always deny it and the Holt family would label it a hoax. Indeed, the family believed it was a hoax. So, what you had was a true story that Angela would never be able to *prove* was true. Am I right?"

The agent started to react but held back. Instead, he slowly put his black coat back on. "One suggestion for you, Mr. Dabovitch," he said finally. "Check out the murder of a tourist in Sydney around the time Ms. Flanagan supposedly drowned. It might help you put all the pieces of this puzzle together. Must say it is quite a tangled web."

The agent smiled for the first time, fully revealing his crooked, nicotine-stained teeth. "Give Mr. Levitsky our best," he said. "MI6 loves his London office. Great place to land when we're sent out to pasture. I'm going to need him myself soon. His contracts are too good to pass up."

He laughed and, without bothering to shake hands, did an about-face with Sandhurst-like precision and disappeared out the door into the rainy London night.

Gotta love the invisible hand, Rem mused. Ask the spooks if it doesn't make sense. They'll get it.

CHAPTER 68

Internet Road-Kill

Black Lion Pub
Hammersmith, London, England
Wednesday, Sept. 29, 2010
1:44 p.m.

The early fall sun shining gloriously on the Thames, running silent and deep a few yards away, Kellen Williams and Rem Dabovitch sat contently on the outdoor patio, washing down the last of their breaded English fish with red Irish ale.

The outdoor lunch crowd had thinned out, last sips taken, cigarettes snuffed out. Time for the salarymen to get back to their cubicles. Only ones left were the two American journalists and one attractive forty-ish couple who couldn't keep their hands off each other.

"Those two need to get a room," Rem said, eyeing the groping twosome, oblivious to the world around them. "If they're married, it's not to each other."

"Yeah, ain't lust grand," Kellen said with a chuckle, turning to look at the passing parades of boats—tourist, pleasure, industrial. "I love this spot. I live just around the corner. This place was remodeled while I was back in New York. Like the old place inside a lot better."

"I hear you, Kellen," Rem replied. "The whole world is being remodeled and old guys like us are being tossed out with the trash. Beat goes on."

"Tough to swallow when you do something your entire life that you think is a great public service, only to find out most people could care less, especially the younger ones," Kellen mused. "Long-form newspaper journalism is damn near dead. If you can't say it in 140 characters, it ain't worth saying."

Rem laughed and shook his head. "Nothing worse than two old dinosaurs sitting around complaining about climate change," he said. "So, give me the dirty details about the fight Maggie and Ari had the night the infamous story ran. I got Maggie's version the other day, but I need corroboration. Probably will lead off the book."

"No direct quotes," Kellen said. "I'd be fired and probably lose my pension if Ari III knew I was talking to you."

"Got it," Rem said. "I'll protect you. The book will be in my voice. Besides, I doubt Ari III will be around very long once the bombs start landing. There's going to be a direct hit on the House of Steinberg."

"Ok," Williams said, sitting up and pulling up his chair to the table. "I remember coming into the newsroom the night the story ran. Still recall it like it was yesterday. Wednesday, January 1, 2003. First thing I noticed was the panic and fear in the air. The paper was being bombarded with calls from around the world demanding to know if the story was a hoax. The top foreign editor on duty that night was just a low-level copy editor whose head looked like it was going to explode.

"Anyway, Maggie and I went from her office up to 15, where Ari was standing at this picture window, hands in his pockets, staring down at the New Year's night crowd below. Maggie was so angry she could barely contain herself. Her worst fears about Angela Flanagan had come to pass and she knew she was going to take the hit for it. I recall her hands shaking, face twitching. I knew it was going to be bad."

Kellen paused, took a long drink of water and launched into the action scene.

"As soon as we all sat down, Ari III began screaming, literally: 'How could the senior editors of this great newspaper have allowed such a stupid story to get into print, how you should all be ashamed of yourselves, how we are going to be the laughingstock of late-night TV.' I remember him saying specifically: 'Jon Stewart is going to kill us on this.' And on and on. Totally unhinged.

"Well, Maggie took it for a while. When she did try to talk, Ari cut her off. I could see her face getting redder as she took this stream of abuse. It literally went on for five minutes.

"Finally, in his own imperious way, he said: 'Maggie, I want a full written report on this on my desk by tomorrow evening. You better get to work. You, too, Kellen. You've got 18 hours.'"

Kellen interrupted the narrative again, taking another long drink of water and wiping his mouth with a white paper napkin. He took a deep breath and kept going.

"Well, that put Maggie over the top. She completely lost it. Started screaming, shrieking almost: 'Ari, you stupid bastard. I told you not to promote that woman. She's a bloody incompetent. Her only talent was she knew how to suck your pathetic dick.'"

"Whoa, she said that?" Rem cut in. "Called his dick pathetic? She left that little nugget out when I interviewed her."

"She was so mad she probably doesn't even remember what she said," Kellen replied. "You should have seen Ari's face. Turned a nasty shade of pale. Like he was going into shock. Underlings just didn't talk to Prince Ari that way.

"Then she screams: 'Write the fucking report yourself. You caused this mess; you clean it up.' By this time, she's throwing everything she can at him—newspapers, books, magazines. She even took off her right shoe and threw it at him—just like that Iraqi did with Bush a couple of years ago. All the time yelling: 'Ari Steinberg, you're a complete fraud and you know it.' Stuff like that. Mother of all meltdowns."

"I'm loving this," Rem said, writing furiously.

"So," Kellen continued, "Maggie storms out of the office with her left shoe still on and Ari is there fumbling around with all the debris on his desk, and he hands me back Maggie's other shoe. He looks pathetic. Then, he says, and this is a direct quote: 'I can assure you Mrs. Flanagan is not incompetent. Please find her as soon as possible. I am very concerned for her well-being.'"

"That's all," Rem asked.

"Yep. Back in his lord of the manor persona. I never spoke to him after that. He apparently left the building and sulked for the next few days at his weekend home in the Hamptons. Ninety-six hours later, they found Angela's 'So Long' note. About 96 days later, I was sent back to London, this time as 'senior European culture correspondent' and Maggie was ousted with a $2 million severance."

"And Ari survived to rule another day," Rem said, putting down his pen.

"Yep," Kellen said. "America launches its idiotic invasion of Iraq March 19, 2002, and the *Herald* wins five Pulitzers for its news coverage. And this tempest is totally forgotten."

"Until now," Rem said with a smile.

"Yeah, until now," Kellen said, raising his glass. "Cheers. What a story."

CHAPTER 69

Rogue Reporter

Harry's Pub, Marriott Hotel
El Gezira Street, Cairo, Egypt
Friday, October 1, 2010
1:33 p.m.

As North African bureau chief of the *New York Herald*, Katharine 'Kit' Harrison was a rare figure in a very catty business: someone about whom you almost never heard a negative word. In her mid-40s, she had already received one Pulitzer from her reporting days in Northern Ireland, was a Pulitzer finalist for dispatches from South Africa during apartheid and won the Polk Award for her reporting in Bosnia, named for a CBS correspondent murdered in 1948 during the Greek civil war.

Affectionately nicknamed 'Miss Kitty' by her Egyptian support staff, Harrison spoke flawless Arabic, had Muammar Gaddafi's personal cell number in her i-phone, and was on Hosni Mubarak's shit list of reporters "hostile to the best interests of Egypt." She dove deeply as a reporter, wrote fast and fluidly on deadline, and managed a high-strung office staff in Cairo with skill, style and firmness. She never preened, complained or bragged. Her work spoke for itself—and it spoke volumes. In the never-ending newsroom handicapping over who would eventually replace Maggie Maye as the paper's top editor, the highly moral bureau chief was always on the short list. She said she had no interest.

"So, Kit," Rem said, pushing away his lunch plate of kushari and taro, "let's talk about Angela Reilly Flanagan. Great Irish name if there ever was one. Tell me something about her I don't know, as Chris Matthews would say."

"Well," Harrison began, "for better or worse, I probably knew her better personally than any other reporter on the staff. For some reason, she confided in me. Said I was her role model."

"Good role model," Rem quipped, "bad execution."

"I actually felt sorry for her," Harrison said. "Tough life. Mother was a drunk. Badly beaten in a botched drug deal in college. Began snorting coke as a teenager and never stopped. Hated by her peers. Thought she was a management suck up totally unqualified to be a foreign corre- spondent. Always shunned at correspondent meetings held once a year in the Middle East and Asia."

Harrison paused for a drink of ice water. She glanced at her watch and continued.

"Her husband didn't help much. He thrived in those Third World spots where they were posted, and he paid no attention to her work or well-being. So, she was incredibly lonely and isolated. Most tandem couples work out ok. Couples help each other. This one was a disaster."

"Sounds like it," Rem quipped, furiously taking notes.

"You can't have a neat-freak personality and a society-girl nervous system and thrive in a place like Cairo or Delhi," Harrison said. "That's why she contacted Ari III to reopen Sydney. Great for her, terrible for Raffy. He was never the same."

Harrison pushed her plate away and looked at her watch again. "Look, I gotta go. On the 4 o'clock to Tunis. Lots of stuff going on over there. Talk about a so-called Arab spring. Color me skeptical."

She stood to go. "Look, I know you want to talk about her relation- ship with Ari III but count me out, even off the record. Sorry. Their relationship was sordid and perverted from what I heard. She cracked the whip on him, and he loved it."

Harrison laughed and shook Rem's hand. "Nice to finally meet the 'Serbian Assassin' in person. Admired you from afar for years, Rem. I can only imagine what you are going to find out. Hear you're heading to Hong Kong to see Peter Lynch. Please give him my regards. Tell him we miss him a lot. He was good."

With that, Miss Kitty turned and headed out into the furnace-like mid-day heat. Lucky woman, Rem thought. Still has a good job.

CHAPTER 70

The 3Ms

Offices of Osbourne, Simon & Li
Hong Kong Island, Hong Kong, China
Monday, October 4, 2010
5:15 p.m.

Peter Lynch stood and walked slowly over to the picture window overlooking a teeming Victoria Harbor that sits at the center of one of the most populated places on earth.

"Just think of Angela Flanagan as opaque," Lynch said. "Very Asian. Operated on several levels. A real piece of work. I couldn't stand her. Not someone you could trust and that doesn't work in this job."

"Do you still think of yourself as a journalist?" Rem asked. "Sounds like it. How's the PR gig going?"

Lynch grimaced and walked back to his desk, sitting back down again. "It's a job," he said. "Pays me a ton of money so I can send my kids to college back in the States and pay my lazy ex-wife $10,000 a month in child support. In return, I spend my day sucking up to clients, most of whom are obscenely rich, impossibly spoiled and have little respect for what we do. They think favorable news stories are something you dictate to reporters. So other than that, I love it."

"So, you miss the newsroom?"

"Every day," Lynch replied. "Always will. Had to jump to the dark side, though, because the business is failing so fast. Either abandon ship today or drown in the typhoon tomorrow."

"Yeah," Rem said, "sounds familiar."

"You know," Lynch said, "I have an MBA from Northwestern—same school Angela went to—and at one point a few years ago I offered to move over to the business side for a while. Try to figure out how to remain relevant and profitable in the digital age and keep profits from tanking too much. Prepared a detailed proposal and sent it directly to Ari. He never answered. I don't even think he read it. Man is clueless."

"So I've heard," Rem said.

"Much as I hate PR—and I do hate it—I've learned something the last few years," Lynch said. "Image matters. Optics matter. We never explained in any detail to the American public exactly why newspapers are so important. How important it is to keep public figures honest, how expensive good reporting is, how long it takes to drill down to the truth."

Lynch paused to catch his breath and climbed one step higher on his soap box.

"Going back twenty years, our leaders—the publishers and editors—were so blasé when we were attacked by the wingnuts on the right—mainly Rush Limbaugh. They just said: 'Our work speaks for itself.' Sorry. Doesn't work that way anymore. We needed our own version of Herb Schmertz—the legendary Mobil Oil flak in the 1970s--telling our story every day, battling it out in the trenches with those who hated us. John and Josephine Public needed to be told why we still mattered in the new digital age, and we dropped the ball."

Lynch paused again before adding: "I want to write a book about how a 400-year-old business in America withered away through myopia, mismanagement and malpractice. The 3Ms, I call it. Makes me want to cry."

Which, to Rem's astonishment, was exactly what Lynch looked like he was going to do.

CHAPTER 71

Fuck Me Twice...

Newsroom, Sydney Morning-Telegraph
Darling Island Road, Sydney, Australia
Friday, October 8, 2010
7:07 p.m.

Stacey Simpson stood tall in her cluttered cubicle and stretched hard to get her six-foot-three-inch frame loose after a workday that began 10 hours earlier and included so many phone calls the receiver still felt like it was glued to her left ear.

God, she thought, that interview with the mother of the dying surfer was pure heartbreak. Always jarring when a close relative is so eager to talk to a police reporter, a total stranger who sounds like they care what happened. I'm good at that, Simpson thought. By the time I'm done, they usually can't shut up. And I do care, she thought defensively—up to a point.

As she scanned the high-tech newsroom, she reminded herself yet again how she was glad she had to work at the sterile main office only on Fridays. All the multi-media platform crap, the ubiquitous flat-screen TVs, the newsroom itself eerily quiet and antiseptic. Christ, she thought disgustedly, the Sydney morgue has more energy than this place. News reporters everywhere—all over the modern world--used to rely on dramatic interviews to get the big story on a tough deadline, but now they sort through tweets, emails, and Facebook postings, and watch the tube. Where's the fun in that?

Thank God, the cop shop is still old school, she mused gratefully. Most of the time she was working the streets, operating out of her car or a police station and filing from her laptop. I'm the best god-damn cop reporter in New South Wales, she reminded herself, because I get down and dirty in bad-ass King's Cross. Know all the key boys in blue by their first names and—most importantly—they all know me. I know who's driving the ambulances and who's chasing them, which sex workers are cross-dressers and which ones sent their customers back to Munich and Montreal with an STD.

Love playing darts with the homicide cops at John Barleycorn's, drinking them under the table and letting them win occasionally if it loosens lips for a possible scoop. Even a little intimacy occasionally if it feels right. Hey, a girl's got to compete.

"Jerry," Simpson yelled over at Jeremiah O'Connor, the city editor, seated a few yards away, back to her, eyes locked on this desktop screen, "I just updated the shark story from Perth. Put some comments in from dear ole mum. Talked to the hospital off the record. They're saying the surfer dude probably won't last the night. Lost too much blood."

"Ok, Simpson, thanks," O'Connor replied, looking back over at her. "Keep the Blackberry with you. If he carks it on deadline, you'll have to call mum back. Have a nice weekend. I can't make it to Barleycorn's tonight."

"Got it," Simpson replied, heading off to the ladies room to freshen up and put on her game face for the weekly Friday night follies.

As she eyed herself in the mirror, combing her shortish dirty blond hair and retouching her eyeliner, she told herself yet again how she had to get serious about curbing her ravenous appetites for food, drink, and lust in all the wrong places. How she had gained 25 pounds in the last year alone and how she could barely touch the rim anymore, let alone dunk the ball. Sure, the boobs are enormous now but, looking in the mirror, so is the backside. It's spreading faster than a Tasmanian brush fire, she noted disgustingly.

As she put on her spring jacket back at the cubicle, the landline on her desk roared to life, giving her an unpleasant jolt. She eyed the phone suspiciously, wondering whether she could slip away without anyone noticing. Oh, what the fuck, she thought on the fourth ring, it could be a game changer.

"Simpson here," she barked into the phone. "Make it fast. I'm off duty."

"Simpson, so glad I caught you," said the voice on the other end, accent clearly American east coast, probably Boston or New York. "Rem Dabovitch here, free-lance reporter from the States. Here in Sydney on business. I have a great story for you. We need to talk."

"No, we don't," Simpson spat. "I have no idea who you are and frankly, my dear, I don't care to find out."

She slammed down the phone and hurried to the third-floor elevator, joining the other reporters heading out for the night. Bloody Americans, she thought. Took me years to get over what those assholes did to me last time. Fuck me twice, she thought, shame on me.

CHAPTER 72

What Would Stella Do?

John Barleycorn's Pub, King's Cross
Sydney, Australia
Friday, Oct. 8, 2010
9:49 p.m.

Simpson felt dizzy, sick, disoriented—like when she got whacked in the head with an elbow playing basketball. Glaring hard at this Rem character who somehow tracked her down to her secret lair, she couldn't completely absorb what he was saying.

"You're fucking with me," she snarled, stepping a couple of feet back from the bar. "That Holt story was true? Get the fuck out of here. Can't be."

"Yep," Rem replied evenly, sitting on one of the wooden, high-backed bar stools, while Simpson remained on her feet, looking pale, unsteady. "Confirmed it in London this week with British intelligence. Got a copy of the original report. You just got the authors wrong. You were set up."

"Don't know whether to cheer or cry," she said, taking a seat, darts still in her left hand, voice quiet and nearly inaudible in the Friday-night din. "Story haunts me to this day. Lump in my stomach that's never gone away. We were so ashamed and humiliated."

"Yeah," Rem replied sympathetically, "it was a cruel hoax that worked. Angela was the target. You were just collateral damage."

"I need some air," Simpson said suddenly, grabbing her huge leather purse off the bar and bolting through the back exit door into the alley where all the smokers were hanging out.

"Oh, my, I thought I was going to be sick in there," she told the trailing Dabovitch, wiping away beads of sweat on her forehead, color returning to her face. She took a Marlboro from her purse and lit it, inhaling deeply.

"So, what do you want exactly?" she demanded. "I don't like surprises and I don't trust you fucking Yanks. Nobody down here gives a rat's ass about this anymore—except maybe me and Angela and she's gone. And, frankly, I'd rather not relive the single worst experience of my entire life."

"I know, I know," Rem said reassuringly, briefly placing his hand on her arm. "But this is your chance to set things right. That's why I came down here all the way from New York. We need your help. You know your way around and we don't."

"Who's we?"

"Glad you asked. Believe you know her. Your old boss at the *New York Herald*, Margarite Maye."

"Whoa, you buried the lede, mate," Simpson shot back. "Maggie Maye? The editor? The Stella Steele author?"

"The one and only," Rem said, smiling.

"Jesus, I love Stella," Simpson said. "She is my hero. Why didn't you say so?"

Simpson lit a new cigarette off the old one, which she threw a few feet away still lit. A homeless man in the alley quickly picked up the discarded butt and took a long hit. Simpson smiled at him and waved.

She returned her gaze to Rem, suspicion back in her green eyes. "I've heard this siren song before, you know, just down the street at O'Rourke's Ale House," she said. "That's where the smooth Conor McCann hung out. I still don't know who that bloke was. The bloody bastard."

"Tell you what," Rem said. "Meet Maggie and me over at Bondi Beach tomorrow afternoon and I'll show you a copy of the real report. Has MI6 stamp at the top of the page. That should make you feel a little better. We'll be at Pedro's Café on Hall St. And we'll explain the story on Angela that we're working on. And you can have the exclusive on the Holt stuff. Nobody in America cares about him."

"Nobody in Australia cares about him," Simpson shot back.

"Whatever. Story is yours if you want it."

Simpson's Blackberry buzzed and she took it off her belt. She studied the incoming message and said nothing for a time.

"Gotta run," she said finally. "Have to update a front-page story before the final deadline. This Blackberry is killing me. I work 24/7."

Rem nodded. "So, what do you say? In or not?"

"Don't hold your breath," she replied. "I don't appreciate ambushes. Tell Maggie I'm going to have a séance with Stella and ask her what I should do."

She laughed sarcastically, flipped away the second cigarette in the same direction as before and disappeared back into the bar without another word.

CHAPTER 73

Bondi Beach Mellow

Pedro's Café, Hall Street
Bondi Beach, Australia
Saturday, October 9, 2010
5:25 p.m.

A few klicks east of downtown Sydney, Bondi Beach is the Aussie version of hip urban sand—like Miami Beach or Rio. Tourists flock there year-round but it's particularly colorful during the holidays when the pasty-faced rain birds from the UK come en masse to see Santa Claus surfing on Bondi Bay. If I can milk the reporting on this story for another couple of months, Rem mused, maybe I'll still be around to see it for myself this year.

Rem looked at his watch and frowned. "Afraid she's not coming," he told Maggie, sipping a Shiraz in the chair next to him. "She freaked last night when I mentioned the Holt story. I thought she was going to pass out."

"Can't blame her," Maggie said, watching the passing human parade at the outdoor café, eyes hidden behind Prada sunglasses. "Nothing more painful for journalists than bringing up past mistakes, particularly the worst ones. Can we do this without her?"

"Yeah," Rem said, 'but not as well and not as fast."

"Tell me more about her, Rem," Maggie said, sitting up straight and removing her glasses. "To me she was just a rookie reporter Angela hired to do Raffy's job. A real free spirit, I take it. I did finally see that 1999 photo of the dirty dozen. Pretty cheeky, pun intended."

"Gino Carella told me about her," Rem replied. "Got to know her well when he worked here. Says she busts all the molds. Drinks too much, openly bi-sexual. But she's also a great police reporter. Has great sources. Cops adore her."

"Sounds a little like my Stella," Maggie said, chuckling. "How did you find her?"

"Carella told me she hangs out every Friday night in a dive bar named Barleycorn's in King's Cross. I waited a while before approaching her just to see how she acts in her native habitat, so to speak. Quite a show."

"Go on."

"Well, she's like an oversized ballerina—tall, athletic, graceful but overweight. Everybody in the bar seemed to know her. Calling her name, giving high fives, hugs. The men, the women, some I couldn't tell."

"I love it," Maggie said, laughing and clapping her hands. "It's a cop bar, right?"

"According to Gino, it's cops, prosecutors, journalists, flacks, politicians, sex workers, hustlers of all kinds. You name it, she knew them."

"Then you had to go and spoil everything," Maggie said.

"Yeah, skunk at the garden party," Rem said. "Do that a lot."

Maggie stayed quiet for a time, putting her sunglasses back on and focusing on the passing human parade. She pursed her lips, lost in thought.

"You know, Rem," she said finally, "I see yellow lights flashing everywhere. We're going to be exhuming some deep, dark stuff in a place we know nothing about. Could be tricky—ugly even. We really do need her help."

"I hear you," Rem replied. "Got to nail everything down six ways from Sunday. Gonna take time. This is no rush job. If I fuck anything up, Ari and his lawyers will pounce on me like tiger sharks on a tuna."

"Hope I'm not interrupting anything," Stacey Simpson said, appearing at their table, seemingly out of nowhere, wearing a revealing white sun dress and extending her hand toward Maggie. "Margarite T. Maye, I presume. I adore Stella O. Steele. She is my hero. What can I do for you?"

CHAPTER 74

Who Was That Dead Man?

Room 333, Bondi Beach Hotel
Sydney, Australia
Sunday, October 10, 2010
10:10 a.m.

My God, Maggie thought, the woman looks like an unmade bed this morning. Same skimpy white sun dress she had on yesterday afternoon, no makeup, hair a mess. Who on earth might we be going into business with, she wondered?

"So, Stacey," she said, wiping her mouth with a cloth napkin and tossing it onto the food tray, "we need an answer. You in? Great stories like this are like February 29th. Only come around once every few years."

"We can probably make it work," Stacey said evenly, guard gate high. "My city editor says I can work on it in my spare time. And he wants our own story separate from what the *Herald* is doing. He still remembers the Flanagan fiasco. Everyone here does."

Ouch, Maggie thought. Seated on the hotel-room patio with its unobstructed view of Bondi Bay, she didn't respond for a time, hearing only the growing sounds of the Sunday morning beach traffic three floors below. Rem was also quiet, standing in the doorway, wearing cutoffs, flip-flops, and tee shirt showcasing a spongy gut. He doesn't look so hot either, Maggie noted, but men usually get a pass on that stuff.

"Right you are then," Maggie said finally, standing up and taking charge. "That's ok with me. Let's get started.

"Rem, I want you to interview *every* single person of note named or quoted in *every* major story that Angela Flanagan wrote while she was in the South Pacific bureau. Been almost eight years now and time unseals a lot of lips. Her files were way too puffy. Something was amiss there. Do the interviews in person if it helps. Fly, drive, run, walk wherever you must go. Report back to me as soon as you can on how long this will take. I'm guessing you'll need at least a month or two. We have one chance to get this right."

Maggie may look a lot differently than the old days, Rem mused, but the famous gunny-sergeant style hadn't changed: here's what you're going to do, here's why you're doing it, and here's your deadline. Back in the day, her no-bullshit persona was legendary among those who worked for (or competed against) her.

" Stacey," Maggie continued on, turning her gaze to Simpson, "I want you to write me a memo on everything—repeat everything--you know about Angela. The personal, professional, the kitchen sink. Write what we know and can print, and what we think we know but still need to report out. Give me the sex, the drugs, who and how she loved, what and whom she hated. I want this yesterday. Rem needs it."

"Right you are, luv. I'm on it."

"Now," Maggie continued on, "our operating assumption is this is all a giant insurance scam and the Flanagans are alive, well and living together somewhere in the South Pacific, probably southern New Zealand or western Australia."

"You can forget that, luv," Stacey blurted. "Those two loathed each other. Besides, Angela told me Raffy had turned into a fag."

"Stacey," Rem said, "I got a tip from British intelligence about the murder of a foreign tourist in Sydney about the time Angela disappeared. First few days of 2003. Was told the identity of this guy would help us figure out what happened back then. Can you check it out?"

"Was he a fag?" Stacey asked.

"Can we please stop using the term 'fag,'" Maggie snapped. "I believe 'gay' is the respectful term of art now, even here."

"Sorry, luv," Stacey said, not sounding it, "I spend too much time around cops."

Stacey looked at Rem: "Well, was he? A wonderful gay gentleman, I mean."

"Dunno," Rem replied, trying with limited success to avert his eyes from her prodigious cleavage. "Does it really matter?"

"Yes, it does," Stacey shot back. "There was a string of gay sex-worker murders in Sydney that began back in the mid-1990s involving foreign tourists looking for lust in all the wrong places, mainly King's Cross. Bodies found about once a year in a bunch of different places. All bound, gagged, sodomized. Never found any identification or money on any of them."

"What's King's Cross?" Rem asked.

"A raunchy nightclub district," Stacey replied. "Lots of crime, drugs, seedy characters. Seems like half the stories I write come from there.

"Anyhow, it turns out the perp was a Bible-thumping sheep farmer from New Zealand who eventually confessed to at least nine murders from 1994 to 2003. Angela even wrote a story about it when the police investigation was going on before the guy was nailed."

"I thought that story sounded familiar," Rem said. "I read it in her clips. Can you check who he was?"

"Sure," Stacey said confidently, "I know just the person to ask. But the person you should be talking to is a guy named Jack Quinn, one of Angela's boy toys. If she's alive—and I'm certain she is—Jack will know how to reach her. Runs a travel agency near the beach, not far from here. I'll pay him a surprise visit tomorrow morning."

"Great," Maggie chimed in. "See, we're already making progress."

"Quinn would do anything for Angela," Stacey said. "He just worshipped her. She'd say fetch and he'd ask where. It was soooo embarrassing."

Maggie and Rem both laughed.

"Listen," Stacey said, "gotta pickup basketball game down at the beach in a while. Mind if I use your bathroom to change into my sweat clothes?"

Anything to get you out of that disgusting sun dress, Maggie thought. "Sure thing," she said. "Mind if I join you? I'd like to watch how you play."

"No problem," Stacey said. "I've got to sweat this booze out of my system. Had a hard night. British Navy's in town."

CHAPTER 75

What are Norks?

Basketball courts, Bondi Beach
Sydney, Australia
Sunday, October 10, 2010
1:44 p.m.

Oh yeah, I could get used to this, Maggie thought approvingly: lovely day at the beach, temperatures nearing record highs in the 90s, beautiful bodies everywhere. If this city weren't so bloody hard to get to, she mused, I'd come all the time. L.A. minus the smog and traffic.

"Stacey," she deadpanned, turning to look at Simpson next to her on a wooden bench by the sand, "all the booze gone? You look like you're about to have a stroke."

Red-faced and sweating buckets, Simpson laughed and took another long drink from her Coke can. "Best way there is to get rid of a hangover," she said. "Do it all the time. Headache hurts a little at first but it's all good after that. I feel almost normal now."

Give her this much, Maggie thought: she's got game. After last night's carousing, she plays pickup basketball for two straight hours, kicking male butt up and down the court. Only woman playing and easily the best performer.

"I knew you were on the Aussie Olympic team," Maggie said, "but I had no idea you were still so good. You were fabulous, girl."

The two laughed and did a single high five.

"Should have seen me ten years ago," Stacey said, smiling at some friends on the beach nearby. "Lot lighter then. Could dunk a basketball from a standing start."

"But you hurt your knee?" Maggie asked.

"Yep, just before the 2000 Olympics right here in Sydney. We got the silver medal. Yanks beat us in the final game. Really embarrassing. I had to watch on crutches."

Simpson belched loudly without apology and drained the final sips in the Coke can. She threw the can ten feet toward a trash can and didn't even hit iron.

"See," she said, "I really have lost my touch."

Both women laughed.

"Listen, Maggie," Stacey said seriously, picking up the can and putting it in the trash, 'we need to be straight with each other. What you get with me is what you see. I'm not going to change just because I'm going to partner with some big-time writers from New York. Did that once. Never again. Been living it down ever since.

"You guys saw me this morning. I looked like hell; I know it. I saw Rem leering at my norks. I like it when men do that. Makes 'em so easy to lead around. That's just how I am, Maggie. Ain't changing. I don't care what you bloody feminists think."

"Well," Maggie noted politely, "to each her own. What on earth are norks?"

"Aussie for tits, luv."

"Oh, ok. Never heard that one before."

"Listen, Maggie, I agreed to meet with you guys only because I want closure on what happened on New Year's Day, 2003. I want to find Angela and do the first exclusive interview on what happened to her. We can help each other. Just business. Nothing else. We're not going to be friends."

"You sound like Stella," Maggie said, chuckling.

"Exactly, Maggie. I know Stella by heart. I've read all three books and can't wait for number four. She is my hero. Works too hard, drinks way too much, personal life a complete mess. But nobody tells her what to do, and she always, always gets her story. That's me, Maggie. I'm the real Stella Ophelia Steele."

OMG, Maggie thought, how is this going to end?

CHAPTER 76

Angela's Other Butt Boy

Sun&Fun Travel, Bondi Beach
Sydney, Australia
Monday, October 11, 2010
9 a.m.

Jack Quinn punched the key code and opened the green door of his small travel agency, just as he had done six mornings most every week the past seven years. (He only closed on Tuesdays.)

Hey, he would often muse, it isn't being chief flack at the Aussie visitors bureau, but it pays the freight---kids' college, ex-wife's alimony, Mykonos in August with his latest Sheila. Opening satellite offices in Belfast, Glasgow and Liverpool was pure genius. Those cockney working stiffs love spending Christmas Down Under watching some bozo surf Bondi Bay in a Santa Claus outfit. ('Mum, you wouldn't believe what we saw in Sydney.') Next planned expansion: Oslo, Stockholm, Helsinki."

"Hello, Jack," a female voice said brightly, following him through the door. "Remember me? Stacey McKenzie? Stacey Simpson now. Police reporter with the *Morning-Telegraph*."

"What?" Quinn growled, startled by the rude interruption of his morning routine and looking back at this Amazonian dirty blond towering over him in a skimpy blue sun dress. "Have we met?"

Putting on his glasses, he looked more closely at the uninvited intruder, who was already well into his office and studying the photos on the wall. She turned and smiled menacingly.

"Yes, we've met, Jack," she replied. "I worked for Angela Flanagan, your old friend and business partner. Surely you remember all the hot times on the roof of that Diplomat Road mansion?"

"What?" a startled Quinn blurted again, stepping back and starting anew at the cheeky intruder who had the temerity to park herself in the leather chair next to his roll-top desk.

"Mind if I sit, luv?" Simpson asked as an afterthought, taking a cigarette from her purse and searching her purse in vain for a light. "Got a match?"

"I do mind, and no, I don't have a bloody match," Quinn yelped, face reddening. "Please do not smoke in this office. I do remember you now. You were on that infamous women's Olympic basketball team, weren't you?"

"Bingo," Stacey said. "Guess you didn't recognize me with clothes on, eh? Not to mention how fat I've gotten."

"What do you want, Ms. Simpson?" Quinn snarled, not buying the attempt at levity while trying not to stare at her sun dress. "I'm really busy this morning."

"Jack, I want to interview you about Angela Flanagan. We're doing a story about her magnificent life and mysterious death. We need your help."

"Bulldust," Quinn barked. "You're up to no-good. I know it. All you reporters are pond scum. Besides, who cares? She's been dead a long time."

"Jack, we're doing the story," Stacey replied evenly. "You can help us or not. We can't subpoena you."

"How's this?" Quinn spat. "I have no comment for your story and, what's more, I have no comment on my no comment. Now, please leave Ms. McKenzie, or Ms. Simpson, whatever your name is."

"Here's my card," Simpson said firmly, moving toward the door. "I'm available 24/7 if you change your mind.

"Not likely," Quinn snapped.

"Last chance," she replied, standing in the doorway. "Could be off the record. People came all the way from New York to do this story."

"What people?" Quinn couldn't help himself.

Stacey wrote Maggie's name on a piece of paper in her reporters' notebook and handed it to him.

"Jack," she said, whispering in his ear and leaning over in such a way he could see all the way to Pasadena, "tell Angela we got it right on Harold Holt. He really did defect."

"What?" Quinn shrieked, drawing back and staring. "What do you think I am? A bloody psychic?"

"Just tell her, Jack. We're going to clear her name as well."

With that, Simpson glided out the door with great style and disappeared into the passing foot traffic headed down to the beach. She waved without looking back.

CHAPTER 77

It's King's Cross, Jake

Botanical Gardens, Sydney, Australia
Monday, October 11, 2010
4:44 p.m.

Vic Cox was totally blind-sided by the e-mail he received the night before from Stacey Simpson, police reporter for the *Sydney Morning-Telegraph*. Though the retired New South Wales homicide detective generally had no use for reporters, Simpson was *the* exception. She always got it right in her stories, carefully protected her unnamed sources, and loved cops unapologetically in every way. Every with-it cop in Sydney knew the S.I. Simpson byline.

So out of the blue she asked him about the one murder from the King's Cross strangler era that didn't fit—the one that had stuck in his craw all these years. What could she possibly know about that case, he kept asking himself, and how could she possibly know it?

Seated on a park bench near the entrance to Sydney's famous botanical gardens, Cox watched as several male Frisbee players—probably students--tried to strut their stuff for the benefit of some females sunning themselves nearby. It wasn't working.

Probably should have finished my degree at the University of Sydney, Cox mused, instead of joining the Australian Army after a couple of years. Fuck it, he thought. Water under the dam. Or was it over the dam? Makes more sense.

Out of the corner of his eye he saw Simpson in the distance, coming toward him with her unmistakable swagger in her trademark sun dress. Feeling a mild surge down below, Cox took a deep breath and stood to greet his old friend, her face and chest sweating profusely in the prolonged heat wave that showed no signs of letting up.

"Stacey," he said affectionately, holding out his arms, smiling broadly, "come to Vic. If I didn't know better, I'd think you were a hooker in King's Cross."

The two amigos laughed and hugged for several seconds—a comic sight since Cox was only five-feet-five.

"Oh, Vic, I miss you so much," she cooed, finally releasing his head from her chest. "How come you don't come to John Barleycorn's anymore? Everyone always asks about you."

"Ah," Cox sniffed, "nothing worse than a retired cop hanging around pretending he still matters."

"But you're still doing the cold-case stuff on contract, right?" she asked, as both sat on the wooden bench.

"Yeah, yeah, when I'm not out fishing. Gives me a little extra income. I just don't have the shield anymore—or the Glock. BlackBerry is about all that's left."

Cox felt his left side and took the device off his belt. "I hate these bloody things," he said, checking his messages, "but I'm hooked now. Got your message last night. Really caught me off guard."

"Why?" Simpson asked, taking her reporter's notebook out of her purse.

"You first," he shot back. "Why this murder? You know we wrapped up the Strangler case years ago. Why bring this one up?"

"Ooooh, me thinks I have touched a nerve," Stacey replied excitedly. "Don't bullshit me, Vic Cox. Give it up."

"Give it up or get it up?"

They both laughed.

"Ok, this victim was never identified," Cox said carefully. "We tied him to the strangler, even got the conviction, but it was bogus. Strangler wasn't even in Sydney at the time. Had receipts to prove it. But what the fuck, we got him for nine murders. What was one more? Chief didn't want any loose ends hanging out."

"So you think it was a copycat?" Stacey asked, really animated now.

"Who knows?" Cox shrugged. "Bloke was drugged, supposedly sodomized and strangled, all in that order. Problem was the perp's semen wasn't found—unlike the other cases."

"What did this guy look like?"

"Middle-aged, beard, white hair, good build. No wallet, clothes, jewelry anywhere. Motel room also wiped down for prints."

Cox held out his palms, indicating why he was so mystified.

"Anything else?" Stacey asked.

"Well, his hands were bound behind him with handcuffs from the New York Police Department. Vintage 1980s. NYPD verified that for us. None of the other murders had anything like that."

"So, what does that tell you?"

"I don't know," Cox shrugged, annoyed at the one-sided interrogation. He usually asked the questions. "Maybe he was a gay cop from New York City. Frankly, I haven't a clue."

"Not likely," Stacey said absently, mind racing through the possibilities, the clues ringing bells in her head. "Did you bring the report?"

Cox handed her a large, thick tan envelope that he pulled from a badly weathered brown leather briefcase. "This is my own unauthorized copy, everything going back to January 3, 2003, the day the body was found. Police reports, coroner findings, morgue photos, crime-scene pictures. I want all this back. I could lose my pension if the brass knew I was talking to you. I can assure you; they don't want this particular case exhumed."

"What did happen to the body?"

"Buried in a pauper's grave in Rookwood Cemetery after a year. I was there when they put him in the ground. Not much of a sendoff."

"Wrong time, wrong place," Simpson said. "It's King's Cross, Jake."

Cox laughed. "Chinatown" was his favorite movie too.

"Your turn," Cox said. "Why do *you* care? What do you know that I don't?"

"Can't tell you yet," Stacey said, standing to go, both arms wrapped around the case file. "Tip is that if we can ID this guy, heavens will open up on another story we're working on—a really big one."

"What other story?" Cox demanded. "Come on, Stacey. You get, you gotta give."

"You gotta trust me on this one, Vic," Simpson said, starting to head back the way she came. "I'll call you when I'm done reading this."

She returned and gave Cox a quick kiss on the cheek. "Adore you, luv," she said brightly. "You're the best. I'll pay you back, I promise."

She laughed sexily, did a shimmy-shake and headed off. Cox stood and watched her figure recede until she exited the gardens and disappeared.

How on earth did she unearth this nugget of information almost nine years later—a secret that appeared sealed shut for the ages, he wondered. Who the fuck cares now? Why do they care? She needs to tread lightly here, he mused. Be careful what you seek but, more importantly, be careful *how* you seek it.

CHAPTER 78

Brave New World

Stacey Simpson's flat
Apartment #8, Dover Heights, Australia
Tuesday, October 12, 2010
6:56 a.m.

Simpson bolted upright on the pullout bed in her tiny studio apartment, head throbbing, upper body coated with grime and sweat, mind already in fifth gear. My God, that police report was a shocker. This tortured tale is finally starting to make sense, she thought. Why couldn't I see it before? Rafer Flanagan, aka Conor McCann, found dead in a seedy King's Cross motel room 16 months after he supposedly died at 9/11. The morgue photos prove it. The body markings are unmistakable. What a story.

Simpson sighed and went into the tiny bathroom, where she stared at her body in the full-length mirror on the back of the door. As she searched for the latest imperfections, she recalled the journalism chestnut that the first draft of a big enterprise story is like seeing someone naked for the first time.

Occasionally, the first take is a real work of art: terrific top, taut middle, great bottom that rounds everything out perfectly. Alas, in the real world, the top is often off point, the middle riddled with the flab and the only virtue of the bottom is that it mercifully ends the story. Try this one again, mate, the editor will tell the resentful reporter/writer. Needs another go.

Simpson laughed to herself as she recalled the news editor who told her that story, an old sea salt named William "Bad Moon" Rison, whose three loves in life were news, sex-starved spouses and Australian beer— probably not in that order. Died last year of a heart attack at age 68 in the arms of the French attache's wife. Poor man, Stacey recalled, he went out with a full-blown, Viagra-fired erection, semen still loaded in the chambers below, according to the autopsy report.

God, I still miss him, Simpson thought. What would he advise me today? Probably tell me to go after the Flanagan story on my own. 'Fuck the Yanks. You don't need them. Bunch of wimps and wusses. I served with them in Vietnam. Left messes wherever they went. They fucked you once, they'll do it again. You have this nearly figured out now. Go back to Jack Quinn. He's got the last key you need.'

Simpson sighed and walked over to the picture window overlooking Sydney Harbor downtown, bathed in the dawn's early light. So lovely and peaceful out there, she mused, so messy in here.

CHAPTER 79

The Big Break

Sun&Fun Travel, Bondi Beach
Sydney, Australia
Wednesday, Oct. 13, 2010
9:30 a.m.

Jack Quinn was fully expecting the enquiring reporter this time, happy even, as she showed up unannounced on his doorstep for the second time in three days.

"My, my, Ms. Simpson," he said with mock formality, "why am I not surprised to see you again? Have a seat. To what do I owe the pleasure of your visit this time?"

"My, who gave you the chill pill, Jack?" Simpson replied, smiling slightly. "Let me guess."

"Please do."

"Angela has agreed to be interviewed and you're going to lead me to her."

"Tell me," Quinn said slowly, "why are you so sure I know where she would be and why I would even care? She disappeared eight years ago."

"Come on, Jack. You adored that woman. No shame in that. A lot of people did. I did."

"I'll say," Quinn replied. "Woman had more lovers than Ava Gardner."

"Who?"

"Never mind. How about Samantha Jones? Your generation gets that."

Neither spoke for a time, each waiting for the other to make the second chess move.

"So?" Simpson said finally.

"So? So what?"

"Will you take me to her?"

"What else you got?" Quinn shot back. "You gotta give a little and, then just maybe, ye shall receive."

Stacey reached into her oversized leather purse and removed a large brown envelope. She pulled out four black-and-white photos and handed them to Quinn, one by one.

"Take a look," she said. "I now know who this John Doe is, and I want to find out what happened to him and why. You know him too."

Quinn eyed each photo carefully, saying nothing, examining them under a magnifying glass that he had in his desk drawer. They showed the naked victim in the motel room on the bed and at the morgue lying face up on a metal gurney. His aqua-blue eyes were wide open, a look of dismay frozen on his face.

"This is the first time I've seen these," Quinn blurted. "Not a pretty picture what you look like after you leave this world. Date rape drug didn't work very well. He fought us a lot harder than we thought."

Adrenalin surged through Simpson but she said nothing. The big story is almost mine, she thought, a cop reporter's dream. Edna Buchannan, legendary Miami Herald police reporter, take note.

"Go on," she said.

"Tell me about these Yank reporters you're working with," Quinn said. "How much do they know? What have you told them?"

"Not a thing," Simpson said. "They don't even know these photos exist. They just want to ID this guy. I haven't told them."

"I remember how the Yanks hung you out to dry on that Holt story," Quinn said, turning the knife. "That was bloody cruel. Why do you trust them this time?"

"I don't."

"Good," Quinn barked, voice hard, leaning forward. "Don't start now. Let me see what I can do. Be ready to travel on a moment's notice. Don't tell *anyone* what you're doing. Not your mother, not your boss, not the Yanks. Breathe a word to anyone and the deal is off."

"Ok. For the record, my mother and I haven't spoken since my divorce five years ago."

"Pack for at least a week's stay."

"How about where?"

"Think camel rides on the beach at sunset."

"Broome," Simpson said excitedly, clapping her hands. "I just knew she was on the West Coast. I just knew it. She loved it there."

"Just know," Quinn cautioned, "that the person you're going to see has a new life, new look, new identity. Angela Reilly Flanagan really is gone and so—most definitely, as you have discovered—is her husband. RIP, both of them."

CHAPTER 80

Cut the Crap

South Head
Watson's Bay, Australia
Friday, October 15, 2010
1:33 p.m.

The brutal heat wave in Sydney was showing no signs of abating. The temps downtown were headed toward a record shattering 100 degrees. Only people out in weather like this are mad dogs and American tourists, Vic Cox mused.

Why couldn't Simpson just talk to him on the phone? Why meet in person again? All the bloody hell out here at the south entrance to Sydney Harbor—even if it was a gorgeous spot. He was seated on a wooden bench next to the old lighthouse.

As Simpson approached him on the foot path, wearing a flimsy green sun dress, Cox stood up from the shaded bench and gave her a hug—a brief one. Both were ringing wet from the heat.

"What's so important we have to meet in person?" Vic asked. "Only the NSA listens to my calls."

"Who?"

"Never mind. Bad joke."

"Vic, listen," Stacey said excitedly, "I know who this guy is. I had to tell you in person."

"Fabulous," Cox relied. "Name, please."

"I can't, luv, not yet," Simpson said, sitting down on the bench. "I'm going out of town for a few days. I'll have the whole story nailed when I get back."

"Cut the crap, Stacey," Cox said. "I need the name. You make me come all the way out here on the ferry from downtown and now you won't tell me what's going on. This is bullshit."

"Vic, this is the biggest story of my sorry life," Simpson said, taking his hand. "I've got to do this right. No screw-ups this time. I must make sure I have everything nailed first. I just wanted to tell you in person."

"You haven't told me anything."

"I just love this spot. It's cooler and the harbor looks so beautiful. Sometimes I come here and just sit. It calms me down. Besides, I can't afford anyone seeing us together."

Cox stared at her hard, withdrawing his hand. "Stacey, are you alright? You're acting paranoid."

"Maybe with good reason," she said with no elaboration.

"Tell me you're not in danger," he said.

She laughed, kissed him on the cheek and stood. "Look, if I'm not back in a week, call out your old search-team buddies in the Australian Army. And you know where the hide-a-key is to my apartment. Your file is on my desk near the front door."

Cox stood but said nothing. I need a beer, he thought.

"Look, luv, this will be great for you as well," Simpson said. "Great publicity for the cold-case unit. You'll be the hero of my story, I promise."

"Yeah, yeah," Cox replied. "Action talks, bullshine walks. Don't call me again til you got a name."

Cox walked away without saying goodbye or looking back. He would regret that one day.

CHAPTER 81

Four Faces of Angela

Room 333, Bondi Beach Hotel
Sydney, Australia
Monday, October 18, 2010
5:15 p.m.

Rem Dabovitch slammed down the hotel phone, stared out at Bondi Bay for a few seconds and walked out onto the balcony, where Maggie Maye was reading the *New York Herald* on her laptop.

"Fucking Julie," Rem groused, in his usual off-duty cut-off jeans and tattered t-shirt, "now he wants to publish *The Searchlight* story this year so he can submit it for the 2010 Pulitzers. Says he wants a final version of the story on his desk by Christmas Eve. Christ, that only gives me a little more than two months for all the reporting and writing."

"Poor baby," Maggie said. "I never had two months to do a story in my entire reporting career. Two days, two weeks max, was more like it."

"You were a foreign correspondent, Maggie," Rem said. "I'm an investigative reporter. Two entirely different animals. Hell, it took me two years to do that mob story. People don't understand how hard these stories are--the degree of difficulty involved. Even other reporters don't understand. They think we're lazy. Newsroom penis envy."

"Stop whining," Maggie replied. "This story won't be that hard to report. If people won't talk to you by phone, just show up on their doorstep and see what happens. My guess is once you get started, you'll have trouble getting them to shut up."

"I suppose," Rem replied, not convinced. "Julie also told me just now he's worried things will start to leak if we don't get the news story on the record as soon as possible. Ari III knows I'm working on the story and Julie's worried he might try to sabotage it with a bogus preemptive announcement."

"Ari's not that creative," Maggie said. "And Julie worries about everything. The man is completely paranoid. Pulitzer timing makes sense, though. If you can win number three, it will do wonders for the book and movie."

"You sign up with people like Julie and you gotta live with their insatiable demands," Rem groused. "They pay you a ton of money and they think they own you. They do, I guess."

"Ok," Maggie said, taking charge. "here's the real news: Stacey sent me the Flanagan memo late last night and it's terrific. Great background info. Nobody knew Angela better than Stacey. By the way, she also left me a voice mail saying she's leaving town to check out a hot tip. Said she'd be back in a week."

"A hot tip?"

"That's all she said. It was very curt."

"We can't depend on her," Rem said. "The woman's a total flake."

"She told me you liked her norks?"

"Her what?"

"Never mind," Maggie said, laughing. "The memo said Angela was like a layer cake: charming and beautiful on top; artistic and creative one layer down; cunning and selfish on layer three; and deeply neurotic and insecure at the bottom."

"Hmmm," Rem said. "I like it. Four Faces of Angela."

"We can be more original than that," Maggie said. "Anyway, memo had all kinds of detail about how the rape in Chicago went down, how the cops treated her like a drug addict, how disgusted her mother was, how she had to fly to Switzerland for an abortion. No wonder she's a little unhinged.

"Anyway, the memo's a great road map for you. Between this and the Carella Report you've got the research 90% done."

"Yeah, yeah, typical editor," Rem said. "You guys never get it. I got a million holes to fill, and I have to double and triple confirm everything important. Story must be bullet proof."

"Better get cracking then," Maggie said unsympathetically. "You should try to interview everyone important in person and this is a big bloody country. Good for the air miles. Let's give Julie exactly what he wants. Figure eight weeks for the reporting and a week to write a 5,000-word news story. I'll set up a meeting on 24 December in his office at Trump Tower. We'll show him a rough draft then."

"And what exactly are you going to do in the meantime?"

"I think I'll sit on my butt in this lovely hotel room and rewrite S.S. 4.0. My editor says Stella needs a change of scenery. Wants the murder set in Martha's Vineyard, her old stomping ground, instead of stale old DC. What better place for me to write that than Sydney, Australia?

Maggie laughed. "Doesn't matter. I know the Vineyard like the nose on my face. Bernie and I rented a home on South Beach every August for years."

She laughed again. "God, this is fun. Back on the trail of a hot news story on a mysterious continent south of the equator and I get to rewrite my novel in a hip hotel by a cool urban beach. Is this real? Pinch me, please."

CHAPTER 82

Hell's Paradise

King's Cascades, Prince Regent River
Western Australia
Saturday, Oct. 23, 2010
4:11 p.m.

The 77-foot cabin cruiser was in idle mode, engine purring quietly, the 88-degree day simply picture perfect. It was a scene in paradise to die for.

The couple on the top deck—protected from the sun by a blue canopy, each sipping a can of beer—traded the binocs back and forth, straining to make out the details playing along the riverbank 400 meters away.

"Oh, my," she said, "looks like they're fighting over her. Had no idea. I can even see the basketball tattoo on her lower back. Happy Birthday, Stacey."

He took the binoculars back and focused for a long time, maybe a minute. "Pretty sure she's gone," he said finally, putting the glasses down. "She didn't even see him coming. She didn't say a word—no scream, no nothing—when he took her down. Not before he held her up in his mouth like some sort of trophy."

"I'm glad I stayed below deck," she deadpanned.

The couple continued sipping their beers. Fat free and muscled, she was wearing a brown Aussi sun hat, designer sunglasses and cheap flip-flops. He had on a Chicago Cubs baseball hat and a blue speedo that showcased his flabby physique.

"Just think of it," she said finally, wonder in her softly accented voice. "You're celebrating your 33rd birthday and you're swimming near a beautiful waterfall in one of the most pristine places on earth. You just finished reporting a story that is going to make your career and you're so excited you forget the about the salties. Big mistake. There you are, floating on your back and, boom, a reptile whose ancestors date back 75 million years hits you like a Japanese bullet train. Waive bye-bye, darling. Bye-bye."

She thought for a moment and smiled. "Worked out well. So much for her stupid scoop."

The couple clinked cans. "You're truly evil, you know that," Quinn said, smiling. "Telling her it was safe to go swimming here. Didn't hurt she was buzzed."

Angela shuddered and wrapped a beach towel around her. "Let's get out of here. This place is creeping me out."

CHAPTER 83

No Backing Out Now

Offices of LC&J
57ᵗʰ Floor, Trump Tower, Manhattan
Friday, Dec. 24, 2010
4:30 p.m.

The Jackal closed the story on his Apple computer screen and exhaled loudly. He stared hard at the bedraggled pair sitting across from him. Numb from their 20-hour flight from Sydney that landed two hours earlier, Maggie and Rem looked like—no other way to say it—shit.

It was the Julie Levitsky show from here on out, they knew. The 5,000-word news package had to be fully edited, illustrated, lawyered and launched by 11:55 on New Year's Eve. Get it done, holidays be damned, they knew.

"Okay," the Fat Man said. "The good news is I like the bottom 90% of the story, the narrative of how all this went down. Great reading. Riveting. Ari III will be toast and I'm sure the family will sell out once this shit hits the fan. They won't have a choice."

Julie paused and looked directly at both journalists. "The bad news," he continued, "is I don't like the top. Rem, this ain't no feature story. I don't want a long windup. If this were a baseball game, the runner would have stolen home and be back in the dugout by the time you let go of the ball.

"Get to the point. This isn't the *New Yorker* or *Vanity Fair*. Think *New York Post*. Each of the first 15 graphs should have tightly packed nuggets of news that explode and blow the readers away."

"*New York Post*?" Maggie asked.

"Fucking A," Julie shot back. "At least for this story. Lots of smart people read the *Post*. It's entertaining and it doesn't waste the readers' time. By the way, did I ever tell you I was an investigative reporter at my high school newspaper in suburban Chicago."

"Yes, Julie," Maggie replied, "but I'd love to hear that story again. For the 16th time."

"Don't be sarcastic. We did some great exposes," he said. "The *Evanston Review* was always quoting our stuff after we scooped them."

"I'm sure," Maggie deadpanned. "It was journalism's great loss when you went to law school."

"That was Loyola Law School, by the way," Julie said. "Great Jesuit school. Train real lawyers there. Not like the blood suckers and sycophants that come out of the Ivy League.

"Ok, back to business. Rem, when is your interview with Ari?"

"Tuesday at 3 p.m., in his office."

"Be prepared for anything," Julie said. "Ari's desperate. You've got him cornered. The Steinbergs are the gold standard in this business. Be tough but respectful. Don't provoke him to do something rash."

"Like what?"

"Run out and hold a press conference denouncing the story before it even appears. Put his own spin on things before we even publish.

"Maggie, I want this story posted on *The Searchlight* web site at exactly 11:55 next Friday night East Coast time. Then, I want you to send out a press release the next morning, on New Year's Day around 11 a.m., saying the story is out there. Hit the highlights in the press release and say Rem will be available for interviews. Rem, you might want to send out a tweet telling everyone the two-time Pulitzer-Prize winning Serbian Assassin is back in the game."

"Hah," Rem said. "Usually takes me 140 characters just to clear my throat."

"So I noticed," Julie shot back. "Maggie, make sure all the cable news producers know the story has been posted. It will be New Year's Day. They'll be dying for news. Give CNN a head start. They're the lead steer. The rest will follow.

"Rem, be ready to do the Sunday morning talk shows. Maggie, call Howie Kurtz at CNN. This is right in his wheelhouse, and it will be breaking news on Saturday afternoon. Just what he loves. Also call Bill O'Reilly's guys. Roger Ailes hates the *Herald*."

Levitsky paused for a moment to catch his breath.

"Now, come Tuesday morning, Jan. 4, the *Herald's* stock will be in free-fall. Like a dead body thrown from an airplane. That's where my investors step in. Buy as many market shares as possible on the cheap and make an offer for the rest at a slight premium to the daily close. Include the *Herald* and the three regionals. Price will be a third of the market cap three months ago and a tenth of the value three years ago."

"What's our potential jail time for this kind of scheme?" Rem asked, trying to smile.

"Let me handle that," Julie shot back. "What's legal depends on the quality of your lawyers and I have the best in the business. Don't go wobbly on me now, Rem. You're in this up to your eyeballs."

Levitsky walked over to the coat rack and put on his black fur-lined London Fog overcoat, tailor made for his prodigious frame.

"I gotta go to another one of these fundraisers at the Plaza," he said sourly. "On Christmas Eve, for God's sake. These political types have no shame. Maggie, make it happen. I want a revised top on my desk Monday morning. Merry F-ing Christmas."

Levitsky roared with laughter and disappeared out the door without further ado.

CHAPTER 84

Lovesick Prince

Office of the Publisher, New York Herald
Herald Tower, Midtown Manhattan
Tuesday, Dec. 28, 2010
3:03 p.m.

His world crumbling, Ari Steinberg III had the look of someone about to walk the plank. His eyes radiated dread and his pallor was ghostly. He hadn't shaved in days.

Seated across from him was the infamous Rembrandt T. Dabovitch III, who dressed as you might expect for an investigative reporter: standard-issue blue blazer, gray slacks, wrinkled white cotton shirt, light-blue striped polyester tie, badly scuffed black loafers. Typical attire in the newsroom.

"Mr. Dabovitch," Ari began, slowly, formally, "allow me in the best tradition of our business to cut right to the battle scene. I am prepared to offer you a job as an investigative reporter on our national staff at an annual salary of $190,000. Starting Jan. 4."

Steinberg paused only briefly before landing the real bombshell. "I only ask that you cease and desist on the Angela Flanagan story. As they sometimes say in the newsroom: 'No story here. Let's move on.'"

Dabovitch didn't react at first to an offer he had been expecting, albeit not so soon and not so directly. He looked away for a few seconds, shifted positions in his chair and looked back at the *Herald* publisher.

"Mr. Steinberg," he replied, "with all due respect, you know I can't do that. We both know this is an important story. Killing it wouldn't pass the smell test."

"Hah," Steinberg shot back, tone hard now, "funny you say that. How can an unemployed investigative reporter afford to spend two months on the other side of the world researching an investigative story for a website that has yet to publish its first story? Talk about flunking the smell test."

"I have terrific backing from private investors," Rem replied. "Public-spirited types who prefer to remain private."

"I'll bet," Steinberg sneered.

He paused and looked across the office suite at the huge oil painting of the original Ari T. Steinberg—the patriarch who published the first edition 122 years ago as a journal for the New York shipping industry.

"You know, Mr. Dabovitch, that's my grandfather over there," Ari said. "Never met the man. Died the day before I was born. Tough time for my dad. I was third in line for the throne at the time, so I wasn't that big a deal. Mom wanted a girl."

"Your grandfather is a legend," Rem observed. "I loved reading those histories of the *Herald* in journalism school. Your grandfather led the way in keeping public officials in New York City honest and corruption free."

"That's a load of crap, Mr. Dabovitch," Ari said, springing out of his chair and walking over to the picture window, hands in his gray-striped trouser pockets. "My grandfather was a ruthless bastard of a businessman who wrote unflattering stories about his enemies and flattering ones about his friends. Good journalism had nothing to do with it. It was survival of the smartest and most cunning in the spirit of those times. Those J-school histories are just PR. For all the money we give these schools, they better say that."

"But I digress, Mr. Dabovitch. You did not come here for a history lesson. Here's what I must tell you: there is no way I can answer your questions on Mrs. Flanagan. The practical statute of limitations has expired on that tawdry saga. Seems like a hundred years ago now--different era, different business, different values. It's Century No. 21 and we're fighting for our financial lives—for my grandfather's public legacy, if you will. That's what matters now. You can quote me on that. Other than that, I have nothing more to say."

"All right, sir," Rem said, standing to go, "I'll give Betsy Wright a heads-up later this week on what you should expect."

"You found her, didn't you?" Ari blurted out.

"Pardon?"

"Mr. Dabovitch, I know a lot of people think I'm clueless, but I am not, I assure you. I know Angela's alive. I can feel it."

"We found no hard evidence of that. I looked, believe me. I also think you may be right. My gut tells me the same thing. Underestimate that woman at your peril."

"God help me, but I'm still haunted by what happened down there," Ari said, still gazing absently at the holiday crowds below, his voice starting to quiver. "I cared for her very deeply. She was an amazing woman."

"If she is indeed still alive, Jack Quinn would know where she is," Rem said. "You know him, right? He wouldn't talk to me."

"Yea, I remember him," Ari replied with no enthusiasm. "One of my many rivals for her attentions."

Whoa, Rem thought, now we're getting somewhere.

"Please go now," Ari said, realizing candor was not his ally here. "Please see yourself out. I can't say it was nice to meet you. Just know an unfair story will destroy this great newspaper. Do you really want to live with that?"

Hmm, Rem mused as he headed to the corporate elevator, shades of the wimpy, lovesick King Edward VIII and the scheming trollop Wallis Simpson. Abdication will be his only recourse when this story breaks, he thought, smiling to himself. Adios to the House of Steinberg.

CHAPTER 85

Clock is Ticking

Office of the Publisher, New York Herald
Herald Tower, Midtown Manhattan
Tuesday, Dec. 28, 2010
5:55 p.m.

Ike Citron stood abruptly and held his hands in the sign of a T, like a basketball coach managing the clock in the final minute of the game.

"Ok, Ari, time out," Ike said sharply. "I've heard enough. You're right. This is bad. Real bad."

Ike paused, letting his admonition hang in the air for Ari to fully absorb. "You need to get ahead of this story," he opined. "Otherwise, it will eat you alive. You won't stand a chance."

"Will you help me, Ike?" Ari asked plaintively. "I've got no place else to turn."

Working perfectly, Ike thought. Never seen Ari looking so bad—and that's saying something. Misery usually adorns his face like those tattoos on Mike Tyson's forehead.

"Not til you pay up," Ike said coldly. "You know the paper still owes us $500,000. Can you make good on that?"

"That was Dad's doing," Ari replied, shaking his head. "Wilbur Ross told the board your fees were 'obscene' and had to be renegotiated. Dad always listens to Wilbur."

"Guess we have nothing further to discuss then," Ike said, putting on his coat. "We don't work for free. The only obscenity here is that your firm did not pay its bills."

"Ike, please," Ari pleaded, grabbing Citron's arm and holding him from leaving. "I'll pay you out of my own pocket on this one. Dad won't even know."

Ike looked up at the ceiling, mentally mapping the next move. "Can you and Roberta go to Chicago tomorrow?" he asked finally.

"Guess so. Why? What for? What does Roberta have to do with this?"

"Trust me," Ike said, moving out the door. "Get the corporate jet ready to fly out of Teterboro at 9 a.m. Tell Roberta to dress like a Republican. And wire $100,000 to my personal account by midnight. No money, no deal."

CHAPTER 86

Just Like Tiger Woods

The Zoe Z. Zelinsky Show
ZZZ Productions, Chicago, Illinois
Wednesday, Dec. 29, 2010
2:33 p.m.

As the unrivaled doyenne of afternoon blather, 'Girl Talk' host Zoe Z. Zelinsky was always seeking gossip from the powerful and infamous that would make the evening news, set Twitter afire or impact the stock market shortly before the afternoon close in New York. A former edgy fashion writer on Fleet Street in London, she sought a talk show with a female flavor and 60 Minutes edge—ones with 'pop, crackle and snap,' as she liked to put it.

Today, she knew, mixing metaphors, she had a ten-strike.

"Now, audience, listen up,' she said in her best Brit accent, gliding across the stage in regal style, microphone in left hand, "I've got a big scoop for us this afternoon, something hot off the presses."

She smiled slyly and plunged ahead: "We've devoted so many shows to coping with life's addictions—alcohol, gambling, food, no food, drugs legal and illegal—but there is one we have never addressed because it is so taboo. It's the one that got Tiger Woods into so much trouble. Yes, audience, sex addiction. It's real, it destroys families, and it's treatable. Men are 95% of its victims. Audience, please welcome two brave souls, talking for the very first time, Ari and Roberta Steinberg, whose family owns the *New York Herald*, must reading every day for anyone who is anyone."

The all-female audience rose to its feet and cheered on cue as the Steinbergs strolled hand-in-hand across the stage to their seats, each giving Zoe a brief hug.

"Ari, Roberta, so nice to see you on such short notice," Zoe began. "Your decision to go public is a true profile in courage. Let's get to it. Ari, I believe you have something to say to America and the world."

"Thank you so much, Zee," Ari began, slowly, formally, looking ever so upscale in an open-necked white shirt and dark-blue pin-striped suit. "I watch your show all the time and I'm always moved by the candor of your guests when they so openly and so honestly discuss problems that are so personal and so painful."

Ari halted for dramatic effect, allowing the poetry of his 'sos' to marinate for a time. He smiled at Roberta next to him on the guest couch. She was wearing a dark-pink St. John knit dress and matching shoes. She didn't return the smile. Ari took a long drink from his water glass, breathed deeply and took the plunge.

"I'm announcing today that I am taking a 90-day leave of absence from my job as publisher and CEO of the *New York Herald* and will enter the renowned Hazelton Hospital in Minnesota. I am seeking treatment for my long-time addiction to sexual intercourse. I need to deal with this once and for all."

A few in the audience snickered, some others applauded politely. Ari glanced at Roberta and reached for her hand without success.

"Mrs. Steinberg, what say you?" Zelinsky asked. "Standing by your man?"

"Zoe," she replied, looking like she was about to undergo a wisdom-tooth extraction, "my husband is a good father. He doesn't drink, smoke or do drugs. Unfortunately, he is trying against long odds to save a dying family business. He needs help. He is under great pressure. That is all I have to say at this point."

"Ari, your turn," Zoe said.

"That's right, Zee. I never expected to run the family business, but when my two older brothers were killed in a plane crash, I was thrown into a role for which I had no formal training. I was a lawyer and venture capitalist, not a newspaper executive. And let me tell you: when you are the publisher of the world's greatest newspaper, smart, beautiful women swarm to you like moths to light. Hey, I'm just a nerdy Jewish kid from Bronxville, New York. What could I do?"

A few in the audience laughed along with Ari, but Zelinsky held up her hand, indicating the interview niceties were over and it was time to get real. The trap was set.

"Ari," Zoe said, "I can just hear the women of the world saying: 'This is just lame. He's just another cheating husband caught with his clothes off.' Your response?"

"Hah, good point," Ari replied weakly, smile starting to curdle. "All I can say to my lovely wife, my family, my employees, my stockholders, my stakeholders is watch what I do from now on. I plan to return to work in a few months rejuvenated, refreshed and ready to take the *Herald* to new zeniths in the 21st century. Tiger Woods got through this. So can I."

"Why are you doing this now?' Zelinsky asked coldly.

"No reason," Ari answered, smile all but gone now. "There were some rumors and gossip out there, something to do with a female reporter who died years ago in the line of duty. Just rubbish."

"Audience, Mr. and Mrs. Ari and Roberta Steinberg," Zoe said, rising to her feet. "Give it up for the man dealing with his demons and the woman standing at his side. Good luck, Ari. You're going to need it."

The audience applauded politely as the Steinbergs exited stage right —not holding hands.

CHAPTER 87

As Clueless as Hillary

Aboard the –30—
Glide Path to Teeterboro Airport
Teeterboro, New Jersey
Wednesday, Dec. 29, 2010
8:18 p.m.

Ari Steinberg fastened his seatbelt and lightly tapped his wife on the shoulder as she sat with her back to him, sobbing quietly, incessantly, head on a pillow against the bulkhead.

"Bobby, honey, please,' he said quietly, 'we're about to land. Fasten your seat belt. You know the rules."

"Fuck my seatbelt, Ari Steinberg," she hissed without turning around, "and fuck you too while we're at it. You made a fool out of me this afternoon on national television. I looked as clueless as Hillary Clinton. You were supposed to admit you are a sex addict—not addicted to sexual intercourse, you dumb bastard. Don't you know the difference?"

"Honey, please," Ari pleaded, "let's not quibble over wording."

"If that's the case," she spat, sitting up and looking at him, eyes red with rage and hurt, "why haven't we had sexual intercourse in three years?"

"Honey, honey, you did great," Ari replied, trying unsuccessfully to hold her hand. "Even Zoe said later what a trooper you are."

"Fuck her too and that phony accent. She's just a low-life Aussie pretending she's English. What a fraud. That awful Ike Citron arranged this stunt, didn't he? I thought you fired him years ago."

"He just thought it would help us get ahead of the story," Ari said lamely, inadvertently opening another Pandora's Box. "That's what they do in his world."

"You asshole," she hissed. "I don't even know what story you're talking about. Must be that awful Flanagan woman. That slut. May she roast in hell. But you know what, Ari? I don't give a damn anymore. You've abused me for the last time."

She sat up straight, fastened her belt and dabbed at her watery eyes with the warm towel handed out by a flight attendant.

"As soon as we're on the ground," she said quietly, "I'm going to hire the meanest, nastiest, most expensive divorce lawyer in New York City and sue your ass for all it's worth. Mark my words, Ari Steinberg the 3d. I'm going to get my 10 pounds of flesh out of this sorry family business before it goes broke. Meanwhile, fuck all the groupies you want—all the ones flying so close to that randy flame of yours. Maybe if I'm lucky, you'll run into Lorena Bobbitt."

CHAPTER 88

Return of the Serbian Assassin

Press Release, PR News Wire
Saturday, Jan. 1, 2011
1 p.m.

Veteran Scribe Launches Web Site;
Pulitzer Winner Exposes Major
Wrongdoing at New York Herald

New York (*PR Newswire*)—Two-time Pulitzer Prize winner Rembrandt T. Dabovitch III, one of the nation's premier investigative reporters, has founded a website dedicated to exposing corruption and wrongdoing at all levels of society public and private.

The news site, known as *The Searchlight*, published its maiden story late last night that detailed extensive malfeasance and corruption in the publisher's office of the *New York Herald*. To read the story, go to: www.thesearchlight.com.

Dabovitch's reporting unmasks a scheme of kickbacks, which was carried out in partnership with one of the paper's foreign correspondents, Sydney-based Angela Reilly Flanagan. She reportedly died in a drowning accident eight years ago near Melbourne. Flanagan and Steinberg were secret lovers, according to the story.

The Searchlight story says that Flanagan wrote the copy for a long-running series of full-page ads known as "Fyi South Pacific" that promoted Australia and New Zealand as business hubs and affordable tourist destinations for North Americans. The ads were paid for by the Australian visitors' bureau, with which Flanagan had a very close relationship. Mrs. Flanagan received cash payments for her work, which she used to support her cocaine habit, the story said.

Mr. Dabovitch won his Pulitzer Prizes as an investigative reporter for the *New York Daily News.* His web site includes his full resume and links to all his major stories.

Mr. Dabovitch is available for interviews. Requests should be emailed to <u>RemDabIII@hotmail.com</u> or texted to 212-HOTTYPE (468-9873).

The Searchlight is being funded by public-spirited private investors who wish to remain anonymous and are trying to breathe new life into investigative journalism in America at a time when the nation's metropolitan newspapers are experiencing severe financial difficulties.

For more information, e-mail Ike Citron at <u>DrSpin666@gmail.com</u>.

---30---

CHAPTER 89

The Final Goodbye

Home of Ari Steinberg Jr., Palm Beach, Florida
Sunday, Jan. 2, 2011
9:49 p.m.

Ari Jr.'s facial expression said it all: disgust his only living son and namesake made a giant jackass of himself yet again. Only this time his fuckup couldn't be covered up or papered over. No turning back. It had gone viral.

The *Herald's* stock tanked last week as the sages on Wall Street absorbed the news that the paper's CEO was being hospitalized for sex addiction. What a crock, the Street said in unison. Then, some Woodward-Bernstein type was all over the talk shows this morning detailing how the paper allowed one of its reporters in the Sydney bureau to write advertising copy for the Australia visitors bureau.

Ari III said nothing, squirming on the leather couch in his dad's library, the only place where the family's most sensitive secrets were discussed. Outsiders were never allowed in, including lawyers and financial advisers.

The stillness in the room was deafening. "Say something," his father finally demanded. "Defend yourself, for Gods' sake."

"It wasn't that bad, Dad," Ari III said miserably, curly brown sticking out every which way, bloodshot eyes drooping badly from days of little sleep. "Everything's being taken out of context."

"What on earth was that interview on "Girl Talk"? the father demanded. "Sex addiction? Are you insane? Comparing yourself to Tiger Woods? Lamest thing I've ever heard."

Ari III stared at his 83-year-old father, a man who still intimidated him after all these years.

"Roberta wants a divorce, Dad. I got a hand-delivered letter last night at the Dakota. She's hired Oscar Rodriguez. One of the B-52s of the New York divorce bar. Mean as a salt-water crocodile."

"I don't blame her," Ari Jr. replied coldly. "You made a complete fool of her—and yourself—on national television. Let me tell you about a hand-delivered letter that I received here this morning. It's from O'Malley, Blankstein, Cruz and Sebastiani. You know them?"

Ari III shook his head.

"Well, you should. Talk about mean as a crocodile. Brendan O'Malley has represented every ruthless corporate raider going back to the days of Mike Milken. They want to know if the Herald's for sale."

"Did they name a price?" Ari III asked, perking up for the first time.

"Didn't say. I'm guessing $300 million for everything."

"Three hundred million? That's a bloody insult. Honey Shaw just sold that crappy web site of hers for $300 million and they don't produce anything. Last time I looked, our market cap was $600 million."

"Well, you haven't looked lately, son. It's been speeding south faster than drunken college students on spring break. Fell below $400 million Friday. You should really keep track of that."

Neither Steinberg spoke for a time, gloom shrouding the room.

"Look, son," Ari Jr. said finally, "O'Malley and I talked this afternoon and he told me off the record his clients only want the Herald brand, not the newspaper. They'll probably shut the dead-tree edition as soon as possible."

"Look, Dad," III replied plaintively, "I really do need some time off. Rethink everything. I've always done what you wanted but it's never been enough. I'm not cut out for this job. Truth be told, newspapers are going to die sooner or later anyway no matter what we do. You can't swim into a tsunami."

"Are you really going to Hazelton?"

"I suppose. Said so on national TV."

"Ike Citron set up that interview, didn't he?" Jr. said angrily. "The guy's a charlatan. I thought we fired him years ago."

"The audience seemed sympathetic to the addiction angle," III said lamely. "Unfortunately, Wall Street doesn't have the same heart."

"Wall Street doesn't have a heart, you blockhead," Dad barked. "You should know that. So should Ike."

"Dad, listen," III said, standing up for the first time, "That Searchlight story was horribly exaggerated. Made Angela look terrible."

"That woman had you by the balls," Jr. said harshly. "Everyone could see that except you and your clueless wife."

"Dad, forget all that for a moment. I know a guy in Sydney who can tell me if she is still alive. I just *know* she is and I've got to go there. I still miss her terribly, Dad, even after all these years. She's the only woman who's ever made me happy."

Both Steinbergs were standing now, a few feet apart, most of the anger gone from the room.

"You really do need some time off," Dad said softly. "Pack up your office in New York and get going. I'll take over as acting CEO for a while. Sort this mess out. Come back when you're ready."

The two remained apart, tears starting to form. Ari Jr. finally reached out to his third son—the one who always seemed so badly miscast.

"I love you, buddy," the father said, hugging Ari III hard. "Always will. You gave it your best shot. Your mother would be very proud. Go find what you're looking for. Maybe something good will happen."

The men held on to each other a few moments longer. Ari III then stepped back, did an about face and headed out the door without saying goodbye.

CHAPTER 90

Michael Who?

The Rim Gym
Rockaway Beach, Queens, New York
Friday, Jan. 7, 2011
3:13 p.m.

All six-foot-nine, 285 pounds of him, Jim 'The Rim' Robison towered over his client, leaning in slightly, barking in his best drill instructor accent--the one the DIs learn at Parris Island.

"Get it up, you pussyyyy," Robison ordered in that inimical sing-song style. "Get it up. You can do it."

Going from grunt to scream, the weightlifter barely completed the push and let the 350-pound weight crash down on the metal stand, sending a thunderous clap around the cavernous exercise room. A few heads turned and smiled tightly. Got to give that dude some room, they thought. Dion DeStefano is as stone-cold as they come.

"You know, Rim," Dion said, sitting up and toweling off his neck and face, "there's not a man anywhere who called me a pussy and lived to talk about it. I'll make an exception in your case."

The best friends laughed and did a fist bump, *de rigueur* among the muscle heads who patronized the newest Rim Gym in Queens, opened almost a year now. Already it was *the* place to be seen among cops, firemen, construction workers, professional athletes, criminals and all the other testosterone-fueled Lou Ferrigno wannabes. Even a few Jillian Michaels disciples hung out there, beauty for the beasts to ogle.

"So," Robison said, "I forgot to ask. What did that reporter tell you yesterday? Forgot his name. Any sign of Raffy?"

"Nah," Dion growled. "Says Raffy just disappeared into thin air eight years ago when he went back to Australia to get even with his wife."

He paused, then added: "Guess we know something about that."

The hitmen laughed and did another bump.

"I think she got to him somehow," DeStefano continued. "If he were alive, he would have gotten word to me, somehow, some way. He asked for half the insurance money and she iced him."

"Yea, probably right," Robison said. "I saw her run out of the house in her bathrobe that night after we gave her that note, but she sped off so fast we couldn't follow her. Raffy was waiting in the car a block away. It was like she knew we were out there."

Robison shook his head: "Then, early the next morning, Raffy gets a call on his cell phone from some guy who says he knows where Angela is. Says to come alone to some motel in the nightclub district. And that's the last I heard from him. I should have never left him alone."

"She's out there somewhere, having a great time," Dion said, standing up and waiving to one of his muscle buddies across the weight room. "I can feel it. I told that reporter he better let me know if he has any idea where she is. I want an exact address. I don't care how long this takes."

"What did he say?"

"Said he would. He owes me big-time. I'm the one who told him what happened to Raffy after 9/11. He's still reporting this out. Guess some other reporter down there has also gone missing. Could all be connected."

"Well," Robison said, "I got a couple of Yakuzas on call. Man/woman team. Can fly to Sydney on a moment's notice. Speak good English, know Australia well, blend in perfectly. They never miss. Done at least 10 kills down there. All drug stuff. I got other people as well.

Motorcycle gang banger on the West Coast in case we need someone there.”

“Put 'em all on notice,” Dion said. “I’ll put up the 50 grand myself.”

“Sheeeeit,” Rim scoffed. “I’ll do it myself for that kind of money.”

“Not a chance,” Dion fired back. “Six-foot-nine-inch neeeegroes don’t blend in very well in the land of the pale face. Not trying that again.”

Both men laughed.

“Dion, you ever wonder what would have happened if we hadn’t gotten into that fight in the Garden that night,” Robison asked seriously.

“No.”

“I would have gone to UCLA and been an All-American and you would have played semi-pro ball in Romania.”

“Listen to me, Rim.,” DeStefano said, laughing and hocking a big one into his towel. “I don’t want to hear any more glory days bullshit. The next Bill Russell, my left nut. That sportswriter was just blowing smoke up your ass. Michael Olowokandi is more like it.”

“Who?”

“My point exactly,” Dion said, smiling. “My point exactly.”

CHAPTER 91

Staying Behind

Capital Hilton Bar
16th St., Washington, D.C. NW
Friday, Jan. 7, 2011
8:08 p.m.

Maggie sipped her first martini—straight up, two olives—and glanced at Rem, sitting next to her at the bar, drinking a lime and tonic.

"Why the long face?" she asked. "You should be on cloud nine. *The Searchlight* is the talk of the town, the Steinbergs are toast and Julie is about to make you rich. I believe they call that a Hat Trick."

"Yea," Rem replied, "good fortune is raining down on me in buckets and I've got a bad case of the blues. Not exactly sure why. All the criticism on social media, I guess. Both left and right. I'm either destroying a great newspaper or peddling kinky porn masquerading as news."

"Nonsense," Maggie said. "Just background noise. Pay no attention. Focus on facts. Millions of hits on your first story, a possible $500,000 advance on the book and potential movie rights in seven figures. And best of all, you ex won't get a dime because your divorce was final on New Year's Eve."

Rem laughed for the first time. "I really owe you, Maggie," he said, taking her hand. "You're a great friend. I only focus on the negative."

"Typical journalist," she replied. "Disease we all have. Listen, I meant to tell you that you were terrific on Howie the K last Sunday and the O'Reilly interview Monday night was off the charts.

"Thanks," he said. "Truth be told, I didn't watch either one. Cable news isn't journalism anymore. Have to watch the BBC if you want to know what's going on in the world."

"Go with the flow, Rem," she said. "Don't fight what you can't control."

"Listen," he said, changing the subject, "I'm going into hibernation now. Julie wants the first draft of the book by March 31. Already has the title: Fall of the House of Steinberg: How America's leading newspaper empire was undone by corruption, incompetence and debauchery."

"Ooooh," Maggie said, laughing. "Debauchery. I love it."

"Yeah, Julie really does have a tabloid soul. He should be buying the *New York Post.*"

"Speaking of that, you know Julie wants me to be executive editor of the *Herald* once the deal closes in a few months, right?"

"Yeah, you mentioned that might happen."

"Why don't you come work for me once you're done with the book?' she said. "Be my chief investigative reporter in D.C. Document how corrupt Washington has become, how bloated the bureaucracies are, how fascism American style is already here. Julie wants bomb-throwers. Like his boyhood hero, Mike Royko. Chance of a lifetime for you."

Rem said nothing for a time, glancing at the digital clock behind the bar. He took some unsalted peanuts from the pewter tray between them. The lonesome highway is calling, he mused.

"Maggie," he began, "you ever see 'The Paper'?"

"Please," she said, "no more movies. I know. You've seen 'Deadline USA' 50 times."

"Fourteen, but who's counting?"

"Please, *no mas.*"

"Ok, ok," he said, "Point is, I love *newspapers.* I love their history. I love how they impact the daily conversation. I love the pop that comes when they have a monster scoop or investigation. The shit storms they set off, the reforms they set in motion.

"The magnificent 500-ton presses coming alive at midnight, the first editions coming off the assembly line four hours later. I call it the smell of the ink, the roar of the presses. And I love how you start over again every morning. On to the next edition. Gotta a paper to put out."

"Very poetic," Maggie said. "It's a business. Get a grip."

"Listen," he continued, "I know Julie will eventually kill the print edition and I don't want to be part of killing something I love. To what end? The new, new journalism? Tweets, canned interview via email, digital stories that fade even before the sun sets. Bogie was right at the time: being a reporter *was* the world's greatest job. Not anymore."

Rem finished his drink, stood to go and put two $20 bills on the bar. "I don't think so, Maggie. Thanks anyway. I'll just write my books and tend to my investigations. The other side of the river doesn't interest me.

"Thanks for the offer. I'll call you when I'm done with the book."

With that he kissed her on the cheek and exited stage right, waving goodbye without looking back, disappearing through the revolving door into the tony crowd waiting for taxis to their favorite watering holes.

Maggie watched him exit with a touch—just a touch—of sadness and nostalgia. Once an all-star player, she mused, he's now being tossed about in a mad new world where there is no normal and big-city newspaper reporters—society's traditional investigative watchdogs--see their platforms crack and crumble.

Stella, on the other hand, loathes newspapers, she mused. The news is always stale, you kill trees to produce them, the ink comes off in your hands, and the paper often ends up under your car in the driveway in the morning.

Give me my smart-phone app any time, SOS would say.

Maggie laughed to herself. You can't fight a riptide, she knew. Look what happened to poor Harold Holt.

Or did it, she wondered with a smile.

PART THREE

FIVE YEARS LATER

CHAPTER 92

Life at the Bottom

Cleveland Park Ave.
Washington, D.C.
Friday, April 1, 2016
11:11 a.m.

Still dressed in a tattered blue bathrobe, Rembrandt T. Dabovitch massaged his blood-shot eyes and tried to focus his alcohol-fogged brain on the handwritten note that just arrived by snail mail. Postmarked Stockholm, the oversized brown envelope had no return address or other markings other than the 13-krona cost of the letter.

How could someone in Sweden know all this, he wondered. Certainly feels authentic. Got some of my best stories from these kinds of whistleblowers who lurk in the shadows.

Seated on the brick patio overlooking a small backyard on a sweltering spring day, Rem finished off the last of his Guinness draft in a black 15-ounce can, belched quietly and started reading the letter a third time. The atrocious cursive made for slow going. The letter was dated March 26, 2016.

Dear Rembrandt:

Take this letter seriously. It is your last hope to salvage your sorry journalism career. You're drowning fast, mate, but I'm here to help. Get the checkbook out. Plan on six figures American.

Here's some of what I know and can prove:

---Where Rafer Flanagan is buried.

---How much money, down to the penny, was cleaned out of Ari III's brokerage account a year after he disappeared. (He is dead.)

---How Stacey Simpson died. (Where and when)

---Final drum roll: ARF is alive and well on the Aussie West Coast. Different name, different look, different lifestyle but same DNA and criminal mind. The story has only gotten better with time.

That article on you in the recent Vanity Unfair was a fun read. Two-time Pulitzer winner crashes/burns. Alcoholism, drug addiction, screenwriting flop. Total professional meltdown. Great stuff for those who loathe the liberal media.

But I digress. This is no joke. I have your email. I'll be in touch soon. And spare me in advance how you journalists don't pay for stories. You will if you want this one.

Insincerely, YLH

(Your Last Hope)

CHAPTER 93

Help Is Coming

Cleveland Park Ave.
Washington, D.C.
Friday, April 1, 2016
5:45 p.m.

The buzz of the doorbell jolted Rem from a light sleep on the couch. The sportscaster on TV was blathering about how the Nationals should win their division this year. Rem groaned, sat up and rubbed his face. His head throbbed.

He moved to the front door and peered through the peephole. Maggie Maye! Jesus, what does she want? Woman's nagging is driving me crazy. Short drive.

"Maggie, hi," he said, opening the door and letting her in. "Come on in. Sorry the place is a mess. I've got the Asian flu."

"Cocktail flu, you mean," she cracked, moving into the living room.

Wearing Lulu Lemon jogging clothes and hair pulled back into a blondish ponytail, Maggie looked around and recoiled. The stench was overpowering. Newspapers and magazines were strewn everywhere. Trash littered the floor. Clothes were in heaps several feet high.

"Oh, Rem," she said, "let's go out on the back porch. It's disgusting in here. I can't breathe."

CHAPTER 94

Trump Might Win

Cleveland Park Ave
Washington, D.C.
Friday, April 1, 2016
6:26 p.m.

Maggie handed the letter back to Rem and sat back in her deck chair.

"Let me get this right," she said. "Two weeks after Vanity Fair writes this story about the meltdown of your miserable life…"

"Don't sugarcoat it, Maggie."

"I never do. Your miserable life and he wants at least $100,000 for information on the White Whale you've been chasing all these years. I don't think so. Feels like a scam."

Rem leaned over in his chair and put his head in his hands. His body shook and voice cracked.

"Maggie, I need help," he said softly. "I don't know how all this happened. Ever since Julie died—what has it been? Five years? --my life's been a mess. He was my guardian angel. All his plans for me—the book, the movie deal—died when he did. Nobody else wanted to touch me. This letter may be my last shot."

"Ok," she said, getting to her feet, "first thing we need to do is dry you out. Pack a bag tonight and be ready for my phone call in the morning. I know just the place for you. God knows, I've sent enough reporters there. I can get you in *toute de suite.* "

"What about the letter? I need to act fast on this."

"No, you don't. Get healthy first. Besides, this thing has got déjà vu written all over it. You didn't find her before. What's different now?"

She waived toward the wreckage inside the house. "For God's sake Rem, take a shower, wash your clothes, clean this place up. Looks like a typhoon hit it. You look like a hoarder."

With that she disappeared out the front door. No hug, no goodbye wave, no emoting. Vintage Maggie, he thought.

Rem went over to the staircase to the second floor and sat on the third step. He put his head in his hands and tried yet again to make sense of his crash site.

Nothing more irrelevant that a washed-up newspaperman, he mused. An ink-stained wretch from a faded era of newspaper journalism no one cares about anymore. Truth, accuracy, fairness—swept away in a rising tide of ignorance, intolerance and suspicion.

The corporate behemoths now control a 24-hour news cycle and many of the honest watchdogs of yesteryear are dead or dying. Political corruption is surging, and smash-mouth identity politics has torn the country apart.

This upcoming election may not end well, he thought. Donald Trump may have a chance.

The Miracle of Rehab

Spring Valley Road
Washington, D.C. NW
Friday, May 6, 2016
10:10 a.m.

Face red, body oozing sweat, Maggie Maye was finishing her morning Peloton ride—818 calorie burn—in her home office when the doorbell rang. Damn, she thought. Who the hell is that? I look ghastly. Hate seeing anybody before noon.

Once she opened the door, it took her a moment to recognize the clean-shaven white guy on the porch. Wearing a light-green golf shirt and dark-brown stretch pants, he looked like he was about to hit off the first tee.

"May I help..." she started to say. "Oh my God. Rem. I didn't recognize you. Look at you. You look fantastic!"

She hugged him so hard that he almost fell off the side of the porch into some bushes. Regaining his balance and surprised at her show of affection, he hugged back.

"Hi Maggie," he said, beaming. "I just got out of rehab last night and I wanted to see you. It's the new me. Say hello."

"Come in, come in," she said, pointing to the kitchen. "Coffee first. Then we talk."

CHAPTER 96

Let's Do a Deal

Spring Valley Road
Washington, D.C. NW
Friday, May 6, 2016
10:44 a.m.

Maggie wiped her face with a wet hand towel and walked to her kitchen window overlooking a modest backyard. She leaned against the white porcelain countertop and looked directly at Rem with her best Maggie Maye glare. Lips pursed; eyes locked.

"So, Rem, let me get this right," she began. "You're just out of rehab. Bully for you. You're nose-deep in debt. The ex-wife who allowed you to live in her rental property free of charge now wants you out because you trashed the place. And you want to spend several weeks on the other side of the world chasing a woman who was declared legally dead more than 10 years ago."

She paused and smiled. "Makes sense to me."

They laughed.

"Listen, Maggie," he said. "My body is clean, and my mind is clear. AA has my back. I'm ready to launch. That letter was real. I just *know* it."

"Ok," she said, sitting back down next to him at the kitchen table. "Let's do get real."

Rem cut in. "Let me add I got an email a few days ago in rehab from an old source who offered his help finding our elusive redhead. He read that article and suggested he could help money wise. Going to New York tomorrow to meet with him."

"That article said you had $200,000 in credit card debt," she said. "Tell me that's not true."

"It's not. It's $220,000. Interest adds up fast."

"What on earth?"

"You read the article, Maggie. I thought I could sell a screenplay based on Angela's life for $1 million or more. Didn't happen. Lived in LA three years on those cards."

"You have any income now?"

"Little over $1700 a month from Social Security. Took it at 62 last year. That's it. No pension. Paper didn't have one. No IRA. Never got around to setting one up."

Maggie breathed out deeply and looked away for a time. He's a human auto accident—and a bad one at that, she mused. Debris strewn everywhere.

"Tell me about the Vanity Fair piece," she said. "Don't you know what a barracuda Shannon Greeley is? Forget that toothy smile. The woman's a stone-cold killer."

Rem laughed. "That's what they used to say about me. Maybe that's why I liked her. Avoided her for months but she wore me down."

"Wore you down how?"

"I'd rather not get into that too much," he replied. "Let's just say I was lonely out there. She's drop-dead hot and was fresh off her second divorce. We bonded over lines of white powder."

He added: "I was shocked at the tone of the article. I thought it was going to be a puff piece about how I had weathered adversity and was making a comeback. That's what she told me. Not a hit job about how my life had collapsed."

Maggie frowned and stood up. She shook her head, lost in thought.

"Ok," she said finally, "let's forget all that, shall we? Not the first time a man has been led astray by his pecker. As an investigative reporter you certainly should have known better.

"But there is hope. I like to buy low, and I want a new challenge. I'm retired from the W-2 world, and I have more money than God because of the SOS books. I have no husbands anymore, no kids, no relatives I care about.

"So, here's what I propose: we set up an LLC with yours truly as 51% owner. That corporation will fund your return to Australia with $100,000 in cash. The revenues will flow when you finally nail down the definitive story of our red widow. Blockbuster book followed by Netflix movie deal. And, no, you won't be the screenwriter."

Rem laughed. "So, I do all the work and you get most of the money?"

"You got it, pal. I own the gold and I set the rules. Golden rule of business. We can make a lot of money on this—something I love to do—and the truth will finally come out after all these years.

She added: "I'm going to be your editor. Hands-on. We're going to do it right this time. You tried once before, and it didn't work. This time we cross the finish line."

Maggie looked at her watch. "Gotta go. Have a lunch meeting with my publisher. Novel #5. Meet me in the Capital Hilton lobby at 6:30 tonight and give me an answer. Let's get this done."

CHAPTER 97

Bouncing Off Bottom

Capital Hilton Hotel
16th St. NW, Washington, D.C.
Friday, May 6, 2016
5:55 p.m.

Sitting in an overstuffed leather chair in a corner of the hotel lobby, Maggie eyed the comings and goings of the corporate guests with an amusement that came from decades of diving deep into government malfeasance.

The lobbyists with their bejeweled partners--all the hangers-on who live at the public trough-- mingle so smartly, so smoothly, so confidently. All in all, a great display of soft-core corruption, she mused. Always wonder how the fees of the sex workers are buried in the expense accounts.

She spotted Rem coming through the revolving door. She stood and waved him over to the vacant chair on her left. They hugged platonically and sat.

"Probably shouldn't have picked this place to meet," she began, "given our favorite bar is only a few yards away. You want to go to the Starbucks down the street?"

"Nah, it's okay," he said. "Can't let bars freak me out. This is my new life, Maggie. AA meeting every day, maybe two. Take it a day at a time. Don't need to quit drinking the rest of my life, just the rest of the day. Same thing tomorrow."

"Okay," she said, "I know it's daunting. All about new beginnings. Had a few myself."

She smiled slightly, a hint of sadness in her dark brown eyes.

"So, have you thought about my offer?" she asked.

"Very tempting, very generous. Can you give me a couple of days to think about it?"

"Of course. Is Gina serious about evicting you? I thought the kids had persuaded her to help you."

"Yeah," he said. "she's furious. Taped an eviction notice on the front door a few days ago. Won't even answer my phone calls."

"Ouch," Maggie said. "That's serious. You can stay with me for a while. Take the bedroom over the garage. It's private. Has its own bathroom."

Rem started to speak but she cut him off. "You need to take care of your bankruptcy ASAP. Settle with the creditors for 20 cents on the dollar. I'll supply the money. You pay me later."

"Wow,' Rem said, "Talk about an offer I can't refuse. Don't know how to thank you."

"I don't want thanks," she shot back. "I want results. I plan to sell very high."

The pair stayed quiet for a time, watching the free show in the lobby.

"You know Maggie," he said finally, "I never should have taken that offer from Julie. He threw me a life preserver when I was drowning, but it was a deal with the devil. That *Searchlight* story probably would have saved him $200 million on the final sale price of the *Herald*. Only good thing is the deal died when he did. But, without him, no one wanted my book and movie deal either.

He paused for a moment. "I still think about him. He was such a character. A modern-day pirate. I knew the fruit was poison, but I didn't question him too closely. I didn't want to know the truth. Funny thing for a reporter to say."

"Water over the dam," Maggie said. "I was complicit too. The deal died. End of story."

"So, how is your offer different from what he offered me five years ago," he asked. "Aren't you offering the same kind of help."

"Not even close," she said. "Thought you might ask that. We'll have a straight-up business partnership. Completely transparent. I put up the money, you do the reporting and writing, and we sell a blockbuster true-crime book that tops all the best-seller lists. I've already gotten my SOS publisher on board. When I ask, they do."

Rem looked at her a long time, saying nothing. He finally reached and took her hand. "I'll call you when I get back from New York," he said quietly. "I think you know the answer."

CHAPTER 98

Setting the Trap

Home of Dion DeStefano
Staten Island, New York
Saturday, May 28, 2016
9:33 a.m.

Clad in a black silk bathrobe in his back yard, Dion DeStefano finished his croissant and drained the last of his cranberry juice in a small high-ball glass.

Security cameras all around, he scanned the walled compound for anything out of the ordinary. Living near Paul Castellano's old 17-room mansion was a constant reminder to keep enemies close. Brutal world out there, he knew.

He glanced at one of his few real friends, Jim "The Rim" Robison, sitting across from him, drinking coffee and eating a sprinkled donut. He was reading the *New York Post*, his go-to newspaper.

"So, Rim," Dion said, blowing his nose on a white linen napkin and tossing it on the patio breakfast table, "fill me in on our reporter. You've already hacked his email, right?"

"Yep," Robison replied. "Got in on the first try. Password Rem-Dab666. Too easy. Same as his email. Amazing how stupid smart people can be when it comes to computer security."

"Perfect," DeStefano said. "I want his email tracked in real time. He's coming this afternoon, right?"

"Right. 3:30. Driving up from D.C."

Dion glanced at this diamond Rolex. "That works," he said. "What's the plan?"

"Depends on what he needs," Robison said. "We want him to find her. He finds her, we find her. I'll take it from there."

"The guy is $200,000 in debt," Dion said. "Serbian assassin, my ass. Serbian fuckup is more like it. I say we offer him $25,000 in cash. That should cover his trip expenses."

"But start," Rim said, "by giving him that briefcase with all those articles in the *Brooklyn Spotlight* about Raffy's high school basketball days. The ones your parents saved. Good stuff for his book."

"Yeah," Dion said, "my parents loved that kid. A lot more than me."

"Not hard to see why."

The two gangsters laughed and bumped fists.

"I'll just say we're here to help him any way we can," Dion said. "I'll scare him a little. Let him know his ass is on the line. Let him know he owes me."

"Got it," Rim said, taking his yellow aviator sunglasses atop his head and putting them on. He stood to go.

"You're never going to let this go, are you?" Rim said. "Dude wasn't even Italian."

"He was on his mother's side," "Dion shot back. "I was his bodyguard and best friend in high school. I'm certain she murdered him, and I want to know how, where and when. Then I want her head on a stick."

"Suit yourself," Rim said, heading into the house. "I'll never understand you dago motherfuckers. And you think us niggas are crazy. I'm outta here."

"You're not Italian at all," Dion yelled after him, "and I'd do the same thing for you."

Rim's high-pitched laugh echoed around the walled compound as he waved goodbye.

CHAPTER 99

Bye-bye Behans

Home of Dion DeStefano
Staten Island, New York
Saturday, May 28, 2016
3:33 p.m.

What's it been, Rem wondered. At least five years. Hardly recognize DeStefano.

No more leather jacket, gold chains, three-day beard, 300-pound gut hanging over his belt. Now it's a black shark-skin suit, open necked white shirt perfectly ironed, black Italian loafers. Incredibly buff, perfectly groomed. From capo to underboss. Movin' on up in the world.

"Dion, you look terrific," Rem said after they shook hands and took seats on the patio. "No more back of the bar meetings in Behan's, eh?"

"Yeah," Dion said, "life's good. Family's good. Money's good. That place was a dump."

He smiled slightly.

"So, what happened to you," he asked. "I couldn't believe that article. Your career's a mess, your family life is a disaster and you've got no money. What the fuck?"

So much for pleasantries., Rem thought. Dion the Diplomat.

"Yeah," Rem replied. "Been a rough few years. Appreciate you having the Rim reach out to me."

"Article said you're still trying to find the red-haired cunt who killed my best friend," Dion said. "How can I help you? You need a loan. I'll make it interest free."

He smiled again. "I don't make that offer very often."

Rem hesitated. Careful here.

"Thanks Dion. As luck would have it, I just got a new financial backer. I'm going to find her this time. She's still in Australia. I know it."

"Look," the mobster said, leaning forward for emphasis, "what I want here is not complicated. If you find her and write your story, Aussie cops will take it from there. They can't hang her anymore down there, but she can spend the rest of her life in prison. I'd be happy with that."

He held out the palms of his hands as a show of disclosure. "Just know I'll help you any way I can. I'm just a part of your rooting gallery."

"You remember when we first met?" Rem asked.

"Course. Sal's murder trial. He liked you, respected you. Your stories on the labor unions in Manhattan helped us settle some old scores."

Great, Rem thought. So much for the public service part of that Pulitzer.

"You remember how I helped you a few years ago?" DeStefano said, voice suddenly tinged with menace. "How I told you Raffy faked his own death? Lived in my basement for nearly a year? You remember that?"

"Of course," Rem replied. "I broke that story on the *Searchlight*. Triggered a shit storm here in New York. Still get feedback from that."

"Point is," DeStefano said, "I don't do nothing for free. You owe me and it's payback time. Find her and we'll call it even. Justice will be done—finally. Act like your life depends on it."

Rem paused. Holy shit. Dion showing his true colors. Get me outta here.

"One last thing," DeStefano said, pointing a meaty finger at Rem's chest. "Don't ever think about mentioning my name to anyone about any of this. Ever. Ever. Ever. Capiche?"

"You got it," Rem said, hoping his voice didn't betray the dread he was suddenly feeling. "I'll get her this time. Won't come back til I do."

Did he say rooting gallery or shooting gallery?

CHAPTER 100

Enter the 'G-Man'

Office of the Deputy Director
Manhattan FBI office
Jacob Javits Federal Building
Tuesday, May 31, 2016
10:10 a.m.

Shamas Callahan is affectionately known as the ShamMan by the FBI agents who work for him in the Manhattan office.

With a thick Boston Irish accent and a wardrobe off a discount rack, he is an unmistakable figure in an office where his job as deputy director includes keeping an eye on the Mafia's infamous crime families. Thirty pounds overweight and a total workaholic, he has a volcanic temper with the few agents who don't do their job and a soft spot for the most who do. His 600-square-foot studio apartment in Greenwich Village costs him $4,000 a month and has almost no furniture or wall decorations. He spends most of his free time at The Shamrock, his favorite bar down the block. Perfect staggering distance.

After 10 years as deputy director of the Manhattan office, his mandatory retirement date is set for year's end. He tells friends he can't wait. That's a lie. He has no hobbies, no girlfriends and two ex-wives. Children are grown and they live on the West Coast. Bureau is literally all he has. What the fuck am I going to do, he wonders? Get a job in corporate security for Disney World? I'd rather die, he tells himself.

"McGiffin," he barked from the door of his office, looking at a cubicle a few yards away, "in here, please. Now."

Agent Kathy McGiffin pulled away from her computer screen, grabbed her brown leather briefcase and hustled into her boss' office. Her mouth was dry.

"McGiffin," Callahan said after both were seated on opposite sides of his mahogany desk. "how's it going so far? You've been here a month now, right?"

"Two months, sir."

"Whoa, two months. Sorry we haven't had a chance to talk much. You came here from an Indian reservation, right? Buttfuck, Oklahoma, if I remember correctly. Far cry from Manhattan."

"It was Bumfuck," she deadpanned. "Two towns are often confused."

Callahan laughed. I like this woman, he thought. A millennial with a sense of humor.

"Actually, it was Anadarko," she added. "Bills itself as the Indian capital of America. Loved it there. Great place."

Callahan stayed quiet for a time. What does a South Boston blockhead like me know about American Indians, he mused? Tonto ('What do you mean we, White Man?') comes to mind but that's lame.

He picked up the blue folder on his desk and held it up. "Great job on this report, "he said. "How did you get it done so quickly? DeStefano and Dabovitch only met three days ago."

McGiffin shrugged. "Wrote most of it Sunday. Don't have much of a social life here yet."

Callahan stared at her for a time, feeling a slight tightness down below. To be 30 years younger, he thought.

"Get a personal life, McGiffin," he said finally. "This place will eat you alive if you don't."

"Point taken, sir."

She shifted in her chair and held up her own copy of the report she took from her briefcase. It was stamped 'Confidential' in red letters at the top of the cover page."

"I thought the photographs of DeStefano and Dabovitch taken from the so-called hidden camera on the telephone pole outside his house were especially revealing," she said.

"DeStefano gave him a briefcase, probably full of money as some kind of payoff. As the report noted, Dabovitch is desperate. Who knows what he is up to? He's washed up as a reporter."

"So, you think he's dirty somehow?

"Yes, I do,' she said. "I recommend we get a warrant to search his house. It's right off Connecticut Ave. in D.C. Mess with his head a little."

Callahan held up his hands. "Slow down here, Dorothy. You're not in Oklahoma anymore. We don't get warrants for fishing expeditions on members of the 4th Estate."

"Sir, my name is Kathy, not Dorothy."

Callahan gave her an incredulous look but moved on.

"Point is we don't fuck with reporters for no reason. Nothing like charges the FBI is abusing civil liberties and spying on the noble 4th branch of government to get liberal DC panties in an uproar. We don't need Nancy Pelosi on our case."

"I love her," McGiffin gushed. "Those pearls she wears are so classy."

Another incredulous look from the deputy director followed by another no comment.

"That bureau camera," Callahan said. "I see DeStefano still gives it the finger whenever he leaves his house. "

The agent laughed. "Is that what he was doing? I couldn't tell from our photos. Seemed like he was just sticking his arm through the sunroof."

"I've played cat and mouse with DeStefano for years," Callahan said. "Big part of this job is tracking the mob. DeStefano's a killer just like his dad, but he's no street thug. Thinks strategically, always several steps ahead. He's up to something here. I can feel it. Keep an eye on this, McGiffin. Let it develop. These are the cases that make your career."

He added: "I'll talk to our black ops guys to see if they have any ideas. Maybe they can get us started."

CHAPTER 101

Hunting the Red Menace

Spring Valley Road
Washington, D.C. NW
Monday, July 11, 2016
5:55 p.m.

Sweat stains soaking her blue blouse in the dreadful Washington heat and humidity, Maggie looked irritably at the Lady Rolex on her left wrist. Can't wait to get Rem out of the house, she thought. The man is so needy—and such a slob. Hasn't washed a dish since he's been here.

"Rem," she called into the living room from the kitchen, "tell me again when you leave for Sydney. Midnight?"

"11:50," he said, coming into the kitchen. "Going from Dulles. Got an Uber at 7:30."

Maggie poured two lemonades and they clinked glasses. "Cheers," he said. "Been sober more than three months now, Maggie. Feels good. The fog has lifted."

Whatever works, she thought. Time for the pep talk.

"Look," she began, "I've got everything in order. The partnership papers have all been processed and you have the credit cards. I'm having all your old debts renegotiated at 22 cents on the dollar. Pretty much a clean slate for you."

"Fabulous," he said. "You're my guardian angel, Maggie."

"Sit a minute," she commanded, pointing to the chairs at the kitchen table. "We've got to make sure we're on the same page on everything."

"Sure," he replied. "I'm for that."

"I want a memo every few days on your progress," she began. "Doesn't have to be long. Just the highlights: what you know for sure and what you don't, possible narratives. Where you're going, when and with whom. That kind of stuff."

"Got it."

"Take your time," she said. "Turn over every stone, spare no expense, be prepared for surprises. God knows, we've had enough of those."

"Check."

"Sometimes when we fail, great things happen. Remember, Stella Steele was born when I got fired by Ari Steinberg. Thank you, Ari, wherever you are."

She laughed. "You took a chance on Hollywood that didn't work out. It happens. Better to have tried and failed than to have never tried at all."

"Thanks," Maggie. "I like that."

They clinked glasses again. "*A ta sante*," she said. "*Laissez les bon-temps roulez.*"

They smiled at the memory.

CHAPTER 102

The Man to See

Lady Macquarie's Chair, Sydney Harbor
Sydney, Australia
Thursday, July 14, 2016
12:44 p.m.

"Nice spot, eh, mate?"

Rem turned quickly, startled at being approached from behind without warning. Shouldn't happen like that, he told himself. Know your surroundings.

"Rembrandt Dabovitch, I presume?" Vic Cox said amiably, extending his hand. "Welcome back to Sydney, the city built by convicts and proud of it."

The pair laughed and sat next to each other on the concrete bench, a hallowed spot and tourist attraction with front-row views of the city's world-class harbor.

"Heard a lot about you, Vic." Rem said. "Thanks for agreeing to meet. Think we have a lot in common."

"Hope so, mate," Vic replied. "Let's walk over to the Opera House and have some lunch along the Harbor. Celebrate Bastille Day. This is a great spot, but the bench hurts my arse. Don't know how Mrs. Macquarie stood it."

"Terrific," Rem said, standing to go. "That article on you in *Sydney After Dark* really got my attention. You're the man for me to see."

CHAPTER 103

The Flighty Quinn

Oyster Cove Café
Sydney Harbor, Sydney, Australia
Thursday, July 14, 2016
12:51 p.m.

Their plates wiped clean of kangaroo steak grilled in pepper sauce (for Rem) and barramundi baked in pepper bark, Vic looked across the harbor and winced. A 10-story cruise ship a few hundred yards away was setting sail.

"Love this spot, loath those ships," he said. "They're infested with germs. Give me the creeps."

Vic looked at Rem and appeared a little sheepish. "Sorry, mate. You work homicide long enough and you get a little weird."

"No worries," Rem said. "We're all a little mad."

He pulled the handwritten letter from his battered briefcase and handed it to Vic. "This is why I wanted to meet with you in person. Please read this carefully."

Vic put on his reading classes and took them off almost immediately.

"First of all, I know who wrote this," he said. "Don't need to read a word."

"So, do I," Rem said. "At least, I think I do. Please read it."

Vic read the letter carefully, slowly, grunting occasionally, running his index finger down the middle of the page for tracking purposes.

He finally looked up and smiled. "You're back in business, mate. This must be from Jack Quinn and he's giving you the keys to the kingdom. He's finally ready to talk--for a price."

"Why are you so sure it's Quinn?" Rem asked.

"I recognize the atrocious handwriting. He's written me several notes over the years."

"You think this stuff is true?"

"My gut says yes. Jack knew Angela better than any person alive. Loved her dearly and she treated him like an errand boy. Angie's Clown, he was. If anyone has the detail on all this, it must be him."

"Why do you think he's willing to talk to me now?" Rem asked. "Money? Really? He's been avoiding me for years."

"My guess," Cox said. "is she dumped him and he's getting even. You know, hell hath no fury like a man scorned."

The pair laughed.

"Here's the envelope it came in," Rem said, reaching into his brief-case again. "Got a Swedish postmark. What's up with that?"

"Probably just a head fake. He opened an office in Stockholm a while ago. Probably asked one of his customers to mail it to you when he got back to Sweden."

Rem stayed quiet for a time, watching the ferries glide through the harbor. Just like Seattle, he thought.

"Doesn't he have an office near here?" Rem asked.

"Yeah," Vic said. "Same one he's always had. Out on Bondi Beach, a few blocks off Campbell Parade."

Rem stood. "So, let's go pay him a surprise visit. Ambush him at closing time. I've done that a lot in my business."

"He hates reporters," Vic said. "Very bitter how the press treated him when he was with the visitors bureau."

"Lots of people hate reporters," Rem said. "Goes with the territory. And it doesn't mean they won't talk to you."

CHAPTER 104

Truth Time

Quinn's Sun&Fun Travel
Bondi Beach, Sydney, Australia
Thursday, July 14, 2016
5:58 p.m.

Jack Quinn flipped the sign in his office window from open to closed and was pulling the door shut when Vic Cox approached from behind.

"Jack, hold on," Cox said, pushing his hand against the green door. "We need to talk. Brought someone to meet you."

Startled, Quinn wheeled around. It took him a few moments to recognize Cox in the fading sunlight of the late afternoon in mid-July.

"What the bloody hell, Vic," he snarled. "Don't sneak up behind me like that."

Quinn ignored Rem's outstretched hand and pushed back into the office. He left the closed sign in the window.

"Make it fast," Quinn snapped. "I don't like people sneaking up behind me."

Cox and Quinn took chairs near the storefront window while Rem stood looking at a framed photo on Quinn's rolltop desk. A striking woman with long dark red hair was seated at her Apple desktop, eyes locked on the screen, cigarette in mouth, wearing an old-fashioned wide-brim black hat. Angela on deadline, Rem guessed.

"Is this who I think it is?" Rem asked.

Quinn scurried over, grabbed the photo and put it in a desk drawer. "You bloody well know who that is," he spat.

" I do," Rem said. "Great photo. Looks like Rosalind Russell in *His Girl Friday*."

Baffled at the reference, Quinn shook his head, sat back down and looked directly at Cox. "You're not a cop anymore, Vic. I don't have to talk to you. And I certainly don't need to talk to him," pointing toward Rem.

"Cut the crap, Jack," Cox said mildly. "We know you sent Rem that anonymous letter from Sweden. That's why we're here. We both want to find Flanagan. She's a killer and you're complicit."

"Bull feathers," Quinn snapped. "Woman was declared dead more than 10 years ago. You know that. Drowned at Cheviot Beach."

"Jack, look at me," Vic said, pointing two fingers at him and then back at himself. "We want to know where Flanagan is now, what her new identity is and what's the best way to approach her. We both want to interview her."

Quinn stood abruptly, and walked to the window, watching sun-baked tourists passing in review. After a time, he turned and looked at Cox.

"First of all,' he said slowly, formally, "what letter? I admit nothing —which is what you have on me.

"Secondly, there may be some common ground here. You get what you need and I get what I want. Why don't we go into the conference room and hash this out?"

He laughed. "Dabovitch, you want a drink?"

CHAPTER 105

Art of a Deal

Quinn's Sun&Fun Travel
Bondi Beach, Sydney, Australia
Thursday, July 14, 2006
6:44 p.m.

Got to give Quinn credit, Rem mused. We've got him cornered and he goes on offense. Quite a show by a first-rate sleaze ball. Bobs like the Sugar Rays—Robinson and Leonard.

"Word is, Vic," Quinn said, leaning back in his faux leather chair, "you're making a killing—pun intended—on the backs of desperate relatives. Quite the entrepreneur you are, mate."

Cox laughed. "Nice try, Jack," he fired back. "I have a legitimate business and you know it."

"Tell me again how it works," Quinn said, smirking.

"Simple," Cox said. "Thousands of people in Australia go missing every year and my business is to find them if their relatives want me to."

"Nice," Quinn said. "Making money off the misery of mum and dad. You're a first cousin to an ambulance chaser."

"You want to know how it really works?" Cox asked.

"Sure. Why not? I love scams."

Cox frowned but moved on. "The National Missing Persons Bureau in Canberra keeps track of people gone missing as best they can. Who they are, where they're from, when they were last seen. That kind of stuff.

"I offer to find them if their family will cover my costs. I charge nothing if the search fails. If it succeeds, I charge a flat fee of $5,000—but I'll even waive that if the clients can't pay. Not doing this for the money, Jack. Have my police pension and my needs are modest."

"Sounds sleazy to me, Vic," Quinn cracked.

"Fact is, Jack, I've got so much business I've got six retired cops helping me out. I don't even ask anymore. I've got people calling me from all over the world. Word is out. I'm the gold standard on this stuff. Thousands of people out there are missing long-term. Each one has a story."

"I'm just playing with you, Cox," Quinn said. "Don't take yourself so seriously."

Cox ignored the jibe. "Some of these people don't want to be found. They've started new lives and don't want anyone to know where they've gone. King's Cross and the West Coast are filled with people like this. As I think you know."

He paused. "Your red-head included."

Quinn said nothing for a time. No one did. It's Truth Time, Quinn told himself. No more wisecracks. He reached into his desk and pulled out a red passport. He handed it to Cox.

"I believe you're looking for her," Quinn said dryly. "Maybe this will help."

Cox took the passport, open it to the photo page and stared hard for several seconds. He looked up in disbelief.

"Where is she, Jack?"

"What's it worth to you?"

Cox took a deep breath, stood up and walked over to Quinn, his fists tight.

"Is she alive?"

"Doubt it. Don't know for sure."

Rem was riveted by the back and forth he didn't fully understand. No time to ask dumb questions, he knew.

"Lots more where this came from," Quinn said, the smirk still on his face. "Cost you $50,000 American. All $100 bills. On my desk in 48 hours."

Rem looked pained and started to speak but Quinn waived him off. "No bullshit about not paying for stories," Quinn snapped. "That's your problem. No money, no washee."

"What's the washee?" Cox asked.

"Clues, leads about the mysterious Mrs. Flanagan." Quinn said. "I'll tell you where to look, when to look, what to look for, who to talk to. Think of it as kind of a board game."

"What does Inge Hedburg have to do with Flanagan?" Cox demanded. "Did they know each other?"

Quinn smiled smugly. "Face it, mates. You need me a lot more than I need you."

Nobody spoke for a time. It was nearly dark outside.

"Gotta go," Quinn said. "My Sheila is waiting for me in a pub just down the street."

"Let us talk it over and get back to you tomorrow," Cox said. "I think we can make this work."

"One thing I'll tell you now," Quinn said. "Get ready to travel. You are on the wrong coast."

"I could help you with immunity, Jack," Cox said as he and Rem headed out the door. "Looks like you might need it down the road. I know the right people for you to talk to."

Quinn slammed the door and cursed under his breath. How did Cox get involved in all this? What a bloody mess. Immunity, my arse, he thought. Time for a long vacation. Malta's nice this time of year.

"So who's Inge Hedburg?" Rem asked as the pair walked back down toward the beach. "Jack really got your attention with that one."

"Her Dad's a client of mine," Cox said grimly. "Been looking for her. Disappeared somewhere along the West Coast four years ago. Not a good sign Jack has her passport."

CHAPTER 106

Friends of Bill Unite

Bondi Beach Hotel, Room 313
Campbell Parade Ave., Sydney, Australia
Friday, July 15, 2016
5:33 p.m.

Staring at the cloudless sky in the late afternoon from his hotel room balcony overlooking Bondi Beach, Rem extended his right arm straight out and watched his hand shake.

He swallowed hard, trying not to think of the mini-bar in the adjacent room. The AA meetings on the beach in the Bondi Pavilion are a godsend in the early morning, he thought, but they don't stave off the cravings in the late afternoon. Just one beer would really hit the spot, he mused. Just one. Promise.

Vic appeared on the balcony with two cold Coke cans in hand. He handed one to Rem. "You're a Friend of Bill, right?" he asked. "Thought I recognized the look. Let me guess. Three months sober?"

"Four," Rem said grimly. "Gotta make this work. I'm outta do-overs."

"Just get through the day," Cox said, patting him on the shoulder. "It gets easier. Got my three-year chip last month. You get by with friends you don't even know you have. AA is the best rehab org on earth, and it doesn't cost a dime."

"Yea," Rem said quietly. "My brain gets it. It's the body I'm working on."

"Cheers," Cox said, clinking his Coke can with Rem's. "I say we join forces. Two recovering drunks from opposite sides of the world tracking a mysterious female killer on the remote Aussie West Coast. What do ya think?

"I like it," Rem said, brightening noticeably. "Aussie version of Sam Spade meets Seymour Hersh."

"Something like that," Cox said, laughing. The pair clinked cans again.

"So," Vic said, "I'm going to meet Jack at his office in about an hour. Better I do it alone. I'll have $10,000 in cash with me. That is what I'm offering. You can't pay for information but I can. It's a business expense for me."

Rem nodded but said nothing.

"I'm going to make it clear to him that his clues, as he put it, better be good or I'll tip off my old buddies in homicide that he should be investigated for the murder of Stacey Simpson. That would be huge news down here. Cops loved her."

Rem perked up. "Stacey was an odd duck, wasn't she? Only met her once, here in this hotel room but she seemed flakey. Unhinged even."

"She was a good friend," Cox said, "but, yeah, she heard a different trumpet. Last time I saw her she was acting paranoid. Our meeting didn't end well."

"When was that?"

"Fall of 2010, almost six years ago. At the south entrance to Sydney Harbor. Beautiful spot, beautiful day, lots of tourists around. She was very animated. Said she'd just confirmed a tip on a huge story she was working on. A murder victim in King's Cross. Wouldn't give me a name. Needed a few days to put the story together."

Vic continued: "I got mad at her. Told her not to call me again until she could give me a name."

He paused, voice cracking slightly. "She never called. Not a fond last memory."

"You two were lovers, right," Rem asked matter-of-factly.

Irked by the question, Cox glared at this new partner. He said nothing but his tanned face reddened slightly.

"Sorry," Rem said after a time. "I'm nosey. Juicy details are my stock-in-trade."

"I'll just say we were very, very close friends," Vic said. "That's all I'm going to tell you—for now."

CHAPTER 107

Game of Clues

Home of Vic Cox
Eastern Avenue, Dover Heights, Australia
Monday, July 18, 2016
11:33 a.m.

Facts don't lie, Vic Cox always told himself. Write them down, group them by subject in one column after another after another and soon the forest starts to take shape.

As you probe, dig as deeply as possible, follow *all* leads and keep going back to what you don't understand. Beware of the conventional wisdom. It is often wrong. Use imagination, logic and common sense as your guideposts and good things will happen. The bad guys will be caught, and justice will be done.

If you're lucky.

It was that discipline that made Cox a legend in New South Wales homicide circles. Working largely alone, he cracked the case of the Sydney Strangler, the rapist-murderer who terrorized the gay community in King's Cross in the 1990s. Cox was unrelenting. The last of his three wives left him after he began sleeping on a cot in his office.

The huge poster board in the study of his ocean-front home in the eastern Sydney suburbs was vintage Vic—all the clues in one spot provided by Jack Quinn.

The doorbell at his Dover Heights home rang to the tune of the William Tell Overture. Cox answered and waived Rem in.

"Love the doorbell," Rem said. "The Lone Ranger? Guess that's you, buddy. Makes me Tonto, I suppose."

The pair laughed and bumped fists.

"See what you think," Cox said, pointing to the poster board. "It summarizes everything Quinn gave me. Good stuff—if true."

Rem stared for a long time, saying nothing, grunting occasionally at the factoids and revelations. "Whoa," he said finally. "This is quite a roadmap. Think it's legit?"

"We'll find out," Cox said. "He took the $10,000 without argument. Seemed jumpy. Think I spooked him with that immunity comment. He looked like a man with a lot to hide. Seen that face a thousand times."

"Get this," Rem said. "I called his Bondi Beach office this morning and his son answered. Told me Jack left town yesterday with his Sheila and passport. No known destination, no known return date."

"We'll catch up with him later," Cox said. "I think we got our money's worth. Let's go through it."

CHAPTER 108

Anatomy of a Murderess

Home of Vic Cox
Eastern Avenue
Dover Heights, Australia
Monday, July 18, 2016
11:56 a.m.

Standing next to five poster boards on separate easels, black Sharpie in hand, Vic Cox was in his element, a real natural. Just like the old days when he would brief the brass on his latest murder investigation.

"So," he began, his audience of one slumped on a leather couch several feet away, "let's explore what we know and what we don't. All this according to Quinn—something we always must keep in mind.

"Column One: Our Red Widow is living on the Aussie West Coast under the name of Julia Margaret Cameron. She travels on a Canadian passport that has her from Vancouver, British Columbia. We need to confirm she is in the country illegally because we can always have her arrested for passport fraud. That's a serious charge here."

"I'll call the Canadian embassy this afternoon," Rem said. "That should be easy to check."

"Excellent," Cox said. "Now she lives in one place for only a few months at a time before moving on between Margaret River south of

Perth and Darwin in the north, a distance of 2500 miles. Usually stays in Airbnbs or camping grounds. She almost certainly will be in the popular tourist town of Broome in late August/early September for the annual pearl festival, a real tradition on the northwest coast. Kind of an Aussie Mardi Gras.

"Column 2: the best current photo we have of her, taken up close on the camel-famous Cable Beach outside Broome. As you can see, she is heavily tattooed, her long red curly hair in pigtails and she remains in superb condition—something she has always been fanatical about. Note the cold green eyes.

"Column 3: Hedburg's passport. This is huge for me. Last seen in the company of a Canadian woman (who was almost surely ARF) in Wyndham in 2012. Jack found the passport in a secret compartment under her dashboard and kept it for safe keeping. He suspected foul play but never asked her directly why it was there or who she was. He usually visited her on the road once or twice a year. Her wealthy father has offered me $50,000 American if I can find out what happened to her.

Column 4: Photo of a pauper's grave in Rookwood Cemetery in Sydney. Body buried there in late 2003. We need to prove it's Rafer Flanagan and determine the exact cause of death. I'll work my homicide and coroner sources hard on this one."

"This is huge for me," Rem said. "My book rests on proving this."

"Got it," Vic said. "Now, Ari Steinberg. We know he was last seen in Florida in early 2003 telling his father he was on his way to Australia to find Angela. We also know that $4,878,415.14 was withdrawn from his Citibank account in Perth less than a year later. We believe she killed him, dumped his body and looted his account. Not sure in what order. We need to talk to the bank about this."

"Another must-prove for me," Rem said.

"Got it," Vic said. "Now, here's Column 5 and it's off the wall. There's this Toyota salesman in Darwin who sells Julia a new car every year. Name is—get this—Rocco Mazilli. Quinn says he's a real charac-ter—born in Brooklyn--and has become quite friendly with our quarry over the years. Always sells her a new Land Cruiser every year. Top of the line. Tinted windows, steel reinforced floors and doors. A mob-boss car. Specially made in Japan. Retail price around $275,000. Quinn says check Rocco out. May be willing to talk. Has a monster ego."

"I'll call him tomorrow," Rem said. "Italians from Brooklyn are my specialty."

They both laughed.

"That's a start, mate," Cox said. "We've got a lot to check out before we head to Darwin. Should leave by the end of the month at the latest."

Rem stayed silent for a time, eyes locked on the beach photo. "Man," he said finally, "I've been chasing this woman for almost 15 years. Can't believe I may be about to find her. What the hell am I going to say when we finally meet?"

"You got plenty of time to work on that," Cox said. "Let's meet again in a couple of days at your hotel. Got something else I want to show you."

CHAPTER 109

Gotta Prove It

Tuesday, July 19, 2016
Confidential/Your Eyes Only
From: RemDab666@hotmail.com
To: SOS777@gmail.com
Subject: Update #1

Hi Maggie:

Making real progress. Getting amazing stuff.

The highlights:

Confirm ARF is alive on Aussie West Coast and travels with bogus Canadian passport under name of Julia Margaret Cameron.

Estranged husband is likely buried in Sydney pauper's grave, murdered by ARF and perhaps an accomplice.

Robbed/murdered Ari Steinberg III, it strongly appears. Body long gone.

Suspect in the disappearance of a female Swedish tourist four years ago.

Enclosing recent photo of ARF as a pdf. Also a road map of the northwest coast from Darwin to Broome.

More news: I have teamed up with a retired Sydney homicide cop —name is Vic Cox—who's probing the tourist disappearance. We're flying together to Darwin at month's end. From there we drive 1150 miles south to Broome later in August. That's where we expect to find ARF and confront her. Google Aussie cop Vic Cox. Great profile of him in *Sydney After Dark,* local alternative newspaper down here. He's the real deal.

Big Question Now: Once we find ARF, what is best way to approach her and get her to talk? Want to avoid freakout. Thots welcome.

All for now.

Yours in Sobriety

RTD

Tuesday, July 19, 2016

From: <u>SOS777@gmail.com</u>

To: <u>RemDab666@hotmail.com</u>

Subject: Update #1

My Feedback:

Excellent. Carry on.

Be careful. Your quarry is obviously dangerous. I find that photo sinister. Pigtails creepy.

Flattery best way to approach her, imho. She's a pioneering female reporter of immense talent whose genius was never recognized by pig-male bosses or husband. You want to tell that story.

Team-up with Cox ok. Reporters/cops cooperate *tout le temps.* Just don't broadcast it.

XOXOXO

MTM

CHAPTER 110

Victim #10

Bondi Beach Hotel, Room 333
Campbell Parade, Bondi Beach, Australia
Thursday, July 21, 2016
11:10 a.m.

The vacant stare of the dead, Rem mused. Chills the souls of the living.

Vic laid the color photo carefully on the hotel writing table, the body lying face-up on the gurney, aqua-blue eyes wide open, a look of disbelief and panic on his face. He was middle-aged and had long white hair and matching white trimmed beard. He was fair-skinned and buff. His penis was discolored.

"Any recognition here?" Cox asked. "Last thing Stacey Simpson said to me was she knew who this was. Must be Rafer Flanagan, right?"

"Well," Rem said, "I only saw him once in person—at a Pulitzer ceremony in New York 25 years ago—and he didn't look anything like this. He was skinny, clean shaven, had a buzz cut. Looked like a U.S. Marine."

"We know from the original autopsy report that this guy was drugged and suffocated," Cox said. "My guess is the coroner's office took DNA from the body before it was buried. I'll have my old sources run it through the updated data base. That'll be the proof you need."

"Yeah," Rem said, "that would be huge. If Angela's DNA is on the body, that's a daily double."

Rem paused and looked away from the color photo. "Where did you get this anyway?" he asked. "Why didn't you show this to me the other day at your house?"

Cox laughed. "Let's just say I keep this photo and the full autopsy report at a secure location deep inside a downtown bank vault. Just call it a precaution."

"Precaution for what?"

"I never want this case reopened," Cox said. "No file at headquarters, little chance anyone will bother."

"Go on," Rem said.

Look," Cox said, "I'm not proud of this. I lumped this guy in with the other nine Strangler murders but he didn't fit. There was no semen at this scene and the sheep farmer had a good alibi around the time this bloke was murdered.

"It was just a pretty bow on the investigation. We proved he killed nine people. What's the problem with one more? Police found the victim in King's Cross and 10 sounded better than nine in the press releases. The perp was going to get a life sentence without parole in either case. Point is, we never tried too hard to find out who the victim was."

"So, how do we play this when we confirm his real identity?" Rem asked.

"I'll figure that out if and when the time comes," Cox said. "Anyway, they can't do much if they can't find the file. Just don't know what happened to it."

CHAPTER 111

Beware the Salties

Bondi Beach Hotel, Room 333
Campbell Parade, Bondi Beach, Australia
Tuesday, July 26, 2016
5:44 p.m.

Rem stared out at the ocean for a long time from the hotel balcony, Coke can in hand, smoking a cigar, lost in thought about what comes next. So far, so good, he mused, but this is just getting started.

"I love the beach scene here," he said, turning to look at Vic, standing beside him, "but I'm ready to roll. Darwin here we come."

"Yea, me too," Cox said. "Let's go inside for one last update."

After they sat at the writing table, Cox reached into his battered briefcase and pulled out a yellow legal pad with scribbling only he could decipher.

"Ok," he began, "anything new on the passport front?"

"No," Rem said. "I talked to the embassy again this morning. Reconfirmed everything. There is no Julia M. Cameron in Australia as far as the Canadians are concerned and they'd love to have her arrested if she tries to use her passport."

"Ok," Cox said. "let's just hope she's not arrested while we're in the midst of our investigation."

"Don't see much danger in that," Rem said. "Doesn't look like she's going anywhere. She's brazen, not stupid."

"What about our boy Rocco Mazilli?" Cox said. "One z, two ll's, Rocco being his real first name. Can't wait to meet this guy."

"Talked to him again yesterday," Rem said. "Says to come to the dealership as soon as we get to town. I only told him we were working on a big story. He didn't even ask what. We bonded over Brooklyn. If Flanagan was his best customer, he could be a gold mine."

"Jack Quinn?"

"Still no sign anywhere as of yesterday. According to his son, "'he's gone and I doubt he'll be back any time soon.' His exact words."

Rem reached into his briefcase and brought out photocopies of two of the travel articles Flanagan wrote for *The Herald* nearly 20 years ago. He handed them to Vic.

"I want you to read these again," Rem said. "Look at them in light of what we learned lately.

"The one from Broome is a conventional newspaper travel article but it's very well done. It's obvious she researched it deeply. The tourist magnet of the northwest coast, camel rides at sunset on Cable Beach, exotic history as a pearl-diving mecca, population more Asian than white Australian, all the places to eat, shop, drink etc. She was there during the pearl festival and loved it. Gushed about it as a must-attend for any smart traveler. Her photos were sensational as always."

Rem paused for a moment. "But it's the second one I find especially intriguing. It's about a little town way up on the northwest coast named Wyndham that is the unofficial salt-water croc capital of the country. The main tourist attraction at the entrance to town is a concrete statue of a croc that's 10 feet high and 22 yards long! Place is horribly hot, humid, fly-infested, filled with dangerous crocs. All in all, a place you would *not* want to visit. Kind of an anti-travel article.

Cox laughed. "Those salt-water crocs are monsters," he said. "I've never been to Wyndham but I've heard about it."

"Here's the thing," Rem said. "She clearly had a soft spot for these killers. Called them 'must-see magnificent creatures from the dinosaur era' and notes they only attack humans who are stupid enough to be swimming where they shouldn't.

"Not entirely true but close. At the same time, she did describe their ferocity during a kill. Not much left when the salties are done. I suspect it's a good way to get rid of a body. Article also mentioned the infamous Ginger Meadows case not far from there."

"I remember that," Vic said. "Made headlines all over the world."

"I'd like to see Wyndham for myself," Rem said. "What was the attraction for her? Maybe we could stop there on the way to Broome. It's not that much out of the way."

CHAPTER 112

The Back Channel

Manhattan FBI Office
Jacob Javits Federal Building
Tuesday, July 26, 2016
7:44 p.m.

Dressed in black stretch pants, open-neck white shirt and blue windbreaker stamped FBI on the back, agent Kathy McGiffin put her Glock 9mm in her left-side holster and glanced at the clock. The office was deserted, and the boss was the last to leave--as usual. Perfect time to see him. No one around to gossip why they're meeting.

"Pardon me, sir," she said, knocking on ShamMan's opened glass door. "Have a minute? Got something I need to bounce off you. Something juicy."

"Come in, McGiffin, come in," Callahan said, rising to his feet and shaking her hand. "Sit, please. And call me Shamus. Enough with the 'sir' crap. What d'ya got? I could use a good story. Been refereeing turf battles all day with the CIA. Story of my life."

"Well, you remember our little talk about Dion DeStefano and that reporter, right?" she began. "You told me to keep an eye on the case?"

"Of course."

"Well, I just received a one-page typewritten letter, postmarked Hoboken, no return address, no authorship on it at all, that you should know about."

"Go on."

"Letter claims that reporter is now in Sydney, Australia, hot on the trail of a woman—a former reporter herself—who likely murdered Ari Steinberg III, the former owner and publisher of the *New York Herald*. He disappeared years ago and has not been seen since."

"Good stuff," Callahan said. "I know the Steinberg case well. Solving that mystery would be a huge coup for us. I knew Ari's father. A real gentleman. Died years ago. Son was a real low life. Ran the paper into the ground."

Callahan took out his reading glasses. "Let me see the letter," he commanded.

She pulled it out of her briefcase and handed it to him. He read it carefully, taking his time, shaking his head occasionally. The revelations were explosive.

"Stuff about this missing tourist is interesting," he said finally. "You check out this guy, Vic Cox?"

"Yea," McGiffin said. "He's legit."

"DeStefano has to be involved in this somehow," Callahan said. "This *is* the same reporter he met with at his house in Staten Island— the one you wrote about."

"I'll keep digging on that," McGiffin said. "Here's my problem: how much do I believe? How do I know it's not a hoax.?"

"Believe it," Callahan said, without hesitation or elaboration.

"Huh? How can you be so sure?"

"Don't ask. I just know. When I get to know you a little better, I'll explain."

"Is it the black ops stuff you were talking about?" she asked.

"No comment, but that's a good guess," he said. "Here's what I want you to do: write me a memo based on this letter. Make it short and sweet. Say the info comes from a highly trusted CI.

"Then I want you to take this report and put it through your shredder. You do have one, right?"

"No," she said, "but I can get one on the way home from work. There's an Office Depot just around the corner from my apartment."

"Every good agent needs a shredder at home, McGiffin," Callahan said. "Guess they don't tell you that at Quantico. Put it on your expense account. Anyway, this letter no longer exists. Give me your memo soonest and let's talk in a couple of days."

The Darwin Connection

Manhattan FBI Office
Jacob Javits Federal Building
Monday, August 1, 2016
4:44 p.m.

ShamMan spotted McGiffin across the room and waived her over into this office. As she entered his lair, he was rubbing his hands and smiling—rare for him.

"We've got ourselves a hot one," he said, "and things are moving fast. Your memo was first-rate. I faxed it on a secure line to Joe Lockhardt in D.C., the #3 man down there. In charge of ops. He and I go way back."

"Ok," McGiffin said.

"I just got off the phone with him," Callahan said. "He asked: 'Do you really think we can find out what happened to Ari Steinberg? Do you know what a plum that would be? We've been looking for that a-hole for years.'"

Callahan laughed. "I know how Joe thinks. He can just see the front-page headline in the *Daily News* now: 'Newspaper Scion Mystery Solved.' Article says who killed him, why, where it happened and what happened to the body. All solved by the brilliant detective work of the, drum roll here, the Federal Bureau of Investigation!"

He laughed again. "He told me to get a hold of the Australian Federal Police in Canberra and ask them if they know about this and if they could use our help. Maybe they have an investigation of their own going on. We could join forces."

"Great," McGiffin said. "How would that work?"

"Okay, so I called our FBI office in Canberra and asked for an AFP agent in Darwin who could help us. They gave me the name of Clem Murphy, deputy director of that office. Said to give her a call."

"Wow," McGiffin said. "This is moving fast. Clem is a woman?"

"Yep. That's my understanding. It's Tuesday morning in Darwin. Call her now. They gave me her cell phone number."

Callahan paused, beaming to have such a fast-moving story land in his lap. Never seen him look so happy, McGiffin thought.

"I want a report back tomorrow morning," he said. "Pack a bag while you're at it."

CHAPTER 114

Time to Team Up

Manhattan FBI Office
Jacob Javits Federal Building
Tuesday, Aug. 2, 2016
1:11 p.m.

The ShamMan closed McGiffin's personnel file in his office and looked up at her through his half-moon reading glasses.

"You're lucky to be alive, Agent McGiffin," he said. "What the hell happened down there?"

"You mean the shooting?" she said. "No biggie. Got a few shotgun pellets in the butt. Nothing life-threatening."

"Who was the perp?"

"A meth dealer on the res. I was helping the Tribal Police. They had a warrant for his arrest on multiple murder charges."

"He shot you in the back?"

"Looks bad, I know," she replied. "He got the jump on me in the house. Tribal Police killed him a couple of seconds later."

Callahan stayed quiet for a time, staring at CNN on the muted TV screen mounted on the wall behind McGiffin. Dog days of August, news was slow.

"You have any flashbacks?" Callahan said finally. "Nightmares? Other collateral damage? Anything that would prevent you from taking on a sensitive foreign assignment?"

"Nope," she said. "Lucky to be alive, I know. Tell myself that every day. Never know when your clock is going to strike midnight."

Callahan said nothing, waiting for her to elaborate. She declined and answered his stare. Smart woman, he mused. Don't complain, don't explain.

"So, to the business at hand," he said finally, "what do you know now you didn't know yesterday?"

"A lot. I talked to Clem Murphy for an hour last night. Instant mind-meld. They'd love our help. She sounded really jazzed."

"Do they have investigations of their own going on?" Callahan asked.

"She suggested they do but she didn't offer specifics. Didn't want to get too deep in the weeds on an unsecure cell line."

Callahan again went silent, this time staring at the agents outside his office milling smartly about, pretending to be busy. He knew they were dying to know what this newbie agent—with blonde curly hair and drop-dead body—was doing in the boss' office.

"Ok, McGiffin, "he said, "I reread your personnel file last night and I'm going to take a chance on you. You're headed to the Tropics. Darwin, Australia. Opportunity of a lifetime. You find out what happened to Ari Steinberg--and we get credit—your career will take off.

"Remember, you represent the FBI, the best national police force on earth. Don't let me down. Failure is no option."

CHAPTER 115

Ivory & Ebony

Kathleen Q. McGiffin fled an Oklahoma ranch as a teenager and never looked back. Yellow-haired, green-eyed and skin the color of a fresh Montana snow, she tips the scale in double digits and stands 5-3 in stocking feet. Barbie-doll cute, she has two male fiancées on her personal resume but no ceremony to show for either. Age 29, she is a grinding workaholic who paints by the numbers and bleeds FBI red, white and blue.

Clementine Bindi Murphy, 35, is a rising star in the ranks of the Australian Federal Police and on a short list of field agents targeted for big jobs at the AFP headquarters in Canberra. She's 6 feet tall and has the body of a chiseled triathlete. Her blue eyes are stone cold and her hair is curly black. Her flawless medium-brown skin comes from an Irish-born father and aboriginal mother. Gay and proud of it, she finds life on Darwin's Top End tolerant, colorful and diverse—everything she says the federal capital is not.

"Being with you these last few days has been great," Murphy said, as the two federal agents sipped a morning coffee at the Mykonos Café in downtown Darwin. "Haven't been this jazzed in years. You respect what I know and do. Not easy to be a black woman in this Aussie cop culture. Very discouraging and lonely."

"We're the new version of Cagney and Lacey," McGiffin joked. "Loved that show. Part of the reason I became a cop."

"We've got a lot riding on this," Murphy said grimly. "Got a lot of prove here, Sister. Too many dick-head bosses expecting us to fail. Hell, rooting for us to fail."

"Fuck 'em," McGiffin said. "Anything they do, we do better."

The agents laughed and did a fist bump. They didn't feel as confident as they sounded.

CHAPTER 116

The Brooklyn Connection

Top End Toyota
Stuart Highway, Darwin, Australia
Sunday, August 7, 2016
4:22 p.m.

Out of their comfort zone in this part of the tropics and impossibly overdressed in coats and ties, Vic and Rem exited their rented black Chevy Suburban and moved slowly to the front doors of the dealership.

"You sure this is the right place?" Cox asked irritably. "There are more than one of these in town, you know."

"Relax, Vic, I talked to Rocco this morning," Rem said. "He's waiting for us."

"Christ," Cox groused. "Whoever heard of an Aussi named Rocco Mazilli?"

"I told you, Vic. The guy's from Brooklyn. Good friend of Angela's. Certainly, worth an interview."

"I never realized just how bloody hot and humid it is here," Vic groused again. "Give me the weather in Sydney any time."

Sweating profusely, the pair walked through the automatic double doors, where they were loudly greeted by Mazilli, car-sales king of northwestern Australia. He was clad in Hawaiian shirt and unmatching

Bermuda shorts. On his feet were size 12 pink flip flops, on his face a three-day beard and around his neck a gaudy gold chain attached to an oversized crucifix. He looks like a movie character at a gangster confab in Vegas, Rem thought.

"Gentlemen," he roared, "come in, come in. Welcome to Darwin, Australia, the city that keeps coming back. The Japanese bombed the shit out of us in 1942 and Cyclone Tracy flattened us in 1974 and we're still here. Who knows what's next?"

Mazilli roared with laughter, clapping his meaty hands and showing his visitors to his sparse sales office. The only decoration on the wall was a faded black-and-white photo of an elderly couple in formal dress in front of a small Old-World Catholic church.

"What a treat," Mazilli said, flashing a toothy smile. "Vic Cox, the Columbo of New South Wales homicide and Rem Dabovitch, the Carl Bernstein of the New York underworld. How did you two ever hook up?"

"You have any idea why we're here?" Cox asked.

"I believe I do," Rocco said without hesitation or elaboration.

"Do tell," Vic said.

"Her name is Julie Cameron, she's from Vancouver, British Columbia, and she's got something to hide," Rocco said. "Am I right or am I right?"

"Bingo," Rem said.

"Tell us about the car you sell her every year," Cox said.

"Ah, yes, I see you've been talking to Jack Quinn," Rocco said. "Toyota Land Cruiser. Floors and doors steel reinforced, windows bulletproof and tinted, 5.7-liter V-8 engine. Vehicle fit for a gang banger in a drug war."

Rem shook his head and exhaled quietly.

"She even scares me," Rocco added. "Something about those green eyes. Hard. Cold. Think they've seen a lot."

Rocco laughed. "Hey, she's my best customer. I don't ask and she doesn't tell."

"What else do you know about her?" Cox asked.

"How much time you got?" Rocco asked. "Settle in. I'll get us some iced tea. You two look like you could use it."

CHAPTER 117

Top End Tornado

Top End Toyota, Stuart Highway
Sunday, August 7, 2016
7:37 p.m.

A striking East Asian woman who works in finance and leasing knocked on Rocco's closed door and opened it slightly.

"Hi Tony," she said brightly, "Sorry to interrupt. You going to Shenanigans tonight? Bunch of us heading over now. Irish band starts at 9."

Rocco took his flip-flopped feet off a chair and sat up straight. He looked at his Apple watch.

"Holy shit," he said. "*Tempus fugit.* I don't know, doll. Save a seat for me."

"Got it," she said and shut the door.

Rem stopped writing on his legal pad. "Tony?"

"Oh, man," Rocco said, laughing. "That's what everybody calls me up here. You know, like Tony Soprano. Everybody says I talk like him."

"You do," Vic said.

"Listen," Rocco said, "I'm a rock star up here. Got commercials on late night local TV where I dress up like a gangster, put on my best

Brooklyn accent and tell the folks I'll give 'em an offer they can't refuse. Corny but they love it here."

They all roared with laughter.

"Jack Quinn gave you my name, right?" Rocco asked. "Poor bastard. Julie's butt boy."

"We can't confirm that," Rem said. "Don't reveal our sources. You get that. We'll do the same with you."

"I met Quinn a few years ago when she was here buying her new car," Rocco said. "They were not getting along at all. She told me when he wasn't around that he wasn't worth much because he didn't have enough lead in his pencil. Told him to get some Viagra. Actually said that to me in front of him."

They laughed again.

"You really believe she's a stone-cold killer?" Rocco asked.

"Looks that way," Rem said. "We're heading out soon to find out."

"Broome, right?" Rocco said. "End of August? The pearl festival?"

"Yep," Cox said. "That's our general direction. May make one stop along the way."

"What makes you think she'll talk to you?" the car salesman asked. "What's in it for her? She doesn't buy cars with bullet-proof tinted glass because she's an open and friendly person."

"Good question," Rem said. "We're hoping you might have some thoughts on that."

Rocco didn't answer right away. He stood up and walked over to his window overlooking the car showroom floor, deserted now except for the aboriginal cleaning crew.

"We have an odd relationship," he said finally. "She likes talking about New York and so do I. But she never talks about herself. She seems very isolated to me. Don't think she has a lot of friends."

"You know where she lives?" Vic asked.

"Her car mainly, campgrounds, Airbnb's if she is staying in a place a week or two. She'll probably be staying at the Roebuck Hotel in Broome. She generally stays around Darwin and Broome in the dry season (that's now) and then heads south to Perth and Margaret River in summer. She's a real gypsy. Quite a few people like that on the West Coast. Gray nomads, they call 'em."

"Why don't you come with us to Broome?" Rem suggested. "All expenses on me. Maybe if you introduced us, she'd be willing to talk."

"Hmmm," Rocco said. "Let me think about that. Might be fun."

He suddenly looked at his watch. "Gotta go. I've got a beautiful Japanese woman waiting for me in an Irish bar and she loves *all* things Italian."

He laughed. "See you tomorrow."

CHAPTER 118

Road Trip

Tuesday, August 8, 2016
Confidential/Your Eyes Only
From RemDab666@hotmail.com
To: SOS77@gmail.com
Subject: Update #2

Hi Maggie:

Greetings from Darwin, Down Under. If you like humidity and nasty crocodiles, you'll love this place. Brief historical note: the same Japanese aircraft carriers that attacked Pearl Harbor on 12/7/41 were deployed a few months later to flatten Darwin. They call this place the Top End and the shoe fits. This is the End of the Road—in this part of the world anyway.

Speaking of Japan, our killer lady is likely winging her way down the coastal road toward Broome in a black Toyota Land Cruiser, license plate number ARF 1960 (Hmm, not too hard to figure that one out.) She'll be staying at the Roebuck Hotel the last week of August.

We hope to have a CI traveling with us who knows the target well and, we hope, will introduce us to her at the pearl party. He thinks your flattery approach is our best shot. We must keep his identity secret.

We're traveling in a black Chevy Suburban rented from Avis at a cost of about $2,000 a month. Has nondescript license number of 252 477. So should not draw any undue attention around here.

Just so you know, it ain't cheap here. Estimating my total expense tab at north of $25,000. Everything going on the credit cards, so you can review costs as you like.

Lastly, no word yet on DNA from Rookwood Cemetery in Sydney. That's a big one.

Bill's Devoted Friend

RTD

From: SOS77@gmsil.com

To: RemDab666@hotmail.com

Subject: Update No. 2

Thanks for the history lesson. 10-4 on expenses. Get it done right and it will all be worth it. –MTM

CHAPTER 119

Bad to the Bone

The ZZK Garage
Melbourne Avenue, Darwin, Australia
Thursday, August 11, 2016
11:30 a.m.

Zbigniew Zeke Koslowski is Mongol to the bone. Polish-born, South Africa-bred, 'Ziggy the K' heads the Darwin chapter of the fearsome motorcycle gang named after the most notorious Mongol of them all, Genghis Khan.

A huge portrait of the 13th Century marauder adorns the wall above the metal desk in Ziggie's motorcycle garage. The Mongol motto—*Fear Nobody*—is stitched in black letters on a purple quilt under the color painting.

Ziggie's a motorcycle man sent from Central Casting: tattoos everywhere; huge battle-scarred fists; bowling-ball gut; scraggily black-and-white beard extending to his sternum; hair long, stringy and dirty.

A retired member of South Africa's special forces, he learned some valuable lessons in the military—namely how to blow things up without leaving a trace and how to kill quietly and efficiently. He also learned how to fix machines that are mobile—which is why he is the man to see in the Northern Territory on motorcycle repairs. Doesn't matter who you are—Hell's Angel, Comanchero, Mongol—his place is gang neutral. Only cash accepted, no receipts given.

"Ziggy," his wife yelled from the sales office next to the garage, "pick up on 2. It's your call from New York."

"Ziggy here," he barked into the cream-colored landline. "Talk to me quickly and carefully."

Silence for several seconds. He fiddled with the cord on the wall phone, his greasy hands staining the receiver.

"Yep, got all the emails," he said. "Keep 'em coming. Good stuff. Set to go. Will GPS her car when she gets there. Won't let her out of my sight."

Silence for several more seconds. "Stop with the questions, mate. Let me do my job. Text you when I'm done. Will verify with photos."

With that, he slammed down the phone. "Bloody blackfella," he muttered. "Nobody tells Ziggy how to roll."

He looked around the filthy garage, motorcycle parts everywhere, concrete floor covered with grease and oil.

"Sheila," he bellowed, "saddle up. We're heading out."

CHAPTER 120

It's Getting Complicated

Mykonos Café, Cavenagh Street
Darwin, Australia
Wednesday, Aug. 10, 2016
9:19 a.m.

Wearing yoga pants and tank tops, the federal agents blended in easily with the informal crowd at the Mykonos Café—best known as the place Darwin's arty types go for great breakfasts.

Cavenagh Street once formed the heart of the city's China Town, a ramshackle collection of shops and opium dens with a decidedly frontier feel. Today the colorful Asian handprint of 100-plus years ago is gone, replaced by bland office buildings, art shops and cafes like the Mykonos.

Eating her veggie omelet with a fork in her right hand and reading her iPhone with her left, McGiffin suddenly breathed in loudly, putting her hand over a wide-open mouth.

"Don't look now," she told Murphy, eating an Indian dish of dahl, roti and yogurt, "but those guys over your right shoulder are that cop from Sydney and that investigative reporter from the States. Don 't know the third guy."

"What?" Murphy said. "How do you know?"

"I just got their photos from the FBI. Plus they sent me an update on our fugitive: where she's headed now, the car she's driving, even the license plate on her car."

"Jesus," Murphy said, "where are they getting this stuff? You Americans scare me sometimes. All the spying you do. Is it legal?"

"Listen," McGiffin said, trying not to look in the direction of the three men, seated about 30 feet away, "that's way above my pay grade. I was basically told: 'You never ask, and we'll never tell." They have a lot riding on this arrest. End worth the means."

"Let me see those pictures," Murphy said, taking the iPhone and scrolling through the attachment.

"Holy shit," she said. "I've met this cop. Vic Cox, homicide detective in Sydney. Can I look over my shoulder now?"

"No!" McGiffin said. "They seem to be looking over at us."

"Okay," Murphy said. "I'm going to visit the little girl's room. I'll see if I can get a glimpse on the way back."

She reappeared three minutes later.

"Christ," she said. "I know the third guy. Know of him anyway. He's a car salesman here in town. Does funny late-night commercials on local tv. Don't remember his name. What the fuck is he doing with those guys?"

"Haven't a clue."

"Let's get out of here," Murphy said. "This could turn into a circus if we're not careful. Our job trumps theirs and we may need to let them know that at some point."

CHAPTER 121

RIP, Slim Dusty

Mykonos Café
Cavenagh Street, Darwin, Australia
Wednesday, August 10, 2016
9:49 a.m.

Eyes locked and loaded, Rocco Mazilli followed the woman as they arose from their table on the outdoor patio, each leaving a $20 bill on the table. They began a stroll down Cavenagh Street, stopping to look in the shops and headed in the direction of Government House, an architectural gem that survived the bombs and storms of the past 75 years.

"Whoa," he said," "look at those two. Must be here for the marathon this weekend. I'd enter but pretty sure I wouldn't last a mile."

Vic and Rem laughed.

"The tall woman looked familiar to me," Vic said. "Just can't place her. Never seen the other one."

"She looked familiar to me too," Rocco said. "I'll bet the other one is American. You can just tell. Blonde and perky."

"So Mr. Rock Star, whatya think,?" Rem asked. "You in? By the way, I saw one of your commercials last night. They *are* hilarious."

Rocco was quiet for a time, standing and looking down the street for the female joggers, who were nowhere in sight now.

"Look," he said, "I want to go but you guys need to know a little about me. You might have second thoughts. I've never been a candidate for the priesthood."

"Let's have it," Vic said.

"Well, I left Brooklyn about 20 years ago," he began, "after I got a call in the middle of the night advising me to leave town yesterday. I was in my early 20s at the time and getting into some bad stuff on the street— you know, loan sharking, drugs, pimping. Not sure why I was targeted but I didn't stick around to ask many questions. Had something to do with violating family boundaries.

"Family boundaries?" Vic asked.

"You know, like you see in the movies. Marlon Brando. The God-father."

Vic nodded. Rocco paused and took a sip of water before continuing.

"So, I set out for Vegas in the middle of the night driving my beat-up Honda. No goodbyes to anyone—parents, sisters, girlfriends, old pals. Had $500 in cash and some names to call when I got to Sin City."

"Sin City?" Vic asked again.

"Yeah, that's what they called Vegas in those days. So anyway, I get a job as a bouncer at one of the strip clubs, doing drugs, different woman every night. Not a bad life, but I knew I had to get out. Go far away from everything I'd ever learned. Otherwise, my next landlord was going to be the Nevada Board of Corrections."

He laughed.

"So, I buy this world map and tape it to the wall of my dumpy apartment just off the Strip. I circled all the places that looked like the end of the road: tip of South America, Baja California, Key West, tip of Cape Cod."

"And Darwin, Australia," Vic chimed in.

"You got it," Rocco said. "I came here on a tourist visa, got a job in a copper mine down south and eventually applied for citizenship. Started selling cars here about 10 years ago."

"Man," Rem said, "that's why you're such a natural with those commercials."

"I love this country, man," Rocco said. "Or I should say: I love this country, mate. Gave me a second chance. I love listening to Slimy Dusty singing Waltzing Matilda. Know the verses by heart."

"Me too," Vic chimed in. "Love his version of Pub With No Beer."

"To Slim Dusty," Rocco said, raising his water glass as a toast. "The Australian Johnny Cash. Rest in peace, brother. You were the greatest of them all."

"To Slim Dusty," they all said in unison, even Rem who'd never heard of the guy.

"What are we waiting for?" Rocco cried. "Onward to Broome. The camels await!"

CHAPTER 122

Who Are Those 2?

Mandalay Hotel
The Esplanade, Room 515
Darwin, Australia
Thursday, August 11, 2016
4:54 p.m.

Binoculars in hand, Vic stared at the lot below where their black Chevy Suburban rental was parked in one of the hotel spaces. Two women were giving the car the once over, taking photos with their iPhones, trying to look inconspicuous.

"Rem, come here," Vic barked. "Take a look down there. Isn't that Ebony and Ivory, the joggers we saw at breakfast this morning?"

Rem took the glasses and trained on the pair five stories below. "Yeah," he said quickly. "Hard to miss those two. What the hell are they doing?"

Cox motioned Rem back into the hotel room. "You remember I told you the tall one—the black woman—looked familiar?

Rem nodded.

"It just came to me," Cox said. "I met her at a law enforcement conference in Perth a few years ago. She's an AFP agent."

"A what?"

"The Australian Federal police. The Aussie FBI."

"What the fuck?"

"She was a featured speaker at one of the seminars," Cox said. "Something about how federal and local law enforcement could better coordinate on aboriginal matters. A real snooze but the room was packed because she's such a babe."

Rem laughed. "They're both babes. What about Miss Perky? She ring any chimes?"

"Remember what Rocco said," Cox noted. "Looks American. FBI maybe? What would they be doing here? I'll get my camera. Get a shot of her from up here."

CHAPTER 123

Bingo!!!

August 11, 2016, 11:59 a.m.
Confidential/Your Eyes Only
From RemDab666@hotmail.com
To: SOS77@gmail.com
Subject: Update #3

Maggie:

Hi. Need your help fast. Please look closely at the attached photo. We think she may be an American federal agent: FBI, ATF, Homeland Security, whatever. Any data base you could run her photo through? Use your old FBI sources maybe? Need positive ID asap.

All Best

RTD

From: SOS77@gmsil.com

To: RemDab666@hotmail.com

Subject: Bingo

Name is Kathleen Q McGiffin. FBI agent attached to Manhattan office. Shot and wounded in a drug raid on an Indian reservation last year. Photo was in all the Oklahoma papers.

XXXOOO

MTM

CHAPTER 124

God Bless DNA

Mandalay Hotel, Room 515
The Esplanade, Darwin, Australia
Friday, August 12, 2016
11:22 a.m.

Vic Cox put down his cell phone and answered he knock on his door. He let Rem in.

"Got some great news this morning, mate," Cox said. "Come in. Sit."

"All ears," Rem said, taking a seat at the writing table in the corner.

"First of all, my Sydney homicide mates really came through," Cox said. "This is still unofficial, but the coroner confirmed that the body in Rookwood Cemetery is Rafer Flanagan. His DNA is in the system from his days as Sydney correspondent and it matched the guy found strangled in that King's Cross motel in early January 2003.

"Terrific," Rem said. "Can we get that in writing?"

"Yes, but there's more," Cox said. "DNA on the throat was found belonging to our Angela and guess who?"

"Jack Quinn."

"Bingo," Cox said.

"Christ," Rem said. "They apparently drugged and strangled him. Autopsy shows he had a potent date-rape drug—something called GHB--in his system."

"No wonder Jack's gone missing," Cox said.

"There's even more," Cox said. "I just got a slew of Q&A interviews from Hedburg's whole family that gives a much better look at the woman I'm chasing. Guess what?

"I don't guess," Rem deadpanned.

"The last time the family heard from Inge was in a letter postmarked Wyndham, in the middle of nowhere way up on the Top End. Known as the hottest place in Australia. Filled with human-eating crocs.

"Here's the news: Inge was supposedly hitchhiking down the coast with a quote cool Canadian woman and everything was good. No worries. Guess what? Never heard from again."

"This time do let me guess," Rem said. "This cool Canadian woman had red hair and a great body. Her name was Julia and she drove a Toyota Landcruiser."

"Bingo again," Cox said.

"Holy shit," Rem said. "ARF is rising from the dead. We now know she killed her husband; we suspect she robbed and killed her publisher-boyfriend and we have strong circumstantial evidence she killed this tourist. This woman is truly a monster. What else has she done?"

"Good question," Cox said. "I'm having my guys comb through the records for any other female tourists gone missing on the West Coast going all the way back to 2003, the year she disappeared."

"Tell me more about Inge," Rem said. "How did she get all the way out here, anyway."

"Well," Cox began, "according to these interviews with the family, she dropped out of Stockholm University and came to Australia on a 30-day tourist visa with her boyfriend Max, a real low life. Both were druggies. They lived for a while in Nimbin, a hippie town north of Sydney. They got bored and decided to hitchhike across Queensland to the Northern Territory and then north to Darwin. But it's monsoon season, Max hates it there and heads back home. Inge sticks out her thumb and heads south along the West Coast to Broome."

Cox reached into his briefcase and pulled out a photo of her that Max had taken of her just before the pair split up. He gave it to the family when he got home.

"Look at her," Cox said. "Scrawny dirty blonde, vacant blue eyes, pouty lips. Looks like all those runaways in King's Cross and all over the West Coast. Act stupid, party hard, die young. What a waste."

"Inge, we hardly knew ya," Rem said quietly. "Guess there wasn't a whole lot to know."

CHAPTER 125

Proof Positive

August 12, 2016
Confidential/Your Eyes Only
From: RemDab666@hotmail.com
To: SOS77@gmail.com
Subject: Update #3/Bulletin

Maggie:

This just in: we have DNA proof that Rafer is buried in Rookwood Cemetery and wife's DNA is also on the body. Coroner's office has already ruled the death a homicide.

This is huge. More stuff TK.

RTD

CHAPTER 126

Canberra, We Have A Problem

Federal Police Headquarters
Darwin, Northern Territory, Australia
Friday, August 12, 2016
3:33 p.m.

Federal agent in charge of the Darwin office, Peter Keating could not contain his fury. Face bright red, hands shaking, he stared daggers across his desk at Clementine Murphy, his No. 2.

"How could this happen?" he hissed. "You're running a task force on a West Coast murder investigation involving the publisher of the *New York Herald* and I don't even know about it? What the bloody fuck is going on?"

"Peter, calm down," Murphy replied evenly, keeping cool. "I'm just taking orders from Canberra. I thought they had talked to you already."

"The FBI is involved?" Keating raged on. "What the fuck are they doing here? We don't need those shitheads. Arrogant arseholes. This is a bloody outrage."

"Peter, please. Calm down. You look like you're about to have a stroke."

"Calm down, my arse. You don't fool me, Murphy. You have no loyalty to anyone other than yourself. You think being an abo dyke makes you special. Got news for you, sister. I think it makes you a bloody pervert."

"Peter, I'm warning you," Murphy shot back. "This kind of name-calling is actionable. My race, gender and personal life are none of your god-damn business."

"I don't want anything to do with your little investigation," Keating hissed. "I'm sure you'll fuck it up. And don't bring the FBI anywhere near this office. Now get out of here, Murphy. I have work to do.

CHAPTER 127

This Magic Moment

Casuarina Beach
Darwin, Australia
Friday, August 12, 2016
6:16 p.m.

A spectacular sunset looming on their left, the fearsome thunder-clouds pierced by steaks of fading sunlight, the two agents strolled along the deserted beach, saying nothing, lost in thought. Their gym clothes--soaked in sweat from the 5-mile jog from their hotel—were in a pile nearby.

"I had a terrible row this afternoon with my boss," Murphy said quietly. "He says he wants nothing to do with our investigation. Called me an abo dyke. He was just horrible."

"Abo dyke?"

"An aborigine who is a lesbian."

"Oh my," McGiffin said. "That was nasty. What was the fight about?"

"He's furious he wasn't in the loop. He didn't even know the FBI was involved. His face was so red I thought his head was going to explode."

"Why wasn't he told?"

"Canberra doesn't trust him," Murphy replied. "He likes to leak to the press, and we absolutely can't afford that here—not now. He's also a terrible manager. The troops loathe him. His office door is always shut—unless he's yelling at someone at their cubicle. Then I have to be the peacemaker. Tell the young agents: 'Oh, that's just Peter. He didn't really mean that.' The man has zero social skills."

McGiffin laughed.

"One thing about Peter," Murphy added, "he's magic when it comes to technology. Computers, cameras, wiretaps. Has terrific night-vision goggles that we use on drug stakeouts. We could use his help down in Broome if we want a wiretap."

Murphy stopped and stared out at the Timor Sea. She put her hand on McGiffin's shoulder and guided her to the water's edge.

"I just had to show you this before we leave," the Aussie agent said. "This sky is my Higher Power. My aborigine mum is looking down at me. That's why I love this place so much and probably won't ever leave."

The couple shared a platonic hug as the sun sank into the Timor. A warm humid wind was blowing softly on a perfect 80-degree August evening.

Half a kilometer behind the beach, at a well-hidden trailhead surrounded by vegetation, a Nikkormat camera on a tripod, with a long-range lens and special night-vision capabilities, clicked quietly away.

CHAPTER 128

How Do They Know?

Mykonos Café, Cavenagh Street
Darwin, Australia
Saturday, August 13, 2016
8:18 a.m.

The two agents sat at their table on the patio of the trendy Mykonos Café, lingering over their expressos and nibbling the last of their veggie omelets.

"Kathy, tell me again how Vic Cox approached you yesterday at the pool," Murphy asked. "This is driving me crazy. How on earth did he know who you were?"

"Good question," McGiffin replied. "I'm so new to the New York office most people there don't know who I am. I was sitting by the pool reading the newest biography of J. Edgar Hoover—de facto required reading for all agents—and he comes up behind me. Puts his business card on the table and says: 'Agent McGiffin, we need to talk. Call me. Give Agent Clem my best. I'm a big fan.' That's it. He walked away back into the hotel."

"He referred to me as 'Agent Clem?'"

"Yep, like he was your old friend."

"Jesus," the AFP agent said, exasperated. "We know all kinds of things about them and now they know about us. What's the connection there? What don't we know?"

McGiffin didn't answer right away as she watched the human parade passing in review on Cavenagh Street. She finally shook her head.

"Wish I knew," she said finally.

"Where do your FBI sources get their information?" Murphy asked. "You have any idea?"

"Nope. Not a clue. They tell me it's black ops and never, ever use the information in any official way. Everything you get from us must be verified and confirmed through second and third sources.

McGiffin shrugged. "All I know is they really want to find out what happened to that New York publisher. Do that and it's Mission Accomplished. Fuck up and hello Fargo."

The agents laughed and did a fist bump.

Detour to Wyndham

August 15. 2016
Confidential/Your Eyes Only
From: RemDab666@hotmsil.com
To: SOS77@gmail.com
Subject: Update No. 4

Hi Maggie:

Heading soon to Broome. Have rooms there at a hotel on the beach north of town. Stopping on the way at a tiny town named Wyndham. Trying to figure out why Angela was so enamored of the place. Probably take our time and get there in a couple of days.

Events may move quickly in Broome. Surprise is our best friend there.

All Best
RTD

CHAPTER 130

Wyndham: A History

A slightly mad American journalist named Roff Smith wrote a travel book in the late 1990s about his misadventures riding a bicycle around Australia. Titled **Cold Beer and Crocodiles**, *the book was a tale of astonishing endurance and discipline mixed with wanderlust gone wild.*

Smith started in Sydney, where he had worked for Time magazine, and ended some nine-plus months later back in the same place. When he took a side trip 60 miles off the main highway to visit Wyndham, he was not impressed.

"Never in my life," he wrote, "have I seen a more forbidding place—a cluster of iron sheds and a jetty, blocked off from the rest of the world by the stony shoulders of the Bastian Range and looking out on a vast steamy swamp of crocodile-infested mangroves and tidal mud flats."

The temperature the day he visited was 120 degrees and "the noontime glare was blinding. The view from the hilltops above town was haunting, pre-historic. Five primordial rivers slither through distant deltas before emptying sluggishly into the Gulf of Cambridge. It was a scene from the dawn of time."

Yet, not far from Wyndham is the eastern edge of the Gibb River Trail, which one guidebook described as providing "one of Australia's wildest outback experiences. The largely unpaved road is an endless sea of red dirt, open skies and dramatic terrain. Side roads lead to remote gorges, distant waterfalls and million-acre cattle stations."

Wyndham itself is a town of less than 1,000, mostly aborigine, that is the northern-most population center in the state of Western Australia. Its modern founding dates to the 1880s when gold was discovered, and 5,000 miners descended on the town.

At its zenith Wyndham had six pubs—always an Aussie bellwether of economic health—and the harbor was crammed with ships headed for the open seas to the north. Unfortunately, the boom collapsed after only two years and the town went bust—the first of several in the decades to come.

Hope did return in 1919 when a meat-packing plant opened and was a town mainstay for decades. A favorite time of day occurred when the blood and meat scraps were dumped into the Harbor and the salt-water crocs went into feeding-frenzy mode. Great tourist attraction by all accounts.

In 1985, the plant closed but the salties--by then protected by federal law and exploding in number--stayed. Unlike their more benign freshwater cousins, they will rip apart and eat anything meaty—farm animals, birds, humans. All taste good to these primordial terrors of the northern coast.

Rather than play down the fearsome croc connection, Wyndham built a concrete replica of a monster salty at the edge of town: 66 feet long, 10 feet high and weighing thousands of pounds.

Now, Sydney has its Opera House, Cairns has its Great Barrier Reef and Wyndham has its "Big Croc."

CHAPTER 131

'I'm Somebody Here'

Road to Wyndham, Australia
Victoria Highway
Wednesday, August 17, 2016
4:44 p.m.

Pointed southwest on the Victoria Highway, about 100 miles from the Western Australia state line, Rem stared at the beauty of the Kimberly from his left-hand passenger seat. Vic was snoring quietly in back.

With Rocco at the wheel, Rem eyed the bad lands known as the Bungle Bungles—behive dome sandstone formations rising some 600 feet above the heated terrain. Aussie version of red-rock Arizona, Rem mused.

Gotta love these colorful Aussie names, he thought. Bungle Bungles, Waga Waga, Goodiwindi, Wee Waa. And what's with these stubby-looking Boab trees? Legend—partly true—has it one of them near Wyndham is 1500 years old and is so large its insides were used as a jail in the 1890s.

Speaking of colorful, Rem mused, look at Rocco behind the wheel. Hadn't shaved in days, a black bandana covered his forehead and long curly hair, and he wore yellow-tinged goggles for sunglasses. Something out of those Mad Max movies, Rem thought.

"What do you think, Rocco," he asked. "This is about as far from Brooklyn as it gets. You ever miss it? Can you ever take the Brooklyn out of the boy?"

Mazilli didn't answer right away. He kept his eyes on the road, the Chevy Suburban roaring through the dust, heat and glare at 30 miles an hour over the speed limit. He gripped the steering wheel tightly, looking slightly demonic, hands in the 10/2 position.

"Do me a favor, Rem," he said finally. "I'm helping you guys with Julie. Only thing I want in return is for you to visit my father when you get back to the States. He lives in a nursing home in Long Island City. Doesn't have much time left. My sisters keep me posted. He just turned 88.

"Tell him I'm making an honest living now. People like me here. I make 'em laugh. Tell him I'm somebody now. He'd be proud of me."

His voice cracked and he cleared his throat.

"Would you do that for me, Rem? You'd make my year."

"Sure, Rocco, no problem," Rem said. "I'll do it first thing I get back. He should be proud of you."

"And, to answer your question," Rocco added, "no, I don't miss it. Brooklyn was a mess when I was growing up. Drugs, crime, riots. It's better now, so maybe I'll visit one day. You know, going back to the old country to see where you came from one last time. But I'll come back here. This is my home now."

CHAPTER 132

An Aussie Original

If there is a Man to See in Wyndham, Australia, pop. 780, it's Michael 'The Ice Man' Scanlon, a grizzled ex-cop who walks slow, talks slow, thinks fast and never shows his cards.

He moves elegantly through the dusty, fly-infested 100-degree heat like it's the most natural habitat on earth. His civilian uniform seldom varies: yellow nylon golf shirt, dark brown khaki shorts, high-top hiking boots and, of course, the wide-brimmed Aussie sun hat. His lined leathery face is right out of an old Marlboro commercial and his crewcut is military ready.

He retired from the West Australia state police force several years ago, took his 30-year pension and bought the Big Croc Motel. Needed something to do.

At the time, the mining industry was thriving and film crews were coming to town because of its authentic Outback feel. For a time the little town was actually hip in its own eccentric way.

But as always happens in Wyndham, the mini-boom went maxi-bust, motel traffic tanked, and Scanlon's long-suffering wife left him for a new life down south in Perth.

In her parting words on a hand-written note, she wrote: 'My Darling Michael: I can stand it here no longer. This place has finally driven me mad. I love you dearly and always will, but that is not enough anymore. Your beloved Claribel.'

"This place gets in your blood," Scanlon tells visitors when asked why he stays. "I know everyone in town and my pension pays the bills."'

The ex-cop never heard directly from Mrs. Scanlon again. He signed the divorce papers and moved on.

Never complain, can't explain.

CHAPTER 133

Who's Chasing Whom?

The Croc Bar, Wyndham Hotel
Wyndham, Western Australia
Saturday, August 20, 2016
5:05 p.m.

The air conditioner crashed again and a new compressor was on order from Darwin. Might take a while; it's the tropics up there. Meanwhile, the six ceiling fans in the outback pub were churning furiously to little avail.

"Mike, can I have another?" Murphy asked, pointing to her empty pint glass and fanning herself furiously. "How can you stand it here? My skin's on fire. I want to jump into a tub of cold water."

Scanlon laughed and nodded. "Hear that a lot," he replied in his slow drawl, wiping his red face with a damp white towel. "Drove Claribel mad."

Murphy laughed. "That woman was a saint," she said. "How did you ever let her go?"

"Didn't have a choice," he said mildly. "She wrote me a note and left. Her Dear Michael letter. Probably best. She hated it here."

"I miss you, you old coot," Murphy said. "Our task forces vs. the bad guys—drug dealers, motorcycle gangs, all the other scum bags up here. God, that was fun. We always got our man."

The pair laughed and did a fist bump.

"Why are you here, Clem?" Scanlon asked. "You didn't really say in your email. And who's your traveling companion?"

"She's American FBI."

McGiffin was seated across the bar near an open window, drinking a Coke and reading her phone.

"We're here on a huge murder case," the AFP agent said. "Mike, I could really use your help. Case is complicated. All kinds of people are chasing this woman."

"Woman?"

"Yeah."

"She hangs out around here?"

"Yeah."

"Let me guess," Scanlon said, smirking slightly. "Her initials are JMC.

Murphy didn't answer at first, surprise clearly showing on her face. She took a long drink, halfway through her second pint of the late afternoon.

"Mike, I've always thought you were really smart," she said finally, smiling, thinking furiously about whether to confirm his suspicions. How on earth could he know this, she wondered.

"You don't have to answer that," Scanlon said. "Your face pretty much says it all. Sorry, Clem, but you should avoid the poker tables in the casinos."

"I'm not confirming or denying anything," she shot back. "Just curious: why do you say that?"

"Julie's an odd duck, to put it mildly," Scanlon said. "She's a gypsy riding around in a $250,000 SUV fit for a Colombian drug kingpin. Something ain't right there."

"Mike," she said earnestly, "this case is out of control. I'm afraid it's going to blow sky high."

"What's the problem?"

"Well, first, my partner over there. She's not very experienced. Seems afraid of her own shadow."

"Not good. Why would the FBI send someone like that on a foreign assignment?"

"Here's the real issue," Murphy said. "There are three guys chasing the same person we are. An investigative reporter from the States, a retired homicide cop from Sydney and a car salesman from Darwin. Don't ask. I don't know what his deal is.

"They're working together and they seem to have inside info on what we're doing. They've told us they want to talk and they're literally following us to Wyndham. Should be here tomorrow.

"What the bloody hell should I do, Mike? You used to do great liaison work for the state cops on the big cases. The feds loved you and so did the reporters. I've never been neck deep in anything like this before."

Scanlon stayed quiet for a time, wiping down the bar and handing her a third pint. "Meet me at the pool at 9 tonight," he said finally. "I've got some ideas. I'll bring the beer. Come alone."

CHAPTER 134

United We Stand

Wyndham Hotel
Wyndham, Western Australia
Sunday, August 21, 2016
12:12 a.m.

Murphy opened the hotel room door as quietly as she could, trying not to disturb her sleeping partner, with whom she was sharing Room 7.

She needn't have bothered. McGiffin was wide awake, roasting naked in the midnight heat, looking angry and sweating head to toe.

"Where have you been?" the FBI agent demanded. "We were supposed to have a strategy session tonight."

She got up off the bed, grabbed a towel and dried herself off. She threw the towel across the room.

"My God, I can't believe it's midnight, there's no air conditioning and the temperature is 95 degrees," McGiffin said. "What the fuck are we doing in this hellhole anyway?"

"Shhhhh," Murphy said quietly, putting her index finger to her lips. "It's all good. Mike says he'll help us. We've got a plan."

"What kind of plan," McGiffin hissed. "I don't like the sound of that. Scanlon's just a washed-up outback cop."

"Hear me out," Murphy said. "Your black ops guys are telling us the Three Amigos will be arriving tomorrow afternoon. They have to stay here. No other motel in town."

"Yeah. Go on."

"Mike will take Vic Cox aside and suggest—one retired cop to another—that we should pool our resources."

"Pool how?"

"Disclose what we are all up to. Put everything on the table. Co-operate and coordinate as best we can. Cox has already said he wants to talk to us. Let's see what he's got."

"Don't like it," McGiffin shot back. "Too risky. FBI agents don't work that way unless the bosses OK it. And I have no such clearance."

Murphy took a deep breath and exhaled audibly.

"Look, Kathy," the AFP agent explained, "you're not in America anymore. Aussie turf, Aussie rules. Go home if you don't like it.

"Secondly, this makes perfect sense. The reporter wants his story, the cop wants to find his missing person and we want our arrest. They're all connected. One plus one plus one equals six.

"You're playing with fire, Agent Murphy," McGiffin spat. "What if they say no?"

"No problem," Murphy replied evenly. "No harm, no foul. We go our separate ways. They say yes and Mike will broker the ground rules. All on the super qt. No one will be the wiser."

"I thought we were equal partners," McGiffin said. "Why did you do this without me? I would not have agreed to anything like this."

Murphy laughed. "That's why I didn't invite you. You need to lighten up, luv. Throw away the training wheels. We need to improvise as we go along. There's no manual for this type of operation."

CHAPTER 135

The Odd Bunch

Wyndham Hotel
Wyndham, Western Australia
Sunday, August 21, 2016
6:06 p.m.

Big Mike Scanlon looked around the shaded white plastic table by the hotel pool and prepared to call the meeting to order.

Inside the Ice Man was boiling.

I just *knew* something was not right about Julie Cameron, he told himself. Should have checked her out while I was still on the job. Like clockwork, she comes through here every year on her way to the pearl festival, driving a tinted-glass gangster wagon, young hippie companions often in tow. Appearance unforgettable: long red pigtails; arty tattoos adorning muscular arms and upper body; cold green eyes; facial expression of a professional gambler. Ex-pat from Vancouver, my arse, Scanlon thought. Should have asked Murphy to have the feds check out her entry status. That would surely have blown her cover. Maybe save lives.

Scanlon shook his head. "Ok guys," he began, "let's get going. You're headed south in the morning, and this is our chance to meet as a group. Unofficially, of course. If you have concerns, speak now."

He looked down at his notes on a yellow legal pad and kept going.

"Just so you know, I have been deputized for the remainder of your mission. Talked to my old boss in Perth this morning and she okayed my request."

McGiffin cut in, clearly alarmed. "So, you told her what we're doing?"

"Nope," Scanlon replied, cool as always. "Not a word. It just means I can act as a cop if you need me. She doesn't know and she didn't ask. She trusts me."

McGiffin scowled. Murphy smirked. Scanlon continued.

"So, let's go around the table. Vic, you first."

"Good to hear, mate," Cox replied. "We may very well need you—and the rest of the state police for that matter. I'm good to go."

"Rem," Scanlon said, looked at the American reporter seated next to him, "thoughts from the 4th Estate, as you Yank journalists so immodestly call yourselves? "

Rem laughed. "All good. I get the exclusive, I'm happy. And, yes, we take *ourselves* very seriously. One reason the public dislikes us so much."

Everyone laughed, even the petulant McGiffin.

"Rocco? What say you?"

"Here's my headline," the car salesman said, holding up a sheet of white paper with block letters in black Sharpie ink:

'Operation Killer Lady
Ready to Launch on
Remote Aussie Coast'

A cheer erupted from the group. "Operation Killer Lady! Great stuff," Rem said. "Rupert himself couldn't beat that."

"Let's roll," Rocco said, giving Rem a fist bump.

The light moment didn't last long. "I'm glad you're taking this so lightly," said McGiffin, the clear outlier at the table. "This is no joke."

Scanlon looked at her and frowned. "Little levity never hurts at moments like this," he said. "Anyway, your turn, Agent McGiffin."

"First of all," she began, "this is not how the Federal Bureau of Investigation operates. My bosses in New York have no idea what's going on here, and I'm not supposed to tell them because of operational security, according to Agent Murphy here. But if this blows up, I'm fucking roadkill."

"Kathy," Murphy cut in, "if it blows up, it's my black ass on the line. Your white tush will be fine."

McGiffin laughed sarcastically. "Play the race card," she snapped. "That helps."

She turned and looked directly at Rem. "Another problem is I don't trust reporters. Haven't met an honest one yet. Never let the facts get in the way of a good narrative and never fail to blow everything out of proportion."

Rem started to object but McGiffin cut him off.

"I got ambushed on an Indian reservation last year and the stories made me look clueless for getting shot in the back. Suggested I was a rookie way out of my league. So humiliating. And sexist, I might add."

"Playing the gender card," Murphy said. "That's helpful."

Rem stepped in, like a referee in a prize fight. "Agent McGiffin," he began, "two points here. I've done this longer than you've been alive, and you need to know I've cooperated with the FBI on the qt many times. Both my Pulitzers were reported with their help. When their interests aligned with mine, we cooperated—quietly and professionally. Our interests align here. I'm 100% certain of that.

"Secondly, you must realize bad journalism is a fact of life and it's not getting any better. Get used to it. It's the Age of Twitter."

"Well, Professor, thanks for the lecture," McGiffin fired back. "Glad you got those Pulitzers, but from what I read, your best days are long gone."

Dabovitch winced but said nothing. He threw up his hands and leaned back in his chair. "You're still a rookie," he said under his breath.

"So, Kathy," Scanlon said, "does this mean you want out?"

"No," she shot back, "I'm just saying this little novel plan you and Agent Murphy came up with last night had better work."

"Can I say something here?" Rocco said. "With all due respect, Agent McGiffin, plans are just that: plans. The real question is: what do you do when the plan goes off the rails. I learned that the hard way from my crime days in Brooklyn."

"Your gangster shtick doesn't impress me," McGiffin snarled. "It may be a big hit in Darwin but that's about it. By the way, I happen to live in Brooklyn, thank you very much."

"Kathy," Murphy said sharply, breaking her silence, "stop with the insults. Rocco has been a huge help. We couldn't do this without him."

"One other thing I don't get," McGiffin said, looking at Cox. "How did you know who I was at the pool that afternoon at the hotel in Darwin. You addressed me by name. How did you know who I was?"

Cox shrugged and looked to Rem. "Sorry,' the reporter said. "Can't reveal our sources."

"Speaking of that," Vic said, "how did you know who *we* were? Why were you taking pictures of our rental car? How did you know it was ours?"

"None of your business," she snapped. "We're the law here, not you. You're not a cop anymore. Don't pretend like there's some bullshit equivalency on this."

Hmm, Scanlon mused, this has gone well. So much for Aussie/ American cooperation.

"Ok, everyone," he said, with as much cheer as he could muster, "time to get this done. Class dismissed. Godspeed to all."

The group clapped and stood to adjourn. McGiffin looked at her partner and scowled again. "Fuck you," she mouthed.

CHAPTER 136

Bad Boy 'Speaks'

Big Croc Monument
Wyndham, Western Australia
Monday, August 22, 2016
6:36 a.m.

The early morning air still blessedly cool, Rem sat on a shaded park bench, drinking coffee in a Styrofoam cup from the hotel, staring at the concrete edifice known as Big Croc a few yards away. Leaving for Broome in a couple of hours, and I need some alone time to think, he mused.

The crack yesterday by that FBI agent was truly nasty but maybe she's right, he thought. Certainly in her 21st Century eyes, I am washed up. The Pulitzers were won decades ago and what's my more recent track record: laid off from my newspaper job and failed as a screenwriter. Portrait of a Loser. If it wasn't for Maggie Maye—who still believes in me—who knows where I'd be. Certainly not here on the story of a lifetime. Bless you, Maggie.

Rem stood and walked over for a closer look at the infamous Bad Boy, who stands 10 feet high. Look at those teeth, Rem thought. Look like bullets for an AR-15. Why did Angela so admire these ferocious creatures? Because they're such deadly killers and ruthless survivors? Like her? Besides, what other breathing creature dates to the dino era?

I keep going back to that mysterious travel article she wrote for the New York Herald 20 years ago, he thought. Why write a travel article for an American newspaper about one of the hottest towns in Australia where the killer salties roam free? Travel stories in a Sunday newspaper are supposed to attract visitors, not repel them.

Yet, he noted, this *is* the unofficial salt-croc capital of Australia and it's a place where intrepid tourists can feel the winds from Hades without actually having to go there. And where else can you photograph salties sunning themselves in the backyards of homes 90 feet away? A third of an American football field! Where else do you have such a contrast between humans owning the solid ground and salt crocs the wet stuff? All of which Angela captured so creatively in her article and photos. She did have real talent, Rem mused, in this area anyway. Very few correspondents have that kind of range, he knew.

So how do you go from that kind of professional to a monster on the lam. The biggest mystery? Where is Ari Steinberg III, the love-sick scion who ran away to Australia to find her and left a media empire crumbling in his wake. We know she looted him, Rem thought, and almost certainly murdered the girly man who loved her so unconditionally. But where did she do it and how did she do it? Where did she dump the body?

Not much chance she'll tell me when I do find her, Rem thought, but you gotta try. The die is cast. The trap is set. Angela, time to fess up. We've got you surrounded.

Rem looked up at Big Croc and patted his spotted underside. "Who you rooting for, Big Guy?" Rem said out loud. "I'll bet your money's on her."

The Bad Boy didn't answer. He didn't have to.

CHAPTER 137

Road to Broome

August 22, 2016
From: RemDab666@hotmail.com
To: SOS 777@gmail.com
Subject: Update #4

Maggie:

Off to Broome this morning. About 400 miles south of here. Staying at the Cable Beach Resort Hotel north of the town center.

Here the big news: My Sydney cop partner, Vic Cox, and I are working with two federal agents—one FBI, one Aussi—who are also tracking our quarry. The plan is for our CI to bring ARF/JMC to our hotel suite where we will ambush interview her. Unbeknownst to us :), the agents will have the room bugged. Once the interview is over, they will act as they see fit. They believe they already have enough evidence to charge her with multiple murders, including that of her husband but not (yet) ASIII.

I will file my news story—at least 4,000 words—once she is formally charged and is in custody. Most of the story is pre-written—I'll send you a copy—and it will be exclusive. Am expecting story will spark huge shit storm worldwide. Should have lots of good folos.

Please call Peter Gallagher at the AP in Washington. Give him a heads-up. We go way back. Just emphasize what a huge scoop this will be for AP.

Reuters, eat your heart out.

Stay Tuned

RTD

August 21, 2016

From: SOS77@gmail.com

To: RemDab666@hotmail.com

Subject: Update #4

Hi. Talked to Gallagher at AP. You should talk to him directly. He sounds skeptical. Not willing to pay til he sees top of the story. Bad sign. No way we can do that. Asked about your drug/alcohol issues. Not good. Didn't seem particularly impressed by your rehab. We may have to revive *The Searchlight* for the news stories from Broome.

Be careful. Prepare for everything, be surprised by nothing.

Go Get 'Em

MTM

CHAPTER 138

Broome: A History

Late in the 19th Century, the exotic frontier town of Broome on the far northwest coast of Australia was known as an "Outpost of the Empire." That was, of course, the British Empire, at the zenith of its glory and might in those days.

It was a time when more than 400 pearl-diving boats—known as luggers—patrolled the bathtub-warm turquoise waters off the coast, harvesting 80% of the world's natural pearls.

The streets of Broome teemed with fortune hunters, adventurers, and assorted scoundrels from all over the world. The town was rich, sinful and tolerant, more Asian than Australian in appearance and ethnicity. China, Japan and Malaysia supplied most of the divers while Afghans drove the supply camels through the streets. Road signs were in Japanese, Chinese, Arabic and English. Commercial sin and brawling helped define the bars in Chinatown.

Life was always unpredictable there. Cyclones periodically flattened the town and its economy tanked in 1914 with the start of World War I in Europe. But it was the start of World War II that caused the most turmoil. Japanese Zeroes bombed the harbor in 1942, sinking 16 Aussie flying boats. It was Broome's version of Pearl Harbor and the savage attack on Darwin farther up the coast at roughly the same time. As in America, citizens of Japanese ancestry in Broome—who ran the pearl business—were incarcerated in the wake of the attacks.

Fast forward to 2016 and Broome remains an outpost of great color and fascination in all its steamy tropical splendor. It is now a tourist mecca, visited by 300,000 people a year from all over Australia, Asia, Europe and North America.

It was the rise of the cultured pearl industry and the arrival of regular commercial air service that changed the town so dramatically. But its major attraction remains Cable Beach, north of town, a 15-mile stretch of untouched sands where the iconic tourist camel rides take place every night at sunset.

The serious partiers in town gather at the 125-year-old Roebuck Hotel in Chinatown on Caravon Street. With its nightclub, multiple bars and palm-fringed pool, the Roebuck is a typical outback pub—authentic, rough around the edges and a must visit for tourists and townies alike. It's Broome's version of the fictional Rick's Café in Casablanca or the very real Hussong's Café in Baja California.

Then there's Broome's mysterious attractions at night—the green flash that sometimes appears on the horizon as the sun does its daily disappearing act into the ocean on its way to Madagascar. Or the so-called Staircase to the Moon light show that occurs when a full moon shines on the mud flats at low tide. Another must-see is the Sun Picture Garden, the world's oldest outdoor movie theater. It was built 100 years ago.

The town is now about to embark on its annual Festival of the Pearl, also known as the Shinju Matsuri. It's a weekend-long orgy of drinking, eating and celebration of the town's unique heritage. It's a main reason why Broome remains an outpost well worth visiting.

CHAPTER 139

Dilemma of a Hitman

Cable Beach Resort & Spa, Room 333
Broome, Australia
Thursday, August 25, 2016
8:08 a.m.

What the bloody hell is going on here, Ziggy the K thought miserably. This job can't get any more fucked up. Seated on a 3d-floor balcony beach chair, he could not stop rereading the email he got from blackfella in New York.

Let me get this right, he thought to himself. Not only are a reporter and ex-cop chasing my target, now two federal agents from America and Australia are hot on her ass. How am I going to score the kill in the middle of this gang bang, he wondered?

"Sheila," he bellowed into the hotel room, "get your arse out here. We gotta talk."

Sheila Donovon Koslowski appeared on the balcony in short order, clad in a hotel-issue white terrycloth bathrobe, hands on her wide hips, face red, neck veins bulging.

"Keep it down," she hissed. "Don't yell at me like that. This is a classy place. Not like those dumps we usually stay in."

Ziggy looked at his frumpy wife with a long dull stare, head pounding from last night's bender at the Roebuck.

"Sit," he commanded. "We've got real problems."

She remained standing, arms folded, disgusted look still on her face. "For God's sake, put some clothes on," she snapped. "This isn't a nudist colony. I'm not going to talk to you when your donger's flapping in the wind."

Ziggy stood, farted loudly and disappeared into the room. He reappeared moments later in his own hotel robe.

"Sheila, just bloody listen," he began again. "I've just learned the feds from two countries are tracking our target. She's wanted for murder."

"Jesus Christ," she snapped. "What feds?"

"Agents from the FBI and AFP. They're coming to Broome. In fact, they should be here now, in this hotel."

"What?" she hissed. "You bloody idiot. What have you gotten us into? Did you tell the people in New York this?"

"They told me," he shot back. "And don't call me an idiot, you bloody hag."

He paused and breathed out hard. Her eyes fired daggers.

"We're fucked," he continued. "They've already paid us $25,000 American. Got to finish the job. These dudes don't mess around. Not like the idiot meth-heads we normally deal with."

Calmer now, Sheila sat next to him. "So we still get the other $25,000 when the job is done, right?"

"Right. They want visuals of the kill."

"Okay," she said. "We have her picture. I'll try to find her around the Roebuck today, maybe at the pool. Try to strike up a chat. Maybe get her to tell me something about her plans. Something to indicate when she might be alone."

"Yea, I like it," Ziggy said. "We can find her car at the hotel and GPS it. Then hang back and wait. No rushing in. Only fools do that."

Ziggy laughed uneasily. "If we can't do the job, we'll refund their bloody money. No reneging on these guys. They know where we live."

No More Running

Cable Beach Resort & Spa, Room 414
Thursday, August 25, 2016
5:55 p.m.

They sat on the fourth-floor balcony of the toney resort overlooking Cable Beach, West Australia's most famous stretch of sand.. It was close to sunset and the tourist-toting camels were making their leisurely stroll back home—an iconic image from the Aussie West Coast known round the world.

Both had vodka tonics in their right hands but she was more interested in the small vial of white powder in her left. "You want a hit, luv?" she said. "Good stuff. I bought it this morning in town. My favorite dealer got it special just for me."

"Nah," he replied, as he watched her line up two lines of powder and inhale them in one fluid motion. "Quit that stuff long ago. It'll fry your brain."

"Darlin'," she said, lapsing into her old Texas twang, "my brain's already fried. That train left long time ago."

They both laughed and went quiet for a time. Exhaling deeply, he was finally ready to launch. "Julie, can I ask you a personal question?" he began.

"No," she shot back. "I don't do personal questions. Certainly not with a guy who sells me a new car every year."

They both laughed again.

"Seriously, what are you running from? Why do you need a car fit for a gangster? I mean, what are you afraid of? I don't get it."

Her poker face didn't change much, just a slight smile, the Mona Lisa kind. She fiddled with her pigtails and took a drink. She stared at the fading light on the western horizon.

"Let me first ask you a question," she said finally. "Our so-called chance meeting this afternoon at the Roebuck was not an accident, was it?"

"No."

"And you're here at the Festival because of me?"

"Yes."

She sat back in the chair and took another drink. Her eyes focused on the camels several hundred yards away.

"Do you know I've never taken one of those camel rides?" she said, chuckling. "I detest camels. They're nasty and disgusting. The outback's full of them, running wild."

Rocco said nothing, his eyes also focused on the passing parade.

"I like you, Rocco,' she said, reaching for his hand. "You remind me of New York City. You know, I don't sleep with men anymore. They're not worth it."

She let go of his hand, adding: "You know, I might make an exception for you. Just say the word."

Mazilli laughed uneasily. "Let me think about that," he said. "But you didn't answer my question, Julie. What are you running from?"

"You know," she said, ignoring the query, "I should have never left New York. I was happy there. My colleagues liked me. I was good at what I did."

Her voice started to crack. "I sold my soul for a man," she said quietly. "Big mistake. I didn't really love him. Just went along for the ride."

She started to cry quietly. "I'm tired of running, Rocco. I don't know how much longer I can do this. I've done some terrible things in my life and I'm tired of looking over my shoulder."

"Tell me what you're running from, luv," he said, squeezing her hand. "Maybe I can help. I'm a runaway myself."

Before she could answer, there was a knock at the door. "Hold that thought," he said. "I'll be right back."

CHAPTER 141

Wired for Sound

Cable Beach Resort & Spa, Parking Lot
Thursday, August 25, 2016
6:44 p.m.

The agents took off their headphones in the sound truck and did a high five.

"Coming through clear and loud," Murphy said. "Our tech guys got it just right."

"Rocco's doing great," McGiffin said. "Sounds like she wants to come clean."

"Let's listen back in," Murphy said. "Cox and Rem should be in by now."

CHAPTER 142

High Noon

Cable Beach Hotel & Spa, Room 414
Broome, Australia
August 25, 2016
Thursday, 6:45 p.m.

About to confront his elusive *femme fatale*, Rem's nervous system was on fire. Defcon1 time for this enquiring reporter, he told himself. An interview 13 years in the getting. Don't blow it.

Got to be calm, he told himself. Got to be cool. You've interviewed all kinds of characters—hit men, Mafia dons, Wall Street charlatans, you name it--and Angela Reilly Flanagan is just another name in that gallery of rogues.

But she's not, he knew. She's my version of David Livingstone and telling her complete story once and for all is my road back from ruin. The first paragraph of my obituary will either say I was one of the best investigative reporters of my era, or it will say I died a broken man, undone by drugs, alcohol and late-career failure and hubris.

He entered the hotel room and approached his target from behind.

"Mrs. Flanagan, I presume," he said loudly, full of faux cheer and offering an outstretched hand. "Rem Dabovitch here, at your service. You're a hard person to find."

Momentarily nonplused and ignoring his hand, she looked at Mazilli and gave him a hard stare. He shrugged his shoulders.

She looked back to Rem. "What took you so long, Mr. Dabovitch?" she countered smoothly. "I thought you were a good reporter."

They both laughed, breaking the ice.

"You know," she added, "that line is bullshit, don't you? That reporter from the New York Herald who found Livingstone made that up. Never said: 'Dr. Livingstone, I presume.' It was a line he later concocted to embellish his story and boost his reputation."

She added derisively: "Just one of the many useless things I learned in journalism school."

"Didn't know that," Rem replied. "But then again, I never graduated from college."

They both laughed again.

"Mrs. Flanagan," Rem began, "I want...."

She cut him off. "The woman you are referring to was declared legally dead years ago. You must know that. My name is Julie Cameron."

"Of course," Rem replied. "As I was saying, this is my associate, Vic Cox. I believe you know of him."

"Ah, yes," she sneered. "Heard a lot about you, luv."

"What happened to Stacey Simpson, Ms. Cameron," Vic asked pointedly. "We know you know. She's been gone for six years now. Her family still clings to the hope she may be alive somewhere."

She ignored the question and turned back to Mazilli. "*Et tu, Brute?*" she asked, green eyes on fire.

"Sorry, Julie," Rocco replied sheepishly. "You just told me you're tired of running. This is your chance to own up. Worst that can happen is life in prison."

"Sit," she commanded, pointing to the chairs around a writing table. "I've got some things to say."

Vic, Rem and Rocco all took seats. They said nothing as she glared at each. She looked cornered.

"I'll talk," she said finally, "but I set the rules. Not deep background. No background. No notes, no recordings. This conversation never happened. Got it?"

The three murmured their assent.

"I know nothing first-hand," she said, her first lie. "I'll tell you what I've heard. Just hearsay. I admit to doing nothing wrong. Not today, not yesterday, not 10 years ago. Capiche?"

The three nodded again.

"So, what are you waiting for?" she sneered. "I ain't got all night. Let's get this over with."

"What happened to Stacey?" Vic asked again.

"Killed by a saltie in the Prince Regent River, not too far from here," she replied matter-of-factly. "Having a swim and the croc took her down."

"How do you know that?" Vic asked hotly.

"Next question," she replied.

"What about Raffy?" Rem asked.

"Who cares?" she snarled. "He ruined his wife's career and then demanded half her 9/11 insurance money. He should have died in the Tower collapses anyway. Whoever killed him just finished the job."

"Where's Jack Quinn?" Rem asked. "He's disappeared."

"Good riddance," she snapped. "He's a coward and a traitor. Don't believe a word he says."

"Traitor to whom?" Cox asked.

"Nice try," she sneered.

"Where is Ari Steinberg," Rem asked.

For the first time, she didn't spit out an answer. She almost teared up but caught herself.

"Poor Ari," she said softly. "So weak, so pathetic. Ruined his family business and then ran away. Hard body, soft mind."

"Where is he now?" Rem asked.

"Haven't a clue," she said straight-faced. "Don't think he'll be back." She smiled derisively.

Cox handed her a photo of Inge Hedburg. "You recognize her? he asked.

She examined the photo quickly and handed it back. "Looks like a lot of Western tourists on this coast," she said. "Grubby low-lives-- staying in youth hostels and campgrounds, doing drugs and odd jobs, fucking their way down the coast to Margaret River. Glued to their smart phones, living on Daddy's dime. They disappear all the time and nobody cares where they went. Good riddance, I say."

Vic pointed to the picture. "Ms. Cameron, you were seen in her company several years ago in Wyndham," he said. "She was said to be carrying a large amount of cash—around $20,000 in Aussie dollars. Never seen after that."

"Sorry," she replied coldly. "Don't recall her. She looks like a sex worker—or drug dealer. Probably both. Great cash businesses. You'll probably find her in King's Cross."

"Ms. Cameron," Rem cut in, "now that we have finally met, can we cut the crap? We know who you are, obviously. Angela Flanagan is not dead. She's right there. Your life is a great story and I want to tell **it.**"

She stared at Rem for several moments and looked out at the sunset. The last of the camel trains was heading home.

"What's so great about it," she deadpanned.

"Do you know who Martha Gellhorn was?" he asked.

"Of course," she said. "I told you: I went to journalism school."

"Well, then," he continued, "you know she was a terrific foreign correspondent in the 30s and 40s but she lived in the shadow of Ernest Hemingway, her husband. She never received the acclaim she deserved. She covered the invasion of Normandie by stowing away on a hospital ship while Hemingway was off partying somewhere.

"Same goes for you. Your husband got all the glory and the prizes and front-page play and you got the shaft. No respect for your great photography. It was an outrage. I want to write that story. You were the real talent, not him."

She looked at Mazilli. "Rocco, will you take me back to the Roe- buck? You and I need to talk."

She turned to Rem and Vic. "Meet me back here tomorrow night, same time. You've given me something to consider. I need to think about it. Maybe it's time to come clean."

She paused suddenly, looking sad. "You know," she added, "I *was* a good journalist once upon a time. I loved my job. I was just coming into my own as bureau chief. Then my supposedly dead husband ruined everything. I miss it to this day."

With that, she stood and abruptly exited the room without looking back. Mazilli was close behind.

CHAPTER 143

Listening In

Cable Beach Resort & Spa, Parking Lot
Broome, Australia
Thursday, August 25, 2016
7:30 p.m.

The agents took out their earpieces in the sound truck and shook their heads. The mystery murderess had spoken for the first time and the words were chilling.

"Oh my God," McGiffin said, "We've got her."

Murphy held up her hand. "Not so fast," the AFP agent said. "She admitted nothing directly. Certainly not anything we can use in court."

"I say we play it safe and take her now," McGiffin said. "Charge two counts of murder and passport fraud. That's a start anyway. I don't trust what this woman will do next."

"Let's wait one more day," Murphy said. "Says she's done some horrible things and is tired of running. See what that means. She's not going anywhere. Rocco can keep an eye on her at the Roebuck."

"Bird in hand, as we like to say back home," McGiffin said. "Take what you can while you can."

"I got this, Kathy," Murphy replied. "Don't go wobbly on me. We're almost home."

CHAPTER 144

Jail Break

Cable Beach Resort & Spa, Rom 202
Broome, Australia
Friday, August 26, 2016
2:12 a.m.

Sheila Koslowski looked over at her husband, buck naked and snoring like a train. No wonder I can't sleep, she thought.

"Ziggy, Ziggy," she said breathlessly, "wake up, wake up. She's gone, she's gone. Headed north up the coast."

She dug her fingernails into his side, once, twice, finally a third time as she also squeezed his testicles.

Ziggy sat up straight, shocked, rubbing his eyes, groaning over his usual hangover.

"What the fuck, Sheila," he groused. "I don't feel like it now. Go back to sleep."

"Ziggy, look at this," she said, showing him a map on her Apple laptop, a car emoji 100 miles northeast of Broome on the Great Northern Highway.

Ziggy focused on the screen, trying to absorb was happening in his slow-witted way.

"Holy fuck," he said finally. "She busted loose. What time is it?"

He farted and looked at this watch.

"She must have left a couple of hours ago. Pack it up, sister. We're going after her. This is our shot."

CHAPTER 145

Where's Rocco?

Cable Beach Resort & Spa, Room 414
Friday, August 26, 2016
8:08 p.m.

Grim-faced all, the four sat around the hotel suite, saying nothing, reading their smart phones. A sense of dread choked the air.

Finally, agent Murphy took charge. "Ok, let's face it," she said. "She's not showing up. She should have been here two hours ago."

"Anything from Rocco?" McGiffin asked.

"Nope," Vic said. "Never came back last night and couldn't reach him all day. Cell goes right to voice mail. Manager told me this afternoon her room at the Roebuck has a Do Not Disturb sign on it."

"Shit," Rem said, "I got a bad feeling on this."

"I know the Roebuck's owner." Vic said. "We go back a while. I'll give him a call."

"I know him too," Murphy said. "Vito Papadakis. A real piece of work."

Of All the Gin Joints

Roebuck Hotel, Room 137
Broome, Australia
Friday, August 26, 2016
9:09 p.m.

A legend in his own mind, Vito Papadakis struts around the Roebuck like he owns the place—which he doesn't. But anyone who knows anything about the Roebuck Hotel knows Vito is the manager and man to see in Broome's most notorious hotel and bar.

He's seen *Casablanca* 33 times. Humphrey Bogart is his hero.

You can't miss Vito in the hotel at night: 6-6, 240 pounds; long dirty blond hair combed straight back; tight black t-shirt covering 6-pack abs and bodacious biceps; yellow yoga stretch pants; and low-top black converse gym shoes, no socks. Some nights he breaks up fights in the bar between rival motorcycle gang members. Some nights he shuts down loud parties in the rooms. Most nights he yuks it up in the bar with guests who lap up his stories about his time as an Australian Army commando.

Reporters love him too. He'll give an opinion on almost anything. Need quote, call Vito.

Tonight, however, Vito didn't feel much like talking. Of all the pubs in all the towns all over western Australia, this had to happen here tonight, he mused. Buck up. Gotta get through this.

Standing by the pool, shaped like a pentagon and encircled by palm trees, Vito waived to the federal agents as they appeared in the courtyard.

"Agent Murphy," he said, reaching out and shaking her hand. "it's been a while. Vic Cox told me you were on the way."

"Nice to see you, Vito," she said. "Sorry it had to be because of this. This is my associate, Kathy McGiffin."

They shook hands, Vito giving the FBI agent the once over with his amber-colored eyes.

"In there," he nodded toward Room 137. "Brace yourselves. It's ugly. I was just about to dial up the local cops when Vic called."

"Yeah, please hold off for a few more minutes," Murphy said.

"Let me get this right," Vito said. "First, I get a call from ex-Sydney homicide to check out this woman's room, then two federal agents show up at my door looking like they just came off a Hollywood movie set. What's going on here?"

"We'll let you know in a minute," Murphy said.

The agents drew their Glocks and pushed the door all the way open. They entered slowly. They gasped in unison at what they found.

CHAPTER 147

Bye-bye Roccco.

Cable Beach Resort & Spa, Room 414
Broome, Australia
Friday. August 26, 2016
10:20 p.m.

Stunned, Rem disconnected the cell call and stared at Vic. Dread filled his lungs and froze his mouth.

"Mate, what's the matter?" Vic asked. "What did Murphy say?"

"Rocco's dead," Rem whispered, burying his head in his hands. "Angela's gone. No one's seen her since last night. Oh my God, have we ever fucked this up."

Vic recoiled. "What do you mean, dead?" he asked. "How? Where? What happened?"

"Shot in the back of the head," Rem said. "Found on the floor of Angela's room. A .22 caliber revolver with a silencer found next to him. Christ, like some sort of Mafia hit."

"Fuck me," Vic spat. "She thought Rocco betrayed her. Said as much in that interview."

"Here's the kicker," Rem said. "She left a message in lipstick on the bathroom mirror. Guess what it said?"

Vic shrugged.

"Martha Gellhorn: Yeah Right."

The homicide cop looked ill. "Stone-cold killer, she is," he said.

"Murphy says we should get over to the Roebuck now," Rem said. "Get a tour of the crime scene before the local cops get there. We gotta move fast. I think I know where she went."

CHAPTER 148

WTF

Cable Beach Resort & Spa, Room 333
Broome, Australia
Friday, August 26, 2016
11:41 p.m.

How could things get any worse, Murphy mused. But guess what? They just did.

"Read that email to me again," she told McGiffin. "It's from your boss in New York?"

"It says **WHAT THE FUCK** (all caps in bold) are you doing over there? Is this really you? Respond ASAP."

"And he sent the attachment?"

"Yep."

"Let me see it again."

McGiffin clicked on the pdf. Up popped the clear color image of two naked women embracing on a deserted beach at sunset. One black, one white. One tall, one short.

"Christ," Murphy groaned, "I should have known that bastard would do something like this."

"Who?"

"My boss in Darwin. The one I told you about who was so angry I got this assignment without his knowledge. He wants me to fail."

"He's a good photographer," McGiffin deadpanned.

The women laughed, punching a hole in the gloom.

"Fuck it," Murphy said. "No way to really explain this now. Email him back asking for a resend. Message garbled; attachment blurred. Blah, blah, blah.

"I'm guessing she's headed to Perth. Could be halfway there by now. We need to ask the state police to set up roadblocks on the highway that parallels the coast. We have her license plate number and vehicle make and model."

"But no tracker," McGiffin noted.

"No. Never got around it to it. Too busy making sure the wiretap worked and was legal."

"Poor Rocco was right," the FBI agent said. "It's not the plan that counts. It's what you do when everything goes south."

"Well, south is where we're headed," Murphy said. "Saddle up. If we can get her in the next 24 hours, we're good. That photo does look bad, I know, but we can explain it. Just a friendly hug. You just tell 'em you don't do lesbians."

The agents laughed, their mojo coming back.

"What about the Lone Ranger and Tonto?" McGiffin asked.

"Who?"

"Vic and Rem."

"They're on their own," Murphy said. "Told Vic we had to part ways."

CHAPTER 149

Swimming Upstream

Cable Beach Resort & Spa, Room 414
Broome, Australia
Saturday, August 27, 2016
1:24 a.m.

No rest for the stupid, they knew. This hour really *was* darkest before the dawn, and they needed to move fast.

"She's headed north, I just know it," Rem said. "It's counter intuitive, I know. But that's how she rolls. Does what you don't expect."

"North where?" Vic asked. "Darwin?"

"Wyndham," Rem said. "You know how salmon swim upstream to die? That's what she may be doing. Be with her beloved salties. She knows it's over."

"Hmmm," Vic replied. "Makes for a good story anyway. A bit far-fetched for my liking."

Rem looked at his watch. "We need to move now. I'll text Mike Scanlon. Ask him to keep an eye out for her."

"What about the girls?" Vic asked.

"What girls?"

"You know: Cagney & Lacey."

Rem laughed. "Clem told me they're headed south. Said to stay in touch. One of us must be right. There's no other major roads out of here."

CHAPTER 150

The Final Kills

Five Rivers Lookout
Wyndham, Australia
Saturday, August 27, 2016
5:45 p.m.

Dressed in green army fatigues and brown Australian bush hat, the woman emerged from behind a giant Boab tree and pulled a .38 caliber Smith & Wesson revolver from the holster on her waist band.

She walked up to the rusted Winnebago camper that pulled up to the lookout. She pointed the pistol directly at the driver's head.

"Hands up," she snarled. "Out of the car, both of you. Slowly. Let me see your hands."

She looked at the woman on the passenger side. "Move it, sister," she ordered. "Drop your hands and you're toast."

The couple exited the cab awkwardly, trying to maintain some semblance of dignity. It wasn't easy.

"Luv," the man said, voice unsteady and cracking, "there must be some mistake. What's the problem?"

"Shut up," she said harshly. "I'm not your luv, luv. I'll ask the questions. Who the fuck are you?"

The couple stayed mum but began to tremble visibly.

"I said: who the fuck are you and why are you following me?"

She fired a shot into the camper door, causing the woman to scream.

"We're nobodies," he croaked. "Just a couple of retirees touring the country. You know, gray nomads on the lonesome highway."

"Bullshit," she snarled. "That's lie number one."

She fired another bullet into the door of the cab. They both screamed this time.

"Take your clothes off," she ordered. "Now. Face me."

Both disrobed quickly, throwing shorts, t-shirts and underwear in a pile next to the right front tire.

"Jesus," the gunwoman said, "you two haven't missed many meals, have you? Turn all the way around. Slowly. Let me have a look. Keep the hands high."

As they went around, she moved a step closer and examined his heavily tattooed torso and back. "Who's that Asian dude on your back?" she demanded.

The man said nothing. His wife could barely stand. She sobbed uncontrollably as mucus and spittle poured out of her nose and mouth. Urine flowed down her legs.

"You see, Sheila," the gunwoman said, "you made a big mistake coming down to see me at the pool that day. Asking me all those questions and showing me those stupid pictures of you and Dumbo here.

"Problem is I recognized him from his trial for murdering that meth dealer in Darwin. His picture was in the local paper all the time. I mean, duh. How stupid do you think I am? I know he got off."

She turned to him. "You're the head of the Mongol motorcycle gang up here and you've been hired to kill me. Am I right?"

"Please," he begged. "You must have me mistaken for someone else. Maybe my brother. We're identical twins."

She laughed derisively. "Nice try. That's lie number two."

She fired another round that hit Sheila in the abdomen, severing her femoral artery. She collapsed in a heap, blood spurting like a geyser.

As she moaned loudly on the pavement, now lying flat on her back, the gunwoman aimed her revolver at Ziggy's head.

"Who hired you?"

"Please don't shoot," he pleaded.

"One more time: Who hired you?"

"Name is Rim. From New York. Never met him in person."

"Jim the Rim," she said quietly, almost to herself, smiling slightly.

"Turn around and put your hands on the truck," she ordered. "Spread your legs."

As his wife lay dying at his feet, Ziggy did as told and lost control of his bowels.

"That's disgusting," she said. "You can tell a lot about a man just before he thinks he is going to die."

"Mother of God," he wailed. "Please forgive me. I'm sorry for everything."

She paused for a moment, mulling the horrific scene, Sheila's moans growing quieter as all life escaped her body. Time to go, the gunwoman thought.

"Death before dishonor," she said. "That's what my husband always used to say. Tell Dion he wins. God have mercy on my soul."

She raised the revolver to her temple and fired.

CHAPTER 151

End of the Line

Five Rivers Lookout
Wyndham, Australia
Sunday, August 28, 2016
3 p.m.

Only the intrepid and adventurous find their way to the lookout 1500 feet above Wyndham town in the hottest part of the day.

On this winter day of our Lord in the year two thousand and sixteen, the thermometer hit an unseasonably high 105 and the humidity index broke 90. The glare from the western sun obliterated the horizon.

Vic and Michael Scanlon stood next to the Toyota Land Cruiser, burnt to a blackened shell.

"This has to be her car, right?" Scanlon said.

"Yeah," Vic replied, kneeling to be a better look at the underside. "The steel reinforced floor nearly melted. Looks like an expert torch job."

Vic looked at Scanlon. "So, what happened here, Mike? Best guess."

"Double murder," the Aussie lawman said, wiping his forehead with a white hand towel from his motel. "Got two separate trails of dried blood up to the lookout. Bodies dragged there and thrown over the side. Parking lot hosed down. Had to be where the murders occurred."

"What's over the side?"

Scanlon shrugged. "Not much. Swamps, mudflats, flies, crocs of course. They're everywhere. Not much left when they're done."

Feeling numb and standing several yards away, Rem kept reading and rereading an anonymous email he'd just received. It was written in the style of a front-page newspaper headline:

She Sleeps With The Crocs;
Rest In Peace, Brother Raffy,
Your murder has been avenged

A photo attachment showed a staged crime scene. Angela Flanagan lay on her back, lifeless green eyes staring skyward, red pigtails at 90-degree angles to her head. Blood pooled next to her left temple. Her arms were folded on her chest.

"What's the matter, mate?" Cox said, walking over to his partner. "You look like you've seen a ghost."

Rem stared straight ahead. "In a way, I have," he mumbled.

He showed him the attachment. The ex-cop examined it for several seconds, shook his head and handed the phone back.

"You know what happened here, don't you?" Cox asked. "You know who did this."

Rem didn't answer right away. He finally nodded slightly.

"It's complicated, Vic," he said quietly. "I've been had. They hacked my computer. How could I be so stupid? My God, what have I done?"

Vic patted him on the shoulder. "It's okay, mate. You'll figure it out. We'll talk later. Remember, there are things we all have to carry to our graves. Even journalists. Cops too."

Cox turned toward the rental car and started walking. "Let's get out of here," he said. "This place creeps me out."

Rembrandt T. Dabovitch III Died of a heart attack in 2017 shortly after he won his third Pulitzer Prize for his biography of Angela Reilly Flanagan, the infamous Red Widow whose whereabouts remains a mystery. The book sold more than 1 million copies.

Vic Cox: Runs Sydney-based PI empire specializing in locating missing persons. Operates virtual offices throughout Australia and New Zealand. Reality tv show based on his business is in production.

Angela R. Flanagan: Vanished without a trace. Only a handful know what happened to her and they've never told.

Ari Steinberg III: Declared legally dead 10 years after he was last seen in Florida with his father. Family sold the *Herald* to a vulture fund in 2019. Newsroom decimated by crippling layoffs.

Margarite T. Maye: Still writing novels about Super Blogger Stella Ophelia Steele and her endless battles with DC corruption and hypocrisy. Dabovitch dedicated his biography of ARF to her.

Kellen T. Williams: Fired in a house-cleaning after the 2019 sale. No more need for a European Cultural Affairs reporter. Received 3 months pay as severance for his 27 years at the paper.

Dion DeStefano: Killed in 2020 by 3 gunmen in broad daylight outside a crowded deli in Bensonhurst. Motive unknown. No witnesses came forward.

Jim "The Rim" Robison: NYC fitness guru with 'Rim Gyms' across city. Named minority entrepreneur of year in 2019 by local business magazine. Refused to talk to FBI about Dion's murder.

Kathleen Q McGiffin: Quit the FBI when she received a transfer to Fargo. Owns a winery in southwest Australia. Never returned to America to live.

Clementine B. Murphy: Ousted from the AFP, she runs winery in Margaret River when she's not surfing, hiking, running and supporting native art and culture. She and McGiffin are business partners.

Zbigniew Zeke 'Ziggy the K' Koslowski: Killed in 2020 in a gun battle between rival gangs in a Darwin motorcycle bar. Shooting made news nationwide. Choice headline from memorial mass: 'Requiem for a Hit Man.'

Sheila Donovan Koslowski: Husband told friends she left Australia and returned to her native South Africa to care for her ailing mother. Never seen again in either country. Mother died 20 years ago.

Rocco Mazilli: Cremated and ashes scattered on Darwin's Fannie Bay. Outdoor memorial service along beach drew thousands. "Tony, We Loved You," read one sign in the crowd.

Mike Scanlon: The Ice Man Stayeth. Still runs Wyndham's only hotel and remains the man to see when it comes to anything connected to the unofficial saltwater croc capital of country. Failed to find any remains from 2016 double deaths at Five Rivers Lookout.

Shamus Callahan: Awarded FBI Metal for Meritorious Achievement when he retired at end of 2016. Moved to the west coast of Ireland where he is a fixture in the pubs of Galway.

Jack Quinn: Still on the lam. Supposed sightings on islands in Greece and Hawaii. Wanted as an accomplice in multiple murders. Travel business went bankrupt.

Gino Carella/Candy Garcia: Married and living in a mansion outside San Juan on their NYPD pensions. He plays golf and she runs her own lucrative private investigations firm. Her business motto: Puerto Rican Proud, NYPD Tough

ACKNOWLEDGEMENTS

After a long newspaper career chronicling real events and obsessing over facts and accuracy, I found that writing fiction is more fun than I ever would have thought. No daily deadlines. The freedom to do the all the research I needed to make this fictitious narrative believable. Facts matter but it's not the same as real life. In this case I spent years researching all aspects of the decline of American newspapers, a main theme in this book. I also read dozens of books—fiction and non-- about that colorful country Down Under where much of this book takes place. Australia is an endlessly fascinating land and the weeks I spent there were a great help in setting the scenes for this book.

In no particular order, I'd like to thank the following people who helped this book come alive:

1) **James Castle Furlong**, my older brother and himself an accomplished journalist and author. His wise counsel and encouragement were a huge help from the very beginning.

2) **Jim Elsener**, my old pal from Chicago newspaper days of long ago. An author himself of two novels. Jim was a sounding board, advisor and manuscript editor. He is a Master of all Trades when it comes to the published word.

3) **Martha Little Campbell**, an old high school friend who may be the most literate and well-read person I know. When she gave me her blessing on the final draft, I knew I had cleared a high bar.

4) **Jayne Dodds Furlong** , my beloved wife, best friend and valued copy editor. A meticulous person, her tolerance of the mess and chaos of my home office during this long writing was a huge comfort.

5) Two young Australian women—**Suzy and Melissa**, last names unknown, from either Sydney or Melbourne—who rescued me from a fearsome car crash on Bastille Day, 1966 in the French resort town of

La Ciotat. Their rescue salvaged my European vacation and allowed me and my two traveling companions to appreciate up close those adventurous Aussies who wander Europe in their camper vans for months on end before returning to their distant homeland. Australia has had a special spot in my heart ever since.

6) Lastly, and probably least, **Charlie Dodds Furlong,** my late Orange tabby cat who slept at my side every day in the early stages of my writing in Seattle. When I would hit a writing speed bump, I would pet Charlie and he would meow irritably and eventually go back to sleep. End of writers' block. Charlie, Jayne and I will never forget you.

T. Castle Furlong—aka Tom Furlong—is a journalist and fiction writer who read his first sports story in the Chicago Tribune at age 6—the start of a life-long love affair with American newspapers. A native of Evanston, Illinois, Furlong spent decades as a reporter and editor with top-of-the-line newspapers in Chicago and Los Angeles. He is an honors graduate of Denison University and a proud U.S. Naval veteran. He lives on a lake outside Minneapolis with his two favorite females—wife Jayne and border-collie rescue Lucy. He and Jayne have five adult children between them.